THE LONG, LONG TRAIL

THE LONG, LONG TRAIL

War at Home, 1917

Cynthia Harrod-Eagles

SPHERE

First published in Great Britain in 2017 by Sphere

A CIP catalogue record for this book
is available from the British Library.

ISBN 978-0-7515-6556-0

Typeset in Plantin by
Palimpsest Book Production Limited, Falkirk, Stirlingshire
Printed and bound in Great Britain by Clays Ltd, St Ives plc

Papers used by Sphere are from well-managed forests
and other responsible sources.

THE HUNTER FAMILY
of The Elms, Northcote

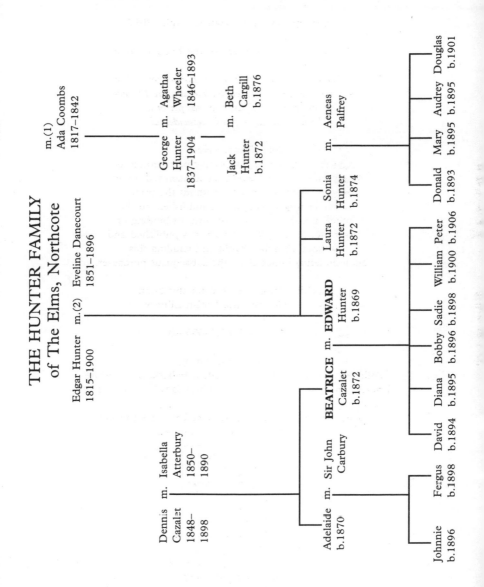

CHAPTER ONE

Sadie jerked awake from a deep sleep with the realisation that there was someone in the room. She sat up, heart thumping, and realised it was only Peter, standing in the doorway, the light from his 'air-raid' torch partly obscured by his fingers.

'What is it?' she asked.

'It's Christmas,' he said.

Beyond Peter's back, the house was in darkness. If the servants had been up there would have been light from the hall below.

'It's too early,' she groaned. 'Go back to bed.' It was bitterly cold, too. Peter, in his pyjamas, was shivering, shifting from foot to foot. 'Hasn't Father Christmas been?' she asked.

'I know it isn't Father Christmas,' he said. 'I know it's Mum and Dad.' He was ten years old, and the war had been going on for more than two of those. Childhood was different, these days. Illusions were harder to hold on to.

'What's the matter, then?' she asked.

He was silent a moment, then said mournfully, 'It doesn't seem a bit like Christmas.'

She softened. 'Do you want to bring your stocking in here? Don't make a noise, though.'

He scampered away. She put on her bedside lamp, and reached for her dressing-gown, which she had spread across the bed for extra warmth, to put it on. Nailer had been

1

curled under it, across the foot of the bed. He lifted an enquiring head, then lowered it again, sticking his nose back under his belly like a cat. Down in the hall, the Vienna clock struck a slow, thoughtful five. Her own stocking was hanging on one of the bed-knobs, but she could happily have waited until morning for it. She was too old for a stocking, really – she would be nineteen in a few weeks' time – but she knew her parents were making an effort to keep Christmas as much like itself as possible, for all their sakes.

But Bobby was dead – the realisation hit her all over again, with astonishment and pain, as it did almost every day on waking. And David had been wounded, invalided out of the army, and who knew if he would ever walk properly again? Peter was right: it didn't seem a bit like Christmas.

He came back with his stocking and jumped into bed with her, his icy feet making two sharp shocks. 'Don't you want yours?' he asked.

He was the youngest, and they must all try to protect him. 'Of course,' she said. So they opened them together.

The family walked to church, crunching through a fresh fall of snow, the servants tramping behind, stepping in their footprints like King Wenceslas's page. The congregation was smaller than usual for Christmas morning. Perhaps the snow had kept people at home. And there were no bells to remind the slugabeds: the rector had ordered them silenced when the war began, and since then, most of the ringers had volunteered or been called up. But the joyful sound of the bells ringing the Christmas carillon across the snowy fields was sorely missed.

The rector gave a thoughtful sermon, speaking of the losses that had hit every household, the pain that would be mitigated only by their collective determination to defeat the foe and rid the world of this modern evil. He didn't say, as he had always said in the early days of the war, that God would comfort them in their grief, and the omission interested Sadie, though she couldn't decide what it signified. Had he stopped believing in God? Had they all? The suffering of the war seemed so horribly man-made, it was hard to think of anything outside it. Why were they fighting? What did it all mean? Of course she knew they had to fight to stop the Germans – but why were the Germans fighting? It didn't make any *sense*.

Perhaps that was why the rector didn't mention God, and why fewer people had come to the service. Nothing made sense any more. The certainties of the old world seemed now like dust that the wind of war had simply blown away. Where was Bobby? His body was rotting in the cold clay of France, but where was *he*? She couldn't believe any more in a Heaven of angels and harps, or the smiling dead beckoning you across the river. Or in God as a benign old gentleman with a long white beard. If there was a God – and she suspected there *was* – it was a God of a distinctly more challenging aspect. A God you would not dare to look in the face.

She supposed they all still prayed when danger threatened, in the 'God help me! God keep my people safe!' manner – after all, what else could you do? But did they any more believe that it worked?

Bobby had always been their Master of the Revels, planning their games and keeping the fun going. Without him, everything was flat. Diana, six months married, was spending Christmas with her husband in London; and in the end, David didn't leave his room. Everyone had assumed he would: they had been working towards it, his first trip downstairs, something to celebrate. But he sat by the fireside in his sitting-room upstairs, staring at the flames, his gramophone playing the same few songs over and over – the sad ones. Among the presents waiting for him under the

Christmas tree were some new disc recordings – everyone would be glad to be spared 'The Last Rose of Summer' and 'Un Bel Di' yet again – but he would not be tempted down.

'I can't manage the stairs,' he said, and, 'My leg hurts too much.' That was always the clinching argument; but, seeing William's and Peter's disappointment, Sadie managed to get a little bit angry with him.

'You have to try,' she said. 'You'll never get better if you don't try.' And, eventually, 'You're spoiling it for everyone.'

But David wouldn't even be provoked. He gave her that silent, flat stare, then turned his head away. 'Leave me alone,' he said.

So it was just the five of them. They took David's presents up to his room but he only pretended to be interested in them, and eventually he asked them to go, saying he felt tired. He had Christmas dinner in his room, leaving two spaces at the dining-table, his and Bobby's, that felt like pulled teeth. You didn't want to look at them, but they drew the eye, as the painful hollow drew the tip of the tongue.

William was wearing Bobby's wrist-watch, which the War Office had sent back and which Father had given to him. The sight of it made Sadie want to cry. When they left the table she made them all play a game, as Bobby would have. They went along with it, even Mother and Father, for Peter's sake. But they were pretending, just as David had been.

There were no Christmas celebrations at Dene Park. Northcote natives were disappointed, having hoped that since a local girl, Diana Hunter, had married the heir, Lord Dene, there would be livelier times in prospect, and a boost to Northcote trade. The Earl and Countess Wroughton were spending Christmas at Sandringham again. Royal Christmases were notoriously dull, but the countess had never let personal feelings interfere with duty, and since the King and Queen had invited them, it was their duty to go.

Lord and Lady Dene were spending Christmas in their new home at Park Place. London was lively, with lots of officers on leave, and many families staying up so that their loved ones need not waste precious time travelling. Rupert's determination was to have the liveliest parties in Town, and the younger set seemed happy to help him achieve it.

Diana was heavily pregnant, expecting her first child in March. She felt huge and ungainly; and she had an uneasy feeling that pregnant women were not *supposed* to go about in public. Surely it wasn't the done thing.

'I don't want people to see me like this,' she told Rupert.

'But, darling, you look wonderful! Magnificently fecund,' he said, catching her hands and stretching them out to survey her. She really did seem awfully large in her loose breakfast gown. Like a very well-dressed seal. He increased the warmth of his smile. 'And more beautiful than ever. Really, it's an unkindness to other women for you to be seen beside them, but I can bear it if you can.'

She was only half placated. She wasn't sure what 'fecund' meant but it didn't sound proper. And she was beginning to suspect that her husband didn't mind what means he used, as long as he got his own way. 'I am in mourning, you know,' she said.

'Nobody does mourning any more.' His mobile features changed rapidly from glee to solemnity. 'It isn't patriotic in time of war. Everyone's lost someone, but we just have to carry on. Can't have spies telling Fritz we've lost heart. The more we eat, drink and make merry, the worse it makes the enemy feel. It's our *duty* to have as much fun as possible.' Diana looked at him doubtfully, and he added, 'I've lost a brother too, you know.'

There was nothing she could say to that. He saw that she had yielded, and pressed home his advantage. 'I know you get tired, darling, and when you've had enough you can

5

make your excuses. But you must be seen on my arm. I don't want anyone to think my wife lacks pluck.'

Diana felt uncomfortable about her shape, but fortunately the tubular style of the pre-war days was going out and fashions were favouring fuller skirts and long tunic tops, which made concealment easier. There was no shortage of money for clothes – Rupert positively encouraged her to be always buying. And he had proved unexpectedly knowledgeable about corsets.

Before her marriage she had rarely given them a thought, happy simply to buy a basic '8s. 11d. small' from Whiteleys. But Rupert had raised his eyebrows at that. He had sent her to an expert at Marshall and Snelgrove's, and had thought 15s. 11d. a perfectly reasonable price for white coutil trimmed with silk Swiss embroidery. It had embarrassed her at first to have him know about her undergarments, but after a while she had found it rather exciting, a little warm secret they shared that set them apart from the world.

Pregnancy, however, seemed to require even more from a foundation garment, and he had directed her to an obscure place in Leicester Square to have an adjustable corset made to measure. 'You must have the proper support, darling,' he had told her, when she had murmured that three guineas seemed an awful lot to spend on one set of stays. 'It's a small price to pay for the well-being of our son and heir.' In the end he had insisted she have two made, so that she would always have one to wear while the other was being cleaned – he was a stickler for cleanliness. With a bill for six guineas winging its way towards him, she could only hope that she would not let the side down by producing a girl.

In the end, she did enjoy the Christmas season, though she found the endless fun tiring and generally had to excuse herself early. But Rupert was running with a different pack, these days. Before their marriage he had favoured a rather

6

Bohemian set, and she had found some of his friends distinctly odd. Now he seemed to have reverted to the circle of his own class and connections, people he had known all his life. Diana didn't always like them, but at least they were understandable. What she liked best was when they entertained at home, with a quiet dinner for a dozen old friends. Then she found she could relax and enjoy herself, and didn't always long for her bed at nine o'clock.

She did miss her family, though. There was never time to go over to Northcote. She felt guilty that they must be having such a sad, quiet Christmas, while she was surrounded by cheerful company. The best she could do was to send a telegram of greeting on Christmas Day, and to order a basket of hothouse fruit to be delivered from Dene Park, with her love.

'You must persuade your father to have the telephone put in,' Rupert told her. 'It really is shockingly medieval that he hasn't got it. If he had the telephone, you could have rung up on Christmas morning and spoken to everybody, which would be practically as good as visiting them.'

Diana had found it an intriguing thought, that one might use the telephone for 'chatting' rather than for communicating essential information as concisely as possible. Only Rupert, she felt sure, could have come up with such an expansive idea.

David was having a nightmare. Ethel, now sick-room maid, had the next room to his, and always slept with her door ajar in case he needed her, so she was with him before his screams reached full pitch. He was sitting up, clawing at his face. She hurried to him, leaned over and grabbed his wrists to stop him hurting himself, but he was strong in the arms and knocked her flying. The tumbler on his bedside table went flying too, and the sound of breaking glass penetrated his clouds. His eyes opened.

7

'Wake up,' she said firmly and calmly, getting to her feet. 'You're dreaming. Wake up.'

He was staring blankly, and making 'Uh? Whu?' sounds. There were tears on his face, and he had scratched his nose and one cheek, and drawn blood.

'It was only a dream,' Ethel said. 'You're safe at home. It's all right.'

'Lice,' he said, with a look of horror. 'There were lice. Oh, the *stink*!' His hands flailed, making brushing-off movements.

But she saw he was coming back. 'No lice. No stink,' she said. She helped him to sit up more, punched his pillows, straightened his bedclothes. 'Just lovely clean sheets, smelling of lavender. Smell – go on. See? Lavender. You're home.'

He gave a long look round, and drew a shuddering sigh. 'I'm sorry,' he said. 'Go back to bed.'

'I'm up now,' she said briskly. She fetched a damp flannel, wiped his face and inspected the scratches, which were only shallow. He had been sweating, despite the cold of the night, so she rinsed the flannel and wiped his neck and his upper body inside his pyjama jacket. He allowed her ministrations, passive now. 'Is your leg hurting?' she asked. He nodded. 'Do you want something?'

'No morphine,' he said. He was terrified that if he took too much, it would lose its power.

'I'll make you up some Collis Browne's,' she said. 'That always soothes you.'

The small dark bottle of Dr Collis Browne's tincture stood with the others on his medicine table, and she mixed him a dose in his tooth-mug. When he had drunk it, she picked up the bits of broken glass and said, 'You just rest quietly, and I'll go down to the kitchen and make you some Horlicks. Do you want me to call anyone?'

'No,' he said. He tried to smile at her, but his mouth wouldn't obey him. 'You're all I need,' he said. 'Thank you.'

She nodded, pleased, and went away.

He leaned back against his pillows, feeling himself trembling lightly. Sadie always said if you had a bad dream, you had to go through it in your head when you were properly awake, to recognise that it was untrue, and banish it. He couldn't remember how it had started, only a confusion of noises and voices. The war again – always the war. Only the end bit was vivid. He'd been lying down, in bed somewhere, and the lice had begun crawling up from under the covers and over his face. And when he had lifted the bedclothes and looked inside, the whole bed had been full of them, millions of them, a seething mass covering his body. That was when he had started screaming.

No, he had started screaming when he had seen that, under the lice, he had no legs. Not even stumps. His body ended with his trunk, and beyond that there was just a heaving, pullulating infinity of lice.

He shuddered, swallowed, finding his mouth dry, and tried to shake off the horror, looking round his familiar room, thanking God for electric light, which did not make moving shadows to torment you, like the candle stubs they relied on in the dugouts. It was only imagination, he knew, but he could still smell that smell. Trench mud. It had a stink all its own – *once known never forgotten*, they used to joke. In his dream it was *he* who smelt like that. The stink seeped out of his pores. They brought it with them when they came out of the line, had all been morbidly conscious of it until they got to a proper bath and carbolic soap. But the memory of it haunted him. Sometimes he felt he would never get rid of it, that when people came near him they would catch its whiff and be repelled. Another reason he did not want to see people.

He was awake now, and the familiar depression had sunk back to its accustomed place. Some people spoke of it as a black dog that followed you, or a raven that perched on your

9

shoulder, but to him it was like a boulder that rested on his chest and made it hard to breathe. It filled his view: he could not see past it.

He thought of his younger self, remembered how he had sat beneath the trees in the summer of 1914 with his best friend Oliphant, how they had talked of wanting to do something noble. The war had seemed to offer endless possibilities of shining heroism. They had dreamed of glory, even of honourable death. What fools they had been! There was nothing honourable about death, just filthy, stinking rags of flesh trodden into the mud and forgotten. There was no glory in war, just pain and horror and degradation.

Bobby had gone to war, cheerful, handsome Bobby, whom everybody loved, and Bobby was dead. Well, at least he was a hero. David had achieved nothing. His name would not go down in history. He had gone to war and come back a wreck, a hopeless cripple; he would never walk again, never live a normal life. He had no future but pain and dependency.

He felt as though he was in a dugout after a shell explosion: the roof had collapsed and the entrance had fallen in. He was trapped, buried alive – but no-one knew he was there. He could hear them outside, moving about, talking, living their lives, but no-one could hear him screaming. Buried alive. It was a joke, wasn't it? A hideous joke. Like his leg, which throbbed like a rotten tooth. How much trouble had the doctors gone to, to save it? That was a joke, too.

Ethel came back with the mug of Horlicks, and a fresh glass of water for his bedside table. He took the mug from her and said, 'Thanks. You can go back to bed now.'

But she had brought some sewing in with her, and sat down with it in the armchair by the window. 'That's all right. I've got this shirt to do. I'll sit here until you drop off again,' she said.

He didn't want to feel grateful. He told himself roughly that it was her job, she was paid to be the sick-room maid – and that was another joke, wasn't it? He, David Hunter, inhabitant of a sick-room.

He sipped the Horlicks, and the familiar taste was soothing. And the Collis Browne's was warming away his cold dreads. 'What time is it?' he asked.

'Half past three,' Ethel said, turning the shirt to find the tear.

William's, David thought. Too big to be Peter's. His brothers, alive and well, free to come and go, to plan for their futures, to be normal and useful and whole. Tears pushed up to the back of his nose, and he fought them down, sipped more Horlicks.

'Plenty of time to get back to sleep,' Ethel said, without looking up.

And he thought that, when he had finished the drink, he probably would, with her there to guard him. He watched her sewing, and knew she would not speak unless he did. She knew the value of silence. Or perhaps she just knew her place. But he was glad she was there. Wasn't that pathetic? He was glad the sick-room maid was there.

CHAPTER TWO

Edward had felt guiltily glad to be going back to work. He had known it would be a sad Christmas without Bobby, but he had pinned his hopes on David coming downstairs. Sister Heaton, who had looked after him for the first few weeks at home, had been very firm that he must aim for that, and he had seemed to improve under her stimulating briskness. Now she was gone, he seemed to be sinking into a Slough of Despond. Edward did not know what to do to reach him, and it troubled him to feel so helpless. At least at the bank he knew what to do; at least *there* problems had solutions.

When he went down to breakfast, he was surprised to find Beattie, dressed to go out.

He'd been sleeping in the dressing-room for some time now. From the beginning of the war, she had been withdrawing from him; and the consecutive blows of Bobby's death and David's wounding seemed to have shattered the delicate web of connections between them. When she looked at him, her eyes passed over him blankly, as if he were a stranger. It was worse in its way than his inability to help David, for it meant that each of them had to bear their grief alone.

To pretend that things were normal seemed to be all that was left to do, so he said, 'Good morning, my dear. You're up early.'

'I'm going up to Town,' she said, sipping coffee.

He poured himself some. It seemed distressingly weak. 'I wish you would speak to Cook about the coffee,' he said.

'Williamson's couldn't fill the last order,' said Beattie. 'We only had a little left, so I told her to make it last.'

'I'd sooner have it less often, and have it strong,' he said. In some places, he'd heard, they were eking out coffee with ground acorns, or the French subterfuge, chicory root. The notion made him shudder. What was civilisation, if a man could not have a proper cup of coffee at breakfast time? 'I will do without coffee after dinner, if necessary.'

'I'll tell her,' said Beattie. She still had not looked at him.

'What takes you to Town?' he asked carefully.

Now she looked up, but her eyes did not meet his. 'The canteen. There are soldiers on leave, coming and going. And I thought I would call on Diana. It was her first Christmas away from us. I did hope they would at least drop in,' she added.

'I expect the snow put them off,' Edward said. 'Driving would have been difficult.'

'The trains were running,' Beattie pointed out.

It made Edward smile. 'I can't imagine our son-in-law travelling all this way on the Metropolitan Line – not now he's Lord Dene.'

That did at least attract her attention. 'It's so strange that she's Lady Dene, when we thought all that was over and done with.' Diana had been engaged to Rupert's older brother, Charles, but he had fallen in France.

Edward said, 'I admit I was worried when she accepted Rupert. It seemed too hasty – perhaps a wartime thing. But they seem happy enough. If the magazines are anything to go by, they are seen everywhere together.'

'I think she's outgrown Northcote,' Beattie said. 'London's her playground now.'

Ada came in with the tray. Cook appeared on her heels.

'If you was going up to Town, madam, and happened to be passing any shops . . .' she began wheedlingly.

'What is it that you want?' Beattie asked.

'Well, madam . . .' She hesitated.

'Coffee?' Edward suggested, with faint acerbity.

'Oh, no, sir. There was a message came with Williamson's boy just now,' she replied. 'They're getting some in today, and they'll send it up later.'

'What, then?' Beattie asked impatiently.

Cook took the plunge. 'Suet, madam,' she blurted.

'Suet?' Beattie's eyebrows shot up. 'You can't expect me to walk about London clutching a lump of suet.'

'Oh, no madam, perish the thought! They do it ready prepared now, shredded, in nice clean cardboard boxes. Just if you was to happen to pass a grocery shop, and it wasn't any trouble . . .'

Beattie sighed. 'Very well. How much?'

'As many as they'll let you have, madam – or as many as is convenient to carry,' said Cook, humbly. 'You just never know what's going to go missing in shops nowadays. There doesn't seem to be no sense to it. Only the other day—'

'Thank you, Cook,' Beattie interrupted firmly. 'I'll see what I can do.'

'Very good, madam.' Cook knew herself dismissed, and turned away, but she could not suppress the *sotto voce* grumbling, any more than a volcano could. 'I don't know what things are coming to. No coffee, tea as dear as gold dust. And that boy of theirs! Whistling at the back door, same as if I was a dog! "Keep yer hair on, Ma," he says. Twelve years old, and he calls me "Ma". *Me!* Never in all my born days . . .' She mumbled her way out of the morning-room.

Edward regarded his wife with mock admiration. 'I didn't realise until now the trials you have to bear as a housewife. I tip my hat to you.'

In the old days she would have laughed, and a conversation would have bloomed between them. Now, however, she just looked distracted, as though he had called her from important thoughts. 'Have you any message for Diana?' she asked at length. He couldn't help feeling that that was not what she had been thinking.

'Just my love,' Edward said. 'And I hope we'll see her soon.'

The door at Park Place was opened by a middle-aged man in livery. Male servants were getting ever harder to come by, thanks to conscription, but Beattie noted the man had a slight limp, which might explain his presence. He seemed to know his business, anyway, looking at her with the polite blankness of a well-trained servant.

'I do not believe her ladyship has left her room yet, madam,' he replied, to Beattie's query, 'but if you would care to step in I will enquire for you.'

Her ladyship, Beattie thought. Her little Diana was now *her ladyship*. And she lived in a grand house in St James's and had a footman to answer the door. The fulfilment of her youthful dreams. Beattie hoped it answered. At least when the war was over she would still have all this, however her marriage turned out.

The house was bright and smart and smelt of newness and fresh paint. There were flowers in a vase on a stand, the hall table gleamed with polish and the big looking-glass behind it sparkled. Her daughter had good servants.

The footman had gone upstairs, but it was a woman who came down, in the plain black dress of a personal maid. 'Her ladyship will be glad to see you, madam, if you don't mind her being undressed. She's still in bed.'

Diana was sitting up against a mound of pillows, in a bed-jacket of some kind that was a froth of lace and chiffon. Her hair looked sweetly ruffled, her face was glowing with health, and the bedclothes only partly concealed the bulge of the baby.

She smiled at her mother. 'How lovely to see you! But you're so early – is everything all right?'

'I had to come up to Town, so I thought I'd call. You have a new maid,' she commented, as the door closed behind her.

'Yes. Padmore. She's much better. I never liked the one Lady Wroughton chose for me.'

Beattie wondered how Diana's autocratic mother-in-law had liked having her choice superseded. 'Are you well?' she asked.

'Oh, quite! Rupert says I should rest as much as possible, that's all. There's never anything to do in the mornings anyway, so I just stay in bed. Isn't that dreadful?'

'It's very wise.'

'How is everyone? I missed you all at Christmas. How was it?'

'Quiet. Thank you for the fruit, by the way,' Beattie said.

'They have all sorts of fruit at Dene, and there was no-one there to eat it. But afterwards I thought it must have looked odd. You weren't offended?'

Beattie laughed. 'Not at all. Hothouse fruit is always acceptable. We were sorry not to see you, but we understood.'

'I hoped you would,' Diana said. 'I'm so uncomfortable sitting in a car, except for a short journey. And then, with the snow and everything . . . Really, I wouldn't go out at all, except that Rupert insists on having me with him. But I wished I could have visited you.'

'It doesn't matter, darling, as long as you're happy,' Beattie said. 'You *are* happy, aren't you?'

'Oh, yes. Rupert's so sweet to me. I just wish this baby would hurry up and come, so I can see it. Didn't you think it strange, when you were in my condition, that you didn't know what it looked like?'

'It's too long ago. I can't remember,' Beattie said. But of course she remembered. David, her firstborn, her dearest – she remembered everything about it.

Diana read her face. 'How is David? Did he come downstairs?'

Beattie shook her head. 'He's very low. But it was a hard time for all of us.'

'Our first Christmas without Bobby. I can't believe he's gone.'

'Try not to think about it,' Beattie said. 'You should have nothing but happy thoughts, until the baby comes.'

'Does it really make a difference?'

'They say it does, so better to be on the safe side.' She stood up. 'Now I shall go and leave you in peace. I've lots to do.'

'What sort of things?' Diana asked.

Beattie chose a safe one. 'Cook's run out of suet, and Williamson's don't have any, so I'm to look for some if I pass any shops.'

'I'm sure we must have some downstairs. I'll ring for Padmore.'

'No, no! What would she think, if you sent her for suet?' Beattie said, smiling.

'Rupert says we ought to challenge the servants every now and then, to stop them taking things for granted. He says once they start anticipating you, they think they control you.'

'Your husband does have novel ideas!' She rose and kissed her daughter's cheek. 'I must be off. I'm glad to see you looking so bonny,' she said.

In the time between Christmas and New Year, Edward traditionally reviewed his clients' portfolios, and looked into new investment opportunities. It was usually a quiet period, with Parliament in recess and most of his clients out of Town. But the war had changed many things. Weather was

17

too bad at the Front for anything other than routine activity, so the leave rotas were being worked through, and London was lively, with uniforms everywhere and the restaurants full. Many people had stayed up; and some parts of government could not stop.

So, he was not too surprised to receive a visit from Lord Forbesson of the War Office, on the morning of the 3rd of January. He came in out of a dismal, sleety rain and said, 'I was just passing and saw your lights, and a longing for a glass of sherry came over me.' He glanced at the fireplace and rubbed his hands. 'Glad to see you have a decent fire. Let's hope we don't have a hard winter, or we'll all have to start economising on coal.'

Edward gestured him to a chair by the fireside and poured the sherry. 'Please don't mention economies. My breakfast coffee was so weak I could see the bottom of the cup.'

'That will never do,' said Forbesson. 'Can't have you flagging for want of a stimulating beverage! We all depend on you a great deal.' A sheet of hail hit the window, and the fire jumped as the gust came down the chimney. 'Wretched day,' Forbesson said. 'Still, thank God for bad weather, eh, or our men at the Front would get no rest. Imagine waging war twelve months a year! Poor devils in Russia have it much worse, of course,' he went on, holding his glass up to the firelight to admire the colour. 'Makes you wonder how anybody ever settled in places like Siberia. Why they didn't take one look and move on. Nothing so curious as the human race.'

'Speaking of Russia,' Edward prompted.

'Ah, yes – our biggest headache at the moment. Will the Russkis stick? They've suffered terrible losses, their soldiers are short of bullets, boots and bread. And the Tsaritsa has her pet lunatic whispering in her ear to make peace—'

'Rasputin, you mean?'

'More than one lunatic in her entourage, I grant you, but

18

yes, Rasputin. He comes from Siberia, by the by. I suppose livin' in a place like that for any length of time, you're bound to end up hearin' voices. He urges her, and she nags the Tsar, who's always done what she wants. And if they make peace with Germany – well, it doesn't bear thinking about.'

Edward nodded. If Russia dropped out of the war, Germany would be able to move all its Eastern Front troops to the Western Front.

'We've just given Fritz a pasting, put him on the back foot, got a real chance of rolling him up this year,' Forbesson complained. 'We need the Russkis to keep biffing it out, whatever it costs them. And the Tsar's got enough on his hands, with the Duma and the Soviets and industrial unrest, without his wife stirring up scandal and bad feeling. Trouble is, Nicholas has no backbone, otherwise he'd have controlled his wife – and had someone put a bullet through the madman.'

'You really think the Germans are down?' Edward asked.

'Lord, yes! We took big losses last year, but theirs were far worse. And they don't have the benefit of good morale back home. Our people are sound, and they know they're fighting for a just cause. Our blockade is hitting the Germans hard. We've got the upper hand over the Zeppelins, and we've proved we can force them back in the line. It's a matter of keeping going now, holding firm. The Germans are on their last legs – they're so anxious to get the Russians out of it, that they're . . .' He paused. 'This is in the strictest confidence?'

'Of course,' Edward said.

'The Germans are secretly financing the Red revolutionaries in return for a pledge that if they succeed in taking over they'll make peace.'

'Revolution in Russia?' Edward said. 'Well, we've talked about it often enough. Do you really think it's likely now?'

'It's always just under the surface,' said Forbesson. 'It

hasn't been successful until now because the revolutionaries have never had the organisation, and the Tsar has always had the only disciplined troops. But if the *army* turned against him – and the Reds stopped quarrelling with each other long enough to co-operate . . .' He shrugged. 'We must hope that it blows over, as it always has.' He drained his glass and stood up. 'Which reminds me, I must be off. War cabinet meeting with our new chancellor of the Exchequer. How to pay for it all.'

'Like God, the Treasury never sleeps,' Edward said, rising to show him out.

Forbesson gave him a considering look. 'You're a good fellow, Hunter. Can't tell you how much I appreciate having you as a sounding board. You see things as they are. Politicians always end up thinkin' crooked, no matter how good their intentions.'

'Mathematics can't be corrupted,' Edward said. 'At the end of the column, the number is right or it isn't. There's no area of doubt.'

'Must be a happy state,' Forbesson grunted. 'Government is *all* doubt.'

Remembering that Beattie was in Town, working at her coffee stall in Waterloo Station, which meant she would be late home, Edward went after work to see Élise de Rouveroy at her small flat in Soho Square. He took with him the papers relating to her investments, which he'd had under review.

She greeted him eagerly. 'Oh, Édouard! I have not seen you for such a long time! Christmas is for families, it is sad for those who have none.' She was already tugging at his coat, to make him take it off, afraid that it might be a flying visit.

He let her divest him. 'Where is Solange?' he asked. 'You should not be answering the door yourself.'

20

'Oh, we are not so nice,' she said. 'Solange is more a friend than a servant. In any case, she has gone to the International Store in Shaftesbury Avenue to see if they have any coffee.'

'I suppose we must get used to these annoying shortages,' Edward said. 'My cook this morning was asking about suet.'

'What is suet?'

'I believe it is animal fat, used in cooking. Beef fat.'

She laughed. 'What conversations we have! It is fantastic. Not poetry, or the opera . . . I will ask Solange about beef fat when she returns. But, come, you are staying for dinner?'

'I can't – I must go home. But I wanted to talk to you about your investments.'

'*Tiens! Les affaires!*' she pouted. 'And I thought you came to see *me*.'

He grew grave. 'Élise, you must not—'

'*Must* not?' she teased. '*Quoi, encore?*'

'You must not flirt with me,' he said, feeling his face grow hot. 'It is not right. I am your financial adviser.'

'And a friend,' she urged, fixing him with bright eyes.

'I hope so. But not – more. I am a married man.'

'I know,' she said, her mouth curled in a tight, mocking smile. 'And if I – what is it? Flirt? Ah, yes, this is also in French the same – if I *flirt*, you will tell me you will not come again. You will threaten me.'

'It's hardly threatening—' he began uncomfortably.

'*Mais si!* It is exactly that. Because I depend so much on seeing you. I have such a dull life, and see so few people.' She looked up at him, and changed her expression. 'I am sorry. It is not fair. I must not provoke you. Come and sit down, and let me tell you my news, and I will be *absolument comme il faut*. You need not fear me, Monsieur Sang-froid.'

He sat beside her on the sofa, and said, 'I am not afraid of you.'

'Well,' she said consideringly, 'I think you *are*, just a little.

21

It is very English. But that is as it should be. A woman should always have – how do you say it? – the upper hand?'

'In England we have a saying, the customer is always right.'

'Of course, I am your customer. Very well. Now I must tell you my news. I have found a job.'

He felt slightly dismayed. She should not have to work. 'What is it?' he asked.

'What is there that I could possibly do, Édouard?' she said, laughing. 'The dance, *bien sûr*! I am to instruct at a school of dance in Oxford Street.'

'I'm surprised that dancing is still being taught in wartime,' he said.

'No, why should you be? Young ladies must dance with soldiers when they come on leave. And young men who go to be soldiers must dance whenever they can. If young people do not dance together, how can they fall in love and marry and make more little soldiers? So they must learn, and someone must teach them.'

'So you will be teaching ballroom dancing?'

'And also ballet, though not so much. But one day the war will be over, and when the world is free there will be ballet again. Little girls will always want to be ballet dancers.' She sounded a little wistful.

'Won't it be very tiring?' he asked.

'It will be good to be tired in that way. I do not like to be idle, me. And in this place,' she waved a hand round the flat, 'there is not much home-making to be done.'

'I have been thinking for some time that you ought to move somewhere nicer,' Edward said.

'We are comfortable here, Solange and me. And there is not a great deal of money,' she said indifferently.

'Ah,' he said, reaching for his briefcase, 'that is what I have come to see you about. Your investments are doing quite well, but I think they could do better. I would like to change some of them. If you'll allow me . . .' He took out a sheaf of papers, and went through them with her. As she bent her head forward, it came close to his own, and a wisp of her hair brushed his cheek. He drew back just a little to avoid the contact, hoping she would not notice.

'But this,' she said at last, pointing to one item. 'You wish me to invest in armaments?'

'It is one of the most lucrative options, in wartime,' he said.

She looked up at him. 'You wish me to invest in guns and shells to kill people?'

He met her gaze steadily. 'My job is to take care of your money, and advise you where it can get the best return. It is for you to decide if you wish to follow the advice.'

'But don't you think it would be wrong?' she insisted. 'Is not killing wrong?'

He chose his words carefully. 'Unfortunately, we are at war. And, unfortunately, war means killing the enemy before they kill us. In a perfect world, we might wage war with words alone, but we have to deal with the world as it is.'

She studied him, as if trying to read his thoughts, to discover what he really believed. 'And if I invest as you advise, I shall be able to move to a better place?'

'I believe so. And it would make you more secure.'

'Then I will do it, and hope my bullets kill only Germans.' She smiled suddenly. 'Come, Édouard, do not look so blue. I have not such a great conscience when it comes to *les sales Boches*. I remember what they did to my poor Guillaume, and Émile. You may make me rich in any way you please.'

'Then you won't need to take the job,' he said cautiously.

'Oh, I shall still take it,' she said lightly. 'One must be prudent. And I like to be useful. But do not despair,' she said, with the teasing smile again. 'It is only for a few hours a day. I shall still be here to have supper with you, and hear all you have been doing.'

'I wasn't thinking about that,' he said with dignity. 'My concern is only for your welfare.'

'It comes to the same thing,' she shrugged.

In a small, shabby house in a street near Waterloo Station, Beattie lay in bed in Louis's arms. She would not waste their precious moments together sleeping, but she was drifting on the calm sea of his breathing, in a state of mindlessness.

The mantel clock downstairs struck, bringing her back to the present. She stirred, and sighed. 'I will have to go.'

His response was to tighten his arms round her for a moment, but then he released her. 'I wish it didn't have to be like this,' he said. 'Snatching at crumbs. After the war—'

She interrupted him, putting her fingers quickly to his lips. 'Don't talk about "after the war".'

He kissed the fingers, smiling, and said, 'You think it's unlucky?'

She pulled away and swung her legs out of bed. 'I don't want to think about it.' She could not imagine it. It was like a foreign country, so far away she would never see it. She stood up and turned to face him. 'This is all we have, don't you see? The present. We can't—' She stopped, and started again. 'We had no idea, when it began, how it would be. What would happen.'

He nodded. 'All right.' One of her sons was dead, another badly wounded. She could not look beyond that, and he understood. 'When shall I see you again?'

'I can't come tomorrow. And then there's the weekend.' She had to be at home at the weekend. 'But I might manage Tuesday morning,' she said, frowning over her mental diary.

'I have a meeting at Horse Guards in the morning,' he said. 'Can you stay in Town until lunchtime? I could make an excuse and get out early.'

She nodded unhappily. 'I'll try.'

'The following week,' he said gently, holding her eyes, 'I

24

shall be in France.' He saw the alarm leap into them. 'Not to fight, not yet. But there will be a strategy meeting, with all the generals, and I have to inspect the sites. I shall be away for a week.'

'A week!'

'I know. It seems like an eternity to me, too.'

'How shall I bear it?'

He took her in his arms. She rested her cheek on his chest, and he kissed the crown of her head. 'Keep busy,' he said. 'We must both keep busy. It won't last for ever—'

She jerked her head back to look at him in alarm. 'It won't?'

'The war, I mean. Our love will last for ever. You need never doubt that.'

'That's not what I am afraid of,' she said, in a low voice.

CHAPTER THREE

Sadie arrived at Highclere, propped her bicycle against the fence, and went straight into the isolation box to see how the bay was doing. Someone else was in there before her: a man, with his back to her, at the bay's head. It was a back she would have known anywhere. She stopped, closed her eyes, let the rush of joy have its way with her.

He turned his head, saw her, and smiled. 'I was wondering if you'd be up today,' he said.

His face was thinner, not so much as if he was starving, but as if he was being worn away, like stone by wind or water. He looked tired, and she had the sense that if he had not been so weather-tanned, he would have been pale, too.

'I didn't know you'd be here,' she said.

'I arrived last night. My Christmas leave,' he said. 'It's pretty quiet out there at the moment – or as quiet as *we* ever get. No battle injuries, but there are always accidents. And the sheer strain of the work takes its toll on the horses.' The words seemed to pull his face downwards. 'The cold is terrible, and there's no shelter for most of them. The troopers do their best . . .' He visibly changed his thoughts' direction. '*Your* horses are looking pretty good. Except for this chap.'

'He started a discharge from his nostrils yesterday,' Sadie said. 'It could be just a cold, but he didn't look right to me, so we isolated him.'

'He does seem rather miserable,' Courcy said, stroking the horse's neck. 'A bit glassy-eyed.'

'That's what I thought,' Sadie said. 'Do you think he's got a temperature? Is it just a cold?'

'I'm not sure. I think he may have some kind of swelling under his jaw. Here, feel this, tell me what you think.' He reached for her hand, to guide her fingers.

His was hard and rough and strong. When he took hers, it was like a small electric shock. She tried to concentrate on the horse, feeling through the thin hot skin under the jaw what could be a thickening. 'I think there's something there,' she said, aware of her heart beating too rapidly. 'What is it?'

'It could be an abscess starting,' he said. 'That would account for any fever. Awkward place to get at, if it comes to draining it. Too many large vessels in the area.' He was still holding her hand, frowning over the horse as if he'd forgotten it. 'We'll just have to wait and see if it develops. If it is an abscess, it might burst spontaneously. You can try hot poultices. That might help.'

She nodded, dry-mouthed. He looked down, noticed their linked hands, and let hers go without comment.

'Should we keep him isolated?' she managed to ask.

'Wouldn't hurt. Abscesses like this are quite common with animals in low condition, but it could be symptomatic of something infectious, like tuberculosis or strangles. How long have you had him?'

'Two days,' she said. 'He seemed low when he arrived, but I put it down to the train journey. Then he started the runny nose yesterday.'

'Well, if he has something, he came in with it. You'd better keep a sharp eye on the others, especially those he travelled with.' He stroked the bay's neck again, and it turned its head slightly and nudged him, then looked away. 'He's feeling under the weather, poor old boy. What's his name?'

'Berry,' she said.

Courcy laughed. 'So you're still naming them! I was testing you.'

'It's just easier when referring to them,' she defended herself. 'I don't get attached, as I did with the first ones.'

'I bet you do,' he said. She felt the warmth of his look all the way down into her stomach, like a hot drink on a cold day. 'Is it too late to wish you a happy new year?'

'I think you're allowed to say it the first time you see someone, even if it's days later,' she said. 'So happy new year to you, too.' Her smile faded. 'Not that it feels very new, with the war going on and no end in sight. Or very happy.'

He nodded. 'I'm sorry about your brother. Pilots have a rough time out there. But what they do saves countless lives. You can be very proud of him.'

'I am. But it doesn't bring him back. I miss knowing he's in the world.'

'And your other brother – David, is it?'

'It's a slow business.'

'And what about you?' he asked. 'It must be hard on you.'

'No more than on anyone else,' she said.

'Yes,' he asserted. 'Because you feel it. You take responsibility, even for things you don't have to. I can see in your face how you've changed.'

Once she would have blushed at being the object of a man's attention, but she *had* changed. She had been a child still, when she first met him. Now she had seen and done things she never could have imagined. She met his gaze steadily. 'I feel much older,' she said. 'I suppose partly it's David, and Bobby. But mostly it's . . .' She sought for words. 'The war is everywhere, in everything. It's like having a great heavy pack on your back, whatever you're doing, and you can't put it down, not for a moment.'

He nodded again, as if he really understood. He said, 'It's your birthday soon, isn't it?'

28

'On the nineteenth,' she said, flattered that he remembered. 'I'll be nineteen.'

'Nineteen on the nineteenth,' he said. 'What a great age you've reached, Miss Sadie Hunter.' He looked around. 'Where's my friend Nailer?'

'By the fire in David's room. He said it was too cold to come out today. He spends a lot of time in there – of course we have to keep the fire burning all the time, for David.'

'And a sensible dog will always stay by the fire,' said Courcy. 'Do you want to show me the rest of the horses?'

'Of course,' she said happily. 'And then, perhaps you'd like to go for a ride?'

'I've been counting on it,' he said, and seemed pleased.

She hoped, a little wistfully, that he was pleased not just to go for a ride, but go for a ride with *her*. John Courcy was the vet who had been assigned to them when they first started training horses for the army. Though he had now been transferred to France, he still visited Highclere when on leave, and if Sadie could have believed *she* was the reason for his visits, she would have been the happiest female in England.

The letter came on the Saturday after New Year. David hadn't heard from Sophy since before Christmas, and he opened it eagerly; but from the first words, his heart sank. When a person begins by saying the letter is hard for them to write, you can bet the recipient will find it even harder to read.

It was his old rival, apparently, Humphrey Hobart. The Hobarts owned an estate near the Oliphants' country house in Melton Mowbray, and the Oliphant parents had always wanted her to marry the son and heir. Mr Oliphant had accepted David because Sophy was in love, and he was soft-hearted towards her, but Mrs Oliphant had never given up hope of something better. Sophy's brother, David's best

29

friend Jumbo, had warned him his mother was working against him. Now it seemed she had succeeded.

It had all happened quite suddenly, Sophy pleaded. Hobart had been home on leave. They had gone to a dance together. He had confessed he had always loved her, asked her to marry him. She had said yes before she knew it.

You most generously offered to release me from our engagement once before, because of your wound and your uncertain future, and I refused to consider it. But given that it remains most uncertain when you and I could marry, if we ever could, I feel I owe it to my family to make the best match I can. I know Humphrey will be a good husband to me, and hope that you will be generous once more, and release me as soon as possible. Knowing what a noble soul you are, I am anticipating your kindness, as Humphrey wishes us to get married before he goes Overseas, and my parents are very eager to secure my future comfort. I hope and pray your recovery will be as complete as possible, given the nature of your injuries, and that in time you will find happiness with someone else. I know that you will wish me everything good for the future, as I wish you, and I shall remain always, your firm friend, Sophy Oliphant.

Soon to become Sophy Hobart, David thought viciously, throwing down the letter. She had not mentioned love. He didn't know if that made it better or not. If she'd found she had mistaken her heart, and that she really loved Hobart, would that be less painful to him than her deciding that he, David, was a hopeless case, and hastening to secure Hobart, the good match, while he was still available? Sophy mistaken, Sophy faithless, Sophy calculating? No, it didn't make any difference. It hurt, whichever way it was. He had lost her, his beautiful, his perfect Sophy, his angel, his miracle. He had gone to war for her, as her knight, wearing her favour, intending to slay dragons and lay heroic deeds at her feet. What a fool, what a hopeless, romantic fool he had been! But still she reigned there in his mind, at the heart of a crystal of perfection, untouchable, unchangeable.

And he was left a wreck, a dependent, useless cripple. Sophy had been the one thing he had to look forward to, the one thing he had to live for. Now there was nothing.

The news spread rapidly about the house. They took it hard down in the servants' hall. When they assembled for lunch – as they called their mid-morning tea and cake – there was indignation on all sides.

'And to think she visited him not two months ago!' cried Ada. David had always been her favourite. 'Pretending to love him, promising to stick by him!'

'*Three* months ago,' said Nula, who had come in to over-haul the linen. She had been nursemaid to all the young Hunters but was now married, lived out, and acted as part-time sewing maid. 'Wasn't it October?'

'What's the difference?' said Ada, impatiently.

'A month can be a long time for a young girl,' Nula replied.

'If I had a sweetie, I'd stick by him through thick and thin,' said Emily, the Irish kitchen maid. 'No matter what.'

'Ho, yus!' said Ginger. 'You'd 'ave to! Any sweetie *you* got'd be your last chance.'

'None of your cheek,' Cook rebuked him automatically. 'How's he taking it?'

She addressed the question to Ethel, who had been allowed out of her bad books sufficiently to take her meals with the other servants again, though she occupied the lowest seat, at the far end from Cook, next to Munt, the gardener, and opposite Ginger, the boot boy.

Ethel feigned not to know she was being spoken to, and

31

Cook was forced to answer herself. 'He'll take it like a gentleman, o' course, but it must hurt all the same.'

'He'll go into a decline and die, and then she'll be sorry,' Emily sighed.

'None o' that talk,' Cook said hastily. 'Nobody's dying. Anyway, he's well out of it, in my opinion. That Craven, their chauffeur, said in this very kitchen that she wasn't good enough for him. Said she never stuck at anything. In this very kitchen!'

'I thought she was a very pretty young lady,' Lilian said timidly.

'Handsome is as handsome does,' Cook returned.

'Ask me,' Munt growled, 'he saw it coming. Must've. Girl like that's not going to wait for ever.'

'I'd wait,' Emily asserted. 'I'd wait until – until the earth frozed over.'

Munt ignored her and carried on: 'What's in it for her? You got to look at that. This other character's got land. Land always trumps.'

'Nobody wants to know what you think,' Cook snapped.

Munt stared her down. 'Where's the cake, anyway? We're s'posed to have cake.'

'No cake,' she said. 'Flour's short and sugar's got to be used careful.'

'Jam for the bread, then,' Munt said, poking at the slice on his plate with disfavour.

'No jam! What did I just say? Got to economise on sugar. Be grateful you got bread and butter. Haven't you heard there's a war on?'

'I've heard you got a larder groaning with pots o' jam what *we* don't get a sight of. Eat it yourself in bed, most like, when nobody's lookin'.'

Ginger sniggered, and Cook mottled with such fury at them both that she couldn't get any words out.

Into the temporary hiatus Ethel spoke quietly, almost as

32

if to herself. 'She *wasn't* good enough for him. But he worshipped her. He won't show it, because he's a gentleman, but he's taking it very hard.'

It was received in thoughtful silence, which Nula broke: 'Let's get him well first, then we'll worry about his heart. Plenty of nice young women to choose from, once he's on his feet.'

Ethel stood up to leave, which seemed to close the subject.

Lilian turned to Emily. They both had the afternoon off. 'Fancy going to the pictures, Em? There's *Oliver Twist* and a Charlie Chaplin at the Electric Palace. You like Charlie Chaplin.'

'I can't. I got something to do.'

'What's that?' Lilian asked, but Emily only shook her head, and wouldn't say.

'She's got a squeeze!' Ginger crowed. 'Look at her goin' all red! She's after the bread man, that's who.'

Emily, whose unrequited passion for Con Meyer, the deliveryman for Hetherton's Hygienic Bakery, was well known, jumped up from the table with tears in her eyes and ran into the kitchen. Ethel came back from the other door, which she had just reached, to smack Ginger hard round the back of the head.

'Oy!' he protested, to her disappearing back, rubbing his head indignantly. 'What was that for? I was only 'avin' a bit o' fun!'

Munt swallowed the last of his bread and butter. 'She's going soft, that one,' he remarked. 'Takin' up for Emily? Must be all this mixing with the gentry. Pickin' up their manners. Well, I better be gettin' on. On yer feet, boy – taters to pull.'

''V'you finished the boots?' Cook demanded, as Ginger obeyed.

'Nearly,' he admitted.

'You get back there and finish 'em, before you start messing about in the garden.'

33

Munt grabbed Ginger's collar and turned him towards the back door. 'Taters first, boots after, if you wants 'em in time for upstairs luncheon,' he said to Cook.

'And have him tramping mud all through my kitchen?' she retorted.

'We all got our trials to bear,' he told her, shoving Ginger before him. "A'n't you 'eard, there's a war on?'

On Sunday Frank Hussey, who had once been gardener's boy and was now second gardener at Mandeville Hall, came to dinner. By then, the topic of Sophy Oliphant's perfidy had been eclipsed by the assassination of Rasputin, the mad Russian monk. It was a story that had everything: foul murder, debauchery, mysticism and high-ups. It was said two aristocrats had lured him to their house, plied him with drink and drugs, then poisoned him, stabbed him and shot him – and still he kept getting up. So they battered him with iron bars, tied him up and threw him in the frozen river.

'If the river was frozen,' Ethel objected witheringly, 'how did they get him in? He'd have just bounced off the top.'

'I expect they broke the ice first,' Ada said seriously.

'I wouldn't be surprised if it was all exaggerated,' Frank said, trying for reason. 'You know how stories get embroidered.'

'Well, it seems he's dead, at all events,' Cook said, 'and from what we hear he deserved it, pretending to be a man of God and then carrying on like he did.'

'Carrying on like what?' asked Emily, whose reading of the papers was censored by Cook.

'Never you mind. Nothing you're likely to come across. 'Nother slice o' pork, Frank? And a bit more crackling?'

'Thank you,' he said, passing his plate. 'Can't say no to your crackling, Mrs D. I heard the Earl and Countess Wroughton were expected home today, is that right?'

'Seemingly,' said Cook. 'Back from Norfolk. The earl's got a bad cold so he's not stopping in London, going straight to Dene Park. And our Miss Diana's coming down for a bit, too, to rest from all her gadding about. I just hope he keeps his cold to himself. She don't want to be catching one now, in her condition.'

'Well, you'll be glad to see her, I bet,' said Frank. 'Is Lord Dene coming too?'

'It seems not. But he *is* in uniform. I expect he's got duties in London.' The reproach was faint. She was fond of Frank – he was like the son she'd never had, and was the only person who called her by her name, rather than 'Cook' – but with every man going into the army, it went against the grain to see a great healthy-looking chap like Frank staying out. She itched to ask him how he did it, but was afraid of the answer. The master sat on an appeals tribunal, to decide about people who'd been called up and didn't want to go, and stories filtered down sometimes – generally things Peter had overheard and repeated to Cook when he came into the kitchen looking for something to eat between meals. She didn't want to learn something to make her like Frank less – especially as he was sparking Ethel.

When the first course was ended, Frank insisted on helping to clear the plates, and followed Ethel out into the kitchen. 'You ready for our outing this afternoon?' he asked her. 'Where'd you like to go? Pictures, or for a walk, and then somewhere for tea?'

'I can't go,' she said. 'I can't be away from here.'

'It's your afternoon off, isn't it?' he said.

'Yes, but Mr David's upset, with Miss Oliphant jilting him. He doesn't show it, but he's taking it really hard.'

'I'm sorry for him, but I don't see what it has to do with you,' Frank said.

'I have to answer his bell, if he wants anything.'

'Doesn't Lilian do that when you're off?'

'Yes, but he doesn't like it, and the way he is, if he rings for me and Lilian comes—'

He laid his big hand on her forearm. 'Ethel, don't start getting attached to him. You don't mean anything to him. You're just a servant. He doesn't know you exist.'

'What do you know about it?' she said irritably. 'You don't know him.'

'And neither do you.'

'I've looked after him for months now, ever since the nurse went!'

'You answer his bell,' Frank said gently. 'That's all. Believe me, I'm older than you, and a lot wiser, and I know the gentry. And I know men, which you don't, whatever you think.' He grinned suddenly. 'Yes, you think you can wind us all round your finger, but when it comes to it, men don't take women seriously, and gentry don't take servants seriously. So don't go risking losing a man of your own sort who's dead keen on you for the sake of the young master, who finds it convenient to have his bell answered by the same person each time. That's all it is, girl – convenience. You take it from me.'

She stared up at him impassively through this speech. 'Is that it?' she asked ironically. 'You finished?'

'That'll do for now,' he said. He was giving her the smile that drove her mad, the one that said he knew everything that was going on in her head, and found it amusing. Men didn't take women seriously, eh? 'You think you know it all, don't you? You think you're so clever.'

He closed his hand more firmly round her arm so that she couldn't pull away. 'I know a lot about you,' he said, 'and what I don't know, I want to find out. So have your afternoon off, which you're due, and let me take you out somewhere and treat you like you should be treated.'

'And how is that?' she demanded.

'Like a lovely, desirable woman. Not like a parlour maid.'

His words thrilled her, but she wouldn't show it. 'I'm the sick-room maid, I'll have you know!' she retorted.

'Still got the word "maid" in it, whichever way you dice it. Give it up for an afternoon, and come and be a lady with me. Let's go into Westleigh and walk round the shops, and have tea at Cobb's, and catch the early-evening show at the Palace. Go and take your apron off and put your hat on, and we'll go now.'

'What – now? You haven't had your afters. There's Eve's pudding.'

'I'd sooner have you than afters,' he said.

What girl could resist that? 'All right,' she said. But she wasn't going to kiss him in the dark at the pictures, however much she wanted to. She had to remember her hideous past, the secret stain on her that meant she could never marry – not someone as nice as Frank Hussey, anyway, for all his irritating way of being right and knowing best.

CHAPTER FOUR

Diana was upset when Rupert announced that he was going to France. 'You said you wouldn't have to go.'

'Nothing is certain in war,' he decreed.

'What does that mean?' she demanded impatiently.

'For Heaven's sake, it's only a meeting. It's not as if I'm going into battle. There's no action going on out there, anyway.'

'People still get hurt,' she said. 'Mother says there are wounded coming in every day at Waterloo.'

'I shan't be in the line, foolish. The brass hats are meeting in Paris and I'm on the staff, so if they're safe, I shall be safe.'

'I don't want to be left on my own,' she said. 'Not – like this.' She instinctively cupped her swollen front.

'But you're going down to Dene anyway,' he reminded her. 'You're going to see your family – you'll be surrounded by people.'

'It's not the same,' she said fretfully.

He cocked an eye at her. 'You don't mean to say you'll miss me?'

'Yes.'

'Oh,' he said, and sounded almost disconcerted. 'Really? You'll really miss me?'

Now she was taken aback. 'Of course I will. Won't you miss me?'

He thought about it. 'Now you mention it . . . yes. I will.'

She gave an uncertain smile. 'You needn't sound surprised. We are husband and wife, after all.'

He took her in his arms and held her carefully, like something between an egg and a hand grenade. 'So we are,' he said. 'I was forgetting.'

She took it for a joke. He was always saying odd things. 'You promise you won't get hurt?' she said after a moment, leaning against him.

'That,' he said, 'I can promise.'

It was exhilarating to be getting away, out of London; a change of scene, a change of company. Military life – of the sort he led, anyway – was quite comfortable, but it did tend to a sameness.

There was a large party of military and civilian bigwigs, first-class carriages, and some decent picnic baskets had been provided for the journey. Rupert, being a sociable soul, soon identified a group of like-minded young aides to beguile his journey. In particular there was one Wagstaffe, who turned out to be a cousin in some degree – as so many of the old aristocracy were – and proved a comfortable companion.

Wagstaffe came from a military background, and was very useful in naming the various figures who walked up and down, heading from the bigwigs' carriage to the latrine and back, or just stretching their legs and chatting to fellow staffers. One in particular caught Rupert's eye, a tall man with a hawk-like face and an imposing mien.

'Who is that fellow?' he asked Wagstaffe, as the man paused to chat to one of the aides further down the carriage. 'I feel as if I ought to know him.'

'Which one?' Wagstaffe asked. 'Oh, him. That's Major Plunkett. Tea planter, Irish background. Fought in South

Africa, volunteered in 'fourteen. Said to be a devil with the ladies, too. Can't think how, with *that* beak,' he added discontentedly. He had a considerable beak of his own, but a lack of chin to balance it made him look more duck than hawk.

'Oh, I can see how,' Rupert said. 'It's the *tout ensemble*.' He made a circular motion with his hand. 'And the height. Imposing. I'm envious.'

'You're tall,' Wagstaffe pointed out.

'I'm more your willowy type,' Rupert said. 'He's a mighty oak. I'd fall in love with him myself, if I were a woman.'

'You do say the queerest things,' Wagstaffe commented. 'I suppose it's wit. I never had any myself . . . I say, *cave*, he's looking this way.'

Rupert had been staring, and the major, perhaps feeling the eyes on him, had turned, and was giving him a quizzical look. And then he strolled over. 'Plunkett,' he said in a friendly manner, offering his hand. 'Have we met?'

'I don't think so, sir,' Rupert said, standing to shake it. 'Dene is my name.'

'Lieutenant Lord Dene?' the major said. 'I've heard of you. You're Earl Wroughton's son, aren't you? And recently married, I believe?'

Rupert blinked. 'I didn't know my fame had spread so far, sir.'

'I know your wife's family slightly,' Plunkett said. 'I served with her grandfather in Dublin, many years ago. But that was before she was born. She wouldn't know me.' He seemed to brush aside the connection and hurried on. 'Been to France before?'

'No, sir. I've been in Horse Guards since I volunteered.'

'But longing to get out there, I dare say. It's the place to make a reputation, all right.' Rupert wasn't quick enough with an answer, and the major gave a rueful smile. 'And to lose everything else, you're thinking. You lost a brother, I believe.'

Rupert shrugged it off, as one was supposed to. 'Everyone's lost someone, sir.'

Louis Plunkett nodded. 'So you've never been to Paris before? Well, you'll find it a bit knocked about, but still a fine city. Parisians are great hosts. It's still possible to get a good meal, if you know where.'

Rupert grinned. 'I'm guessing *you* know where, sir.'

'I do indeed. I'll make sure to point you in the right direction. There's a little place in Montmartre – they do a truffled duck that would melt your heart.' He gave a pleasant nod and passed on.

Rupert turned his head and thoughtfully watched him go, wondering why he should be so friendly.

Wagstaffe was indignant. 'All very well, but he didn't so much as glance at me,' he complained. 'Just because you're a lord and I'm only an honourable. Your Irish high-ups are such snobs. I shall think it very poor sport, you know, if you hobnob with him without me. We *are* cousins.'

'Oh, I don't think there'll be hobnobbing,' Rupert said. 'He was just fishing.'

'*Fishing?* What for?'

'Dashed if I know,' said Rupert.

Diana was lonely. The earl's heavy cold kept him to his rooms, and seemed to give the countess an excuse to avoid all company. She decreed they would take their meals in their suite, and since she sent a note excusing Diana from attending church in her condition, it meant that Diana didn't see either of the Wroughtons at all.

She had a motor-car and driver at her service so she had herself driven to The Elms, and it was good to see the family again. But when Monday came, the children went to school,

41

her father to his office, and Sadie and her mother had their war work to attend to. However glad they had all been to see her, their duties now came first.

The Elms was not quite deserted: the servants welcomed her, and Cook would have talked for hours about her Condition and the Little Heir To Come, if Diana could have borne the repetition. The others were too shy to initiate conversation, and once Diana had asked if they were well, communication was at an end.

She climbed upstairs to visit David; but he didn't seem particularly pleased to see her. He stared into the fire, answered in monosyllables, asked her no questions about herself. She hadn't seen him for months, and was shocked at the change in him. He seemed to have let himself go. His face was pale and lined, which was understandable, but his hair needed cutting, he was poorly shaved, and he looked as though he had dressed by guess. There was a raffishness about him at odds with the military smartness she had grown used to in the men of her new circle.

Could it all be attributed to a broken heart? she wondered. 'I'm sorry about Sophy,' she said tentatively. He grunted discouragingly, but she struggled on. 'It's better, surely, to know at once if she's changed her mind, rather than later. I mean, if you *had* married—'

'Oh do stop!' David ground out between his teeth. 'What do *you* know about it?'

Diana flushed. 'I lost my fiancé—' she began.

'I said *stop*,' David interrupted. 'I've heard all the heartening speeches already. I'm not a Boy Scout.'

'That's obvious,' she snapped. 'Boy Scouts are polite.'

He did not give her so much as a glance. 'I'm a hopeless cripple,' he said. 'We're excused politeness. *And* visitors,' he added pointedly.

She wanted to slap him; but he was her brother, and he had suffered grievously. 'Are you in pain?' she asked quietly.

'What do *you* think?' he muttered.

'Can I get you anything?' No answer. 'David, I know things look bleak now, but it will get better. Time does heal, you know. I mean, look at me. When Charles fell, I thought my life was over, but now I'm married and expecting a baby. You're unhappy about Sophy, but you'll meet someone else. As for being a cripple,' she went on hastily, sensing a volcano stirring, 'I'm sure that isn't true. And even if you end up with a limp, that isn't the end of the world. There are—'

'If you tell me there are men with no legs at all, I shan't be answerable for the consequences. I know all about them. Some of them were my men. Go away, Di. You don't know what you're talking about.'

So there didn't seem to be anything to do but leave him, and return to her suite in the big empty house at Dene Park.

She invited some of her former friends to visit, and enjoyed showing off her change of circumstance. But conversation was sticky. They all had sweethearts in uniform, hopes of dances and tennis and outings in the summer, and dreams of proposals to come. She had done all that; she was housebound by her condition; and at this stage of pregnancy she found it difficult to think about anything except the baby.

The weekend came around again, and her family visited, and there was relief. The earl still kept to his rooms – his cold had left him with bronchitis – but Lady Wroughton was gracious, and sat with them for half an hour, asked polite questions, seemed to listen to the answers and invited them to come to Dene Park as often as they liked. Her father, Diana saw, was impressed by her obvious desire to please.

But Rupert did not come. He ought to have been back in England long since, but there was no word from him, and Diana had no idea when she would be going back to London.

And with another Monday came a renewal of her isolation.

Edward almost missed his sister at Victoria Station. He had been told the wrong platform number – something that happened all the time, these days – and had to hurry through the crowds to a different barrier, where fortunately he found Laura still waiting. She had a suitcase, a Gladstone, a brown-paper parcel and a bulging cloth bag, and had she been less laden she would probably have walked off in her independent way before he reached her.

'Laura!' he called.

She turned, and her face lit. 'Teddy! What a treat! I didn't expect to be met.' They embraced. 'And certainly not by the Man Himself. Nothing to do at the office today? Don't tell me you've been sacked.'

He ignored her teases. 'Are you all alone?'

'Oh, yes. Scattered to the four winds, the others – not a moment to waste. If I could have found a porter . . . ' She was still looking around.

'Porter*ess*,' Edward corrected her.

'They probably look less surprising to me than to you,' she assured him. 'But they all seem to be busy.'

'Let's try and manage without. Why have you got so much luggage with you? I thought this was only going to be a short stay.'

'Bessie's in the workshop so we had to empty her.' Bessie was the ambulance that she drove in France with a group of friends. 'And we're moving to a new location when we get back, so we couldn't leave things at the lodgings.'

'What's wrong with Bessie?'

'Suspension,' Laura said. 'Those potholes over there are very hard on a girl. Her springs are busted and she's so far down on one side her chassis is touching the rear tyre.' She looked at him and laughed. 'You have no idea what I'm talking about, have you?'

'I'm glad to say I haven't. But I do know they're lucky to have you. Has it answered, your adventure? Has it cured the itch in your feet?'

'I don't know about cured, but I have enjoyed it,' she said. 'Well, perhaps "enjoyed" isn't quite the right word. It's absorbing, and exhausting, and I feel I'm doing good, being useful, making a difference in the world.'

'But you're ready for a rest,' he suggested.

'God, yes! A rest, and a bath, and clean clothes, and a proper bed. All those things. And male company, my dear.' She slipped a hand through his arm. 'Much as I like women, one can get tired of hearing nothing but female voices.'

The rush had dispersed by the time they got outside, and they were able to get a taxi. When they were settled in, Laura pulled off her hat, provoking a cry from Edward. 'Your hair!'

She gave him an affectionately exasperated look. 'Now don't begin! You saw I'd cut it last time I was home.'

'Yes, but not this short! It's like a man's. My dear!'

'*My dear*,' she mocked, 'you can't imagine what it's like. We have little enough time to wash our faces and hands. Long hair takes a great deal of maintenance, not to mention vast quantities of water and leisure, and frankly, I'd sooner have none than have great coils of filthy, greasy, dusty—'

'Yes, I see,' he said hastily. 'But you will grow it again, after the war?'

'After the war,' she said thoughtfully. 'It's hard to believe there will ever be an "after". I can hardly remember a "before" any more.'

'I know what you mean,' said Edward.

'We've all changed,' she said, and seemed to visit some private thought. While she did, he studied her, and while he abhorred the most obvious changes – the short-cropped hair and her brown, weathered complexion – he had to admit that she looked well. Her face was thinner, and there were deep, fine lines he hadn't noticed before, but she was healthy and fit, her eyes bright and alert. She seemed happy, and full of energy. The war – or, at least, the opportunities provided by the war – suited her.

'So, tell me about the family,' she said, coming back from her reverie. 'How is everyone?'

'They're all busy,' he said. 'Except for Diana, who's growing like a pumpkin. And David,' he faltered. 'I wish I thought he was improving, even slowly.'

'What do the doctors say about the leg?'

'The army's signed him off. They say it's a matter of time. But the worst thing is that he won't try. He seems to have lost heart.'

'I'll have a word with him,' Laura offered. 'He always liked me. Sometimes parents are too close. An aunt is easier to listen to. How's Beattie?'

'Busy,' Edward said, failing of any other word. 'I hardly see her. She often works at the canteen in the evening, which is the only time I'm home. Ships that pass in the night,' he added, trying humour to disguise the hurt.

'Ah,' said Laura. 'Well, if I have to visit her there, I will. I'm not going back to France without seeing everyone. Life is too uncertain.'

'Diana's at Dene Park,' Edward said, 'so you won't have far to go to see her.'

'I've always wanted to see the inside of Dene Park,' Laura said.

'There's a sixpenny tour in the summer,' Edward said, with a smile.

'But I always want to see the bits that aren't included,' said Laura.

For a while, Laura's visit lifted David's spirits. She had come straight from the war and had things to tell him that he could not hear from anyone else. She had been there,

46

in that Other Place where he had lived an unimaginably different life – which, therefore, he could never speak of to anyone at The Elms. But the animation soon fizzled out, like a defective fuse, leaving him to sink back into gloomy silence.

'He does seem depressed,' she reported to Edward afterwards. 'I suppose that's natural. His mind has been wounded as well as his body. We see a lot of it out in France.'

'Do you think . . . ' he began.

She spread her hands. 'My dear, I have no medical expertise.'

'That wretched girl broke his heart. Now he feels he has nothing to live for.'

'They say time heals all wounds. But a broken heart usually needs a new object. It's a pity he hasn't got a nurse. The wounded always fall in love with their nurses.'

'That,' said Edward, 'doesn't help.'

Laura found Diana's gladness to see her almost pathetic.

'I'm all alone here,' she said. 'Everybody's busy with the war.'

'Well, you can be busy, too,' Laura suggested.

'I can't go out like this. I don't like strangers to see me.'

'There are lots of ways you can help with the war, without going out,' Laura began.

'Don't say knitting. I'm hopeless at knitting,' Diana interrupted. 'Not very good at sewing, either, so don't suggest making soldiers' pyjamas.'

'What about your mother's hospital bags? They don't take much skill, and it doesn't matter if they're pretty or not. And they're a *very* good thing. I often hear from the wounded how much they value them.'

'Oh, you're so lucky, doing something exciting,' Diana sighed. 'I wish I were you.'

Laura laughed. 'My dear child, my work is dirty and

unpleasant, and you would hate it. Why do you think I cut off my hair? Can you imagine cutting off your glorious golden tresses? And being covered with mud and other people's bodily fluids all day, then having to wash in a basin of cold water at the end of it?'

Diana was sobered by this, but said, 'All the same, you're doing something important for the country. That must feel good.'

'You're doing something tremendously important for the country, something I can't do.'

Diana frowned. 'You don't mean having a baby?'

'It's the most important job of all. You should feel very proud of yourself.'

By the time she left, Diana was looking upon her pregnancy as war work, had agreed to sew hospital bags if the wherewithal was delivered to her. Laura felt quite proud of herself.

One morning Laura travelled into London with Edward, and parted with him at the station to get the tube to the distant bourn of Wimbledon. 'It's a long walk from the station, and I think it's going to snow. And when I get there, it's ten to one that she won't be in,' she grumbled.

'Why do people live south of the river?' Edward said, with a mock shudder.

'I really don't know,' she answered seriously.

He offered her his umbrella. 'Or do you prefer to enjoy martyrdom?'

'Not at all,' she said, taking it quickly. 'I'll return it this evening. Or, if she isn't there, I'll bring it back to the office and make you take me out to lunch.'

The journey was tedious and there was no heating in the carriage, but Laura had grown used to discomfort. She had warm gloves, a book and a small bag of humbugs, all she needed to pass the time. It did start to snow, and by the time she quit the train it was coming down steadily, but it wasn't settling much, and she set off briskly through the empty suburban streets past the identical houses, and soon got her blood flowing again.

When she reached Louisa's aunt's house, there was a shock: the door knocker was wreathed in crape. Having come so far, she knocked anyway, and after a longish delay, the door was opened by Louisa herself, looking pale and depressed, her eyes ringed by weeping.

Laura's heart turned over. 'Oh, my dear!' she cried. 'Your aunt? Why didn't you tell me?' She wanted to take Louisa in her arms, but something about her friend's stiff demeanour warned her off. 'When did it happen?'

'Two weeks ago. The funeral was last week,' Louisa said. Her voice sounded dusty, as though she wasn't using it much. Her brother had been killed the year before, and her elderly aunt had been her only remaining relative. She had rejected Laura's invitation to join the crew of Bessie to look after her – at least, that was the official reason. But Laura had felt they parted in bad blood, and the fact that Louisa hadn't contacted her when her aunt died seemed to confirm it.

'May I come in?' Laura prompted gently.

'Oh! Yes, of course,' Louisa said awkwardly. She led the way through to the back parlour. There had been a fire lit, but it was down to its last embers, and the air was only just warm. There was dust on the mantelpiece and an unused feeling to the room. Laura's quick imagination saw Louisa drifting about the house like a ghost, unable to think what to do, now the benign tyrant who had ordered her days was gone.

'Was it sudden?' she asked, sitting down in the absence of an invitation to do so.

Louisa sat too, winding her hands together. 'She'd been failing for some time, but I didn't know the end was so near.

I'd been reading to her in her bedroom – she didn't get up every day any more – and I went downstairs to warm up some soup for her, and when I took it in, she was gone.' Tears came to her eyes again, with terrible easiness. 'I didn't understand at first. I thought she was asleep. I tried to wake her, and then I realised . . . It was horrid. I didn't know what to do with the soup,' she added pathetically. 'It was mulligatawny. I don't like mulligatawny. Agnes only made it for her.'

'Where is Agnes?'

'I let her go. She stayed until the funeral, but she'd always said when Auntie went she'd go and live with her sister in Kidderminster. She's got a boarding-house there.'

'So you're all alone here?'

'I'm trying to sort out Auntie's things.'

'Did she leave a will?'

'Her solicitor has it. She left Agnes a small amount because she'd been with her for so long, and some gifts to charities, and the rest comes to me.'

'So there's no difficulty about it?'

'No. It will just take time. But it's her *things*, you see.' She made a hopeless small gesture to indicate the whole house. 'What does one do with it all?'

'Sell it,' Laura said briskly. 'You won't want to live here now, will you?'

'It's the only home I've got,' Louisa said.

'It's not your home. It was her home, and she doesn't need it any more. And you won't want her furniture and knick-knacks.'

'The china and linens are good quality,' Louisa objected.

'But not your taste. Sell it all and make a fresh start. I know you loved her. She was good to you when you needed it, and you were good to her in return. Honour satisfied. You've nothing to reproach yourself with. Now it's time to live your own life.' Louisa stared at the miserable fire and didn't respond, stuck in the inertia first of caring for an elderly invalid, then of having that purpose taken away.

After a moment, Laura asked again, 'Lou, why didn't you write and tell me? You know I'd have come.'

Louisa looked up, half defiant, half ashamed. 'I didn't think you'd have time for me, now you've got your new friends.'

'How can you think such a thing?' Laura said hotly. 'Do you think there's only so much friendship to go around, that one person takes it from another?' Louisa didn't answer, looking down at her hands. 'Love is not a finite thing,' Laura went on. 'Did you love your old friends less when you and I became friends?'

Now Louisa looked up. 'Yes,' she said.

It gave Laura pause. Then she said, 'I'm sure that's not true. You have a big, loving heart with room for everyone.' No answer. 'I didn't abandon you, Lou,' she reminded her. 'I asked you to come with me.'

'I didn't think you meant it.'

'I wouldn't have asked if I hadn't wanted you to come. Surely you know me well enough to know that.'

Louisa shrugged, 'I couldn't have come, anyway. I had to take care of Auntie.'

Laura had never been sure that was the case, but whatever the truth, Louisa had done with that obligation now. 'Look here, I've got a proposal. Is there any food in the house – apart from mulligatawny soup?'

That at least raised the ghost of a smile. 'There's the remains of last night's shepherd's pie. And some cheese. And I think there's half a cake in the tin, but it may be a bit stale. Agnes made it.'

'Sounds like a feast,' said Laura. 'So what we'll do is this. We'll have lunch. I bet you're hungry – I know I am – and being hungry always makes one feel sad. Then we'll pack your things, pick out any little mementoes of your aunt that you want to keep, and take it all over to my house. You can move in with me, until you feel like finding a place of your own – though there's not much point in that, to my mind, until after the war.'

'But what about this house?' Louisa asked; but already she looked brighter. The cage door had swung open.

'Tell the solicitor you want to sell it. He'll know of a house-clearing company that can deal with everything. He can pay the proceeds into your bank account, and you need never come back here – unless you want to,' she added, but doubtfully. The heavy, overstuffed furniture, the gloomy Victorian pictures, the pointless knick-knacks and orna-ments infesting every surface, the stained glass in the front door and the stairs window that created a permanent penumbra, the grim garden of sooty laurels and dripping shrubberies . . .

'Come and live in Town, with you?' Louisa mused. She seemed not averse.

Laura struck while the iron was hot. 'Not that I think we'll be doing much living in Town for a while,' she said. 'We'll come back to refresh our spirits and our wardrobes, but in a couple of weeks I'm going back to France, and this time you're coming with me. There's so much to do out there, Lou, and you're just the sort of woman we need.'

'I suppose,' Louisa said slowly, 'it *is* my duty. I mean, Sam gave his life for his country. Helping where I can is the least I can do.'

'You can justify it in that way,' Laura said, with a smile. 'It's also the most tremendous adventure that makes you feel alive every day in a way you've never felt before. You fought for the Cause, my dear, and this is the biggest boost to the Cause there could ever be.'

'Yes,' Louisa said, beginning to be animated. 'I've read

articles saying that, once they acknowledge they can't fight the war without us, they'll have to give us the vote.'

'Quite right. And one other thing – I've missed my friend. I want you with me. So you will come.'

She deliberately didn't frame it as a question, but Louisa answered anyway. 'I will.

CHAPTER FIVE

Rupert telephoned at last, on the 30th of January. There was no receiver in the cadet suite, and Diana was escorted by Worrell, the aged butler, at snail's pace to the machine in the countess's study, which was off the hall that divided the two suites. Worrell drew out a chair for her, saw her settled into it, lifted the receiver and checked that the call was connected from the main telephone downstairs, handed it to her with a bow, and withdrew. Diana could hear the instrument squawking long before she lifted it to her ear and said tentatively, 'Hello?'

'What a time you've been!' Rupert fumed. 'I've been standing here like an idiot talking to the air!'

'You know how slowly Worrell walks,' Diana responded. 'I came as fast as I—'

'Never mind, you're here now,' he interrupted. 'All serene?'

'When did you get back?' Diana asked. 'I thought you were only going for a week.'

'I did. I've been back for a while,' he said.

'But why didn't you call, or send a telegram?'

'I've been busy.'

'I was worried when I didn't hear from you.'

'What on earth for? You'd have heard all right if anything had happened to me.'

Diana felt that was obtuse. 'You could have called anyway,' she said.

54

'There was nothing to say,' he replied. 'I'm calling now – and you're making me wish I hadn't.'

That was a threat. She changed the subject. 'When are you coming to take me home? I hope it will be soon.'

'What on earth do you mean? You're not coming back to London. I thought you knew that. You're staying there until the baby's born.'

'But I don't want to have the baby here. I want to have it at home.'

'You *are* home,' he said firmly. 'You're a Wroughton, and for a Wroughton, "home" is Dene Park. The future earl has to be born at Dene. I was, and Charles was, and Papa was. And Grandpapa. Now don't make a fuss, dear, it's not seemly. Aren't you enjoying seeing your family?'

'I don't see much of them. They're all busy with war work.'

'Invite some friends to stay, then.'

'They're all busy, too. Everyone's busy except me,' she said pathetically.

'Never mind, I'm sure you'll find something to do,' he said impatiently. 'And it's not for much longer.'

'I don't want to be on my own until the baby comes. Can't you come down and stay with me?' she pleaded.

'I'm in the army,' he said. 'My time is not my own. And we're very busy at the moment. Making plans to defeat the Germans. You remember the Germans, don't you? Horrid chaps trying to take over the world? It was in all the papers.'

Diana had no defence against sarcasm, and said nothing.

Rupert softened. 'Just rest, and concentrate on having a fine, healthy baby,' he said kindly. 'I'll send you down some magazines. And I'll be down myself in a couple of weeks. As soon as I get some time off.'

Everyone was saying it was the coldest winter in memory. For a whole week the temperature did not rise above freezing-point,

55

and heavy snow hampered movement all over the country. It was a time to huddle indoors, but Louis insisted they go out to eat.

'I'm not interested in eating,' Beattie said. 'Besides, it isn't safe.'

'It's safe in our little restaurant round the corner, where we went the first night,' he urged. 'No-one we know uses it. I'd like to take you there again. I have something to tell you.'

'You can tell me here,' she said.

But there was a romantic streak in him, which would not be denied. She, like most women, was practical, and cautious rather than dashing, but he wanted his gesture and would not tell her his news except in the restaurant.

It was a Bohemian sort of place, with checked tablecloths, and candles, which made for a place of shadows suited to illicit meetings. It was impossible to see who was at the other tables, which gave Beattie at least the illusion of safety.

'Now, tell me your news,' she demanded, when they had ordered and the wine had been poured. She was afraid that, for her, it was not going to be good news.

But instead of telling her, he raised his glass to her in a toast. 'Seven months,' he said, 'since we first sat here, and I discovered the world was not a blank after all. To you, my darling – the one love of my life.'

'Louis!'

'Don't be impatient. Life is uncertain in time of war, and you have to learn to savour every moment as it comes.'

'It's something bad, isn't it?'

He gave in. 'I've been promoted to lieutenant colonel.' She was silent. 'Now you say "congratulations",' he prompted.

'But – what does it mean?'

'Mean? It means that majors have to call me "sir", now, as well as captains.'

'Don't tease,' she said, and her lips were pale.

He repented. 'I didn't mean to torment you. I just wanted you to be happy for me.'

'I am, but—'

'They're giving me a regiment,' he confessed. 'I shall be going to France as a fighting officer.'

It was a blow. 'When?' she managed to ask.

'I shall be going over next week to inspect them, and to do a little research for the War Office. I'll be back for a couple of days to collect my kit, and then I'll take up my command.'

She nodded. She had no words. He would be a fighting officer. He would be going into danger.

He reached across the table and took her cold hands. 'Germany is on the ropes,' he said. 'They took a frightful beating last year. We'll roll them up this year. There's a big push coming.'

'There's always a big push coming,' she said drearily.

'It's different this time. The Germans are badly over-extended, and their line has a huge salient, which is a serious weakness.'

'I don't really understand that,' she said.

He drew it on the tablecloth for her. 'A straight line is the easiest position to defend, you see. But instead of a straight line, the Germans have developed a big loop into our territory. Imagine it as a bubble, or a balloon. Now, if we attack on both sides at the neck of the balloon, we can cut it off. A large part of the German Army will be isolated and forced to surrender. And then,' he demonstrated by moving the salt and pepper pots, 'we roll up the two ends.'

'And the war will be over?'

'That's the idea.'

'And what then?'

He smiled. 'We'll have the rest of our lives together.' She shook her head, thinking of the difficulties, and he pressed her hands. 'Darling. We'll work something out. We *will*.'

She felt a great weariness. To him, it was simple: he loved her, they should be together. How could she express the immense problems that reared themselves before her, if he would not see them for himself? Pain was everywhere. There seemed no solution.

She couldn't think about it just now. 'Let's not talk about that,' she managed. 'Let's just enjoy the meal—'

'I thought you weren't interested in food.'

'I thought I wasn't hungry,' she said, 'but now I find I am.'

Afterwards, he took her to Baker Street Station in a taxi. They held hands in the dark, cold stuffiness. The taxi wheels hissed over yellow-brown slush. The displaced snow banked at the sides of the roads gleamed faintly in the muted light from the masked headlamps. London was a dark place now: in this, the third winter of the war, black-out had become a habit, no longer thought about.

'We have a little while longer,' he said. 'A few days, when I get back from the inspection. After that, whenever I can get away. Anyway, it won't be for much longer.'

The words hit her in a way he had not intended. *Not for much longer.* She whispered, 'Oh, Louis . . . '

For once he did not follow her thoughts. 'We'll take it one step at a time,' he said reassuringly.

The cab drew up outside the station. Louis helped her out, then turned back to pay the driver. A man was hurrying towards them to take over their cab. Beattie looked up from putting on her gloves, and found herself staring straight into Rupert's startled face.

His expression was instantly masked. He regarded her from under hooded lids. 'What a pleasant surprise,' he said, with a silky smile. 'Mother-in-law, well met.' And as Louis turned round, 'And you, sir. Major Plunkett. No – I was forgetting. Forgive me, isn't it Colonel Plunkett now? Didn't I read something in *The Times*? Congratulations in order, sir?'

'Thank you,' Louis said, a little stiffly. 'Yes, I did receive a promotion. Lieutenant Lord Dene, how do you do?'

'But what a charming thing,' Rupert said smoothly, 'that you seem to know my mother-in-law. How does that come about, I wonder?'

Beattie could not speak for the sickness that was tight inside her. Louis said, 'I think I mentioned to you that I served under your wife's grandfather for a while. Of course, I met – er – Mrs Hunter in Dublin, many years ago. It was a pleasant surprise to bump into her again.' Apart from the slight stumble over her name, it sounded very good. He turned to Beattie. 'May I see you safely to your train?'

Rupert gave them each a long, thoughtful look, and said, 'If you'll excuse me, I must take this cab before someone else steals it. I'm late for an appointment. My regards to the family, Mother-in-law. Your servant, sir.' And he slipped between them and jumped into the cab.

It drove away, leaving the two frozen to the spot. Louis recovered first, took Beattie's elbow and ushered her into the shelter of the station entrance. 'What accursed luck,' he said. 'Another moment and we'd have missed him.'

She turned to look up at him, bewildered. 'You've met him before? He seems to know you.'

'I met him on the train on the way to Paris, for the generals' meeting. He was one of the staff aides.'

'Why didn't you tell me?'

'Nothing to tell, really. We're both officers – hardly unlikely that we'd cross paths at some point.'

'But you told him you knew my father?' she said. 'Why did you do that? Why risk stirring up trouble?'

'I don't know. He – he was staring at me as if he knew me. It was a way to redirect his attention. It seemed harmless. But as it happens,' Louis defended himself, 'it's a good

59

job that I did. It gave a reasonable excuse for being with you now.' She shook her head, staring at disaster. He saw she was really worried. 'Will he tell?' he asked, subdued.

'I don't know,' she said. She couldn't think what else to say. The worst thing, the thing that made her feel sickest, was that he was asking the question. The word 'tell', in this context, was vile. It made her look at the reality of what she was doing. She was the guilty one here. She, and only she. 'I don't know,' she said again, at last. And that was all.

In silence he walked with her to the platform. The train was there, waiting. He kissed her hands, looking at her anxiously. 'Don't worry,' he said. 'Everything will work out all right. If he does say anything – well, what did he see? We bumped into each other by accident, had a chat, and I was escorting you to your train. All completely innocent.'

'Louis, stop talking,' she said unhappily. The train was ready to depart. 'I must go.'

'Yes,' he said, and released her. As she stepped into the carriage, he said, 'But don't worry. It will be all right.'

The train pulled out, taking her away from him. She wanted to weep, but middle-aged, middle-class ladies did not weep in public, on trains.

Now that Louisa had moved back in with her, Laura stayed in Town. She felt that Louisa had been leading a very dull life for the past seven months, and needed diversion, before they went back to France. They did a few shows, met some old friends. Laura arranged a luncheon at the Ritz with Lady Agnes Daubeney – Annie – the leader of their ambulance team; and later tea at Brown's with the other two, Flora Hazlitt and Elsie Murray. All welcomed the new recruit; Annie was at her approachable best; and if Louisa was a little stiff, each of them put it down to her recent bereavement.

Laura had lost interest in the Bedfordite group, and hadn't

intended to go to any meetings. But when the news came out that the Speaker's Conference had made its report on electoral reform, it was natural for Louisa to want to find out what was being said by those still active in the Cause. So Laura made a telephone call, found where some of the principals were gathered, and took Louisa along to a soirée.

It was being held at the home of 'Baby' Melville, who now shared a flat in Lowndes Street with her brother, 'Boy' – otherwise Tom Melville, the novelist. Boy had been called up, but had failed the fitness test, and was instead serving with the intelligence section, which kept him conveniently in London. When Laura and Louisa arrived, the flat was crowded, dim with cigarette smoke and warm with the fug of many bodies – which was fortunate as there was no other form of heating.

'Isn't it a bore?' Baby cried cheerfully as they inserted themselves into the throng. 'The central heating is off – the building has run out of coal, and the caretaker says there's none to be had.'

'Not even for ready money,' Boy finished for her, advancing to kiss the newcomers. 'But there is plenty to drink, thanks to our raid on the parental cellar. Well, with the governor in Palestine and the mater down in the country, it was just sitting there, making itself a target for the Zepps. Better inside us than under the rubble.'

'Don't talk about air raids,' Baby said, punching his arm. 'Louisa, I'm so sorry about your aunt. Is it true you've moved into Laura's house?'

'News travels fast,' Louisa commented.

'Well, Hilary Ogden had it from Harriet Holmes, who knows Laura's next-door neighbour.'

'The house in Wimbledon was too big for me,' Louisa said.

'And too far away,' Tom added. 'You'll want to be at the heart of things.'

Louisa had known Baby for years, through the Cause, but both Melvilles were also Bedfordites, so there was a mixed crowd at the flat, taken from both sets. Laura was not wholly surprised, therefore, when, later in the evening, Rupert came pushing through the bodies, glass in hand, and stopped at the sight of her.

'Aunt Laura!' he exclaimed. 'You don't mind if I call you "Aunt" do you? It is legitimate, even if only by marriage.'

'You can call me what you like, as long as you don't call me Pigeon Pie and eat me up,' Laura replied. 'What are you doing here?'

'Oh, I went to see *Nuts and Wine* at the Empire with Willy Holmes and some other friends, and Willy said Boy had liberated some rather good brandy from his pater's cellar, so we all came to see if it's true.' Wilberforce Holmes was Harriet's twin brother: both their parents were dedicated suffragists and had brought them up in the Cause. They had been named after leading lights in an earlier struggle, so their dedication to some liberal movement had been inevitable.

'*Nuts and Wine*? How jolly,' said Laura. 'I'd have thought you'd be down at Dene holding Diana's hand. She's awfully bored, poor girl.'

'I send her all the latest magazines,' he excused himself. 'Besides, I'm in the army, Auntie dear. My time is not my own.'

'Your own enough to go to the theatre,' she pointed out.

He looked cross. 'Now, don't lecture. Petrol's impossible to come by, and the trains are so uncertain. By the time I got there it would be time to come back.'

Laura travelled back and forth to Northcote on the Metropolitan Line often enough to know how long it took, but it was not her business to quarrel with her niece's husband so she said no more.

And at that moment Louisa pushed through the throng

to join her. Rupert, who had been looking a little sulky, began to smile. 'Well, well, how delightful. Miss Cotton. So you two are back together again.'

Louisa looked puzzled. 'What do you mean?'

'I'd heard there was a little rift in the lute.' And since this plainly failed to enlighten, he went on, 'You've been out of circulation for a while?'

'I was nursing my aunt,' Louisa said. 'But she's dead now.'

'And so you two are back together, as I said,' Rupert concluded. 'I thought you were in France,' he said to Laura.

'I was. I'm going back soon.'

'I'm going too,' Louisa said, with a touch of pride.

Laura saw mischief in Rupert's eyes, and hastily turned the subject. 'Have you managed to talk to Irene?' she asked Louisa.

'That's what I was coming to tell you. She's going to give a speech later,' said Louisa.

'Irene?' Rupert queried.

'Irene Alderton,' Laura said. 'She's sister-in-law to Walter Long, who was on the Speaker's Conference committee, so she knows all about it.'

'Lord help us,' Rupert muttered. 'I must get out before that happens.'

Louisa looked indignant. 'If you aren't interested in the Speaker's Conference, why are you here?'

'Tell us, dear,' Laura said quickly. 'What did the conference decide?'

'Well, they all agreed that there has to be universal franchise for men, because of conscription. You can't force men to risk death for their country if they don't have the vote. And most of them agreed that it was a good opportunity to look at the women's franchise.'

Rupert groaned. 'I liked it so much better when women were merely decorative.'

Louisa ignored him. 'Apparently Mr Asquith said that women's war work gave them the right to be consulted about the running of the country. Although they do say he was really more worried about the militants renewing the campaign if nothing was done. But, anyway, the members agreed they must do *something* for women. The bad news is that they voted by a big majority not to give us an equal franchise. They said it would create a female majority, and they can't have that.'

'So who *would* get the vote?' Laura asked.

'Women over thirty-five, if they're householders, the wives of householders, or graduates.'

'Well, that's something,' Laura said.

'But look at all those women working in munitions factories, and driving delivery vans and so on. They're mostly under thirty-five and working-class. They're not even considered.'

'Fifty years ago, even this much seemed impossible,' Laura said. 'We should be grateful.'

'Don't be grateful too soon,' Rupert said. 'I presume it still has to get through Parliament. There's many a slip, as the old saw says.'

'You sound as though you'd be glad if it didn't get through,' Louisa said indignantly. 'I'm going to talk to Harriet and Baby. At least they make sense.'

'You shouldn't tease her,' Laura said, when Louisa had gone. 'I know perfectly well you don't care about the women's vote one way or the other.'

'How perceptive you are,' Rupert said. 'The two great bores of our time, the women's vote and the Irish Question. Don't care about either. And, talking of the latter, I've an Irish question of my own: what brings my esteemed mother-in-law together with the tall and handsome Colonel Plunkett? I saw them together in Town late one evening, looking most frightfully intimate – and frightfully annoyed to be interrupted by little me. I had no idea they were even acquainted. Do tell, I ask only as a seeker after knowledge in the purest sense.'

Which meant, Laura knew, the exact opposite. What was he up to? What was he suggesting? 'I don't know any Colonel Plunkett,' she said indifferently. 'But you must know Mrs Hunter comes from an army family. I'm sure she will have many army acquaintances, through her father.'

'Funny, that's what Colonel Plunkett said,' Rupert remarked, studying her face.

Laura refused to be unsettled. 'Well, then,' she said impatiently. 'What are you cooking up, Lord Dene?'

'Oh, nothing, nothing. Not cooking at all. Just stocking the larder.' He grinned. 'In these straitened times, one must guard against shortages. On which subject, I shall refill my glass before the good stuff goes. Can I get you anything?'

'Nothing, thank you. I think the speeches are about to begin.'

'Ah, then I think it's time to take my leave,' said Rupert, bowed and sloped away, leaving Laura frowning, with more questions than one.

CHAPTER SIX

However harsh the winter in England and France, it was ten times as bad in Russia. There, the cold was so intense that locomotive boilers burst; and with the railway tracks covered deep in snow, the movement of supplies was near impossible. Both on the Front and in the cities, the people starved, and there were riots and strikes in St Petersburg. For a time the British government held its breath, but the assassination of Rasputin seemed to have drawn a poison: the Duma reconvened and, while noisy in its debates, did not seem to be edging any closer to revolution.

All this Edward had from Lord Forbesson when he called at his lordship's Town house in Upper Brook Street to discuss his investments. For once Lady Forbesson was there, though she was on her way out to a committee meeting at Lady Smith-Dorrien's.

'We're all so busy these days, aren't we?' she said, in gay apology, as they passed in the hall. 'You'll forgive me if I run. Arthur will take care of you.'

From 'Arthur', Edward received the choice between coffee and sherry, and after the talk about Russia, and discussion of investments, Forbesson turned the conversation, surprisingly, to agriculture. 'What do you know about the food-supply situation?' he asked, almost abruptly.

'I know there's a labour shortage,' Edward replied. Agricultural labourers had been among the first to volunteer when the war began – probably, he thought, because their lives were so harsh and poorly paid that they were eager for a change. The army liked farm workers because they were generally fitter than factory workers. He searched his memory for more. 'The harvest was poor last year,' he remembered.

Forbesson nodded. 'Both here and in America. Perhaps you are aware that even before the war we were importing sixty per cent of our food, especially cereals.'

'I knew we were heavily reliant on imports.'

'And the losses in our merchant fleet have exacerbated the problem. On which subject, the intelligence wallahs have it that the Germans are about to step up submarine activity, targeting our merchant vessels. They reckon they can starve us into submission within six months. They took a hard knock last year, and our blockade is crippling them. They see this as the only way they can force us to sue for peace before *they* have to. You see the problem.'

Edward did. One of his clients, Lord Walsham, had told him years ago that it was no longer worth growing cereals in England, when imports from America were so cheap. At the time, self-sufficiency in food had not been a consideration. England had always been a trading nation, and the food of the world came readily to her doors. But if the sea, her bulwark and her main road, could be made her prison wall, the nation might starve.

'We are in very real danger of our running out of food,' Forbesson said. 'We have to supply the men at the Front – they must come first. But the staple diet of the working classes is tea, bread and margarine. You can imagine the riots and disorder that would follow if the bread supply failed. Support for the war would crumble. Our national stocks are down to six weeks' only. The situation is very serious indeed. And if the Germans knock out even more of our cargo ships . . . '

67

'I knew things were difficult, but I had no idea they were so bad,' Edward said.

'Well, we don't want this to get out. Got to keep up morale. Few people know the whole of it. Reason I'm tellin' you, Hunter – have you heard of the Ministry of Food?'

'I heard that one was set up in . . . in December, wasn't it?'

'That's right,' Forbesson nodded. 'Lord Devonport's been made food controller. Well, he's a grocer by trade, so he ought to know what's what.'

'I don't know him,' Edward confessed.

'Hudson Kearley's his name, born in Uxbridge, started life working for Tetley's in London, set up his own tea-importing business, then founded the International Stores.'

'Those I *have* heard of,' Edward said. It was a chain of groceries, prominent on every high street.

'Made his fortune, went into Parliament, served on the Board of Trade,' Forbesson went on. 'Lloyd George was president of the board then, liked the cut of his jib, promoted him. He did good work on the Port of London Authority. Got his peerage in 1910 for that – and not for his services to margarine, whatever the lampoonists may say.' Forbesson's eyes twinkled, but Edward had not heard anything about Lord Devonport, so the joke was lost on him.

'And what are the food controller's duties?' he asked.

'In short, to save us from dependency on imports,' said Forbesson. 'Get more land planted and more crops grown. Liaise with the War Office and get some agricultural workers released from the army. Organise the supply of feed, fertiliser and machinery. Control the distribution of food – possibly the consumption too. If it comes to it.'

'Rationing?' Edward said.

'If it comes to it,' Forbesson repeated. 'Avoid it if possible. Bound to cause bad blood. Neighbour against neighbour, housewives hittin' each other in shops, accusations of

68

cheating, hoarding, under-the-counter dealing.' Edward nodded intelligently, waiting for the point. Forbesson read his face. 'What's this got to do with you, you ask. Well, Hunter, I've heard how you persuaded Walsham to go into pigs. He's become a regular bore – chews your ears off on the superior merits of this porker against that. Taken to it like a duck to water. What he don't know about pigs ain't worth knowing.'

'I recommended it to him as an investment,' Edward said. 'His land is perfect for it, and the market was there.'

'Exactly. But it's good for the nation as well as Walsham's pocket. And what you did there you can do again. You have a lot of clients among land-owners, and in commerce too – all sorts of useful fellers. And everybody likes you. You're in the ideal position to liaise between them and the ministry. And you're brainy – you see your way round things. Solutions to problems. Invaluable skill in wartime.' He nodded encouragingly. 'I've told Devonport all about you and he's itching to have you. Now,' he held up a hand forestalling Edward's possible objection, 'I know you're busy, busier than most, I dare say, but there's nothing more important to the prosecution of the war. Not even munitions matter more. Starving men can't fight. And a starving nation – well, we won't talk about revolution, but hungry men might start to consider capitulation. We can't let the Boche beat us that way, dammit!' He pounded his fist into his palm. 'They won't take us in a fair fight. Damned if they're going to starve us into submission!'

Edward was moved by his grim determination, but he already knew he could not refuse the commission. Duty alone would forbid it. 'If I can serve in any way, I am willing,' he said.

Forbesson looked almost like crying. 'Good feller,' he said. 'Damn good feller. Knew you'd do it.'

'What *do* I have to do?'

'Go and see Devonport. His ministry's been given a

69

suite in Grosvenor House. Awful lot of the new agencies packed in there, but what it lacks in elbow room it gains in views over Hyde Park.' This was a pleasantry, and Edward smiled dutifully. 'Go and see him tomorrow, if you will – he'll be expecting you. Just make your number with his secretary. One thing's for sure,' he concluded cheerfully, 'you'll get a decent cup of tea. Devonport still has the connections.'

He stood up, and Edward stood with him to shake the proffered hand. 'Don't mind telling you,' Forbesson said, in a lowered voice, 'that there could be a knighthood comin' your way for this. You're very well thought of in certain circles, Hunter. I know you didn't say yes in the hope of advancement, but the labourer is worthy of his hire. Don't know anyone who deserves it more.'

'I'm sure that isn't true, my lord,' Edward managed to say, through his surprise. A knighthood? How pleased Beattie would be!

Forbesson saw him out in person. At the door, he asked, 'How's your boy coming along? Any improvement?'

Edward shook his head. 'He seems to have hit a plateau.'

'Damned shame,' he said. 'Our fine men pay with their lives in more ways than one.'

'How is your son?' Edward asked in reciprocation.

'Esmond? Oh, he's doin' very well. Soldiering seems to be right up his street. Mentioned in dispatches in December, up for a promotion now. Dorothy's fiercely proud of him. We both are.'

Esmond was Forbesson's only son. Edward thought of Bobby, and David, and thanked God he had two more at home, too young to serve. Unless the war went on more years than he could bear to think about.

The Germans began their new submarine campaign with Teutonic efficiency on the 1st of February, and the effects were not long in being felt. Almost overnight, it seemed, things that were already in short supply vanished from the shelves.

'Oh, they got 'em all right,' Cook fulminated, at her daily interview with Beattie. 'Keeping 'em under the counter so as they can push the price up. Profiteering, that's what I call it!'

'You shouldn't make a serious allegation like that unless you have proof,' Beattie warned her.

'I don't need proof, madam,' Cook said grimly. 'Not when I see prices double, with my own eyes. Scrag end of mutton priced like it was spring lamb. And fish! Well, if that was cod what the fishmonger was trying to sell me, I'm the Queen of Sheba. A cat would've turned its nose up.'

She was slightly mollified by the fact that they had good stocks of most things in, thanks to Beattie's foresight – which Beattie honestly admitted was due to Edward's urging. 'It isn't hoarding,' he had assured her, 'to be buying things when they're plentiful. In fact, it's good for the country. If everyone did the same, there wouldn't *be* any shortages.'

But shortages there were, and it didn't help that the weather continued wretchedly cold. 'We must economise on coal,' Beattie said. They had enough for now, but who knew if they would be able to get more when it ran out? 'But Mr David mustn't get cold. His sitting-room fire is to be kept in at all times.'

No fires in the bedrooms, it was decided. The morning-room fire was to be lit in the morning, and anyone who was at home during the day would sit there. They would eat in the morning-room, to save heating the dining-room. The drawing-room fire to be lit only in the evening after dinner.

'It's a good job Diana's not still at home,' said Sadie, of the new regime. 'She hates being cold.'

To help eke out the coal, the boys went scavenging for firewood when they were not at school. Northcote, luckily, was surrounded by woods. Peter took to the task with enthusiasm, and proudly called it 'war work'. He had a little four-wheeled wagon – his 'cartie' – and generally managed to fill it up. Some of the wood was too wet to be used at once. Peter cleared a corner of the cellar to make a wood pile where it could dry out, and sometimes went down there to gloat over it.

William could not have it said that his younger brother was doing more for the household economy than he was, so he took his fishing-rod down to the lakes at the bottom of the hill. He nobly risked frostbite sitting for hours watching his line, but so far he had only landed one or two rather trusting carp.

Cook sniffed at them. She had not yet suffered enough from shortages to welcome coarse fish in her kitchen. 'If I'm to be reduced to cooking carp, madam . . . ' she told Beattie menacingly.

'Don't hurt his feelings,' Beattie said. 'He's trying to help us. Can't you find a use for them?'

'I'll give 'em to the dog,' Cook said firmly. 'He'll eat anything. Now, if Master William was to bring in a nice trout or two, it'd be a different story.'

'Oh, please don't say that to him. All the trout streams around here are private. I can't have him trespassing and getting taken up by the law. They'd throw him out of the Scouts.'

The food controller issued a plea for the nation to ration itself voluntarily, in particular for the middle classes to eat less bread, freeing supplies for the lower classes. Mrs Fitzgerald, the Rector's wife, called to support the campaign. So much bread was wasted, she said. Stale crusts thrown out for the birds, or put in the dustbin. Whole loaves thrown away, sometimes, because the well-to-do had ordered too much. Profligacy, she intimated, had no place in a nation at war.

'And I do think it's up to *us* to set a good example,' she said, sitting by the morning-room fire and casting a sharp eye about the room, as if she might spot wasted crusts under the breakfast table; or an illicit side of beef, perhaps, masquerading as a dressmaker's dummy. 'You have a fire in here, for instance. Is that *strictly* necessary?'

Beattie was used to her ways, and bore it stoically. 'I'm sewing hospital bags this morning. One cannot sew with frozen hands.'

Mrs Fitzgerald was ready for that one. 'We ought to get together and do our sewing communally, so that there is only one fire between, say, four or five of us.'

'What a good idea,' Beattie said patiently. 'If only we weren't all so busy, it might be possible to arrange for several of us to be sewing at the same time, rather than doing it when we had a free moment.'

'*I* shall arrange it,' Mrs Fitzgerald said firmly. Whatever you thought of her, she never shirked a task. 'Perhaps at Mrs Oliver's. I'm sure she would be happy to host a sewing-party.'

'Why not at the rectory?' Beattie suggested cruelly.

'Oh, but I'm so rarely at home, the fire is never lit. And you know how long it takes a room to warm up when there's been no fire for a day or two. I have to keep the rector's study fire lit so that he can work, so if I *am* home, I sit quietly in there.' She gave Beattie a triumphant look. 'We even eat in there sometimes, on trays.'

Yes, Beattie could believe that. Self-flagellation was a pleasure in itself to some people. To have the excuse to prosecute dreary economy would make up to Mrs Fitzgerald for any discomfort.

'Now, there is another thing,' she went on before Beattie could make any more inconvenient suggestions. 'As I've said,

I think we ought to set an example to the lower orders, and I'm most concerned that there should be no suspicion of *hoarding* among those of our class. So I am proposing that we should each write down what supplies of food we have in our houses, and I will keep a central register, so that we'll know in detail what is available in the village.'

'What on earth for?' Beattie asked.

'Well, to begin with, it will show up if anyone *is* hoarding. And it will encourage us all to be more economical, if we know our actions are being scrutinised. And if anyone runs short of anything essential, she will know where to apply for it. A friendly exchange can be managed – by me, so that there will be fairness on both sides. Now, don't you think it's a good idea?' She smiled complacently.

'No, I don't,' Beattie said. 'I think it's an appalling idea. It's – it's *socialism*.'

Mrs Fitzgerald recoiled at the word. 'There's no need to be insulting.'

'I'm not going to publish the contents of my cupboards to the world at large.'

Mrs Fitzgerald's eyes narrowed. 'Afraid of what might come out? *Have* you been hoarding?'

Beattie was not shaken. 'What I have is for my family.'

'Don't you think that's rather selfish?' Mrs Fitzgerald said loftily. 'I think we should all pull together at a time like this.'

'Would you be happy to publish what's in your cupboards?' Beattie countered.

'Of course,' said Mrs Fitzgerald, smugly. 'Though, as a matter of fact, there isn't very much there.'

Aha! Beattie thought. 'And who will check that your record is accurate?'

'I *beg* your pardon? *Check?* Are you suggesting I would make a false record?'

'If you wouldn't, there are many who would. Your register would be worthless. As for my cupboards, if a *friend* runs short, I shall always try to help, but I'm not responsible for the whole village, especially for people so imprudent as to let themselves be caught out.' And she looked the rector's wife firmly in the eye as she said it – something she would never have dared to do before the war.

Mrs Fitzgerald took her huffy departure, pausing on the way out to forgive Beattie magnanimously, knowing that Ada, who was holding the door for her, would take the word back to the kitchen quarters and inspire speculation as to what had been the mistress's sin. Beattie almost laughed when she had gone. It had been a transparent ploy. 'But I probably shouldn't have called her imprudent,' Beattie murmured to herself, though without much contrition.

Edward's first meeting with Lord Devonport went well. He was a small man, rather rumpled in appearance, with a high bald front counterbalanced by a large bushy moustache and an oversized bow-tie. He had a friendly, unassuming face, and Edward had no difficulty in imagining him behind the counter. He wanted only the long white apron to appear the essential family grocer.

In his 'office' in Grosvenor House, the mansion on Park Lane that had been requisitioned from the Duke of Westminster at the beginning of the war, he had a good fire going (evidently the coal shortage hadn't reached government departments yet) and he provided Edward with an excellent cup of coffee. When Edward commented on it, he said, 'I've had to bring in my own supplies. I'm afraid the stuff they were serving here was very disappointing, very indifferent. I'm glad you're enjoying it. I have it brought in from India, you know. They grow an excellent arabica in the upper hill country above Chikmagalur. You must let me send you some round.'

Edward had thought it mere politeness, but in due course a messenger arrived at his office with a brown paper parcel, whose stout wrappings could not completely contain the heavenly aroma. Even Murchison, his elderly secretary, lifted his doglike gaze and sniffed openly. Edward waited until he got home to open the parcel, afraid of tormenting anyone else. Inside were six half-pound packets.

'How incredibly kind,' Beattie said. She looked at her husband, a little puzzled. 'What had you done to deserve it?'

'I don't know,' Edward said. He remembered, with an inward blush, Forbesson saying 'Everyone likes you.' A ridiculous exaggeration, of course. He had not told Beattie yet about the possible knighthood, not wanting to speak of it until it was certain. But Devonport had said that as a part of his ministry, it would be helpful if he had the telephone installed at his home, so that he could be contacted whenever needed: 'This war runs for seven days a week, you know.'

Edward, naturally, had wondered how it would be possible, with all the wartime demands on the General Post Office, but official wheels had evidently been set turning, for at the end of the first week, a GPO work crew had arrived at The Elms to do the necessary.

Idlers, children and servants turned out of their houses to watch in considerable excitement, not least because the crew was female and dressed in overalls, like men. Fortunately several houses in Highwood Road already had the telephone, so there was a junction box at the end of the road. A pole already carried the wires just across the street from The Elms, so it was all done expeditiously.

The Elms servants had gathered in a silent, respectful group to stare at 'the instrument' in the hall with a mixture of awe and trepidation.

'What happens if it goes off?' Ada said.

'Goes off? It's not a bomb,' Ethel retorted.

'Well, rings or whatever it does. I wouldn't dare answer it. I wouldn't know what to say.'

76

'Nobody touches it,' Cook ruled. 'It's for the master only. Anyway, you could get a nasty electric shock, if you don't know how to use it.'

'*Some*body'd have to do it, say it rang when the family was out,' Ada said doubtfully. 'It might be important.'

'I seen it on the pictures once,' Emily piped up. 'When the bell goes off, you pick *that* bit up and put it on your ear and then you shout, "Ahoy, ahoy!" into *that* bit.'

Ethel, who had worked in hotels, was scornful. 'You don't shout. And you don't say "ahoy" any more. That was years ago. You say, "Mr Hunter's residence, who is speaking please".'

'Well, you can do it, then,' Cook said. 'I'm not putting electric things against my head for anyone.'

At that moment the instrument rang shrilly, and Cook screamed and leaped backwards.

'Oh, for goodness' sake,' Ethel said, rolling her eyes. She reached out to answer it, but one of the GPO crew popped back in through the door and said, 'It's just us, testing the line.' She picked up the earpiece and spoke into the mouthpiece, and after a brief technical exchange, she hung up and said with a smile, 'That's all working, then. So we'll be off.'

She was wearing overalls and big boots, she had curly fair hair under a man's cap, blue eyes and a smudge of oil on her nose, and was carrying a toolbag out of which a big screwdriver was poking. Emily lost her heart there and then.

'That's what I'd like to do,' she sighed when the girl had gone. 'Wouldn't it be grand, now?'

Cook seized her bony shoulder and turned her round to face the kitchen. 'You got potatoes to peel. Lilian, there's plaster dust on the floor where that female was drilling holes. Clean it up. And, Ethel, you'd better see that Mr David hasn't been ringing his head off for you this half hour.'

'Nobody's rung. I can hear the bells from here. I'm not deaf,' Ethel said, but she stalked off upstairs anyway, so that she could add under her breath, 'Not like some old cows.'

CHAPTER SEVEN

He had gone.

The parting had been wretched. They were to meet at his house, but all the coal had been used up and Waites, his servant, had not been able to get any more at short notice, so it was clammily cold. She had sat in her overcoat and gloves waiting for him for what seemed like an eternity, and when at last he had come, there had been only a couple of hours left.

'I'm sorry, I was tied up at Horse Guards. And I have to get the train at six. Oh darling, come here, you're shivering.' He clasped her to him, and she pressed herself into the familiar comfort of his greatcoat. 'We can't stay here – it's so miserable without a fire. Let's go out somewhere.'

But she was too afraid, now, of being seen, and rejected his suggestions: a café, a cinema where at least they might be warm, just for a walk. It was too cold to undress, so they could not make love, though it might be their last time. So they just sat, in their outdoor clothes, on the sofa, holding hands and talking, until it was time for him to go. She imagined herself waving him off at the station, as by now she had seen hundreds of women do, bravely smiling as their man leaned out of the carriage window and cheerfully pretended he was not going into danger, waving a handkerchief as long as the train was in sight. She could not even do that. At a station they were bound to be seen.

'Seen' – another horrible word, like 'tell'. During that last, limping conversation, he asked her if anything had happened. 'No,' she said. 'I don't think he can have said anything. I'd have seen a reaction by now.' He nodded as though that were good – which it was, of course – but it meant it was still hanging over her. 'I don't know if he just wants to torment me, or if he really will – destroy everything.'

'Darling one, why would he do that? Why would he destroy his own wife's family? No, he won't say anything.'

'Then why did he look at me the way he did?'

'He didn't look any particular way. I'm sure you imagined it.'

They parted in the cramped hall of the little house, with kisses, of which there could never be enough, and finally a straining embrace, her cold cheek pressed against his warm one, breathing in the smell of him, which was like the essence of life. And then, quite abruptly, he put her back, said, 'Goodbye,' and was gone. She guessed that he had been close to breaking down. She waited five minutes to let him get clear, leaning her back against the door, eyes closed, trying to hold on to him in her mind, then went out into the cold dark.

The streets, the whole world, seemed empty without him. She didn't want to go home. She didn't want to *be* anywhere. She wished she could just keep travelling and never arrive, to remain in a state of transit so that no decision could ever be required of her. After the war, he had said – after the war . . . He wanted her to go with him back to the estate he had bought in South Africa, and spoke lyrically about the verdant landscape, the climate, the freedom, the easy way of life. It was paradise, where she could be with him in a state of unending joy. The promised land. But would she be allowed to cross the river? She saw herself on the brink of the flood, staring at the farther bank, shut out from it for ever.

She made her way home slowly, by various buses as far as Harrow, then finally taking the train, too exhausted by then to care any longer. Pain sat deep in her, stiff and intractable, like a malign growth that she must carry about, and which would one day kill her. At Northcote Station a taxi had just deposited a passenger, and it waited for her, its breath smoking up into the cold air. The driver looked at her hopefully, but she turned away from it and walked home, using the time to reassemble herself into the wife, mother and mistress of the house that would be expected. It was a useful exercise.

Beattie had more time now to spend with Diana, and when she saw how grateful her daughter was for the company, she suffered pangs of guilt that she regarded as just punishment.

'Don't you see anything of the earl and countess?' she asked.

'I see her most days, but only for a short visit. The earl isn't at all well. Bronchitis. It's the cold, damp weather. Lady Wroughton says he ought to go abroad, but of course he can't, with the war. I miss Rupert,' she went on. 'If I could be at home – I mean, in Park Place – he'd come home each night. And people would call in. But apparently the baby has to be born here.' She raised hopeful eyes to her mother, as if she might refute this. 'It's tradition.'

But Beattie only said, 'I suppose the birth of a future earl is an important thing.'

Diana sighed. 'There's a christening robe, too – Lady Wroughton showed it to me. So beautiful, satin and silk and lace. I do hope it's a boy. Everyone will be so disappointed if it isn't.'

'Well, it won't be long now.'

'That's what Rupert keeps saying.'

'He visits you? I thought you said—'

'He telephones. Mostly to make sure Lady Wroughton

isn't making any plans he doesn't like. About doctors, and so on. She wants the baby delivered by the same grand doctor who delivered Rupert, but he wants someone young and modern. And there'll be a lying-in nurse and a month nurse. But, Mother, there is one thing I'd like to ask.'

'Anything, dear.'

'Do you think I could have Nula with me, when the time comes? I'm rather scared, and I think she'd make me feel safe.'

'Of course you can,' Beattie said, touched. 'I know she'd be only too happy. But what would Lady Wroughton think?'

A little of the old Diana steel showed. 'Rupert says I can have whom I like, so she'll have to put up with it.'

Lady Wroughton was puzzled with herself and with the situation. Diana was to bear the heir to the earldom, which made her an object to be cherished, deserving of every attention. She ought to seek her out, get to know her, guide her towards her future role. And yet, Diana was so completely alien to the countess that she had difficulty in regarding her even as a part of the family. She was glad of the excuse of the earl's sickness to avoid having to see her, but in the back of her mind she felt an irritating prickle of guilt. She knew she was neglecting her daughter-in-law, leaving her too much alone, and that it was wrong; and since she did not like to be wrong, it made her more uncomfortable with Diana than ever.

As a matter of duty, she made a point of sitting with her for half an hour every day, but it was an effort. Diana could not converse about family, friends and fondly remembered occasions, because they had none of them in common, and they were the only subjects that would have made her feel Diana was 'one of us'. Who *was* this girl, emerged from the deepest obscurity to win Charles's heart, and now, astonishingly, wearing his title but great with his brother's child?

Why had Rupert, in succession, chosen her, when he could have had anyone? What on earth had they both seen in her? The earl, wheezing and coughing, only offered, 'She's a pretty girl,' in explanation, but that did not do. In the course of their stilted conversations, she stared quizzically, tried to make Diana out, and failed.

Hardest of all to contemplate was that she would be there for ever, squatting immovably in the cadet suite, in the receiving line at formal gatherings, unavoidable, unignorable. And what appalling middle-class ideas would she bring to the upraising of the heir? Lady Wroughton would have to be on her guard to make sure that the child, at least, was 'one of us'. An alien grandson was too horrible to contemplate.

The countess liked to be in charge, and it galled her that there was nothing, nothing that she could do about Diana. She would have to suffer her for the rest of her life.

Unless, of course, she died in childbirth. There was always that possibility.

Though she was busy up at Highclere, Sadie was more at home than either her mother or her father, and she made a point of spending some time with David every day, whether he wanted it or not – usually not. So his depression was not only more obvious to her, but bothered her more. It was a burr under the saddle to her; and when her own ministrations did nothing to lighten his gloom, she sought around for another solution, and finally lit on the idea of Miss Weston.

The one time she remembered him cheering up was when Antonia Weston came to visit him before Christmas. He always said he didn't want visitors, but if she simply arrived, he wouldn't refuse to see her, would he? So she wrote to her, but didn't mention Sophy's defection. She just said David was very low, and that a visit from her would surely cheer him up. Antonia wrote back by return, proposing an early date.

Sadie decided not to tell David, so that there wouldn't be time for him to work up an objection. There was no knowing, these days, what he might decide to dislike. One day he had roared that he could not stand that smelly cur in his room a moment longer, and Ethel had been forced to drag the indignant Nailer out; but the next day he had wondered where the dog was and wanted him back. He would be suddenly revolted by some once-favourite dish that Cook prepared specially for him; would refuse food at dinnertime, then be ringing for bread and meat and rice pudding in the middle of the night. And one day he hurled his disc record of 'The Last Rose of Summer' at the wall, breaking it and chipping the wallpaper. Lily said she wouldn't have Ethel's job for a fortune; but Ethel rather liked the distinction of being the one who answered his bell, as sometimes people are proud of fierce, bad dogs that only they can handle.

When Antonia arrived on the appointed day, Sadie met her in the hall, and explained that she was to be a surprise; and also told her about Sophy.

'Oh dear,' Antonia said. 'He was so very devoted to her.'

Something in her tone made Sadie say, 'Didn't you like her?'

'I never met her,' Antonia said, 'and I'm sure she was very nice. But I always thought he idolised her in a very unrealistic way. He thought of her as a goddess, rather than a real flesh-and-blood female, and that's not a good plan.'

Sadie lowered her voice. 'I thought her rather ordinary,' she murmured guiltily. 'I really couldn't see why David was so struck. But I suppose,' she added uncertainly, 'love is like that. I mean, you can't tell who you'll find irresistible until it happens, can you?'

Antonia gave her a humorous look. 'Perhaps that's just as well.'

'Perhaps it is,' Sadie agreed, and had a sudden fierce wish that David had brought home Miss Weston as her potential sister instead of Miss Oliphant. It would have been *so* much more comfortable!

'Do you think we should go up, now?' Miss Weston interrupted her reverie.

'Oh – yes! Of course. But you are prepared, in case he's not pleased?'

'I shall face what comes like a soldier,' she promised.

He scowled when Sadie announced that he had a visitor. Then he saw who it was, and Sadie was afraid for a moment that he was going to cry. But he didn't. He didn't smile, either, but he held out a hand, and said, 'How good of you to come and see me.'

Antonia crossed the room, swift and light as a bird, and took the hand. 'Not good at all. It's my pleasure.'

And then she sat, and they started talking. Sadie left them to it. She noticed that Antonia had not begun with 'How are you?' as everyone else did. Perhaps that was the secret to success.

Edward was away one or two days a week, now, visiting landowners to persuade them to turn pasture into arable – and, moreover, to do it *now*. If the country was to have a bigger harvest in the autumn, the seeds must be sown this spring. Already in February more than a million tons of shipping had been lost to the new German submarine campaign. It was Edward's job to impress on landlords the seriousness of the situation without setting their backs up.

He was not travelling alone. A cheerful young spark from the Board of Agriculture had been assigned to accompany and advise him. Christopher Beresford, with his wiry fair curls and eager freckled face, looked like a schoolmaster's favourite fifth-former, but in fact he was in his late twenties, and it didn't take many moments of conversation with him to discover that he had one of the sharpest minds in the field. He was also delightful company. Edward was soon on such terms with him that they could work in partnership, and rely on each other to speak or be silent as circumstances demanded, the better to persuade the reluctant.

For Edward found that, however patriotic your landowner, there were obstacles to overcome. There was tradition, 'Our family has always done it this way,' and indifference, 'I don't know anything about cereals.' There were the aesthetics of it: verdant parkland cropped by sheep or deer enhanced a great house, whereas acres of potatoes rolling right up to the ha-ha were an eyesore. And there were practical problems: 'We don't have the labour,' and 'We don't have the horses.'

These last were what Edward and Beresford tried to concentrate on, because something could be done about them, whereas an opposed mind had to be worked on at length. But once the practical elements were dealt with, it was harder for the landlord to refuse without looking merely unpatriotic.

Beresford had a passion for, and extensive knowledge of, machinery of all sorts. He could turn plain numbers about the efficiency of tractors into poetry. His particular task would be to make a register of all the machinery in an area, requisition it, and arrange a schedule of use. Horses and mules would likewise have to be shared, but his faith was all in the machine.

'I'm urging the Board to put pressure on the government to buy tractors from America and lease them to our farmers,' he told Edward on their first journey together. 'It will mean a large initial investment, but it will pay dividends in the long run. There's a Fordson tractor over there that's cheap, light enough for our wet fields, and so simple to use a woman could drive it.'

The last was an important consideration, because the other constant objection was the lack of labour. So many agricultural workers had left the land, and elderly shepherds and cow-hands could not be expected to learn new skills overnight. The Land Army had been set up in 1915, training men unfit for combat to work on the land; now Edward was able to tell the landlords that there would be a Women's Land Army to draw from as well. Not just tell them, of course, but persuade them that women could and would do the work. Many owners recoiled in horror at the idea. A girl wouldn't be strong enough. She wouldn't stand the cold, the wet, the mud. She'd lark about, not get on with the work. And it wouldn't be suitable, seemly, fitting for females to be doing dirty manual work.

Here, Edward and Beresford both had their poetry, drawing on the valiant efforts women were making in all sorts of areas so that our brave boys could fight the wicked Hun abroad. Sometimes no words could sway the set mind, but they had plenty of successes. Once the landlord had agreed, other officials would set about organising the distribution of seeds, fertilisers, and labour. It fascinated Edward – who discussed it often with Beresford on their travels – to see how what had been a country entirely made up of separate individuals could, in the fourth year of the war, organise itself on a national level, and do it with astonishing efficiency.

'You only have to look at how the army functions,' Edward said. 'I don't mean in combat, but in day-to-day matters: the men are fed, rations are distributed, arms and uniforms are manufactured and sent where they're needed, all on a scale unthinkable before the war.'

'You're right, sir,' said Beresford. 'The transport alone is a miracle of science. And the postal system: a letter from home to a Tommy arrives in forty-eight hours – and his back to them, of course.'

It happened that Edward was on the road when the news reached England of the Russian Tsar's abdication. Since the 8th of March, bad news had been coming out of Russia, of increasing rioting in St Petersburg, followed, more worryingly, by mutinies. The soldiers in barracks in the city, called out to quell the riots, had turned on their officers and sided with the rioters; and the mutiny had quickly spread to the front-line troops. The breakdown in order was so severe that representatives of the Duma had intercepted the Tsar's train as he travelled back towards St Petersburg and demanded his abdication. On the 15th of March, he had signed the instrument, and abdicated on his son's behalf as well. And on the following day, the next heir, the Tsar's brother Grand Duke Michael, refused the crown, and a republic was born.

What it would mean was hard to determine, and Edward wished he could talk to Lord Forbesson and get the inside information. A provisional government had been formed, which had declared its intention of continuing the war, but whether it would be able to command the loyalty of the troops and put down the riots and mutinies was the question.

'We need Russia to stay in the war,' he explained to Beresford, who hadn't thought much about that aspect – although he knew a surprising amount about Russian agriculture.

'They still use the medieval strip system,' he told Edward. 'Imagine it, in 1917!'

'I don't suppose they have many tractors, either,' Edward joked.

Beresford grinned. 'I think I see a career opening up after the war – tractor salesman in Russia. Think how many thousands one could sell in a country that size.'

'And you'd be the man to sell them,' Edward agreed. 'If you can persuade Sir Henry Duxford to use land girls, you could sell ice-cream to Eskimos.'

At The Elms, the servants were at breakfast, and exclaiming over the business of the Tsar's abdication, which was all over the papers.

'Well, he won't be missed,' Ada pronounced. 'Wicked autocrat, it says here. That's what he was. The blood of his own people on his hands.'

'He was a bloody tyrant,' Emily agreed.

'Language!' Cook reproved.

'It says it in the paper,' Emily protested.

'That's as may be. But what I say is, he's first cousin to our own king. You got to think about that.'

'Well, he didn't act like our king,' Ada said. 'If he had, maybe he'd still be on his throne.'

'Once you start something like that, you don't know where it'll end,' Cook warned.

'Something like what?' Lilian asked.

'Revolution,' she said, with gloomy relish. 'You only got to look at history – what happened in France. Thousands be'eaded on the guillotine, ordinary people like you and me. You take away the king, and the 'ole thing gets out of hand. So don't you start hankering after a revolution, my girl,' she addressed Ada, 'because it's the likes of us that ends up paying.'

'I never,' said Ada indignantly. 'I only said he was a bloody tyrant.'

'No, *I* said that,' Emily piped. ''Twas in the paper.'

'And I'll have no more of that language in this kitchen,' Cook snapped, sensing she was losing her grip. 'Get on with your breakfast. They'll be ringing to clear in the morning-room before you know it.'

It was at that moment that a very small boy on a bicycle much too big for him – he had to stand up to pedal – skidded up to the house and raced to the back door with a written note and a face full of importance. 'For your missus – urgent!' he cried.

Ada jumped up and took it. 'Where from?' she asked the child.

'Dene Park,' he said. 'Gard'ner's boy, I am. That's the

'ead gard'ner's bike,' he added, grandly. 'Tole me to come quick as yer like, and lent me 'is bike.'

Ada was already halfway out of the kitchen, and the others followed to linger in the hall in the hope of hearing. As it was a Saturday, Peter, William and Sadie were at the table with Beattie, as Ada came in and proffered the note. 'A boy's brought this from Dene Park, madam,' she said, with breathless expectation.

Beattie opened it. 'It's from Lady Wroughton.' She read it, and looked up. 'Miss Diana's in labour,' she said.

'Oh, madam! At last,' said Ada.

'I must go,' Beattie said, getting up. 'Is the boy still there? I'll write a note for him to take back. And send someone round to Nula straight away, will you?'

Ada whirled away, and William looked anxiously at his mother. 'Will she be all right?' he asked.

Peter caught his drift. 'Mother, Diana's not going to die, is she?'

'No, of course not,' Beattie said. 'Whyever should you think that?'

'Bobby died,' Peter said, with a wobble.

Beattie paused in her exit to reassure him – both of them. Their safe, unchanging world of before the war was now full of uncertainty. Some of it had been fun, of course, but when it came to members of the family disappearing . . . 'She's having a baby, Peter, not fighting in a war. Women have babies all the time – it's nothing.'

She threw a glance at Sadie, who said, 'I'll stay with them. I won't go to Highclere.'

'Good girl. I'll ring when I have any news. But it will probably take all day. First babies don't hurry.'

She went out, and Sadie looked at her brothers' anxious faces, realising that they had not been reassured. William looked quite pale. If it was going to take all day, it wasn't going to be 'nothing', was it?

She thought Diana would be fighting a war, in her own way. She didn't know a great deal about childbirth, but considering the size of a baby, it couldn't be easy getting it out, could it? And people did die in childbirth. You heard about it all the time.

But she wasn't going to think like that. They'd had enough trouble in the family already. And she had a job to do. She arranged a smile on her face and said to her brothers, 'She'll be all right. Honestly. She'll have Nula with her, and Nula knows what to do. Besides, Mother had all of us, didn't she? And she's fine.'

William recovered his colour. 'Yes, of course,' he said bravely. And, for Peter's sake, 'I saw the sheepdog, Ness, up at Sharpe's Farm, have puppies years ago. She just sort of squeezed them out. It was easy.'

'How many is Diana going to have?' Peter asked, perplexed.

'Just the one,' William said, then, uncertainly, to Sadie, 'Isn't it?'

'Just one,' said Sadie.

'So that'll be even easier,' William concluded.

'What are we going to do today?' Peter asked. 'Do we have to stay in the house?'

'No, you can go out and play, if you like. I'll stay here, in case of messages.'

'I'll stay too,' William said loyally.

'You don't need to. Nothing will happen this morning, anyway.'

'No, I'll stay. You shouldn't be on your own,' he said, sounding very grown-up.

'I'll stay too, then,' said Peter. 'I'll just go along the road and tell Jimmy. We were going to look for tadpoles.'

Jimmy Covington lived at The Lodge, three doors down, and their maid Ruby was a friend of Ada's, and would surely be at the back door before you could say 'knife'. And as she was a noted gossip, the news would be everywhere by eleven o'clock. Sadie got up from the table and went upstairs to tell David, though without the slightest doubt that Ethel would have managed to do that already.

Lady Wroughton had sent a telegram to Rupert at the same time as dispatching the note to Beattie, with the result that although his chosen medical attendant, Dr Fleming, had to travel from London, he still managed to arrive before the baby was born.

Lady Wroughton was peeved that Sir Maurice Enderby, who had delivered both Charles and Rupert, was not to be called, but she was a little wary these days of crossing Rupert, who, since he had become the heir, had grown ever more ungovernable, and had a quick wit that made verbal jousting with him hazardous. He had absolutely vetoed Sir Maurice. Her annoyance distracted her so much that she forgot the Hunters now had the telephone, putting her to the trouble of writing a note, which, when she remembered the fact, only irritated her further. And the arrival of not only Beattie – who in justice could not be expected to stay away at such a time – but the old family nurse turned the whole thing into a circus, in Lady Wroughton's opinion.

The earl, on having the news of the labour conveyed to him, insisted on getting up and dressing with full, formal care.

'You needn't have,' Lady Wroughton said. 'Childbirth is not men's business. There's nothing for you to do.'

'Nothing for you, either,' the earl said, with a chuckle that turned into a cough. 'It's the girl's mother who reigns until the child is born. But it will be my grandchild and possibly heir, so I shall be ready and fittingly dressed, whenever it happens. And now I'd like some breakfast, and I suggest you have some too. Settle your nerves.'

'I am not nervous,' she said, with dignity.

'You damn well should be. The future of the Wroughtons is at stake.'

'I don't agree. If she dies, Rupert can always marry again.'

The earl looked shocked, and the countess, belatedly realising that she had spoken aloud her private thought, had the grace to look ashamed.

'Your nerves *are* on edge,' the earl said. 'Come and have some eggs and bacon with me, Violet, old girl, and you'll feel more settled. And if it's a boy, I think you'll find you like our daughter-in-law a whole lot better.'

She'll have a girl for sure, the countess thought savagely, *and it will all have been for nothing*. But she didn't say anything.

The baby was born at half past three, after a straightforward labour. 'I had nothing to do, really,' Dr Fleming said afterwards to Rupert. 'There were no complications, and that very capable family nurse knew exactly what to do. The patient obviously trusted her, so I didn't interfere. I just supervised.' Though, of course, he had stepped in and cut the cord himself, so as to justify his fee.

It was a boy, a healthy six-and-a-half-pound boy, with a good set of lungs and a thatch of dark hair, which, Nula assured Diana, would soon come away. 'That's just birth hair, doesn't count at all. He'll be fair like you and his lordship.'

Diana felt as though she'd just done several days' hard labour and would have liked to sleep for a week, but otherwise it was not as bad as she had expected. And when the tiny, red-faced child was laid in her arms, she experienced such an upsurge of emotion, she felt as though something inside her might burst from the force of it. 'He's so little,' she said. 'And screwed up – he isn't very handsome?' She looked anxiously at her mother.

'He'll straighten out. By this time tomorrow he'll be perfectly beautiful.'

'He's beautiful now,' Nula said indignantly.

'A boy,' Diana said, looking down into the face, trying to

learn it. She wanted to look and look and never stop. 'I had a boy.'

'That's right, my lamb. You're a clever girl,' Nula said. 'That'll draw their teeth for them!'

'He'll be the Earl Wroughton one day,' Diana said. 'Think of it!' It astonished her, almost as much as the fact that she had a baby, a real baby, her actual own, lying in her arms. 'Does Rupert know?'

'He will soon,' Beattie said. She wanted to hold the baby, and she wanted to weep, but she couldn't do either.

The earl and countess came in, the earl wreathed with smiles, the countess looking grim. *She* could demand to hold the baby, and did, and as soon as she had it, the grimness relaxed into a curious expression, part relief, part sorrow. No-one but her would ever know, but she was thinking that it ought to have been Charles's baby she held. She had never valued her first-born, but now he was gone, she knew he was the better of her sons, and would have made the better earl.

'Is he healthy?' she demanded of the doctor, but without looking at him. *A nobody, to deliver her grandson!*

'Perfectly, your ladyship,' said Fleming.

The earl said, 'That's splendid! Well done, Diana, my dear. I hope it wasn't too gruelling for you? I won't come too close, because of this wretched cold, but I had to see you and say well done. There's champagne on ice – will you take a glass? I believe champagne is good for ladies at times like this - am I right, Doctor?'

'It will do no harm,' Fleming said, hoping that he would be included in the libation.

Beattie was pleased that the earl had remembered his manners and spoken to, and of, Diana. The countess, holding the baby, had not even looked at her.

The champagne was brought in, and they all took a glass, though Lady Wroughton put hers straight down untasted.

The baby was all she cared about. 'It's a good one,' the earl said. 'The '05. Nothing but the best to wet my little grandson's head.' He raised the toast. 'To the next earl-in-waiting! Have we a name yet?'

He looked around the room. Lady Wroughton kept silent, but looked furious. The name should have been decided by the family elders, specifically her, but there again Rupert had got away from her. He was proving as hard to hold as a handful of eels.

Beattie answered the earl. 'I believe Rupert will choose the name, when he comes.'

'Ah, yes, of course. Well, he'll select something fitting, I'm sure,' said the earl, tactfully, with a glance at his lady.

He had better, said the countess's expression.

Rupert arrived just before seven, and from his vinous breath and the sparkle in his eyes, he had been celebrating already. But he called for more champagne, and was as charming and warm towards Diana as even her mother could wish. Diana sparkled for him, pleased with herself, delighted with her child, glad of his attention.

'A boy first time. Clever you!' Rupert said, and bent to kiss her forehead. 'He's a funny-looking little thing, but you can't expect much from new babies. He'll be better by and by. With two handsome parents he's bound to have the looks.'

And Beattie found herself thinking uncomfortably of Charles, who had not been handsome. The baby was Charles's nephew instead of his son. How odd the world was. 'What will you call him?' she asked Rupert, to distract herself.

'I've been thinking about that all the way down. I like the idea of George – what do you say, darling? It's a nice, solid, English sort of name. A good name for an earl.'

'I like it,' Diana said.

'Good. George he shall be. And, since he has to have some other names to play with, a boy in his position, I think he ought to have Edward, after your papa, and Harcourt, my mother's maiden name, and Charles. After Charles. Who is bound to be very much in our thoughts at this moment.'

Diana looked up with tears in her eyes, and nodded her approval.

Beattie had never liked Rupert more than at that moment.

And the Hon. George Edward Harcourt Charles Wroughton, untroubled by these responsibilities heaped on him, continued to catch up on his sleep.

CHAPTER EIGHT

The Spring Offensive was due to start in April, but during March disturbing reports had been coming from the Front. Information was fragmented and hard to verify, but at last it was confirmed that the Germans had been quietly slipping away, back to a new defensive position they had been building all winter. Dubbed the Hindenburg line after the German chief of staff, the new line cut off the Noyon salient, reducing the Western Front by twenty-five miles.

When Edward came home, rather grey in the face, and told her what had happened, Beattie remembered Louis explaining to her about the 'balloon', and how nipping it at the neck was to bring about the end of the war – or, at least, the beginning of the end of the war.

'So that's bad – isn't it?' she said hesitantly.

'Yes,' said Edward. 'It's bad. The Germans will need thirteen or fourteen fewer divisions to hold the shorter line, and all those men will be freed to attack us.'

Beattie thought. 'But won't a shorter line give us extra men, too?'

He looked approving of the question. He hadn't expected her to understand or really care about strategy. 'Yes, it will. But it forestalls our spring offensive. And their new defences will be much stronger – they've been building at their leisure, in their own territory, with no fear of being attacked, so they'll have got them just the way they want them.'

'So what will happen now?' Beattie asked.

'Our generals will adapt their plans and carry on, of course, but I imagine it will be a lot harder to break the new German line.'

'I see,' said Beattie, and turned away. Harder fighting, she thought. More danger. And no end to it. She felt slightly sick.

Edward was concerned at her obvious upset. He went after her, touched her arm. 'You mustn't worry. We will win. Never doubt that.'

'But at what cost?' she said, keeping her face averted.

He turned her gently to him. 'I know we've paid heavily already. And you're thinking of William and Peter. It won't come to that.'

'William's seventeen,' she said in a flat voice.

'They can't send him abroad until he's nineteen. The war won't last another two years.'

'You don't know that,' she said. 'And you don't know that they won't change the rules.'

Edward paused. He hated to see her unhappy, but what could he tell her that was true and honest? At last he said, 'We can't change what will happen to us. We're fighting to save the world from a horrible evil. If it takes sacrifice, we have to face that. But we'll face it together. We'll give each other strength. I love you, Beattie. I love the children you've given me. For all the pain of losing Bobby, it's worth it to have known him for those twenty years. And to have been your husband is the greatest privilege of my life. Whatever happens, they can't take that from us.'

Beattie's mouth trembled. She wanted to howl and weep and rend her hair, but now, of all times, she must keep control. 'Thank you,' was what she finally said. It wasn't much, it wasn't what he deserved, but it was safe.

True to prediction, in a week the new baby had straightened out, paled to the colour of a pearl, lost the black thatch, and become without question the most beautiful baby that had ever lived. Dene Park was *en fête*, receiving visits from neighbours and relations, and friends of both generations of Wroughtons. Rupert was down almost every evening to praise his clever wife and dote on his little son.

'I never knew I'd feel like this,' he said wonderingly to Diana. 'I always thought babies rather repulsive. But this one . . .'

'He *is* very handsome,' Diana said. 'More so than most babies.'

'He's perfection,' Rupert said. 'I'm so grateful to you, darling, for letting me have this experience. I never thought I would.'

'Even second sons are allowed to get married and have children,' she pointed out.

'Oh – of course! But there wouldn't be much point, would there? Now, we must have a terrific party for the christening. Mother wants to have him dipped next week, but I want you to be able to enjoy it. What about the week after that? Will you be out of bed by then?'

'I think so,' Diana said. 'Actually, I feel all right now, but Nula says if I get up too soon my insides will slip.'

Rupert's face contorted. 'Don't tell me things like that! I want to believe this baby floated down from Heaven on a cloud of swansdown. Reality is too cruel, sometimes.'

Diana laughed. 'You're funny! Will the party be at home? I mean, at Park Place?'

'No, darling – last concession to the Aged Ps, it will have to be here. But after that we can go back to London. I've seen the most delicious wallpaper for the nursery – let me describe it to you . . .'

Christening gifts of all sorts were arriving. Diana discovered that, among the upper classes, the gift was not usually something the baby could use, but rather in the form of an investment for his future. Her own circle gave baby clothes, rattles and toys, but Rupert's godmother, Lady Teesborough, for instance, sent an exquisite little early Boucher landscape.

'Don't let the baby suck on that,' Nula advised.

Nula was busy interviewing nursery maids for when the baby went back to Park Place. 'I can't come with you,' she had told Diana, as soon as she thought she could bear it. 'I've me own husband here, and me own life. And I'm too old to be coping with a little baby.'

'Nannies in the Wroughton family always seem to be old, from what I've heard. Much older than you,' Diana said wistfully.

'It's not what I agree with. A sensible, mature woman, yes, but not some old mothball with a creaky back that'll drop the baby on its head. Maybe that's why so many of your aristocrats are not very bright. Have you thought of that?' It made Diana smile, but guiltily. 'Don't you worry, my precious, I'll find you a nice nanny and a good clean country girl to help her, and that's all his little lordship will need for now.'

'He's not a lordship,' Diana reminded her. 'He's just an honourable.'

'He's a lordship to me,' Nula said firmly. 'Who'd have thought my baby Diana would rise so high? Your boy's going to be an earl. Isn't that something?'

Diana rather thought it was.

In the first week of April, Donald Palfrey, the eldest son of Edward's sister Sonia, had his embarkation leave. The Palfreys threw a big party in their Kensington house on his last night to 'send him off in style'. In truth, the Palfreys loved to hold parties, with or without an excuse, but this was a momentous occasion. Donald, with his lieutenant's pips proudly on display, was pink with excitement, and solemn under the weight of his new responsibilities, to his country and to 'the men'.

He and his father emerged from a private talk in Aeneas's study, both looking a little moist about the eyes. Laura, who was back in London for forty-eight hours, thought it adorable. 'We might see each other out there,' she told her nephew. 'Do you know where you're going?'

'I'm not allowed to say,' said Donald.

'Of course you're not,' Laura said indulgently. 'Well, I'm not under the same restraint. We're moving north, towards Ypres. We've heard that's where the action is going to be in the near future.'

Aeneas was interested. 'Haig has been wanting to break out of the Salient since last year, but what makes you think he's about to try again?'

Laura smiled. 'I couldn't possibly tell you. War secrets. But if you find yourself in that sector, Donald, look out for our ambulance. Just,' she added hastily, 'in the social way, you know.'

'You take care,' Edward told her. He and Beattie had come for the party, with William and Peter. Sadie had stayed at home to keep David company, and Diana had sent a telegram. 'I know you think it all a great game,' he went on, but she interrupted him.

'No, Teddy, I don't think that,' she said seriously. 'I've seen enough to know exactly how careful I have to be. But we haven't been hit yet – and I wouldn't have asked Louisa to come out with me if I thought it was too dangerous. I feel a sort of responsibility towards her. We – Bessie's crew – are her only family now.'

The following Monday, Aeneas was in his office at the factory going over some production figures. His door stood open, as it always did unless he was holding a private meeting, and Audrey tapped politely on the frame. 'Poppa? Are you busy?'

It had been a leap of faith for him to let her take over

101

Donald's job when he was called up last May. There was no doubt she was extremely bright – brighter than her brother – and had a determined character, but she was, after all, a female. Yet she had done so well that he often found himself forgetting her sex. He was aware that there had been grumbling from some of the men, but he thought they would settle down in the end and get used to her, as he had.

She was as neat as wax, in a grey flannel tailor-made over a plain white shirt and a dark blue tie, and her hair was drawn into a severe bun. Her hem was a conservative four inches above the ground. Some women in active pursuits were now wearing skirts eight inches above. Aeneas appreciated her restraint.

'Never too busy for you, my pet,' he said. 'I wanted to talk to you, anyway. Come in and close the door.' She complied, and stood directly in front of him, hands folded, as composed as a nun. 'We have a little problem in the bottling plant, do we not?' he said. 'I have a report from Barrett that he's had to slow down the jam production because it's not going into the jars fast enough.'

'That's what I came to talk to you about,' Audrey said. 'I want to take some of the women from the jam section and put them on to bottling temporarily, until we even things out. We'll have to recruit some more hands for the long term, but it'll take a little time to find suitable women. The best of them are going into the munitions factories.'

'More women,' Aeneas sighed.

'No use recruiting men if they're going to get called up the moment you've trained them. Besides, women are quicker to learn and easier to handle. They work hard and don't cause trouble.'

'Why not school-leavers? They still have the habit of learning, and the war will be over before they're of age.'

'Most of them are not tall enough or strong enough,' Audrey countered. 'And those who are don't want to work in confectionery. They want to be making bombs and aeroplanes. It's no use, Poppa,' she said kindly. 'You'll have to get used to it.'

'I've got used to *you*, haven't I?' he defended himself.

'I wish everyone was like you,' Audrey said.

Aeneas raised an eyebrow. 'What's the trouble now?'

'It's McDuff again. He's objecting to my moving women into his section.'

'What's his reason?'

'He has no reason,' Audrey said impatiently. 'He objects because *I* suggest it. He simply wants to be obstructive.'

Aeneas frowned. 'I've known the man for years, and I've never seen that in him.'

'Of course not! When he's with you he smirks and wriggles like an ingratiating dog. But he won't be managed by a woman, that's the long and short of it. He wants to force me to quit and, if possible, to see me cry.' Her father was looking uncomfortable, and she softened her tone a fraction. 'Poppa, I try not to bring these problems to you. If you have to repeat my instructions before anything happens, you might as well do the work yourself. Mostly I get round it. But I can't get round this one. I can't shift McDuff, so I'm *having* to come to you.'

Aeneas pondered; then said, 'All right, we'd better have him in. Can't accuse a man behind his back without letting him put his own side.'

'He *has* no side to put,' Audrey began, but Aeneas held up his hand and stopped her.

'We'll hear what he has to say,' he said firmly.

McDuff, when he came in, looked sullen, which was not a good start.

Aeneas didn't waste time. 'McDuff, what's this I hear about you refusing to have extra hands to shift the backlog?'

'Not hands, sir, *women*.' McDuff's tone was respectful, though taut with suppressed feeling. 'Untrained hands around machinery are a danger to themselves and others. You know that, sir, well as I do.'

Aeneas looked at Audrey.

'I have three women who've used similar machines before. A demonstration is all they need. In an hour, they'll grasp it, I guarantee it.'

'*You* guarantee it?' McDuff muttered.

'Within the day, they'll be quicker than the men. Their hands are more nimble, and they have more sense of rhythm.'

McDuff looked outraged. 'Rhythm? What's rhythm got to do with it? This is not a dancing school for young ladies!' He appealed to Aeneas: 'Sir, these women are ruining the business. They don't know what they're doing. They should be at home minding babies, not taking honest men's jobs from them!'

Aeneas said mildly, 'Jam production is up. Sounds as if they know what they're doing.'

'The men are carrying them,' McDuff argued. 'It's been nothing but trouble since the women came, and this damn-fool female thinks she can just walk in and take over from men who've been twenty-five years learning the business!'

'This damn-fool female is my daughter,' Aeneas reminded him sternly, 'and it was my decision to put her in charge. Are you questioning my authority, McDuff?'

'No, sir. But your decision I do! Putting the factory in the hands of a chit of a girl barely out of pigtails—'

'That's enough!' Aeneas snapped. 'I won't have insolence from you.'

'I beg pardon, sir,' McDuff said. 'I mean no disrespect, but I can't bear to see you throw away your company like this. She's your daughter so you don't see the harm it's doing.'

Again Aeneas held up his hand for silence. To Audrey he said, 'Can these women do the job?'

'Yes,' said Audrey.

'Then that's all that matters.'

'I won't have them!' McDuff said hotly.

'You will do as you're told,' Audrey replied.

McDuff slipped over the edge of some personal precipice. 'Not by you, I won't! I've never taken orders from a female, and I'm not starting now! If one of my womenfolk spoke back to me like that, I'd give them such a skelp they wouldn't sit down for a week! Go home where you belong! Go home to your dollies, and keep your nose out of men's business!'

Aeneas stood up. 'Get out!' McDuff, taking one look at his face, left in a hurry.

The room seemed very quiet. Audrey, a little pale but quite steady, said, 'You'll have to dismiss him, Poppa.'

Aeneas, who had been deep in thought, started slightly, and looked at her. 'Now, let's not be hasty,' he said, after a moment.

'You can't keep him after he's spoken to me like that,' Audrey said. 'I'd have no authority left.'

'I'll talk to him. He'll come round. He'll take the women.'

'But he'll never take orders from me. He'll have to go.'

'McDuff's been with us twenty years. He knows his section inside out. How would we manage without him?'

'I've got a woman, Aggie Semple, she'd make an excellent foreman. She's ready for promotion – in fact, if she doesn't get it I'm afraid she may leave.'

'A woman foreman? That's going too far,' said Aeneas.

'You've already *gone* too far by putting me in charge. There's no going back now. You needn't be afraid of Aggie. She's a steady hand with a cool head, and she gets on well with the men in her section, not just the women. And she's got ideas for making things run better. Give her the job, Poppa. McDuff's a bad influence. He unsettles the men.'

'I'll think about it,' Aeneas said; and when Audrey began to speak, he stopped her. 'I said, I'll think about it. I don't make decisions lightly, you know that. Run along now, pet. Leave it be for now.'

Audrey knew her father well enough to know he would not discuss it further, and left him alone.

Aeneas put his head into his hands and cursed the war for taking Donald away. But later that day he was seen about the factory floor, moving silently from section to section, observing the work, and the people doing it. He asked a few questions. He found out which one was Aggie Semple and watched her without appearing to. And by the end of the day he had made his decision. The three women, plus Aggie Semple as foreman, were moved to the bottling side.

He did not dismiss McDuff, but moved him to deliveries where, driving alone, he was unable to upset any other worker, and was free from the irritation of having women around him. It seemed to Aeneas a reasonable resolution to the problem.

Audrey was disappointed that her father had not publicly sacked McDuff for defying her; but she also knew that women had to move carefully in a man's world, and be sure of their foothold before they loosed a landslide.

Their time would come, she thought.

One day in April Ada came into the kitchen and said, 'The missus has just asked me to make up the guest-room. You'll never guess who for.'

Cook looked up from her pastry. 'Not Miss Laura?'

'No, she's gone back to France. She was only over two nights. No, it's for that Miss Weston. Coming to see Mr David, and the missus says if she's travelling all the way from Hampshire the least we can do is offer her a bed.'

'How long's she staying?' Ethel asked sharply. She was at the stove making David's mid-morning coffee.

'Don't know. She never said.'

'Well, I hope she doesn't go upsetting him,' Ethel said crossly.

'Why would she upset him?' Ada asked, surprised. 'He's liked having her visit, the times before.'

'Liked it *too* much,' Ethel muttered.

'I know what she's worried about,' Emily piped up from the scullery. 'It's 'cause he had his heart broke by that wicked siren Miss Oliphant, and she doesn't want it broke again.'

'What's a siren?' asked Lilian, coming in from cleaning the bathroom. 'I thought it was that hooter they let off at the factories at dinnertime.'

'Pay no attention to that girl,' Cook said. 'It only encourages her.' She looked at Ethel with narrowed eyes. 'And what's it to you who he has visiting?' Ethel didn't answer, lifting her shoulders a little, like a defensive bird, as she poured hot water. 'Not getting fond of him, are you? Because I won't have any carryings-on of that sort in my kitchen.'

'Oh, mind your own beeswax,' Ethel muttered under her breath.

'And you mind your lip,' Cook retorted. 'You're a servant in this house, and he's the master's son, and don't you forget it. No good ever came of a servant getting fond of one of the family. Not fond *that* way,' she added, thinking of Bobby, whom she had loved.

'Anyway, what would Frank say?' Emily piped up irrepressibly. 'Ooh, if he knew he had a rival for your affections, what'd he do, eh? He might challenge Mr David to a duel, and they'd meet at dawn and fight, and one of 'em'd lie a bleeding corpse on the cold ground ere the sun reached its zenith.'

'*Emily!*' Cook snapped.

'What's a zenith?' Lilian asked.

'You're soft in the head,' Ada said. 'How could Mr David fight a duel? Even if he wanted to. Which he wouldn't.'

Ethel poured the coffee into the cup and headed for the door. 'You're all mad,' she said dispassionately. 'Ought to be locked up, the lot o' you. Load o' barmies.'

'You didn't let that stand long enough 'fore you strained it,' Cook called after her, to keep her end up. 'There'll be grounds.'

'I know how to make coffee, thank you.' Ethel's retort floated back from the passage.

Antonia had brought books with her. She had a new scheme. 'I know it must be boring for you, not being able to move around much, but there's no reason not to keep your mind active. So I thought we could do some Latin and Greek together. That way, when your leg's healed, you could go back to university, finish your degree.'

'That will never happen,' David said. 'Even if my leg ever gets better, I can't see myself going back to Oxford.'

'Well, it would help me,' she coaxed. 'I've got awfully rusty. And it will be fun.'

He didn't ask her why she needed Latin and Greek, and he doubted it would be fun, exactly. But, in the event, it was. It was good to use his brain, to face a mental challenge and overcome it; and anything he did with Antonia seemed to be agreeable. It was good to look up at the clock and find the hours gone, when usually the hands crept with painful slowness. It was good to have Ethel come in with enquiries about the next meal, and actually to feel a spark of interest in it.

He didn't ask Antonia how long she would be staying, but he didn't in the least object when each evening she didn't announce that she would be leaving the next day. In fact, it was a strange relief, when Ethel had settled him in his sitting-room in the morning, to see her coming in through the door, fresh as a daisy, carrying the newspaper, which she was making it a custom to read with him. Having someone intelligent to discuss the news with was an unaccustomed pleasure. Sophy had known nothing and cared less about current events. His parents were too busy, and Bobby—

'I miss Bobby,' he said to her abruptly one day.

They had been discussing America. The papers were full of the exciting news that America had declared war on Germany on the 6th of April, joining the conflict at last. It seemed that it was all to do with the Zimmermann Note, as the papers called it. This was a telegram that had just come to light, from the German foreign secretary, Arthur Zimmermann, to the Mexican government, proposing an alliance between Germany and Mexico against the United States. Germany would provide generous financial support if Mexico attacked and, when the USA was defeated, would make sure Mexico regained her lost territories in Texas, New Mexico and Arizona. The telegram had also announced the resumption of unrestricted submarine warfare which, it said, would force England to make peace in a few months.

The telegram had been sent in code to the German ambassador in Washington for onward transmission to Mexico. At the start of the war, Britain had cut the German transatlantic telegraph cable, but the United States, as a neutral country, had allowed Germany limited use of its cable for diplomatic purposes. What neither side realised was that the signal passed through a booster station in Cornwall; that all traffic through Porthcurno was being intercepted; and that British intelligence had long since cracked the Germans' cipher code.

When the contents of the telegram were first revealed to the Americans, they had refused to believe it was genuine; but on the 29th of March, Zimmermann himself gave a speech in the Reichstag in which he admitted the telegram *was* genuine, and this, plus the terrible shipping losses through February and March from submarine warfare, was enough to tip the balance of American sentiment.

'It will make all the difference,' Antonia said. 'It must bring the war to a speedy conclusion.'

'You think the Americans are such great fighters?' David

asked. 'They haven't much history of warfare. I don't think they even have more than a tiny standing army.'

'Nor did we when all this started. But they have red-blooded young men, the same as we do, and they'll rush to the standard. But most of all – don't you see, David? – they have almost limitless resources. My father was talking about a war of attrition—'

'Yes, yes, I know the theory. You wear each other down, use up each other's resources, and the last one standing wins. It wasn't the sort of war I joined up for in 'fourteen.'

'I know,' she said gently. 'It wasn't what anyone expected.'

'I thought I could do something noble,' David said. 'What a fool I was!'

'You mustn't say that. It *was* noble—'

'It achieved nothing – except to leave me a hopeless cripple.'

'*Not* hopeless,' she said firmly. 'You have a first-rate mind, and it's your duty to keep using it. As for your leg—'

But he wasn't listening. It was then he interrupted her, saying, 'I miss Bobby.'

She stopped. 'I'm sure you do,' she said at last.

'Every day. All the time. How is that possible? When he was alive, I wasn't aware of him particularly. He was just my younger brother. He could be annoying, the way younger brothers are. Taking my things and spoiling them. Tagging along when I went out with my friends. But he was funny. Full of life. Everybody loved Bobby. It seems impossible that someone like him could – just not be *there* any more. And I keep thinking, I want him *back*. I want him back but there's no-one to ask and it's not going to happen.'

Antonia laid her hand tentatively on his, and he surprised her by gripping it. 'Bobby died, but at least he *did* something,' he went on. 'He shot down German aeroplanes. He was a hero.'

'So are you. You mustn't underestimate what you did. The man who finally kills a German depends on all the others around and before him. The victory belongs to *all* of them.'

His grip loosened, but he did not entirely abandon her hand. He smiled wryly. 'A good effort, Miss Weston. I think I detect the influence of your father behind those words.'

Antonia smiled back. 'Indeed, you are mistaken, Mr Hunter. My father and I discuss the war, of course, but I assure you I'm quite capable of original thought.'

'I know you are,' he said; and seemed suddenly to become self-conscious. He let go of her hand and picked up one of the books from the table beside him. 'Hesiod!' he said, a little too heartily. 'We haven't had a look at him. In fact, I think we've been neglecting the Greeks lately. What do you say we tackle him before luncheon?'

'Good idea,' Antonia said. If she looked at his bent head with a touch of disappointment, he was not to see it.

Beattie had no objection to Antonia's extended stay. She was glad to have secured some diversion for David, relieved to see him look brighter, to hear from Ethel that he and Miss Weston talked together all day long. And she knew that Antonia had done him good, when she persuaded him to come down to dinner on Friday evening. It still pained him to put any weight on the injured leg, but with her help, and by reverting to the crutch rather than the walking-stick, he managed to get down the stairs, and even looked as though he was enjoying the change when he sat at the dining-table. The boys were excited and pleased, clearly thinking this was the beginning of a new regime. Sadie, in her way, was quietly attentive, seeing to his comfort without drawing attention to the fact, bringing him a cushion for his back, a footstool for his injured leg, moving his water glass within reach. Edward understood his son well enough to know he must

111

not make a fuss, but he sent discreetly for the best claret, and covertly watched David with an expression that made Beattie's heart ache.

So, Miss Weston was still occupying the guest room when the day of the christening came round, and since David had adamantly declared himself against any public exposure, it solved a problem for Beattie: Antonia could stay with him while the rest of the family went to Dene Park. She had not liked the idea of leaving him with nothing but servants while they feasted and celebrated.

'That is a very excellent young woman,' Edward said, in the motor-car that had been sent to convey the five of them to the Park. 'What do you suppose makes her so very good to our son?'

'It's her war work, I suppose,' Beattie said, rather more sharply than she had meant.

'She's in love with him,' Sadie said, almost at the same moment.

'Do you think so?' William asked, with eager interest. 'What about him?'

'I think,' Sadie said slowly, 'he just sees her as a friend. But perhaps I'm wrong. It's hard to say, when so much of what he thinks must be affected by his leg.'

'She's too old for him,' Beattie said abruptly.

'There can't be much difference in their ages,' Edward protested.

'Several years. A man needs his wife to be younger than him,' she insisted.

Edward said, 'How like a woman to leap straight to marriage.'

'That's the way men have shaped the world, Papa,' said Sadie. 'Women *have* to think about marriage.'

'Perhaps things are changing because of the war. We may be forging a whole new world.'

'I'd like to get married one day,' William said seriously,

'but not for a long time. There are so many things I want to do first.'

'I'm never going to get married,' Peter declared. 'I'm going to stay at home and look after you, Mother.'

'*Little suck-up!*' William whispered to him indignantly.

Edward was amused. 'What about you, Sadie? Any thoughts on matrimony?'

Peter was pleased by the impact he'd made already, and said boisterously, 'Sadie's going to marry a horse!' So she was saved from having to answer.

The christening was a lavish occasion, with a dinner afterwards of pre-war splendour, proving that all manner of delicacies could still be procured if you had the money. Diana was in the loveliest of looks. Rupert was at his charming best, the earl and countess were regal, though Beattie thought the earl was looking very worn after his struggle with influenza and bronchitis. And the Hon. George Edward Harcourt Charles Wroughton did his best for all concerned by remaining resolutely asleep throughout the whole ceremony, and not being sick on the priceless old christening gown.

CHAPTER NINE

Sadie and Private Stanhill had taken a batch of horses down to the station in Northcote, each riding one and leading two. There had been some kind of mix-up, and the railway horsebox sent for them had been delivered to the Northcote siding instead of their own branch line at Rustington.

Sadie was glad of the excuse to get away. They had taken on two new girls up at Highclere, and the responsibility for training them fell largely on her, which increased her work and frayed her nerves. It was a cold day, very cold for April, and the sky was numb and grey, threatening snow again. Sadie had a thick jumper under her army greatcoat (*coat, warm, mounted service*, as it was listed), which had been 'acquired' for her by Captain Casimir, their helpful liaison with the Army Remount Service; with a woollen hat, which had been Ada's birthday present to her, pulled down over her ears, she was comfortable. Except for her hands. Gloves were always a problem: they could not be too thick or heavy or you could not handle ropes and reins effectively.

The horses jogged, smelling the snow, perhaps; the country looked wintry, the trees still bare, the grass not springing, a sad lack of primroses in the hedgerow. 'It's more like February than April,' she said to her companion, who seemed annoyingly serene. 'Why aren't you feeling the cold?'

'You forget, I was a master at an English boarding-school,' he said, straight-faced. 'Draughts, unheated rooms, icy baths, blankets so thin you could read *The Times* through them. Survive that, and you can survive anything.'

'I don't believe your stories about school hardship,' she said. 'What's your real secret?'

'I hardly like to discuss underclothing with a lady,' he said, 'but I have a very warm vest under my shirt, and a leather waistcoat over it. As Matron used to say, keep the core of your body warm, and the extremities will take care of themselves.'

'Did she really say that?'

He gave her a sidelong look. 'Not to me. We weren't on terms of such intimacy. She said it to the boys when they came to her to have their chilblains treated.'

'And what was her treatment for chilblains?' Sadie indulged him.

'I believe it was vigorously thrashing the affected digit with a stinging-nettle,' he said.

'My goodness! Did it work?'

'Must have. The boys didn't go back a second time.'

Sadie laughed. 'You should write novels. I'm sure most of what you tell me is invention.'

'I think I might, after the war. Write school stories for boys. It would be an agreeable way to earn a living.'

They clattered into the village, and Sadie said, 'It's so much busier than before the war. It used to be such a sleepy place, a few housewives with baskets, delivery carts clopping along, a servant walking a dog. No more than two or three motors in the whole day. Now look at it!'

Army vehicles and officers' cars roared past. Messengers on motor-bikes slipped past them. Men in uniform seemed to be everywhere. A motor-bus pulled up and a chattering crowd of munitions girls coming off shift alighted, trousered legs appearing below their coats, hair tied up in headscarves, and white powder over their yellowed faces. At every shop, a patient queue of women huddled into their coats, while children, taken out of school to deputise for their mothers, shifted from foot to foot and thrust their hands into their threadbare pockets for warmth. The shortages were getting worse, and queuing for meat, butter and other staples was becoming a part of life.

The horses jerked up their heads as an ambulance came by, passing too close, heading from the station towards the District Hospital up the Walford road. This close to London, all such old general hospitals had been pressed into army use. On the 9th of April, another offensive had begun in France, and the ambulance would be full of wounded.

The battle was at Arras, and her father had told her that its purpose was partly to draw German attention away from the big French attack further south on the Aisne, and partly to break through the German line so as to force them out of their cosy trenches and into a war of movement. There had been big gains of territory on the first day, which had raised everyone's hopes, and the battle was still going on.

They reached the station yard, which these days was closed off with a barrier guarded by an army detail – usually helped, whether it liked it or not, by several Boy Scouts or WVR girls. The private on duty was expecting them and beckoned them through, and two Boy Scouts rushed to lift the barriers out of the way.

'Shouldn't you be at school?' Sadie called to one, whom she recognised as Toby, grandson of Platt the carrier.

'School's shut, miss,' he called back to her gleefully. 'They said 'tis too cold, and there's no coal for the boiler. Shortages!' It sounded as though 'shortages' would soon be the new word among juveniles for 'hooray'!

Sadie and Stanhill helped settle the horses in the box, piled the tack at the barrier to be collected, and walked back out into the street. It seemed colder than ever. Sadie's eyes were watering so much, she had to take off a glove and fumble out her handkerchief to blow her nose.

Stanhill looked at her thoughtfully. 'Podrick won't be here

for half an hour. It's too cold to stand about. How about a cup of tea in the station café? We'll be able to see him arrive through the window.'

'Good idea,' Sadie said; and then, 'Oh, but I've no money with me.'

Stanhill jingled a hand in his pocket. 'I can afford two cups of tea and two buns.'

'Buns! Now you've persuaded me. I'm starving.'

'My treat, though,' he said sternly.

She grinned. 'I think my self-respect can withstand a cup of tea and a bun. Your treat it is.'

Inside, the café was warm and steamy and smelt of hot fat and cigarettes. There were soldiers in there, and carters, and railway men, and two munitionettes, smoking self-consciously, and eating baked beans on toast. Two of the railway men, Sadie noted belatedly, were in fact women. Dressed like the men under their coats, in dungarees and heavy boots, with railway caps concealing their hair, and grease on their faces, they were indistinguishable, until you heard their lighter voices. One had the *Daily Mail* folded open, and was reading out bits about the fighting at Arras to her companions; the other seemed absorbed in a letter – from a sweetheart at the Front, Sadie guessed.

She secured a table by the window, just vacated, while Stanhill went for the tea. When he returned, he sat down opposite her and pulled off his cap, and while he fiddled about taking off his gloves and putting his change away, she studied him, and wondered if other people in the café thought *he* was *her* sweetheart. But he was older than her by, she supposed, twelve or so years. He had a nice face – kind and, while not exactly handsome, still pleasant enough to pass for it if you liked him, which she did. She realised suddenly that he was looking at her and, having been caught staring, she blushed, looked away, and asked, for the sake of speaking, 'Isn't there any sugar?'

'They put it in at the counter,' he said. 'Because of the shortages. Only one spoonful each.'

'Oh,' she said. He seemed to be studying *her* now. 'I suppose we ought to get used to having it without, in case it gets worse.'

'The time may come,' he agreed easily. 'But the buns look good.'

'They make them at Hetherington's,' she said. 'I wonder what will happen to *them* if the sugar shortage gets worse. You can't make cakes without sugar.'

'Didn't you say your uncle makes jam?' he said. They'd had many long conversations in the course of exercise rides.

'Yes, but he has an army contract, so he'll get supplies from them.'

'That was a smart move of his,' Stanhill commented, sipping his tea.

'Uncle Aeneas *is* smart. If anyone comes out of the war to the good, it'll be him,' said Sadie.

'Brains run in your family,' he suggested.

'Well, Papa's very clever. And Aunt Laura is as sharp as a whip. She told us before Arras started that the war was moving north. She's moved with it – her and her ambulance. I think Papa said they had based themselves at Hazebrouck to start with, because there'd be bound to be the earliest intelligence so close to Headquarters. But that's no distance from Arras, so they'll be on the spot.' She took a sip of tea. 'Aunt Sonia's not terribly bright – she's Papa's other sister – but they say she was a beauty when she was young.'

'And you've inherited the brains *and* the beauty,' he said, looking directly at her.

Sadie averted her eyes. 'Not me,' she said. 'David's heaps cleverer than me, and Diana's the beauty.' She took a bite of her bun. 'I didn't see the paper this morning – is there any more news from the Front? They don't seem very excited over there,' she nodded towards the railwaymen having the paper read to them, 'so probably not.'

He accepted the change of subject. 'I only just glanced at *The Times*. It seemed to be saying that having taken our first objective, we now have to have a period of consolidation – building new roads across the battleground, bringing up guns and ammunition and so on. Rapid advance from here on won't be easy, more a case of attacking individual strong points, and taking hold bit by bit.'

'The way a bulldog does, I suppose, hanging on, and shifting his grip an inch at a time.'

Stanhill laughed. 'You have a graphic way of putting it. Perhaps *you* should be the writer.'

'Not me. I was an awful dunce at school.'

'I don't believe that for a moment.'

'It's true. Besides, the only thing I could ever write about was horses. Miss Cartwright used to complain that my compositions always ended up being about them, no matter what the subject. What will your boys' school stories be about?'

'Pranks and midnight feasts and cricket matches, I suppose. What interests boys.'

'What sort of pranks?'

'Apple-pie beds and rubber snakes. Drawing-pins on chairs. Soot round the eyepiece of the telescope.'

'Did they play tricks on you?' Sadie asked, elbows on the table, ready to be entertained. But he had hardly got started when Podrick went past in the van. 'There he is. You'll have to finish some other time,' she said, buttoning up her coat again.

'I'd be delighted to,' he said, holding the door for her courteously. 'Perhaps we can arrange something. I'd love to take you out one evening when we finish.'

Sadie stopped in the doorway, startled by the idea. She looked at him almost in alarm. 'What – you mean, just the two of us?'

'I don't think anyone else would be interested in my stories.'

She had no idea what his invitation connoted, but while she was pondering it, there came a testy bellow from inside the café – '*Door!*' – and she had to move forward to allow him to get out and close it behind him. And then there was Podrick leaning out of the window and saying, 'Missus wants you back quick, Miss Sadie. There's going to be an inspection. Official-like.' So there was no more leisure to consider the matter.

While Edward had been visiting landowners up and down the country, to persuade them to put more land under cultivation, others from the Ministry of Food had been consulting with local councils, to see what common land – such as parks and public gardens – could be put to use.

He invited his colleague Christopher Beresford to dinner on Saturday, the 21st, and there was a discussion on the subject. Antonia, who had gone home for a week, was back, at Beattie's invitation, and since she had persuaded David once again to leave his room, there was a full set of lively minds around the table.

'It would be a shame to dig up the village greens,' Antonia said. 'Some of them go back hundreds of years.'

Sadie agreed. 'The green at Chartley, for instance, with its lovely old elms, and that pretty flint-knapped church behind it.' John Courcy had taken her to Chartley once for tea – it was one of her favourite memories. It made her wonder again, briefly, about Hugh Stanhill's suggestion of meeting after work. He'd said nothing since, but she had a sensation of the invitation hanging over her. What did he mean by it? Probably nothing. She shook away the thought. 'It looks so timeless,' she went on. 'Think of it being turned over to cabbages and beets and muddy potato mounds.'

'But think of all the good food you could get out of it,' William countered.

'I don't like cabbage,' Peter mentioned. 'We have too much of it, in my opinion.'

'You never eat it anyway,' William accused. 'I've seen you, hiding it under your knife.'

Peter had to divert attention from himself. 'Are you going to plant vegetables in the graveyards?' he asked Beresford.

Beresford laughed. 'I don't think we'll have to go that far.'

'But cemeteries are public land, like the parks,' Peter insisted.

'It'd be awfully *good* land, wouldn't it?' William said seriously. 'I mean, well-fertilised and everything. All those bodies—'

'William!' Sadie protested. 'Not while we're eating.'

Peter looked at her slyly. 'Full of bones, I'd have thought. Like a kipper.'

'Boys!' Beattie reproved. 'Behave yourselves.'

'We've a lot of other land to concentrate on, before we need to disturb the dead,' Beresford said kindly.

'Mrs Cuthbert's going to turn her whole garden over to veg,' Sadie said. 'About half of it is already, but she's going to have the other half dug up too. Of course, she really doesn't care for flowers,' she added in fairness, 'so it won't be a hardship for her. And she does have a house full of hungry girls to feed.'

'I thought the army fed them,' said William.

'They do – basic rations,' said Sadie. 'Anything more than that is up to her and Mr Cuthbert. And vegetables don't feature very much in basic rations.'

'I don't see why everyone shouldn't contribute in their own small way,' Antonia said. 'Of course people with great sweeps of parkland have the most to offer, but cottagers have always grown what they can in their little gardens – runner beans and onions and so on. Even someone living in a flat might have room for a couple of window-boxes to grow some lettuces and tomatoes.'

'What a very good idea, Miss Weston,' said Beresford, approvingly. 'I must put that into my report to Lord Devonport.'

Antonia smiled with pleasure at being taken seriously. David, who had not spoken until now, looked from her to Beresford, and frowned. 'There's a lot of empty land along the sides of railways,' he said abruptly. 'What are you doing about that?'

Beresford turned to him, which at least meant he wasn't looking at Antonia. 'There are problems. The railway companies like to keep the vegetation cut down beside the tracks to prevent fires. But beyond the safety strip, I agree the railways own a lot of land, in a linear sort of fashion. I'm sure some of it could be cultivated.'

Peter piped up. 'Munt says there's always tomatoes growing beside the railways, 'cause of the lavatories emptying onto the tracks. You see, he says tomato pips don't get—'

'That's enough, Peter,' Beattie said hastily. 'Finish your dinner and don't talk so much.'

The conversation turned to the war, the ongoing struggle at Arras, and there was discussion of the action at Vimy Ridge and around Bullecourt. Antonia had something to contribute because her father knew a number of retired military men, who in turn had contacts in the House and Horse Guards, and he discussed everything with her frankly and freely, as though she were his son rather than his daughter. Beresford seemed to find her grasp of the situation remarkable, and gave her his full attention. Most of the conversation was between them and Edward.

It was Beattie who noticed that David was looking uncomfortable. Leaning across, she asked him quietly if his leg was hurting. He denied it at first, but when Antonia broke off what she was saying and pressed the question, he admitted he was in some pain, and was tired besides, and thought he should go back to his room. Ethel was rung for, and Antonia insisted on helping him upstairs, taking one side while Ethel had the other. Some time later, Ethel came back to pass on Miss Weston's apologies: she would not be rejoining them, as she would be reading to Mr David until bedtime.

'What a pity,' Beresford said politely. 'I'm so sorry your son is suffering, Mrs Hunter.'

He was a nice young man, and probably meant it, but Beattie thought he was as sorry as they were to be deprived of Antonia's company. She met Ethel's eyes, and the two of them exchanged a slightly sour look as the maid went out.

Beresford's visit spurred Edward into doing something he had been thinking of vaguely for some time. After breakfast on Sunday, he lit a pipe – he still liked one when he had the leisure for it – and walked down the garden to see Munt.

Munt was not supposed to be there on a Sunday, but he often was anyway, not to work, but to sit in his shed and ponder great matters undisturbed. He and his wife had successfully maintained their marriage by agreeing that they would see as little of each other as possible. As the house was her domain, he had made the Hunters' garden his.

He watched Edward's approach all the way up the garden without appearing to. He had a certain respect for the master, but it was not in his nature to kowtow to anyone, so he did not stand as Edward reached the door, or remove his own pipe from his mouth. The closest he got to acknowledging that something was afoot was to nod slightly, his eyes in their wrinkled pouches directed at a spot an inch to the left of Edward's ear.

'Ah, Munt. I'm glad you're here. I'd like a word,' Edward said. He knew the ballet by now, from eleven years of being Munt's employer. Instead of plunging in, he turned side-on to the old man, made a leisurely business of knocking out, scraping and refilling his pipe, then stood, hands in pockets, surveying the garden.

Nailer, who had followed him from his place of exile on the mat outside the kitchen door, sidled closer, looking for company and the possibility of food. He was generally hurled out into the cruel world in the morning and not let back in until David was settled by his sitting-room fire. Munt, he knew, had an oil stove and sometimes sandwiches, but he was unpredictable, and quite capable of throwing a flower-pot at Nailer rather than cherishing him. Edward did not feature largely in Nailer's world, but what was unknown might be turned to profit. Two or more humans gathered together often meant food, and in the dog's experience, food eaten outside not infrequently got dropped.

It was still unseasonably cold, and though there had been no snow for a couple of weeks, the frost at night was still sharp. It lay in white lines along the edges of paths and walls, and tipped the crests where the soil had been turned, like foam on a brown sea. Edward mentioned that it was cold, to which Munt assented with a grunt. Then Edward remarked that it had made a late start to the planting year. 'I suppose the soil's still cold.' Another grunt. 'And digging must be difficult.'

'Where I've not put down straw,' Munt agreed. Then, ''Tis all in the scheme of things. No two years are alike.'

'That's very true,' Edward said. Getting a reply meant that the gardener was prepared to receive applications. But he still needed to approach sidelong. 'It's a pity that this year, of all years, should be late. With the U-boat depredations. And the consequent shortages.'

'Ar,' said Munt, noncommittally. He sensed some interference with his garden approaching, and was not going to encourage it.

'It's lucky that we have a good vegetable garden here,' Edward went on.

''S'not bad,' Munt allowed. 'Soil can be a bit heavy. Still, better that than sand.'

124

'More fertile, I suppose?'

'Can't grow nothin' worthwhile on sand. Potatoes, mind, they don't object to a lighter soil. And the slugs and them sort o' cattle ain't such a pest as here.'

Edward was aware he was being led aside, and tacked back towards the point. 'But we could all do better,' he said. 'Everyone who has a garden. And with the country facing a desperate food shortage this year, it's up to all of us to do our bit.'

'No shortage in this house,' Munt said. ''Cept out o' season. Can't grow veg out o' their season, stands to reason. Can't have peas in Feb'ry.'

'No, of course not,' Edward said. 'I wasn't proposing we tried to pervert nature.'

The 'we' had Munt pricking his ears. He sought a diversion. 'What's that dog sniffing at in that pile o' pots for? Better not be a rat. Rats'll go through a tatie clamp 'fore you can say "knife".'

Edward ploughed on: 'When I say, we could do better—'

'Mice can be near as bad. Course, you can cut the nibbled bit orf, but Her in the kitchen gets sniffy about "spoiled veg" – as if it'd poison you! Don't know the meaning of hardship, some people.'

Edward leaped at the opening. 'I'm afraid we may all become acquainted with hardship before this year is out. There's going to be a serious food shortage, and it's up to every one of us to do what we can to help.'

Munt eyed him cautiously. 'Plant the rows closer together, you mean? Crowd up your rows, you just get smaller plants, any gardener'll tell you. Can't get a quart out of a pint pot.'

'It's not a matter of that. It's rather getting a pint out of *every* pint pot. That's why we're going round the country – we at the Ministry of Food – persuading landowners and local councils to cultivate every possible scrap of land. Big estates. Municipal parks.'

'Too late in the year to be starting that sort o' caper.'

'The season *is* late anyway. We'll have to do the best we can. And it's a case of necessity. We must *all* make a contribution.'

Munt came slowly to his feet as he caught Edward's drift, and didn't like it. 'Big country estates and the like, and public parks, that's one thing. A person's own garden's a private matter,' he said warningly.

'In my case, it isn't,' Edward said. 'I am a spokesman for the food controller. I can't go about urging people to do what I won't do myself. It's a matter of setting an example. Like it or not, the flower garden will have to go, Munt. It must all be planted with vegetables.'

'Dig up my flowerbeds?' Munt said indignantly. 'I don't think so.'

'It has to be done,' Edward said.

'My chrysants? And my dahlias? And my glads – best glads in the 'ole county, this garden, what I've toiled over all these years, getting the plot just right.'

'I'm sorry about that,' Edward said, 'but this is more important than winning prizes at flower shows. This is the nation's security at stake. It's our patriotic duty—'

'I'm as patriotic as the next man,' Munt said hotly, 'but I ain't digging up my flowerbeds and chucking out my prize plants for no-one.'

'They are *my* flowerbeds, as a matter of fact,' Edward said. He didn't want to say, 'I pay your wages,' but he was on the brink of it.

Munt's bristly, Sunday-unshaven jaw stuck out. 'I *made* this garden, 'fore you ever came to Northcote. Just an ole cow-field, it were. Mr Peckwood, the builder, hadn't even finished the 'ouse when he took me on. "Make me a garden," he says. Give me free rein, he did, just drew some squares on a bit o' paper where he wanted lawn and shrubs and suchlike. I done the rest. Planned it and made it, every inch.

Back-break. Blisters – had more water on me hands some days'n a washerwoman. Tended it like me own baby. Dug it and turned it and fertilised it, and dug it again. There's my sweat in every inch o' this garden – *and* my blood – and I ain't a-digging of it up, not if the King himself was to ask me.'

Edward was alarmed to see what looked like tears in Munt's eyes. 'The King *is* asking you,' he said. 'What's more, His Majesty is having the gardens at Buckingham Palace turned over to vegetables to set a good example. And we have to do the same, take the lead so that everyone in Northcote will look to us. Are you telling me we can't do what the King himself is doing, to save this country from being starved out by the Hun?'

For once in his life, Munt was speechless. He glared at Edward, his mouth open at this twin blow of royalism and patriotism, his face red under the stubble, his eyes moist. Edward was almost sorry for him – he had always known Munt regarded the garden as his own, but he had not appreciated the scalding love that lay under the possessiveness and cussedness.

But he could not, *could* not, put himself in a position where a charge of hypocrisy could be levelled at him. And besides, it was quite simply the right thing to do. 'It is a shame about your flowerbeds – you've always given us a lovely display – but they'll have to go. You can draw up plans for what vegetables to grow in each plot and I'll have a look at them. We must aim for the heaviest croppers, rather than delicacies.' And on the principle of distracting from one pain with another, he delivered the final blow. 'As to the lawns, I think potatoes will be the best crop to grow in such a large space.'

Munt was almost voiceless. 'Dig up the lawns? You're saying dig up the lawns?'

After eleven years of toil, he was finally getting them

almost to the level, close-shaved velvet sward his heart yearned for. A gentleman's garden had to have a proper lawn. It was nothing without that. Doing without flowers was one thing, but it was akin to heresy of the most shocking kind to suggest getting rid of the lawn.

Edward nodded, as if he didn't know he was breaking Munt's heart. 'You'll certainly need some help with the initial digging, and I shall see what I can do about that. I'm sure I'll be able to get a couple of soldiers from Paget's Piece to come up and give you a hand.'

He nodded a pleasant farewell, and walked away, trying not to break into a run. Behind him, Munt stared a moment, then tottered back to his chair and sat down. He was so stunned, he did not notice when Nailer crept in, for the pleasure of the oil stove. And when the dog, sensing his distress, came close and looked up at him, and thrust a nose under his hand, he stroked the rough head absently, rather than rebuking him for taking liberties.

CHAPTER TEN

Sadie's first – she didn't know what to call it: *assignation?* – with Hugh Stanhill was so innocuous, she didn't bother to mention it at home. She was washing her hands in the tack room, ready to go home, when he appeared beside her and said, 'Mrs Cuthbert says she doesn't need me again until late stables. Would you like to go for a cup of tea?'

They walked into Rustington, to the Station Café, which didn't mind people in work clothes, and he bought cocoa and buns – tea had run out – and they sat opposite each other and chatted. She had felt awkward when he asked her, but on the way they had talked about work, which took the tension away. And across the table he was so much at ease that she could not be otherwise. He told her amusing anecdotes from his time as a schoolmaster, and described some of the foibles of the other teachers, which had her laughing incredulously.

'All teachers are a bit strange,' he assured her. 'There are a few devoted to their calling, like monks, but for the rest, they are teachers *faute de mieux* – like me – because they couldn't think what else to do, or because they couldn't get any other job. Those are the strangest. And your peculiarities become exaggerated after a while, because you have a captive audience in the boys – and the odder you are, the better they like it.'

They turned out to like some of the same books, and the

war and the horses were a constant resource for conversation. It was so comfortable talking to him that she almost forgot he was a man. Had he not paid for the cocoa, it would have been no different from having tea with one of the girls.

However, when a few days later he asked her if she would like to go to the pictures on Saturday, she had to ask permission at home, because it would mean staying out late.

Beattie was surprised and disapproving. 'A common soldier?' she said.

'He's a gentleman,' Sadie protested, feeling oddly defensive about him.

'Then why is he just a private?' Beattie countered.

'He was a volunteer,' Sadie said, knowing that would count with her mother. 'And he was injured by a shell and sent to the Land Army. I don't think there's much opportunity for promotion there. But he's an educated man.' She described his background. 'He's really awfully nice,' she concluded.

'And he asked you out?'

'He only wants to be my friend,' said Sadie.

Beattie thought, *They never only want that.* And it seemed he was quite a bit older than Sadie. 'He's not married?'

'No, of course not!' Sadie sounded shocked, and Beattie decided to probe no further. Sadie was very innocent, and she did not want to damage that bloom. And if the fellow worked at Highclere, he could not, surely, expect to get away with any impropriety. Besides, Sadie did not seem at all smitten.

'You really want to go to the cinema with him, do you?' she asked at last.

Sadie understood what was being asked. When Ethel had gone to the pictures with a male person, it had been a walk-out. But this could not be that. She was going to say, *I think he's a bit lonely*, but at the last moment decided it sounded too patronising. 'He's just a friend,' she said instead.

130

'Very well,' Beattie said. 'But he'd better come here first so I can meet him.'

Sadie felt embarrassed about putting this to Stanhill, thinking he might be offended at the idea of being inspected, but he appeared to feel it was quite normal. He called for her at The Elms, freshly shaven, his uniform brushed and his boots polished, and seemed at once to allay any fears on Beattie's part. He talked to her sensibly about the war and the good work being done up at Highclere, and after ten minutes of that, Beattie stood up and said, 'Well, you'd better be off, or you'll miss the beginning,' for all the world as if it were William accompanying her daughter.

Sadie wondered what he would say about his interview on the walk to the station, but all he said was, 'You don't seem to resemble your mother very much.'

'No, I take after my father. Diana and Bobby and Peter look more like her. They're the good-looking ones.'

The moment she said it, she was afraid he'd think she was fishing for compliments, but he only said, 'Bobby was the flyer, wasn't he? You must have been very proud of him.' And then they talked about the war, which lasted them most of the journey.

They took the train to Westleigh, and went to the Electric Palace. She was terribly conscious of him sitting beside her in the dark, and felt every shift of his body in the seat, almost jumped when he cleared his throat, practically heard his eyelids blink. But in the end the film and the newsreels absorbed her, and she relaxed. It was, after all, no different from going to the pictures with any other friend.

Afterwards, they went to Jennings's and ate omelettes and fried potatoes and talked about what they had seen. Sadie rarely ate out, and never so late in the evening. Then they caught the train back to Northcote, and he insisted on walking her home.

'But you'll miss the last train,' she protested.

131

'I don't need it. I bicycled here, left the machine behind your laurels. I can't possibly let you walk home alone. What would your mother think?'

So she submitted. And when she said goodnight to him at the gate, he shook her hand and said, 'Thank you for coming out with me. I really enjoyed it.'

'I did too,' she said.

He mounted his bicycle, and said, 'Perhaps we can do it again some time.'

'Yes – perhaps,' she said.

And that was that.

'It looks so terrible out there,' Diana mourned, on the last day of April. 'Like a – like a battlefield.' She had seen battlefields on the newsreels at the cinema – soldiers running across churned, scarred mudscapes.

Edward had not wasted any time in arranging for some soldiers from the camp to come and dig it all up. He didn't want to give Munt time to think about it.

'It is rather a shock at first,' Beattie agreed, holding her little grandson in her arms. 'Munt's being very difficult about it all. He shut himself in his shed while it was going on, and only came out when they started on the tennis lawn. I thought he was going to attack the poor soldiers with a shovel.'

'I can't believe Father had the tennis lawn dug up! We used to have such lovely tennis parties in the summer. Everyone said ours was the best lawn in Northcote.'

Beattie gazed into the sleeping face of the Hon. George, trying to discern likenesses. With such good-looking parents, he ought to grow up handsome. 'It can be laid again after the war. The ministry is suggesting larger areas like that for crops of marrowfat peas for drying.'

Diana wrinkled her perfect nose. 'Dried peas! This war seems to be getting into everything. Now they're saying we can't even play tennis any more.'

'Digging up tennis lawns is voluntary,' Beattie said. 'But your father says we have to set a good example. It's really rather late for starting some things, but fortunately Mrs Oliver has a lot of seedlings spare and she's letting us have them. If we can persuade Munt to accept them! He did calm down a little when your father said he would leave it up to him what he planted and where. Why do gardeners always get so autocratic?'

'Like cooks,' Diana added. 'Ours is upset about rationing.'

'Oh, rationing!' Beattie sighed. Edward was involved in drafting a campaign of advertisements and articles urging voluntary rationing on the middle classes, which meant that at any moment she was going to have to have a talk with Cook, a prospect she was not relishing. She was sure the oligarch of the kitchen would assert that none of her recipes could be made with less butter and fewer eggs. And cutting back on meat did not only mean for the family, but for the staff as well. Cook was accustomed to preparing large joints or stews for them alone.

Diana had seen the advertisements. 'Rupert says we'll eat out most of the time once I'm home,' she said. She was going back to London at last, and had called in on her mother on the way.

'How does that help?' Beattie asked.

'He says it's much less wasteful,' Diana went on, 'because the restaurants cook just enough for their customers so there aren't any leftovers, the way there are in home kitchens.'

Beattie considered this novel idea. 'Is that really true?'

'I don't know,' Diana admitted, 'but I do know you can get awfully good meals at the Ritz, and I suppose they'd be cooking them anyway, so it's better we go and eat them than let them be wasted. And everyone who's home goes there, so you're always meeting your friends. I'm so glad Rupert has his job at Horse Guards. I'd hate it if he was at the Front – after Charles, and David, and Bobby and everything.'

Beattie thought of Louis, from whom she hadn't heard for over a week. He was somewhere in the fighting around Arras, she knew that. He could not tell her exactly where, but she had grown accustomed to reading between the lines now. He was in danger. He might, even as she sat there holding the baby, be dead. No! She wouldn't think that. It was unlucky.

'I'm glad for you that Father doesn't have to go,' Diana said, unwittingly cutting her mother to the quick. Beattie couldn't speak, but Diana, not knowing of the inner conflict, went on, 'Is David a bit better, or am I imagining it? He seemed brighter when I went upstairs.'

'He is more cheerful,' Beattie said, with an effort. 'That nice Miss Weston seems to do him good. I don't know when she's coming again but I hope it's soon. She's the only one who can get him to walk, and unless he keeps trying, he'll never get stronger.'

'But it hurts him to walk, doesn't it?'

'I believe so. But he has to practise. The nurse said his muscles will deteriorate otherwise, and then he really will be helpless. I've tried talking to him, but he won't listen to me.'

'Perhaps a change of scene would do him good,' Diana suggested. 'The seaside, or something.'

'But who would have the time to go with him?' Beattie said. 'Besides, I don't suppose he'd agree. He hates leaving his room even for meals.'

'You said Miss Weston knows how to persuade him,' Diana said. 'Couldn't she go with him?'

'Darling, that wouldn't be proper at all!' Beattie protested.

'I suppose not.' Diana thought. 'Where does she live?'

'In Hampshire. With her father. You remember, David met her when he was stationed down there during training.'

'Hampshire – so it's in the country? Well, why not see if she would have him to stay? If her father's in the house, it

134

would be proper enough. I just think it *can't* be good for him to be shut in one room all the time.'

Beattie's face brightened. 'Do you know, darling? I think you may have hit on something. He always used to talk with great respect about Mr Weston. He's a scholar, you know, so they could discuss all those books David used to love so much. Yes, it could be just what he needs. He's very short of company when Miss Weston's not here. We're all so busy, and the boys, Sadie and I are such dunces in his eyes. There's only your father who can keep up with him, and he's away so much, these days.'

'You should write to her, see what she says,' said Diana.

'I shall – at once. Oh.' She slipped a hand round the baby's rump. 'I think he needs changing. We'd better give him to that girl of yours.'

The nursery maid, Mildred, was in the kitchen, being regaled by the servants. She was a local girl, recruited by Nula, as promised: only sixteen, but very experienced in handling babies, owing to being the eldest of a family of seven.

Diana got up and rang the bell, and Beattie went on, 'No news yet of a nanny?'

'Nula hasn't found anyone she likes, and now Rupert says we can get someone in London. There are lots of agencies, and Lady Wroughton will be happier if it's a proper, fashionable nanny, rather than a country person. She thinks country people won't teach him good manners.'

'Nula taught you good manners, didn't she?' Beattie said indignantly.

'But you got *her* in London,' Diana pointed out.

The thing was very quickly settled. Mr Weston and Antonia both expressed themselves delighted to have David. Edward thoroughly approved of the idea. The Westons ran a tea-room for soldiers from the nearby training camp, and he thought having other young men about would stimulate David, while the intellectual exercise the Westons could provide would stop him brooding. And when Diana told Rupert about it, he bestirred himself to use his varied wide-ranging influence, and arranged for an ambulance and driver to convey David in more comfort than would be possible by train.

David veered between pleasure at the thought of a change of scene, and of seeing Mr Weston again, and a sort of low, animal dread of leaving the safe cave he had created around himself. But with so many people urgent for the change, he raised no serious objections, and the following Saturday, the ambulance was awaited to take him to Hampshire for a month.

'I still don't see why you got to go, too. You're not his valet,' Cook grumbled at Ethel, when she came into the kitchen looking for some missing handkerchiefs to complete the packing.

'Six of them,' Ethel said, disdaining to answer. 'All with his initial on. I know they were washed but they're not in the linen closet.'

'I ironed 'em meself,' Emily piped up from the scullery where she was scrubbing potatoes. 'They're on the shelf next door, next to the sewing-box.'

'When did you ever do ironing?' Cook objected.

'Did 'em last night,' Emily said dreamily. 'I wanted to do something for him, same as everybody else was. You made him a cake, so you did.'

'That's my job. Ironing's not yours.'

'Well, never mind, they're done, that's all,' Ethel interrupted. 'You shoulda given 'em me, not made me go looking for 'em. I've enough to do with his packing and my own.'

'But why are you going?' Cook reverted. 'Don't these Westons have servants of their own?'

'He's used to me,' Ethel said. 'And their servants will have enough to do. I know his ways. Sick-room's a speciality.'

'Don't you go giving yourself airs, my girl,' Cook warned.

'Pride goeth before a fall. You won't make any friends in the Westons' servants' hall by putting yourself above the others.'

'I know what I'm doing,' Ethel snapped, whisking away out of the kitchen.

'And what'll we say to Frank Hussey, eh?' Emily called after her. 'Sure, he'll break his heart!'

It was only when the bustle of departure had died down that Beattie was able to realise how much she would miss having David in the house. When he had first gone off to war, she had hated his being out of her sight. When he had got engaged to Sophy Oliphant, she had dreaded the day he would be married and Sophy would have the care of him rather than his own mother. And now both were happening at once: he was gone away out of her house, and another woman would look after him. It was only for a month, she told herself sternly. And the Westons were sensible people: they would call a doctor if there were the slightest need. But she was horribly aware of the empty room upstairs, like a bad omen, a hollow feeling in her stomach.

Ada took the opportunity to give David's sitting-room a good clean out. There was no fire lit now he was not there to use it, and Nailer found himself dispossessed, and wandered disconsolately from the empty hearth to the top of the stairs and back, wondering what to do with himself. But fortunately, the weather outside was improving, and once he had adjusted to the idea, it was no hardship to waylay Sadie in the mornings, and ride in the bicycle basket up to Highclere for a day of hunting rats and cadging sandwiches from the grooms.

Frank arrived on Sunday morning with four limp pigeons tied through the neck.

'Lovely!' said Cook. 'The master got back last night, and

he's particularly fond of pigeon. Just the breasts, done in a sorrel sauce. Not much on a pigeon, but they're tasty, if you can fancy game, which not everyone can. The rest'll go for soup. The way things are going, we'll all be drinking soup 'stead of eating like Christians.' She sighed. 'Still, I'm not giving up roast on Sundays, say what they will – and it's not as if anything gets wasted. Sunday's beef gets fried for Monday, a nice bit of bubble and squeak, and rissoles Tuesday if it holds so long.' Frank nodded with sympathy, and she warmed to him. 'I got a lovely hand of pork for us today, Frank dear, with sage and onion stuffing, and upstairs is having roast lamb. Thank the Lord we can still get proper joints, being so close to the country. They say in some towns the butchers're all but empty. Are they clean?' she remembered belatedly to ask him.

'I pulled 'em for you,' said Frank.

'Thanks for small mercies,' said Cook. 'Did you keep me the heart and liver?'

'Course I did,' said Frank. Then, 'Where's Ethel?' he asked.

Cook had been dreading the question, but Emily jumped in before she could answer tactfully. Emily loved a drama. 'She's gone! Went yesterday straight after breakfast. She'll be hundreds of miles away by now.'

'Gone?' Frank queried.

'In an ambulance,' Emily said.

Frank paled. 'What the devil—'

'Oh, 'twasn't for her, 'twas for Mr David. She went with him, so she did.'

Frank turned to Cook with disbelief. 'Ethel ran away with Mr David? In an ambulance?'

'Oh, that girl! Pay no attention,' Cook said. 'I was going to tell you, only she has to barge in! Mr David's gone down to Hampshire for a change of air, to stay with the Westons, that Mr Weston what was his wodger-me-call when he was in training – you know, what he looked up to so much. His mental, or whatever it's called.'

'Mentor?' Frank tried.

'That's it. Very clever man, Mr Weston. Book-learned and all. And Ethel went with him because she's used to his ways, and missus didn't want to burden the Weston household with sick-room maiding.'

'I see. How long's this for?'

'Just for a month,' Cook said, eager to comfort him. 'She'll be back before you know it.'

'And she didn't leave a message for me?'

'It all happened so quick, I don't suppose she had time to think.'

But Frank shook his head. There was always time to think, and it didn't take two seconds to say to someone, 'Tell Frank goodbye from me.' It was hard work trying to be Ethel's beau, when it seemed to be all uphill, against her very inclination. But he knew, really, that she cared for him. She just didn't want to show it. And there was something – some secret – that was holding her back, but he couldn't fathom out what it was. If only she would confide in him, he was sure he could get over it for her. But she never would.

Aware of Cook's anxious eyes on him – and Emily's, burning for a tragedy – he walked over to the window, and said casually, 'Can't get used to the look of it, all dug up and muddy. Seems a shame, after all Mr Munt's hard work. How's he taking it?'

'He's not,' Cook said shortly, glad of the change of subject. 'Like a bear with a sore head, he is. You daren't say anything to him. Even Ginger's minding his lip, and you know what a cheek-box he is.'

'Must've broke his heart to tear up the lawns,' Frank said, with sympathy. He had worked on them himself.

'Oh, he didn't do it. We had four soldiers from Paget's Piece, cocky young lads they were, but I will say they worked hard.'

'They was ever such good fun,' Emily said. 'Ever so strong, and full of jokes, and one of 'em looked just like Edward Earle.'

'Edward Earle's dog, more like!' Cook snorted. 'Don't listen to her. They was just ordinary Tommies. And they traipsed mud into my kitchen like you wouldn't believe, *and* making 'em tea and sangwidges all day long, but you couldn't complain, seeing wc got 'em for nothing. Master arranged it with the colonel down at the camp. Poor boys, they was just glad to get away from all that drilling. Longing to get out to France, every one of them. Don't seem to know what's in store for 'em when they do go,' she added, and had to touch a corner of her apron to her eyes. 'Well,' she concluded, with a sigh, 'we shan't want for vegetables this autumn, that's for sure. And the surplus, if it won't store, will go to the poor of the village. Mrs Fitzgerald, down the rectory, she's taken the idea up, and going round the village telling everyone to dig up their flowers and get planting onions and such.'

'But it was Mr Hunter's idea, wasn't it?' Frank said.

'Well, it's hers now. And she's going to arrange classes in wartime cookery. That's the next thing. How to make cakes without sugar and so on. She's got the missus running ragged, trying to find people willing to go and be lectured at. Not,' she added, 'that I object to learning new recipes, if they come from the right place. I've heard you can make cakes with beetroot, but I can't see how. A nice bit of fresh beetroot with a salad in summer, or pickled with cold meat for supper in winter, I grant you. But how you can make a cake anyone would eat with it I do not know.'

The earl, Edward thought, was not a well man. His colour was bad, and he was looking old and tired. Almost, he was sorry to be bothering him at such a time. But questions had been asked – mostly in a polite way, out of what seemed genuine interest. Mrs Oliver had made a joke. And then Mrs

Fitzgerald had waylaid him after church and had supposed in the most arch and pointed way that 'Dene Park is a special case.' It was a pity, she had said, that so much excellent land should be going to waste at a time of national emergency. And she had added that the rector had been asking her about it only that morning, and she had been unable to satisfy him on the question.

'I suppose the Wroughtons, being so close a connection, must have confided in you,' she had concluded, with an acid look. Edward had made a vague noise and hurried away. What she had meant, of course, was that she – and all those under her influence – thought Edward had exempted his daughter's in-laws from digging up their pleasure park, while everyone else was nobly sacrificing their gardens.

The fact was that he had spoken to Rupert some time ago, in a tactful way, about the whole setting-an-example thing, and Rupert had said airily, 'Oh, certainly. Army camp, hospital, wheatfield – whatever you like. I'll have a word with the Aged Ps.'

It was Diana who had objected. 'Surely that's not necessary. We're surrounded by farmland – ploughed fields as far as the eye can see. It's important to have *some* beauty left, or what are we fighting for? And what about the deer?'

'A portion can be fenced off for them,' Rupert had said. 'I don't suppose your father means for us to sacrifice the entire park. I'll talk to the governor, don't worry, Pa-in-law.'

But nothing seemed to have come of it, whether because Rupert had not persuaded his father or – more likely – had not bothered to raise the question in the first place, Edward did not know. The Wroughtons were about to go up to London for the Season, and he wanted to get his word in before they left the country, so here he was, in the dragon's den, facing the dragon in person. Or, rather, two dragons, because the countess had stationed herself firmly at her husband's side, possibly sniffing something in the wind.

It was evident Rupert hadn't raised the subject yet. There was a horrid silence when Edward finished his usual speech, or lecture, or invocation, as you chose to view it. He didn't dare look at the countess, but he could hear her breathing heavily through her nose, a sound of exasperation. The earl, at least, seemed to be thinking.

At last he said, 'I don't know, Hunter. It seems a mite drastic. My tenant farmers are turning pasturage over to arable already. I can't see it's necessary to plough up the park as well.'

'It's a matter of setting an example,' Edward said patiently, as he had said several times already. 'People are turning over their gardens to vegetables. Their sons are laying down their lives abroad. And they see some families – more privileged than they, perhaps – *appearing* not to be fully engaged in the war effort—' He got no further.

Lady Wroughton barked. 'How dare you suggest such a thing? You forget our own son laid down his life for his country. The people of this village know very well what we have sacrificed.'

Edward held his nerve. 'If you had even given up part of the house for a hospital—' he began.

He got no further. 'I will not have the ancestral home of the Wroughtons destroyed by hordes of strangers knocking it about, breaking things and stealing the silver,' she snapped.

'Frightfully destructive beggars, soldiers,' the earl agreed. 'You probably won't have seen it, Hunter, but I have. Reduce a house to splinters in a day. Can't have them in here – unthinkable. I have a duty to my descendants to keep the inheritance safe.'

'Just so!' the countess cried triumphantly.

'I do see that,' Edward said – his own grandson, after all, was one of those descendants. 'Which was why I suggested doing something with the parkland. The owners of some great houses are giving them over as army camps, and you have in the past had the Territorials here for their summer games.'

'Territorials are a different matter,' Lady Wroughton snapped. 'Decent young men from good families whom one *knows*. These soldiers nowadays are drawn from every part of the country, often from the dregs of society. I will not have them sully my home. Once let them in the park, and there's no knowing where you'll find them next.'

'Well, my dear,' the earl said doubtfully, 'perhaps we ought to consider. Perhaps not an army camp – but if Hunter is right, and the nation needs the food—'

'I do not intend to spend the next year looking out of my drawing-room window on a sea of potatoes,' she said. 'And I do not by any means agree that it is necessary. I believe Mr Hunter has yielded to newspaper hysteria. This is an agricultural country, always has been, and if we can't feed ourselves from our farmland, we won't do it by despoiling beautiful landscapes that have been brought to perfection over generations. Generations! Remember, Wroughton, once gone, it cannot be replaced, not within our lifetimes, or our son's.'

The earl seemed struck with this. 'You're right, my dear. I hadn't thought of it like that. This is not ordinary land, Hunter, it's a work of art. It's history. We cannot, we must not, simply destroy it for a short-term gain of uncertain merit. The future will not judge us kindly if we do.'

'Would you have us burn our Rembrandts and Constables on the fire for warmth?' the countess demanded.

'Well said, my dear,' said the earl. 'We are not at that pass yet, not by any means. This country will not fail – and when peace comes, we must have something left of worth and beauty and – and antiquity. No, it will not do. I'm sorry.' He looked suddenly exhausted. 'I'm afraid the thought has quite taken it out of me. I must rest. You will forgive me . . .'

So Edward had no choice but to drop the subject and

leave, and suffer the indignity of having people think he had deliberately exempted the Wroughtons from pressure because of his relationship with them. The most difficult thing about it was that he half agreed with the earl about the spiritual value of irreplaceable beauty and antiquity.

The other half of him knew the shocking figures of merchant-shipping loss, and the real danger that the country might be forced by starvation into making peace.

In the time between the promise of David and his arrival, Antonia turned the parlour on the ground floor into a bedroom and sitting-room for him. Mr Weston raised only one objection. 'Where will we sit in the evening?' They were accustomed to sit there when they were alone.

'With David, of course,' Antonia said. 'He needs the company, and you know you love talking to him.'

'Suppose he wants to be alone?'

'Then we'll use the drawing-room. Or, if it's fine, we'll sit on the terrace.' Outside, the rain drilled down in stair-rods, and it was distinctly chilly, but Mr Weston forbore to point that out. He saw how happy his daughter was. She got some of the young soldiers to help with moving the furniture, while she directed the action, and dashed back and forth with small items, removing their domestic clutter and bringing in a more interesting painting, a useful side table, a less worn footstool; lamps, books, a biscuit barrel for the mantelpiece, a water flask for the bedside, and a little hand bell in case he needed to call anyone in the night.

Mr Weston watched her bustling about, smiling, singing under her breath, joking with the young soldiers, who all worshipped her though she didn't know it. He watched her arrange flowers, a critical frown between her brows as she sought some standard of perfection only she acknowledged; he watched her straighten the counterpane and stroke it smooth with a tender hand. Her happiness made him nervous.

144

'You're in perpetual motion, like a little engine,' he said on the morning of the day on which David would arrive, as she rearranged the books she had selected for the third time. 'You really care for this young man, don't you?'

She looked up, startled. 'He's—' She stopped. 'He's a war hero.'

Mr Weston was not deflected. 'You know the sort of young woman he was engaged to. You've spoken about her to me often enough. His Divine Sophy. I must say, it was the only thing I ever had against young Hunter, his poor choice of female – though in justice to the girl, we never met her, and she may have had many fine qualities we didn't know about.'

'Constancy was not one of them,' Antonia said, her lips hard.

Mr Weston studied her. 'I don't want you to get your poor heart broken, my dear, setting it on a man who doesn't see you clearly.'

Antonia averted her face. 'I know he doesn't care for me in that way,' she said. 'He'll never see me as more than a friend.' Extreme beauty and a mind on which the bloom of youthful ignorance was unblemished, she thought. That was what David could fall in love with. 'I'm too old for him,' she added abruptly.

'Then what do you hope for from this visit?' her father asked quietly.

She folded her hands together, as though keeping something from escaping. 'I can help him, Daddy. He listens to me, where he doesn't to his family. I want to get him walking, so that he can be independent. I can make him practise, get him stronger, and then he'll be truly free to start a new life.'

Mr Weston's heart ached for her. 'You want to set him free, like a caged bird,' he said. 'And do you hope that he will fly back to you?'

Now she met his eyes, hers steady, and full of the pain of reality. She saw things too clearly, he thought. Sometimes

145

a little illusion could be a comforting thing. 'No, Daddy,' she said. 'I'll watch him fly away, and be glad for him.'

He held her gaze a moment, then nodded. 'In that case, I have no further objection. And I will help you all I can in this work of charity. I like that young man very much, and it would be a dreadful loss to the world if he did not fulfil his potential.'

Antonia smiled her thanks, then went from rest straight into movement. 'Towels! I forgot to put a hand-towel by his basin. And I must see what Mrs Bates is planning for dinner. We will have wine, won't we, Daddy?'

'I will go now and select the very finest,' he assured her solemnly, as he went out.

CHAPTER ELEVEN

Vegetables took more tending than established borders and lawns, and Munt could not do it alone. Ginger had to become full-time gardener's boy. He was happy with the change, for it meant he left behind the household jobs, like knife-cleaning and boots, that he disliked most. Of course, he had to put up with Munt's foul temper – the old man stumped about in a continuous rage over the despoiling of his garden – but Ginger had endured seven years of school as a redhead, which had thickened his skin to insult. He kept out of the way as much as possible, and learned that doing things *before* Munt came after him was a good way of avoiding the worst storms. It was making him a better gardener, as he was vaguely aware; he began to think he might go in for it properly after the war. He liked seeing the little pea shoots come up, and the apples set from the blossom, like tiny green baubles. Gardening was a good trade, and you were your own boss a lot of the time. And Frank Hussey was something of a hero to him – big and strong and brown and handsome, all the things Ginger had never been. Well, working out of doors in all weathers, and doing the heavy work for Mr Munt, was making him strong and brown, at any rate. Girls might not laugh at him and call him 'Carrot-top' if he was more like Frank Hussey.

Ginger's kitchen jobs had to be taken over by the others. Emily inherited the knives, and Lilian the boots, and they both had to pitch in with jobs like fetching in the coal and taking the dustbins out, which had been his lot. Ada had to take over some of Lilian's housemaid work, for Lilian was often required to go down to the village and queue for provisions. Williamson's, the grocer's, no longer delivered every day, and some things, like sugar and coffee, had to be queued for.

Stein's, the butcher's, still delivered, but with the general shortage of boys they had taken the plunge and employed a girl, the cheerful, diminutive, buck-toothed Hilda Lane, who was rather too slight for the heavy delivery bicycle, and was often to be found at the side of the road after a spill, picking up the packages and dumping them back into the basket.

She was one of a large family. Lane's, the plasterers and decorators, had gone out of business because of the war: the father and two sons had all gone into the army, and people weren't redecorating their homes for the duration, anyway. The girls had had to find work to help support the mother and the family home. Before the war, they would have gone into service, but there was more choice now: Frederica was a munitionette, Doris was a conductorette on the bus between Rustington and Harrow, Marjie was a cook up at the Walford War Hospital, Ursie was nursing in London and, most sensationally, Gwen had gone into the railway and was working at the Willesden marshalling yard, doing such mannish things that they didn't dare tell their father.

The changes had made a lot more work for Ada, and she was frequently so tired that when her beau, Corporal Armstrong, came to call, she hadn't the heart to go out anywhere. He took her to the pictures once or twice, but finding she fell asleep, even in the middle of *20,000 Leagues Under the Sea*, he decided it was a waste of money, and instead consented to spend his time with her by the fire in the servants' hall, drinking cocoa. It was rather charmingly

148

domestic, perhaps a foretaste of their life after the war, when he firmly intended to marry her. Cook enjoyed having a man about the kitchen, and even supplied him with a pair of cast-off slippers (Mr David's, worn, but still with some use in them) so he could 'take his boots off and be comfortable' while he was about it.

'Could I have a word, madam?'

Cook looked unusually hesitant and deferential, by which Beattie concluded she had a favour to ask. What it could be she could not imagine. Cook had been in post long enough to know what she could and couldn't do, and Beattie had never known her to have any desires outside her work.

'It will have to be quick,' she said. 'I'm on my way to a committee meeting.'

'Yes, madam. It won't take long, madam. I've had a letter, you see. From my sister Hattie in Folkestone. She's got to have an operation, urgent.'

'Oh, I'm sorry,' Beattie said. 'I hope her life is not in danger?'

'Well, madam, you know what it is. There's always danger with operations. But she says the doctor says it's a routine one, and barring mishaps she ought to be all right. But where it is, madam, she'll need someone to look after her when she first comes out of hospital.'

'Hasn't she any family?'

'Yes, madam, but her husband Arthur and her eldest, Ronnie, they're both at the Front. Her girl Gladys, she works at a hotel, lives in, and she can't get the time off just then. And her youngest, Horry, he's only thirteen. He's at school and it wouldn't be fitting, anyway, for him to be washing her and – other things. So where it is, madam, she needs me. And I was wondering, could I take my annual leave early, so I can go and take care of her?'

'It may not be convenient,' Beattie said. 'When did you want to go?'

149

'She's coming out Monday the twenty-first,' said Cook, absently wringing her hands with the urgency of her plea. 'If I could go down on the Sunday afternoon and get things ready for her . . . I wouldn't ask, madam, if it wasn't urgent, and I was thinking, what with Mr David being down in Hampshire, and the master away such a lot, the household's that bit smaller anyway . . .'

Yes, thought Beattie, and with Bobby dead – that was the one they never mentioned. 'How long would you be away?' she asked.

'A week, madam, all being well. Once she's on her feet and can get down the stairs all right, she ought to be able to manage, and Gladys can pop in on her time off and do her bits of shopping. A week, madam, and if it could be thought of as my annual leave . . .'

It could hardly have come at a worse time, Beattie thought, when she was so busy, and the servants' hall had already been shaken up. Ada would have to do the cooking, which would mean she would need help when Edward was home, and she was already having to do more because of Lilian's absences. But you had to stand by a loyal servant in a crisis. Beattie sighed. 'We shall just have to manage. Of course you can go.'

'Oh, thank you, madam! I'll make sure everything's in order before I leave, and if I can cook some things ahead to ease the way, I will.'

'Yes, I'm sure you'll do everything you can. Very well, Cook,' she dismissed her. 'I must go and put my hat on or I shall be late.'

By the middle of May, it was clear that the French offensive on the Aisne had not been successful. No ground had been gained, no objectives secured, and the casualty rate had been high. Indeed, the campaign had been so mismanaged that its author, the commander-in-chief Robert Nivelle, was forced to resign. It was a severe setback to those who had hoped it would be a stepping-stone to ending the war that year.

Beattie was serving in the canteen one afternoon when some consciousness raised the hair on the back of her neck and she turned to see Louis standing at the end of the counter in cap and greatcoat, looking tired and drawn. She hurried to him. 'How long?' It always had to be the first question. 'You're not hurt?'

'No, it's just a forty-eight. I had to deliver a sensitive report to the minister. I'll have to catch a train tomorrow evening at about six.'

'Then we've time,' she murmured.

'Waites has gone ahead to light the boiler so I can have a bath. Don't worry, I'm deloused. Can you get off? We can go and have something to eat before we go home.'

Home, she thought. The little narrow house left him by his father. 'I suppose so,' she said.

He reached across the counter for her hand before he remembered and pulled it back – an odd little gesture, not the first time she had seen it. 'Stay,' he said. 'Stay all night. I can't bear it when you have to rush away.'

'I can't,' she said automatically; then added, as her mind moved more quickly than her fears, 'Edward's away.' He had gone with Beresford to Yorkshire for three days to see several landlords.

'Then you can,' Louis said urgently. 'Telephone them and make some excuse. Please! We have so little time together.'

'All right,' she said faintly.

'I'll wait for you,' he said, and left.

Beattie turned the other way, and felt so light-headed at what she had undertaken to do that she swayed, and dropped the cup she had picked up without thinking. It seemed to make a shocking noise as it hit the floor and broke, like a shell exploding. Milly Dawson came to her in concern, took her elbow. 'Are you all right? You look quite white.'

'I – I have a splitting headache,' Beattie managed to say. Guilt made it almost true.

'You had better go home,' Milly said. 'Do! We can manage here.' She had seen, over Beattie's shoulder, the tall officer hurrying away, and wondered . . . But it was not her business. In wartime, things happened. 'Go on,' she urged. 'We don't need you.'

Beattie collected her coat, hat and bag, and let herself out. Louis was waiting for her under the clock, and as she hurried towards him, she felt a surge of joy that flooded away everything else.

'There's a telephone office in the station, over there,' he told her.

'I've never used one,' she said.

'You just give the number to the operator, and she puts the call through into the booth. It's quite easy. Do you know the number? Do you have some money?'

'Yes, yes, I'll manage.' Now she was beginning to feel nervous again.

It was the first time she had ever telephoned her own house, as well as the first time she had used a public telephone. The operator showed no particular interest in her, but Beattie was afraid she had seen her with Louis, and would overhear the conversation and judge her. The telephone seemed to ring for a long time. She imagined it in the hall at The Elms, jangling away into the emptiness. It reminded her of a dream she sometimes had, that she rang the bell for a servant and no-one came, because everyone in the world was dead but her. She shivered.

And then the ringing stopped and a voice said warily, 'This is the Hunter residence.'

'Ada!' Thank God it was one of the servants. 'This is Mrs Hunter speaking.'

'Oh, madam! Are you all right?' Servants always thought telephones and telegrams were the harbingers of doom.

152

'Yes, of course. But I shan't be coming home tonight. There's a late hospital train, and I've agreed to stay for it. It means I'll miss my last train, so I'll spend the night at an hotel.'

'Oh, madam! But you've no things with you,' Ada said, as though it were a tragedy.

'I'll manage for one night. Is everything all right there?'

'Yes, madam. Miss Sadie's home. She's somewhere about. Let me find her for you.'

'No! Don't do that. Just give her the message. She'll take care of things. I'll be back tomorrow. Goodbye,' she concluded firmly, and rang off. She was trembling slightly, and her hands were damp. But it was done now. She left the booth, paid the operator, and stepped out into the acrid, sulphurous air of the station concourse, which to her, with Louis standing there waiting for her, was like wine.

'All right?' he asked. She nodded. 'Let's go and eat, then.' As they passed out of the station, he took her hand and drew it through his arm, and said gloatingly, 'All night! Darling, we have the whole night!'

'Yes,' she said. Ada, Sadie, Edward, the lie were all in the past, falling away like a landmark seen from a speeding train.

By the time they got 'home', Waites had got the water hot, and Beattie had the inestimable pleasure of sitting with Louis while he took a bath. She had never done such a thing before, even in the days when she and Edward were at their closest.

It was wonderfully relaxing and easy. She had no shyness with Louis. She loved to look at his body. She washed his back for him, as she had once washed her boys, and let her hands linger tenderly over the contours, feeling the string of beads that was his spine, the smooth muscles, the curves of his ribs under the surface.

He spoke about the campaign at Arras, and the terrible

failure of the French on the Aisne. 'The death-rate up on the plateau was shocking,' he told her, bent forward while she poured hot water over his back to wash the soap away. 'It's caused unrest among the French Army. And the Frogs in any case don't take care of their men. They don't rotate them the way we do – they just stick the poor devils in a trench and leave them to rot.'

'How awful.'

'And when they do get any leave, there's no provision made for them to get home. So, of course, they're at the mercy of rumour-mongers. Since the revolution in Russia, there are Communist agitators all over the continent. Apparently, they're getting into the trenches, and telling the poilus that their wives are being unfaithful to them, their farms are going to ruin, their daughters are being debauched by rich war profiteers – all the usual rubbish. The poor ignorant devils have no leadership and no hope, so of course they fall for it.' He straightened and looked at her. 'There's been a series of mutinies, starting near the Chemin des Dames and spreading along the line from there.'

'Mutinies!' Beattie was shocked.

'Just yesterday, a division in the line refused to leave the trenches,' he said. 'We can't let the Germans find out, of course, so don't talk about it to anyone.'

'No, of course not,' she said. 'Is that what your confidential report was about?'

He nodded. 'Mutiny can be catching – worse than the measles where the men are unhappy to begin with. The French don't have a system for getting the post to the trenches, so they hear nothing but what the agitators tell them. They're not even fed properly, and their pay is always months behind. You can hardly blame them – but if it knocks the French out of action, it leaves us alone to hold the Germans back.'

'What about the Americans?'

'They won't even be arriving until the end of June. And they won't be fit to join the action for months after that. They're just raw recruits – and they have no trained officers. You can knock a soldier into shape in six weeks or so, but it takes six months at least to make an officer. No, I'm afraid if the French fail we're on our own. So we're desperate not to let the Germans find out.'

'What does that mean?' she asked falteringly, though she thought she had guessed.

'We'll have to mount an offensive,' he said, as she knew he would. 'Sooner rather than later. We have to keep the Boche distracted.'

'Of course,' she said, in a dead voice.

He lifted his hands from the water and took her face in them, drew it to him, and kissed her. 'No more talk of war now,' he said, and his voice was husky. She felt a pang deep inside her, as sharp as fear, but it was not fear this time. She reached for the towel, he rose up from the water, she wrapped it round him, and he descended to her, streaming, like Neptune emerging in all his power from the sea. Her arms went up to him, like drowning Helle, and she melted into him.

In the early hours of the morning they woke and made love again. Afterwards, she lay in his arms, content, not thinking; until he said in a low voice, 'Don't go.'

'I must. It's Saturday – the children will be home from school.'

'I mean, don't go back to him. Stay with me.'

'You won't be here.' She made the obvious objection.

'You could come to France. I could find a safe place for you. A house somewhere behind the line. A flat in Paris. Somewhere I could get to see you whenever I had a few hours . . .' His voice trailed away. It was impractical, and he knew it as well as she did. He voiced his real anxiety. 'I

155

don't like to think of you with him. I want you to be all mine.'

'You know it can't be,' she said wearily.

'After the war,' he said, automatically, then warmed to it, 'After the war, we'll be together. We'll go back to South Africa, make a new life together.'

'Louis—'

He squeezed her tighter. 'No! Don't say it. God knows, I don't want to hurt anybody, but you don't love him, do you?'

'Yes, I love him,' she said. 'It's not like the way I love you. I love him because he's gentle and kind, because he's always been good to me, because we've been together so long. You . . .' She struggled to find words to describe it. 'My insides are pulled towards you, like a nail pulled by a magnet, and there's nothing I can do about it. I can't pull away. It's like fire, like an earthquake, something you can't control. I love you for no reason. I just love you.'

'I feel the same,' he said. 'You are the love of my life. We *must* be together. It would be – *wrong* not to be.'

'*This* feels wrong,' she said sadly. 'Oh, not when I'm with you, but afterwards, when I go home. Then I feel bad and guilty and I want – not to see you again.'

'You can't—' he began.

She turned in his arms and kissed his lips and his face. 'But this – this . . . It's life to me. When I'm here, with you, I think I shall die if I'm torn away from you. Why can't we run away – now, this minute – somewhere they'll never find us, and just – be – together?'

It was his turn to say, *It can't be.* 'I have to go back. The war—'

'Yes, the war!' she said, with a laugh that was more like a sob. 'We all belong to the war, don't we? It's like a great gobbling mouth eating us all up. I don't want you to go! I don't want you to die, like Bobby!'

Now he had to comfort her, kissing her eyes, though there were no tears – she never cried – and her cheeks. 'I won't die. I wouldn't do that to you. I'll come back, and after the war—'

'There'll never be an "after the war",' she cried. 'It will go on for ever, until it's eaten us all, everything, and there's nothing left.'

'It will end,' he said. 'And then we'll be together. Hold on to that. It's what keeps me going.'

She said no more, thinking of what he had to endure compared with her trivial woes. She clung tightly to him, and after a bit they fell asleep together. Once, she would have thought it a terrible waste of the little time they had, but now it seemed an inexpressible luxury, simply to sleep in each other's arms.

The servants were pleased when Ethel came back after only two weeks in Hampshire, even though she was in a foul temper.

'What did you do wrong?' Lilian asked unwisely, and only just avoided a slap.

'I didn't do anything wrong,' Ethel snapped, her eyes spitting sparks. 'They decided they didn't need me. That's all.'

'Has something happened to Mr David?' Ada asked, alarmed.

'Course not,' Ethel said scornfully. 'D'you think I'd've left? Miss Weston's doing the fetching and carrying for him, and that's all I'm going to say, so you can all mind your knitting.'

'No call to be rude, my girl,' Cook said. 'If he doesn't need you, we do. There's more work than Lilian can manage on her own.'

'I'm not doing housemaid work,' Ethel objected.

'You'll do whatever the missus says, like the rest of us. And I've to go to Folkestone next week to look after my sister, so it'll be all hands to the pump while I'm away.'

'What pump?' Ethel asked. 'What d'you mean, you're going away?'

Cook explained. 'And Ada will have all she can handle with the cooking, so you'll have to do her share. There's no use making faces. Everyone's got to do their bit in an emergency. Don't you know there's a war on?'

Ethel had enjoyed her time at the Westons' house, even though it had very quickly become clear that Miss Weston intended to take to herself all those cherished tasks that Ethel had been brought along to perform. Attending him, helping him from bed to chair, bringing his trays and supervising in the kitchen what was on them, putting out his clothes – all the many ways in which Ethel had devoted herself to him, as to the tending of an exotic pet, were taken over. There was nothing left for her but making his bed, tidying his room and seeing to his fire – housemaid's work.

The Weston servants were sympathetic but curious. What exactly *was* a sick-room maid? Was she medically trained? Wasn't it odd for a young man of his class to be attended by a maid rather than a man? Was it a wartime thing?

It was not a big household: there was the cook-housekeeper, Mrs Bates; a live-in housemaid, Iris, who doubled as parlour maid and looked after Miss Weston's clothes; a live-out girl, Maud, who did the heavy cleaning in the mornings; and Mr Weston's man, Baxter, who was something of a factotum, veering between cleaning boots and filling lamps, valeting the master and waiting at table. His eye brightened when he first saw Ethel, but he was too old to interest her.

Ethel was obviously on Miss Weston's conscience (or perhaps on her nerves, as she hung about David's room hoping for employment) for after a couple of days, she interviewed Ethel and said rather apologetically that there didn't seem much for her to do. 'I wonder,' she went on, 'whether you would be so good as to help out in the tea-room? It's usually my job, but I must spend time with my guest, and two of my volunteer ladies are away at the moment. It would be tremendously helpful, and the soldiers are so appreciative. It's only a matter of taking their orders, serving tea and taking the money. Could you possibly lend a hand?'

Ethel was not in a position to refuse, but though she resented being pushed out of Mr David's way, she was not unwilling to tackle the new task. In fact, she quickly found she liked it better than anything she had ever done. To be around young men – and young men away from home, and in uniform at that – was exciting. She was very pretty, and years of practice had taught her how to encourage flirting without allowing it to go too far. She was quickly aware that she was a success, and that more soldiers than ever were coming in, simply for the pleasure of seeing her toss her head and hearing her scornful put-downs. Within a week, one of 'the boys' was desperately in love with her, and more of them than she could count had tried to get an assignation with her. She loved all the attention and the thrill of the hunt, but she was not interested in getting herself tied up with someone who had no money or career – and who might be dead within months.

Meanwhile, she observed, out of the corner of her eye as it were, how Miss Weston was working on Mr David, teasing and cheering and bullying him into getting out of his chair and walking at every possible moment. Without the stairs to daunt or to excuse him, he was soon passing through the house and on to the flat terrace behind it, and then for longer walks down the lane, or along the path to the river. Miss Weston would not allow bad weather to be a hindrance. Mr Weston's old greatcoat was pressed into use, along with a tweed deerstalker impervious to anything, it seemed, short of an exploding shell.

And when he tired, she would read or work with him in his room. She had thought, like Edward, that he would wish to spend time in the tea-room talking to the soldiers, but he shied away from that, and she learned not to press him.

They were young, fresh-faced, most of them full of hope, ambition and eagerness to 'do their bit'. He had once been like them. They would have hero-worshipped him, but he could not have borne that. So Antonia kept him away from them, and worked on his physical rehabilitation, while stimulating his mind with serious thought.

After two weeks, Antonia decided she could not in conscience keep Ethel any longer, and sent her home.

David was much more mobile, walking with one crutch. Antonia kept her hand through his other arm, ostensibly to steady him if he hit a stone or an inequality in the road's surface. Soon that became second nature to him, too, and he reached for her instinctively as soon as they started forward.

By the end of the third week, the healing of his mind had come so far that he was able to discuss with her the ideas she had had for what he might do with his life after the war, when his leg had healed. He would probably always walk with a limp, it was agreed, but that would not prevent him from an academic career – he could be a schoolmaster, or a private tutor. Or he might go into his father's bank or, indeed, any other office-based career – solicitor, stockbroker, secretary. His age need not be a handicap. After the war, Mr Weston observed, many young men would be coming back in the same position, having gone into the army at the time they would otherwise have been at university or taking articles. It would be an understood thing.

David brightened, and grew more hopeful under the Westons' encouragement. With the exercise, his appetite improved and he grew physically stronger, too. He felt at home with them, and had no desire to leave; and since they were just as glad to have him there, no end date to his visit was mentioned. On the one occasion he raised the question of going home at the end of the month, Antonia at once started talking, as though she hadn't heard him, about her father's new work, a fresh translation and commentary on the letters of Pliny the Younger, and the moment passed. He forgot about it, and neither Antonia nor Mr Weston mentioned the subject.

'So, you're back,' Frank said, passing in through the kitchen door and finding Ethel collecting cutlery to lay the dining-room table.

She did not look up. 'Smart, aren't you? Worked that out all by yourself?'

'Don't I get a smile, at least?'

'What have I got to smile about?' she retorted.

'Ah, come on,' he said coaxingly. 'You can't be jealous over the master's son. That's not on. He's just a job to you – and you're just a servant to him.'

'Fat lot you know about it.'

'I been in the world longer than you, I know a lot about everything. You were sorry for him, then you got fond of him, like a wounded bird you took care of. But you're too sensible to think it's more than that. This other lady—'

'I don't want to talk about her,' Ethel said.

'Good. 'Cause I don't want to talk about her either. Got more interesting people to talk about, like you and me.'

'I didn't know there was any "you and me".'

He came to her and took the cutlery out of her hands – his were so big, he could take both her handfuls in one, which made her shiver – and put it down. Then he drew her irresistibly to him. 'Then I shall have to teach you better, shan't I?' he breathed into her ear.

She struggled. 'Let me go!'

'Not likely,' he said, nibbling the ear now, making her shiver again.

'Stop it! I'll lose me job!'

'Then you can come and live with me.' His mouth crept round and he managed to secure one kiss before she wrenched her face away.

'Stop that, Frank Hussey!' He let her go, and she faced him, pink-cheeked. He didn't think it was all temper. 'You think you're so wonderful! You think every girl's out to get you.'

'No, I don't,' he said. 'I think a good few would be, if I made a play for them, but I don't want them. I want you, Miss Ethel Lusby, and no-one else will do. So where would you like to go this afternoon? Pictures? It's nice and warm in the dark, and if you're a good girl, I'll let you hold my hand.'

'Oh, you!' she cried in exasperation, landing a slap on his forearm, which had as much effect as slapping the table-top.

'Yes, me,' he agreed. 'Come on, Ethel, you went off to Hampshire without a word, which made me feel as rotten as you could ever want, so you don't need to hold me off any more now. I've had my punishment for loving you. Now you can let me be nice to you without feeling you've let your guard down.'

'What in the world are you talking about?' she said, but she was red with consciousness. The way he could step inside her head was frightening – as well as exciting.

'You're afraid to let anyone love you, I know that. That's why you flirt so hard, because flirting keeps people at arm's length. But I'm not going anywhere. I know the worst about you, and it doesn't bother me a bit.'

For a moment she was very still, looking at him with the eyes of a cornered animal, and he saw there was very real fear, something deeper than the one he had just articulated. It interested though it did not daunt him. He knew she had a secret; he felt he had just stepped a bit closer to it.

Then her eyes were veiled. 'You don't know *nothing* about me,' she said, with her usual scorn. 'You're not as clever as you think you are.'

'All right,' he said reasonably. 'After the pictures we'll get a bit of tea, and you can tell me all the things I don't know.'

Suddenly she was weary. 'Leave it be, Frank,' she said. 'There can't ever be anything between you and me. I've told you. I'm not going to marry you, and that's that.'

'That's all right,' he said. 'You've told me, so I'm proceeding at my own risk. And we can have fun in the meanwhile. You like walking out with me, don't you?'

'I like *you*,' she said, and his heart gave a jump at the unexpected admission. 'But don't get cocky,' she added. 'I like pickled onions as well.'

She was trying to claw it back, he saw, but it was too late. He had banked that one already. And he was in it for the long pull. He had no doubt that he would win one day. She was no match for him, whatever she thought.

CHAPTER TWELVE

Having cooked Sunday's luncheon for everyone, Cook had departed, in tears and her best coat and hat, weighed down on one side with a suitcase. The other servants waved her off from the gate. Monday had passed off all right, and Ada had made a very passable cottage pie from the remains of Sunday's beef for the evening meal. Edward had looked at it in surprise, and poked it gently before asking, 'What's this?'

Beattie's lips had tightened. 'I hope you're not going to be dainty about this sort of thing. You know we must eat simply while Cook's away. And everyone's going to have to get used to eating leftovers, if the food shortages go on.'

'Why can't the servants eat the leftovers?' Edward enquired, but mildly. He knew they had to set an example – but he had never cared for twice-cooked meat..

'They are,' said Beattie. 'They're having rissoles from the remains of the pork.'

'I like rissoles,' Peter said. 'We have them at school. I like cottage pie, too,' he added, with catholic inclusion.

'You are an example to us all, my son,' Edward said. 'I shall try not to be dainty in future. By the way, I shall have to dine at the club tomorrow, my dear. Business.'

'Very well,' Beattie said, but with narrowed eyes. She suspected he was running away from the new kitchen regime.

On Tuesday, Nula came in, and Beattie got her to do the ironing, while she took over some of the essential mending,

164

a sort of domestic General Post. There was quite a pile that had accumulated, but she would always sooner sew than iron, and in fact she quite liked darning socks – she found it soothing. She had just settled herself in a chair by the morning-room fire and pushed the mushroom into a particularly fine effort of William's, when there was a knock at the front door. She paused, listening, and her heart sank when she heard the sharp tones of the rector's wife asking if Mrs Hunter was at home. 'Oh, no,' she breathed. 'Not now!'

But there was no escape. Even Ada, who usually answered the door, was cowed by Mrs Fitzgerald; Lilian, who had taken over door-answering now Ada was cook, was rendered almost speechless by her. Beattie only just had time to stand up and smooth down her dress before Mrs Fitzgerald was in the doorway, sailing past the tongue-tied Lilian and raking the room and Beattie with her eyes for any signs of turpitude.

'My dear Mrs Hunter, good morning.' It was impossible for her not to notice – as Beattie now did for the first time – that the breakfast table had not been fully cleared: the cloth was still on and the toast rack sat there with the cruet, mutely begging forgiveness. 'Am I disturbing you? Rather late this morning, were we? I hope you had finished your meal, at all events?'

Beattie swallowed the implied insult bravely. 'We have a small domestic crisis. My cook is away, nursing a sick relative, so Ada is having to do the cooking.'

'I see. Of course, while the cat is away, the mice will play. Perhaps I have chosen an awkward moment to call.'

'Not at all,' Beattie said, with heroic restraint. She *certainly* didn't want her coming back. 'What can I do for you, Mrs Fitzgerald?'

'I wondered if you had taken note of *this* in the newspaper this morning.'

'I haven't had a moment to read it yet,' Beattie said.

Mrs Fitzgerald proffered a copy she had with her, folded

at the right page, and Beattie took it, but was not obliged to read it, as her visitor told her all she needed to know.

'Yesterday our dear Queen opened the first of the National Kitchens in London – in Westminster Bridge Road – where the working people can get a proper, hot meal for sixpence. Of course, it is subsidised by the government, though I believe charitable donations are taken as well. Soup, meat and vegetables – and, I believe, a sweet, though that is not entirely clear. Perhaps it is more than sixpence with a sweet. However, it will be of the greatest help to the war effort, as I'm sure you can see. Properly nourished employees work harder and stay healthier, and we can't afford our workforce to be falling sick at a time like this. And, as you know, the food shortages are hitting the poorest. Their diet is unsatisfactory at the best of times, and with the German submarines sinking our cargo ships—'

'Yes, indeed,' Beattie said, to stem the flow. 'It is a good idea. Mr Hunter was talking about it last week. The government hopes to have a string of them, all over the country—'

'Wherever there are important workers – important to the war effort, I mean,' Mrs Fitrzgerald finished for her. 'And of course we have the munitions factories here, as well as the new aircraft factory they're building over towards Coneys, and the hospitals. We are a vital little cog in the war machine,' she said with a gay laugh. 'Northcote is *quite* on the map.'

Beattie saw where this was going. 'The munitions factories have their own canteens. The hospitals, too. And I'm sure the aircraft factory will,' she began.

'The filling factories have a canteen, but Darvells doesn't,' Mrs Fitzgerald said, with some triumph. Darvells had made brass fire-irons and ornaments before the war and now made shell-casings. 'And there's the rope works in the Walford road, and the shoe factory and the canning factory. And all the railway workers. And,' she went on, before Beattie could say anything else, '*every one* of our working people is important to the war effort, in whatever capacity they serve. We *need* a National Kitchen in Northcote. And I intend to make the case to our MP for siting one here. They are manned by volunteers, you know – I should say, *womanned*' – she allowed herself a rare joke – 'because of course it is ladies like us, dear Mrs Hunter, who take on the noble task of preparing and serving the meals to these honest working-class heroes.'

'But we all have so many other things to do,' Beattie protested. 'The committees, the war work—'

'*Nothing* is as important as this,' Mrs Fitzgerald interrupted firmly, despite the fact that she had initiated most of the war work in the village. 'The food crisis is going to get worse before it gets better. We are going to see real hardship this year, and we *cannot* allow the Hun to starve us into submission.' Her eyes were shining with fervour. She looked like Joan of Arc leading a charge. 'We must and shall have a National Kitchen, and I want *you* at my side, to take a leading part in persuading the government, and in operating it.'

Beattie felt exhausted at the prospect. 'I really don't see how I can have the time—'

'You must *make* time,' said Mrs Fitzgerald. 'Pass some of your lesser duties to lesser women and *make* time. I know your husband is engaged in this important work, at the Ministry of Food, and he of all people will understand that it is your foremost duty to help feed the workforce. Only speak to him, and I know he will persuade you, if I can't.' She glanced at the clock on the mantel. 'And now, dear Mrs Hunter, I must away. I leave you to think it over, but I know you will come in with me when you have fully considered.'

It was her way not to wait around for argument. It was better to remove the opportunity, in her experience, and come back at a later date assuming she had won. It was surprising how often plain, unbudging assumption worked.

*   *   *

On the morning of the 22nd of May, at the Wroughtons' London house in Belgrave Square, the Earl Wroughton's man, Waysgoose, went in to wake his master – a little earlier than usual, as he had a select committee to attend at the House – and found him dead in his bed.

He hurried back downstairs and sought out the butler, Worrell, who took a few moments to absorb the information, then swung into action. The countess's maid, Pickering, was dispatched to wake her ladyship and break the news to her – 'Gently, mind!' – while Worrell took it upon himself to telephone for the physician, and sent Waysgoose back to make sure his lordship looked seemly and the bedroom was tidy before her ladyship should get there.

The earl had taken a long time, lately, to dress, so Waysgoose had gone to call him in plenty of time. It was therefore still only just past eight o'clock when the news reached Park Place and Diana's maid Padmore woke her with it.

'Oh,' said Diana. She couldn't think what else to say. It was a shock: she knew the earl had been unwell for some time, but it had only been that tiresome old bronchitis, nothing to worry about. She had grown used to thinking of death as something that only visited through the agency of the war, she did not expect people safe at home to become its victims. She knew Rupert had not been expecting it, either – he had never expressed any anxiety about his father. That thought provided her cue. 'Does his lordship know?' she asked.

Padmore was inscrutable. 'Mullet says his lordship is not in.'

'Not in?'

'He did not come home last night,' said Padmore.

It was not unusual, but on this occasion it was inconvenient. 'Does Mullet know where he is? Never mind.' She cancelled the question. Mullet had not long been Rupert's man, but he was very loyal, and seemed to regard Diana as

168

a sort of rival rather than his master's wife. 'Tell him to find his lordship, please. He must know some places to telephone. He ought to be told as soon as possible.'

'Yes, my lady. And will you be getting up now?'

'I suppose I had better,' Diana said. She didn't know what happened when someone died, or whether she might be summoned to do something, but it was as well to be prepared.

She had her bath and Padmore dressed her in something sober. She was going downstairs when she encountered Heating, their footman, on his way up.

'A telephone message from the earl, my lady,' he said.

Diana was startled. 'What?'

Padmore, behind her, whispered, 'He means Lord Dene, my lady.'

Heating continued, 'He is on his way home, my lady, and will be here within the hour.'

'Thank you, Heating.' When he was out of earshot, she turned to Padmore. 'I didn't realise— I mean, I thought there would be some sort of ceremony, or something.'

'The title passes at the moment of death, my lady,' Padmore said. There was a hint of kindness in her professional gaze.

'Yes, I see,' Diana said, and went on down. Rupert was now the Earl Wroughton. And – the thought came to her as a sort of novelty – that meant she was now the countess! She had had a long time to get used to the idea of being Lady Dene, but this was altogether too strange to take in.

Rupert arrived home and went straight to his wife in her sitting-room. She could see he was shaken.

'I can't believe it,' he said. 'It's too sudden. What do they say it was?'

'I haven't heard anything yet,' Diana said.

'But hasn't Mother telephoned?'

'No-one has rung from Belgrave Square, since the first

call, just to say he was – that he had passed away. That was Worrell. I expect your mother's too upset to telephone anyone herself.'

'We'd better go over there. I'll get changed,' he said, and turned away.

'Where were you last night?' Diana asked.

He turned back. 'I had dinner with some friends – Heating must have told you that.'

'Yes. But you didn't come home.'

'Oh, it went on rather late, and then one or two of us went on somewhere, and it got to be the early hours so I stayed over at Tony Lassiter's. You don't know him,' he anticipated. 'He's a friend of Erskine's.'

'Where does he live?' Diana asked.

'He's got a flat in Dover Street. Look, I must dash and get changed. You look lovely, by the way. You've dressed exactly right. But wear some pearls. Pearls are quite suitable, and they make your skin glow.'

And he was gone. Diana, sorting out the jumble of sentences he had flung at her, was aware they were a smoke-screen. Dover Street was not five minutes away. Why on earth would he stay the night there, rather than come home to his own bed? And why did he not want her to know the reason?

By the time they reached Belgrave Square, the shutters on the ground floor of Wroughton House had been closed, and there was black crape round the door knocker. 'You can't catch old Worrell out,' Rupert muttered to Diana, as they climbed out of their taxi. One or two journalists had gathered, and grew more alert as they saw the young couple, who were always good for a story. Rupert acknowledged them with a lift of his hand – his lordship was known to be a very affable young man – and there were some murmurs of sympathy.

Worrell opened the door to them before they reached it,

170

and they could see he was already wearing a black armband, as was the maid standing behind him, waiting for Diana's things.

'A sad day, my lord,' he greeted Rupert. 'My lady.'

'Yes indeed, Worrell. How is my mother?'

'Her ladyship is showing her usual fortitude, my lord. Sir Maurice Enderby is here, my lord. I believe he is – er – with his late lordship at this moment.'

Worrell's old eyes looked a bit watery at this reference to his master, and Rupert patted his forearm. 'Stiff upper, Worrell. We'll go straight upstairs.'

'Very good, my lord.' Worrell preceded them at his usual pace, which gave Rupert plenty of time to ask how it had happened, and to hear all that the butler knew, which was not much. Diana was surprised Rupert was not hurrying them on ahead of the old man – he was not generally one for ceremony – but Rupert knew that today, of all days, everything must be done by form.

In the earl's bedroom, the physician was washing his hands at the basin and talking to the countess, while Waysgoose straightened the bedclothes over the corpse. Diana's eyes flew to it. She happened never to have seen one before. Her grandparents had died when she was a tiny child, and of course Bobby had never come home. It was not a shocking sight. His face looked paler than in life, and seemed to have sunk rather at cheeks and eye sockets, as though life had been padding him out. His hands were folded on the top of the sheet, his thin hair had been brushed smooth over his scalp. He did not look, as she had read in books, as though he were sleeping. In fact, he did not look like a real person at all, but rather like a waxwork model. She found that comforting – at least, it was easier to deal with.

Rupert had gone straight to embrace his mother, and she, for a wonder, allowed it for a moment before pushing him back.

'What happened?' he asked her.

'Waysgoose found him dead this morning,' she said unemotionally. 'He had a cigar last night with his brandy before going to bed, and it brought on a coughing fit. He complained of a pain across his chest, and I assumed he had simply pulled a muscle. It was quite a prolonged fit – you know how he has been these past weeks. But Sir Maurice says—'

Enderby took over the sentence smoothly. 'I'm afraid the constant coughing and the breathing difficulties due to the bronchitis had weakened his heart. I would say the last bout of coughing brought on a heart attack, probably while he was sleeping. He would have known nothing about it, my dear Lady Wroughton. Quite a peaceful end, one might say. You may comfort yourself with that.'

She gave him a gimlet stare. 'He was too young to die. He had many things still to do. There is no comfort to be had. Can you give the death certificate?'

Enderby looked a little startled. He had enjoyed her favour for years, and had probably never been spoken to, or looked at, like that. 'Indeed. Of course. There is no difficulty. Immediate cause, coronary infarct. Secondary cause, chronic bronchitis. It is—'

'Do so,' she interrupted him. 'I shall be in my sitting-room.' She looked at Rupert. 'Come with me.' She did not look at Diana, but Diana did not intend to be left without Rupert's support, and followed closely on his heels; she was rewarded by his taking her hand and squeezing it just before they entered the sitting-room.

Lady Wroughton walked across to her usual chair and sat down, placed her hands on its arms, and stared straight ahead, as though she were waiting to be called for an interview.

Rupert walked to the mantelpiece; Diana effaced herself over by the window.

'I'm sorry, Mother,' Rupert said.

172

'I did not see it coming,' Lady Wroughton said, not looking at him, more as if she were speaking to herself. 'I thought we had time. It was that wretched shoot at Sandringham. Cold, damp – everyone was coughing. He was never well, ever since we came back from there. But I thought we still had time.'

'Time for what?' Rupert asked.

'*You* are not ready. Charles would have known what to do.'

'Charles had years to get used to the idea,' Rupert said, a trifle sulkily. 'Anyway, what *is* there to do? The King is dead. Long live the King.'

'Don't speak in that foolish way,' she rebuked him.

'I don't know what you want of me,' he said irritably, rearranging the cards on her mantelpiece as a way of occupying his hands. He did not dare ask her if he could smoke. 'What would Charles have *done*? I suppose there must be a funeral, the will to be read, legal things to sort out. That's what we employ people for. I can't be expected to engage with the minutiae. I'm in the army, for God's sake. *And*, by the way,' he added, glaring at his mother, 'so was Charles. You ought to be grateful that I'm here, and not at the Front.'

'Don't be impertinent. And leave those things alone. It was my idea to keep you away from the Front. Your father would not have thought of it. I have had to think of *everything* for thirty years. If it weren't for me, do you think this estate would be in as good heart as it is? And now I have to hand it over to *you* to ruin.'

It was said so harshly that Diana saw Rupert flinch. He was hurt. He seemed to grope for words. 'I won't ruin it,' he said, but it sounded weak.

'I shall do everything in my power to see you don't,' she said unrelentingly. 'But I know what you are, Rupert. Charles, for all his foolishness, was the better man.'

They were interrupted by the entry of Pickering, who said, 'His lordship's man of business has called, my lady, wanting to talk to his lordship. He's in the library.'

'That was quick,' Rupert said, glad of the respite.

'I believe Mr Worrell telephoned him,' Pickering said. 'And Lady Grosmore telephoned to say she will be here this afternoon.'

That was Rupert's sister. 'The vultures gather,' he said. 'I'd better go and see Boardman.'

He was past the maid and out before Lady Wroughton could say anything. Pickering went on, 'A number of telegrams and notes are arriving, my lady. Would you wish to have them brought up to you?'

'Is Auden here?' Auden was her secretary.

'I believe she arrived a few moments ago, my lady.'

'Very well. Give them all to her for the moment. And tell her I will talk to her later about the arrangements.'

Pickering went away, and Diana felt horribly exposed, trapped in this room with this woman, who was so frightening, and was also, now, a widow. Ought she to say anything? She wished she had managed to get out of the room with Rupert. She tried to stay still and not draw attention to herself.

Lady Wroughton stared at nothing for a long time. But at length she said, 'It was too soon. But at least there is the child. At least one may be grateful for that.'

Diana felt she ought to stand up for her husband. 'I think Rupert will make a very good earl,' she said.

Violet Wroughton looked at her. 'Is that your conclusion? Yes, you *would* be eager to remind me that Rupert is earl now.' Her expression changed to one of great bitterness. 'And *you* are the countess. God help us all. Ring that bell, and then you can go.'

Diana did not care to be sent out like a dog, but just then she was glad to escape.

Later, Rupert came and found her in her sitting-room in the cadet suite. 'What are you doing here?' he asked in surprise.

'Your mother sent me away. I didn't know where else to go. Rupert, can we go home?'

'Lord, not for ages! People will start arriving, and they'll have to be received, given food and drink. There are letters to write. A notice will have to be composed for the press. The funeral plan's drawn up, thank God – trust the mater to have that done long ago – but it will have to be executed. I've got myself leave of absence from Horse Guards, but if there's a sudden show they may call me back in. So you'll have to get to grips with what needs doing, in case I have to go.'

'Your mother hates me,' was all Diana managed to say.

He dismissed that with a wave of the hand. 'Oh, she hates everybody. Pay no attention. Anyway, you're the countess now.'

'So she reminded me.'

He grinned. 'Made you squirm, did she?'

'So what is she, now, if I'm the countess?'

'The countess dowager – don't you know *anything*?'

'And where will she live?'

'Ah, well,' Rupert said. 'That depends. Officially, this house and Dene and all the others now belong to us. Officially, you're the mistress of the house. But I don't want to throw the old girl out. There *is* a dower house, over on the Eastwood side of the park at Dene, but it's a bit damp and gloomy and I don't think she'd like it there. It's probably not even in repair. And, frankly, won't you need help, to begin with? There's a lot to take in.'

Diana nodded. She had never assumed that they would be able just to get rid of the countess. She had not anticipated this day, but if she had, she would have assumed Violet Wroughton was going to be a part of her life for ever. 'And what happens now?' she asked. 'When will the funeral be? And where?'

'The service will be on Friday, at St Margaret's, and then

175

we take the remains down to Dene on the train, to be interred in the family plot in All Saints. Service of committal only – quite short. Won't tax the old boy's patience too much.'

'Don't—' Diana began.

'Don't what?'

'Don't call him that. Don't try to sound – jolly. I know you must be upset.'

He stared at her for a moment, and then his face crumpled. She was sitting in an armchair and he was standing, and he almost collapsed to a kneeling position in front of her, and buried his face in her lap. He had done that once before, when he was begging her not to break off their engagement. It both moved and frightened her.

'Rupert,' she said, and, at a loss, stroked his hair.

'I feel so guilty,' he moaned, 'that I was at Tony's when he was dying. I should have been at home. I shouldn't have been—'

'You weren't to know,' she said, baffled.

He lifted his face and looked at her searchingly. 'They never loved me, you know, not a bit. I was the spare, that's all. The gov'nor no better than put up with me, and I sometimes think the mater hates me. If you'd married Charles, I could have gone to the devil. They wouldn't have turned a hair.'

'But I married *you*,' she said, hoping it would help. She felt very sorry for him. She had always been loved and cherished. But, then, she had never behaved badly. Perhaps, the novel thought came to her, he had behaved badly *because* he wasn't loved?

He caught her words eagerly. 'Yes! You married me. And *you* love me, don't you?'

'Of course I do.'

'No, not "of course". That sounds as though it's your duty. I get enough of duty from my mother. Do *you* love me – *you*?'

'Yes, I love you,' she said.

'Really?' He was like a child, begging for reassurance.

She gave it to him. 'Yes, really. I, Diana, love you, Rupert.'

For a moment he seemed radiant. Then, perversely, he pushed away from her, stood up, gave her one of his cynical, mocking grins. 'Well, you wouldn't if you really knew me. Lord, I'm starving – it must be well past time for luncheon. Do you think anyone's going to feed us, or have we been forgotten? That would be most unlike Mother's household, but these are unusual times. What say we go out? We could walk down to the Ritz.'

'I'd love to,' she said truthfully, 'but do you think we ought? Shouldn't we stay here?'

He sighed. 'Yes, we should. I suppose we'll have to—'

They were interrupted by one of the maids. 'Luncheon is being served in the green ante-room, my lady.'

'Then we shall come at once,' Rupert said. 'I should never have doubted.' He offered his arm to Diana. 'It will be entertainment, at least, to see my mother conducting luncheon as though nothing has happened.' They stepped out of the room, and his face changed. He spoke in a different voice. 'I keep forgetting,' he said, 'that my father's dead. I can't believe it's still the same day. It seems to have been going on for ever.'

'I know what you mean,' said Diana.

Cook (or Joan, as she was down here) was settled in nicely in the house at Folkestone, which she knew well enough anyway, for she spent her summer holiday there every year. She and Hattie had always got on well. Hattie didn't try to tell her how to cook, and she didn't tell Hattie how to bring up children. They always had plenty to talk about, and Hattie was almost as absorbed with the doings of the Hunter family as was Joan.

She was there to receive Hattie when she was brought

177

home from the hospital, and help her into bed, thinking she looked better than she had expected. Gladys had promised to pop in the next day, when she had her time off. Little Horry was excited and pleased to see Auntie Joan. He gave her a big hug and whispered that he liked her cooking better than Mum's. And there was the big tabby cat Rumpot, who greeted her like an old friend. Joan didn't agree with cats indoors, any more than dogs, but she could not hold out against Rumpot's blandishments, and even allowed him to sit on her lap in the evenings. Well, it did help keep you warm, and coal had to be used sparingly.

She soon found the difference between home and Folkestone, as regards shortages. There was a lot more queuing to be done, and a lot more searching things out. Folkestone had lots of shops, and more fresh fish than they saw in Northcote, as you'd expect, but with a much denser population, it was often a time-consuming business to buy provisions, involving much hiking from one street to another, and Joan's feet, after years of standing up all day in the kitchen, were not her strong point. However, it had to be done, and she was determined to get enough good, nourishing meals into Hattie to have her fit to be left by the end of the week.

She slept well the first night, tired after the journey, but the next day found herself all-ajump, as she told Hattie, with the booms and bangs that seemed to be going on all day, and the flying engines overhead that made her cringe, thinking of the Zeppelins.

'You'll get used to it,' Hattie promised. 'We can often hear the guns from France, you know.'

'So you told me in your letter,' Joan replied.

'But them big thuds you can hear now,' Hattie went on, seeing her sister jump, 'that's the coastal batteries practising. They sound a bit like the navy guns practising at sea, but louder. You couldn't hardly be safer anywhere than here, what with the army camps at Sandgate and Cheriton and Shorncliffe, and six army batteries in Dover.'

Joan considered this, at first with a smile, and then with a frown. 'But wouldn't that be the very reason the Zepps would come? I mean, isn't there such a thing as being a target?'

'Oh, the Zepps don't go after individual targets, dear,' Hattie said. 'They're not accurate enough. And we've got them on the run, anyway. Don't forget we've got air bases at Hythe and Dover, and the air-firing school at Lympne. They'll see 'em off, if they do come. We're always getting aeroplanes buzzing about overhead.'

'I've noticed,' said Joan. 'Makes me all jumpy, it does.'

'Oh, we like it – proves our boys are up and doing,' Hattie said easily. 'You mustn't be such a nervous Nellie, Joan dear. You've never been bombed, have you?'

'No, but our Ethel was – nearly killed, and it killed the young man she was walking out with.'

'I know, dear, but she wasn't at home, was she? You've never even *seen* a Zepp at Northcote, have you? I don't know why you get so worked up about them.'

'I suppose I've got more imagination than you,' Joan defended herself. 'I won that prize for a composition at school, you remember. "What I did in the summer". Daffodil bulb in a pot, I won.'

'Ooh, that prize – I must have heard about it a thousand times!'

'Well, you never won anything, did you?'

'Doesn't mean I got no imagination.'

It was a familiar argument that could go on for hours, but it was conducted in a mostly friendly way. The sisters were too fond of each other to quarrel much. And after a day, Joan became as blasé about bangs and thuds as Hattie. She wasn't going to be outdone by a younger sister.

The reporting of the Earl Wroughton's death in the

newspaper brought their heads together one morning, because as well as photographs of the earl, there was one of Rupert and Diana, and a quotation from Rupert saying his father had been a great man and would be sadly missed.

'She's ever so lovely,' Hattie said – and, indeed, the picture of Diana did her credit. They were walking down the steps of Wroughton House, but the camera had caught Rupert's face at a funny angle and he looked as though he'd got no nose.

'He's very good looking too,' Joan said loyally. 'And the little baby's going to be such a charmer.' What was interesting her most was that the paper had entitled the picture, 'The new Earl and Countess Wroughton'. 'Just think,' she breathed, 'our Miss Diana a real countess!'

'Well, you knew she would be one day,' Hattie pointed out.

'I know, but it brings it home to you when it happens. Who'd have thought? We were all so surprised and pleased when Lord Dene took a fancy to her – the previous Lord Dene, I mean.'

'I thought you said it was no more than she deserved, so beautiful as she was.'

So they wrangled happily through the days, when Joan was not out shopping, or cooking nourishing stews and duffs on Hattie's kitchen stove.

On the Friday, Hattie was so much better that Joan felt comfortable about leaving her. 'I'll see about a train Sunday night,' she said.

'Monday's bank holiday,' Joan said. 'Couldn't you stay on? Gladys has got it off. We could all go for a picnic or something.'

'I've only got a week's leave,' Joan said doubtfully.

'If they've managed for a week, they can manage one more day,' Hattie urged. 'Why don't you ask?'

Joan took a bold decision. 'All right, I will. If I slip a note in the post today, I'll hear back by tomorrow. And now, dear, I'd better pop and do the shopping. What could you fancy for dinner tonight?'

'Whatever you cook'll be lovely, dear.'

'What I want is lamb chops, new potatoes and peas,' said Joan, decisively.

'Ooh, that sounds lovely. Ever so fancy!'

'I've been cooking frugal all week, so we can afford to splash out a bit. I'll pop out, if you're comfortable being left?'

'I could go myself,' Hattie said. 'I'm ever so much better, you know.'

'Yes, but you shouldn't do too much walking yet, not with them stitches. We'll have a little walk down the sea front tomorrow, see how you go.'

To her frustration, though she acquired some nice-looking chops, there were neither peas nor new potatoes in the greengrocer's. He gave her a blank look at requiring such delicate fare, and told her only Stokes's in Tontine Street would be likely to help her. And when she had plodded all the way to Tontine Street, the girl in Stokes's said gaily that there would be both, but not until after the delivery, an extra delivery for the Whitsun weekend, which would not be coming in until six o'clock or thereabouts.

Back home, Hattie said, 'You shouldn't have gone all that way, just for that. We can have something else. I don't mind.'

'Well, *I* mind. Got some lovely chops, and I'm not going to spoil 'em for a ha'porth of tar. I'll just have to go back.'

'I don't like to think of you going twice on my account. I'll send Horry when he gets back from school.'

'It's not on your account, it's me being stubborn,' Joan said, with a smile. 'And Horry's a dear boy, but I wouldn't trust him to choose me peas and potatoes. He's got his head in the clouds half the time. It'd be all empty pods and green spuds he'd bring back. No, I'll have to go again meself.

181

Now, don't you fret, Hattie dear. I'll have a nice rest this afternoon, put me feet up and have a cup of tea with you, and I'll go down after six o'clock.'

'Well, get the tram back then, along the sea front. I know it's not that far, but you want to save your feet.'

CHAPTER THIRTEEN

Beattie saw her daughter as a countess for the first time at the funeral on Friday, the 25th of May. She thought that Diana had already taken on a more regal air – except when she was in the presence of her mother-in-law, who seemed to shrink her.

'So, what happens next?' she asked. 'Will you be coming back to Dene Park?'

'Only for the weekend,' Diana said. 'We go down for the interment tomorrow, and people will call to give condolences, and some friends and relatives will be staying on. I hope you'll all come over to dinner on Saturday.'

'Funeral baked meats?'

'Sort of. It'll be all about him, so Rupert says, old friends telling stories. It'll be nice to have someone of mine there. And you can come over any time, you know, to see George. Oh, and tell Nula she can come and see him. I don't care what the countess says.'

'You're the countess now,' said Beattie, with a private smile at the unconvincing defiance.

'It doesn't feel like it, really. I can't see that she'll ever *not* be in charge. Anyway, I'm determined to spend as much time as possible with my family over Whitsun. Next week, Rupert and I will be going back to London.'

'You're not going to be living at Dene Park?'

'Not yet. Rupert will have all the legal things to arrange,

and he can do those better in London. And he'll have to take up his seat in the Lords. And when his leave runs out, he'll have to go back to Horse Guards. So London makes more sense. And,' she added, wrinkling her perfect nose, 'I'd sooner not be under the countess's thumb at Dene.'

'You're the countess,' said Beattie again.

'Oh, I know! I wonder if I'll ever get used to it.'

After a wretchedly cold April, it looked as though spring had arrived at last, just in time to be bumping into summer. The evening of that Friday, the 25th of May, was lovely, warm and gilded, with the gentlest of breezes ruffling the blue sea, and Joan quite forgot about her feet as she walked along and took in the scene. There were people on the beach, people strolling along the promenade, people riding in open horse-drawn carriages, and soldiers everywhere, many in hospital blue, but others on leave, or with evening passes from the two big transit camps nearby. Joan gave them an indulgent eye. 'Our boys' was how everyone thought of them. They all looked so young. There were a couple of airmen, too, with wings on their khaki tunics, and she thought of Bobby. She said, 'Good luck to you,' as they passed, and they smiled at her and touched their caps and said, 'Thank you, ma'am.' Sweet boys with pink young cheeks and bright young eyes, the sort of boys you knew their mother and sisters were proud of. She sent up a prayer that it would be enough to protect them.

Tontine Street was packed, as you'd expect on the Friday night before a bank holiday, everyone with their wages in their pockets, women and children out shopping for the weekend, and a number of men crowding into the pubs, even bringing their beer out on the street to enjoy the evening sunshine. This was the old part of town, with narrow streets and alleys leading down to the harbour, and cobbles underfoot. Cobbles were a trial to someone with tender feet. And when she got to Stokes's, she found she was not the only person who had come back for the evening delivery: the queue had spread out into the street and was practically blocking it. To add to the problems, the evening delivery itself was still there, a cart with a horse, from the back of which sacks of vegetables were being unloaded by two men and carried in with much 'Oy-oy!' and 'Look out, Ma!' and 'Mind yer backs!' as they squeezed past the shoppers.

Joan almost gave up then. It was bad enough coming twice, bad enough having to queue, but to be jostled as well!

The crowds trying to pass up and down Tontine Street forced her to make up her mind, and when she had been pushed politely but firmly by a passer-by into the queue, she thought she might as well stay there. Those chops, after all, were lovely, and deserved the best. You could have enough of stews, and making do.

Some heavy explosions shook the ground under her feet, but she was an old hand now, and was not to be scared by the sound of shore batteries practising. Nobody around her took any notice, and she felt proud of being like a local. But there was another, seeming nearer, and then another was followed by a huge crash, the shocking sound of breaking glass – much glass, too much glass.

Everyone looked around. 'That was a bomb!' someone said.

'Nah, it was the batteries,' said someone else.

'It was a bomb, I tell yer!'

And then, 'Look, Zeppelins!' someone else cried.

Joan's heart contracted. Her head jerked skywards, even as someone else said witheringly, 'They ain't Zepps, they're aeroplanes.'

She knew that was right because she could hear the

engines, a harsh, heavy, grinding noise, and everyone knew Zepps were silent. She saw them now, a silver-white arrow of them, far up in the blue, looking almost transparent as they reflected the colour of the sky. Quite pretty, really.

Some people started cheering. 'There's our boys!'

'Good luck to 'em!'

A soldier, paused just beside Joan, looked up, and said, 'They're not ours. They're bloody Germans!'

She glared at him sharply, frowning at the bad language. He was not one of the rosy boys: he looked like an older man, and he had sergeant's stripes on his arm. He had a funny accent, too, not like a foreigner, but not like an Englishman either.

She didn't think anyone else had heard him. Their eyes locked. And then there was a horrible whistling sound from above. He grabbed her hard round the body, making her squeak, and the worst noise she had ever heard in her life picked them up and threw them both with the mighty power of a cat swiping a fly. At least, that was how it seemed to her. It felt as though the noise had done it.

All the breath was forced out of her, and as she flew she had just time to think, *That was a bomb. I been bombed*, before blackness, surprising and implacable, fell on her.

She came to, briefly, lying on her back on something hard. There was a queer sort of silence, and it wasn't really silence, because someone was sobbing, and someone else was moaning, and there was a roaring sound from somewhere. But under that, she realised, there was the absence of all the other noises there had been before, of a crowd of people and their talk and their activity.

I been bombed, she thought again. What she had feared ever since the first Zepp was reported. It had happened. Well, now it was over, it wasn't so bad after all. It didn't hurt. I been bombed. I'm dying. She inspected the idea

186

and, oddly, it didn't upset her. But the next thought she had was annoyance: Them chops'll be wasted. Hattie won't cook 'em right.

She found she was looking at flames leaping up towards the blue sky. She could smell burning. She was a cook, her instinct was always to put fires out, quick as quick, but a languidness was over her, and she really just wanted to go on lying here. She heard voices, subdued murmurings, and somewhere, distantly, the bells of an ambulance or police car. Well, someone else was going to take charge, she thought. So that was all right. She closed her eyes and let go.

After the service there had been a reception at Wroughton House, and Diana had offered them all beds for the night, but Edward and Beattie preferred to go home. They saw the first 'extras' on the street as they made their way to the station. *German Aeroplanes Bomb South Coast. Folkestone Badly Hit. Many Feared Dead.*

'Folkestone?' Beattie said, looking at Edward. 'That's where Cook has gone.'

'It's very unlikely anything will have happened to her. They will have targeted the military bases. Remember, the Zeppelins caused a lot of fear, but not many casualties. You'd have to be very unlucky to be one of them.'

'Ethel was one of them.'

'I'm sure Cook is all right,' Sadie said, taking her cue from her father. Only she had come with her parents to the funeral – the boys were at school.

Edward was more interested in the fact that it was aeroplanes. 'Can that really be true? That they're dropping bombs from aeroplanes instead of Zeppelins?' It was a new departure, and possibly a worrying one. Zeppelins were inaccurate, slow, fragile, and the defence wing of the RFC had pretty much got on top of them. But if the

Germans had developed an efficient bomber 'plane, that might be much harder to counteract. 'I think I must go and find out what I can. Lord Forbesson will probably be at the War Office. Can you manage to get home by yourselves?'

'Of course we can,' Sadie answered him.

'But I think we ought to send a telegram to Cook,' Beattie said. 'She was always so afraid of the Zeppelins. She should know we're thinking about her.'

Joan opened her eyes, and shut them again quickly. The light hurt. Her head hurt, now she came to think of it – a massive boulder of pain somewhere behind her eyes.

'You have a concussion,' said a cool voice nearby, and a cool but rough hand was laid on her forehead. She was dead, so it must be an angel. An angel with rough hands? 'Can you move your feet?'

It seemed an odd question. Move 'em where? She wished Cool Voice would go away and let her sleep. She became aware of the smell of clean sheets – well, that was a good thing. Heaven ought to smell of fresh laundry.

And then, another smell, not so good. She knew that smell. Hospital disinfectant. Not Heaven, then. But why am I in hospital? She had a fleeting memory of flames, but it was gone before she could take hold of it. Where was she? What had happened? She couldn't remember anything – anything at all! In a panic, she opened her eyes fully. A nurse was standing over her, holding a thermometer. 'I'm just going to take your temperature,' she said. 'Try to move your feet, would you?'

Joan accepted the thermometer meekly, and moved her feet back and forth. She was becoming aware that there were aches and pains all over the place, including, as she shifted slightly, a very large one on her sit-upon or, rather, that bone just above it. When the thermometer was withdrawn, she said, 'What happened?' It didn't sound like her voice, more like a croak.

The nurse looked at the thermometer, shook it down, and said, 'Normal,' then slid a hand under her head and raised it enough for her to drink some water. 'Don't you remember?' she asked.

'I remember . . .' She scowled with the effort. '. . . walking along the sea front.' Why? Where had she been going?

'Nothing more?'

'No,' Joan said.

'Do you remember who you are?'

'Course I do. I'm—' That was queer. She knew she *knew* who she was, but somehow she couldn't say it. Couldn't lay her tongue to the name The effort made her feel a bit sick. And very tired. 'Can I go to sleep, now?' she said, closed her eyes, and went away.

The pub at the corner a few doors along from Hattie's house had a telephone, and she used that eventually to contact the Hunters. The news hit The Elms like a bombshell: Cook was missing. She had gone out to buy new potatoes and peas for dinner and hadn't come back, and the shop she had been heading for had been hit by a bomb. It had dropped among the people queuing outside. The roof of the shop had collapsed, killing all the staff. The fronts of the shops across the road had fallen outwards. A gas main had burst and shot flames into the sky and set fire to buildings. There'd been dead people and dead horses everywhere.

'If she was dead, or injured, we'd know,' Edward reasoned. 'Her name and address would have been in her handbag. They would have contacted us by now.'

'But she's *missing*,' Beattie objected. 'You can't think she would run off for fun.'

Edward knew that bombs could fragment bodies so that

189

they were unrecognisable, and presumably handbags too, but he didn't want to give air to that thought.

Hattie began the miserable round of enquiry: the police, the morgue, the hospitals. Horry had to stay at home, in case the police came round with information. The next-door neighbour, Mrs Sands, agreed to sit with him, and to send him after her if there were any proper news.

'Well, now, you surely must remember me, even if you don't remember yourself,' said the soldier with the bandage round his head and his arm in a sling. Joan looked at him, and thought he had a nice face. Nice voice, too, though a funny accent. Funny accent . . . why did that ring a bell?

'I've met you before,' she said uncertainly.

'I'm not sure it counts as meeting. We never exchanged names. I'm Fred McAusland. Pleased t'meecha.'

He offered a big hand, and she took it automatically, and said, 'Joan Dunkley. Are you American?'

He grinned. 'Australian. Can't you tell from the accent? Lotta Brits went to Australia, I'm the one who came back. What'd you say your name was?'

'Joan Dunkley,' she said again, and then paused in wonder. 'I remembered.'

'You remember the rest now?' She shook her head. 'You were queuing outside the greengrocer's. You and a hundred other people.' She looked to him as though she were straining after memory. He went on: 'I was just passing. Glad I was.'

She shook her head again. 'I remember . . . Was there a horse and cart? They were unloading something. And then—'

'Yes?'

'You were there. You said, "They're not ours."'

'I wasn't talking about the veg, though, was I?'

She frowned. 'There were aeroplanes.' Her eyes flew open. 'There was a bomb. Was there a bomb?'

'You got it!' he said. 'We got blown up, you and me

190

both. Lucky I grabbed you and jumped just in time. The blast threw us out of the way. It's like that with bombs. You just never know. Bloke next to you can cop it, and you're left without a scratch. Well, we got some scratches, all right, but we're alive, so I count that lucky. And I'm twice lucky.'

'How's that?' Joan asked, busy trying to fit the facts back into the hole in her head.

'Cause I got to meet you.'

Joan was startled. 'Me?' She became aware that she was in bed, in a nightgown – not even hers – and he was a man. She automatically pulled the sheet up to cover more of herself. She'd not brushed her hair. Was her face dirty? 'I must look a sight!'

'I got a wrenched arm and a bash on the coconut, but there's nothing wrong with me eyes. I'm looking at a very nice lady. And if she only tells me she ain't married, I shall be happy as Larry.'

'I'm not married,' she said.

'Nor am I. So that's all right.'

Her hand flew to her mouth. 'Oh, my Lord – Hattie! She'll wonder where I am. What time is it?'

'Nine ack emma, Saturday morning.'

'Saturday? I've been here all night? But – but why's she not been to see me?'

'Nobody knew who you were,' Fred McAusland said. 'Nothing in your pockets—'

'My handbag!'

'No handbag,' he said sympathetically. 'I reckon you dropped it and the bomb did away with it. Who's Hattie?'

'My sister.'

'Well, if you give me the address, I'll see about getting a message to her that you're here.'

'You're very kind.' Weak tears filled Joan's eyes. 'I don't know why you'd be so kind to me.'

'I told you – you're a nice lady and I saved your life. When someone saves your life, they belong to you for ever.'

She thought about that. 'Don't you mean the other way round?'

'Comes to the same thing,' he said cheerfully.

'Concussion, bumps and bruises. Nothing more serious than that,' Edward reported. 'They'll let her out tomorrow morning. I dare say she'll want a couple of days to get over it. She'll be shaken up.'

'She'd better stay down there for the rest of the week, if her sister will have her,' Beattie said. 'We're managing as we are. And we don't want her here in a state of shock, having nightmares.'

'She might not want to stay there.'

'Do you think they'll come back, then? The bombers?'

'Who knows? I doubt Folkestone town was their primary object, though.'

Information about the raid had not been made public yet, but Edward had had it from Lord Forbesson that there had been at least twenty aircraft, travelling at about seventy miles per hour, making them hard for AA guns to hit. Probably London had been their target: they had been heading in that direction, but it had been covered with low cloud that day and they had veered away and been lost to ground spotters behind the cloud for some time, before appearing again over Kent. Bombs had fallen on some villages, on the towns of Ashford and Hythe – the former had a railway works and the latter an RFC gunnery school – before an estimated fifty bombs landed on Folkestone. The aeroplanes had then approached Dover, but the Dover defences put up a vigorous barrage, which seemed to deter the invaders, as they veered away back across the Channel. They had not been hit by a single shot; casualties, mostly in Folkestone, were reckoned at around a hundred dead and two hundred injured.

The newspaper reports so far had not named any specific place that had been hit – a curious piece of government suppression, Edward thought, since the news could not possibly be contained. The popular papers were filled with the usual clamour: why wasn't something done to stop it? There must be more ground defences, more air-raid warnings, and Britain must hit back and bomb the German aircraft at their bases.

'A raid like that must be expensive to mount,' Edward went on. 'They'll want to hit important targets, like munitions factories, not shops in Folkestone.'

'That doesn't make me feel very safe,' said Beattie.

'My dear, we're at war. Safety doesn't come into it.'

'Well, we'll leave it up to her,' Beattie said, sticking to the main point.

The part of the town where Hattie lived had not been hit, but everybody was shaken, whether they had been directly involved or not. The bank holiday weekend was spent clearing up. Some visitors had cut short their stay, to the annoyance of local hoteliers and caterers. There had been an influx of the curious, and of the charitable wanting to help, but they did not spend the big holiday money the town partly relied on. It was doubly a disaster, and Folkestone was angry. On Tuesday the town council held an emergency meeting, and sent a resolution to the government demanding an inquiry into how it could have happened in broad daylight and no warning given. The government must take steps to ensure that 'the wholesale murder of women and children' should never happen again.

Horry, like most other boys, had gone into the town to gawp, and to collect shrapnel or other souvenirs, but Hattie had had no desire to go anywhere near it. Joan had been released from hospital on Sunday with nothing worse than bumps and bruises, and Hattie was grateful for that. She had a husband and son at the Front: she could only cope with the war by not thinking about it.

Much more interesting to her was the presence of the big soldier when she went to collect Joan, and his insistence on seeing the 'ladies' to their home. On Sunday night, when they'd both got their feet up, she said to her sister, 'Well, you've come out of it all right.'

Joan was indignant. All right? She'd been blown up, hadn't she? 'What are you talking about?'

'Got yourself a beau.'

'What? That sergeant? Beau, indeed! Don't talk so far back!'

'He seems a nice enough man.'

'We don't know anything about him.'

'Well, that's wartime for you. Throws people together. Course, he's no oil-painting—'

'He's got a very nice face!' Joan gave herself away. 'Anyway, he'll be off to the war soon enough, and I'll be going home. I'll never see him again, so don't get yourself excited.'

Hattie nodded. 'But you got this week. Might as well enjoy it.'

'What's to say he'll call round?'

'He knows this address, doesn't he? He made sure of that. He'll be round.'

Joan Dunkley had never had a beau, never gone sparking – didn't even know what to call it, let alone how to behave. Luckily, Fred McAusland seemed to know exactly what to do. And he did all the talking. Joan was a considerable talker herself, but found unaccountably that she was happy just to ride along on the flow of his words.

They went for walks – short, easy ones – keeping away from the damaged part of town. They sat in cafés or on benches, and he talked. He told her all about himself, how he had been born in Shepherd's Bush, had worked for a butcher, then got a job in an abattoir in Acton, and then, with his brother, had emigrated to Australia. They had fallen for two sisters. His brother had married his, but Fred's had gone off with someone else, and that had sort of soured things. So, being a strong young man and used to handling animals, he'd gone off to the wild parts – the Outback, they called it, which Joan thought sounded like a privy at the bottom of the garden – and worked on a sheep station, which was bloody hard work—

'Language!'

'Take it easy! "Bloody's" not swearing in Australia.'

— until finally he'd had enough and come home, just in time for the war to break out. So he'd volunteered in 1914 and pretty soon found he'd worked his way up to sergeant.

Joan was rather ashamed of her own meagre history, but he seemed to like the fact that she was in service (kept you safe and warm) and especially that she was a cook. (All women ought to be cooks. It's a natural thing.)

She was nervous at first of being out, especially of the aeroplanes buzzing about overhead from the nearby air base. Perhaps for that reason he talked to her a lot, on their first outing, about the bomb, making her go through it in her own words. It seemed to work. After a bit she found she'd stopped minding about it, and didn't flinch at every loud noise around her. It was odd, she thought, remembering how scared she had been about the Zeppelins, when they'd never come anywhere near Northcote. By the time Sergeant McAusland had finished with her, she was almost proud of herself for having gone through it, proud of being – what was the word? Blasé.

'We got something in common,' he said. 'We both been blown up, and lived to tell the tale.'

'I thought I was done for, at first,' she confessed. She told him, rather timidly, of worrying about the lamb chops, thinking he would laugh, and he did, but not *at* her, so it was all right. It was something else they had in common, him having been a butcher and her being a cook: the proper cut and treatment of meat. It was something else to talk about.

He came to call on her every afternoon. 'You can always get a pass,' he said, 'if you know how, as long as you're not on duty – and I'm excused boots because of me arm.' On the second outing, he begged her to call him Fred, and asked if he could call her Joan.

It was a bit fast, but there *was* a war on, so she assented. 'I never really liked my name.'

'You got anything else, then? I'm Frederick Charles, after me dad.'

'That's nice. I'm Joan Margaret. My sister's Harriet Jane.'

'Margaret! Now *that* I like. That's a real nice lady's name. Pretty Peggy. Mar-gar-et, oh, Mar-gar-et!' He sang it. 'Pretty name for a pretty lady. Joan's too hard.'

'I'm not pretty,' she objected, truthfully.

'Beauty is in the eye of the beholder, ain't you heard that? And I've told you, there's nothing wrong with me eyes.'

She'd never known flattery and it made her uneasy. He seemed to realise it and changed the subject, asking her about the Hunters, about whom she could always talk.

'You don't really know anything about him,' Hattie said. This business seemed to be getting too serious. She'd teased Joan about having a beau, but she hadn't expected him to stick. 'I'm just asking you to be careful, Joanie dear, that's all.'

Joan was amazed at herself, after all her strictures to generations of junior maids about not trusting any man. Men would say anything to get their wicked way. And particularly you should never trust a soldier. She had reduced Ada to tears over her Corporal Armstrong. But she looked at her sister now with an expression of clarity that was almost sad. 'How can I be in danger from him, Hat? He can't want to ravish me, at my age, and I've got no money.'

'What *does* he want, then?'

'I don't know,' she said honestly. 'I think, maybe, just to talk. He does love talking. I don't suppose a sergeant can be pally with the men. And men don't really talk anyway, not like women. Most of 'em don't. I think he just – wants someone to talk to.' Hattie looked doubtful, never having met a man like that, and Joan went on, 'I'll be going home end of the week, and that'll be that. I can't get into trouble in a couple of days, can I?'

On Friday, the 1st of June, Fred met her at Hattie's gate as usual and conducted her to the bus stop, where they took a bus into the countryside, to a village with a nice little café for tea and rock cakes.

'Not a patch on mine, but thank you,' said Joan. It was nice to get away from Folkestone, which couldn't help but remind her, though she could cope with the memories now.

'I'd like to taste your rock cakes,' Fred said, sipping his tea.

Joan wondered for a thrilling and awful moment if he meant something else, but his face was quite serious, so she said, 'Not much chance of that. I'm going home Sunday.'

'And I saw the MO today, and he says I'm fit, so I shall be back on duty tomorrow. This'll be our last outing.'

Joan felt a pang of regret. 'Couldn't you get an evening pass tomorrow? You said you could always get one.'

'*If* you're not on duty. There's no chance tomorrow – too much to do. We're off on Monday.'

'Off where?'

'To the Front,' he said, with a humorous quirk of his lips. 'Where'd ya think, Margate Sands?'

'The Front!' she said, and her voice wavered. 'You won't – you won't be going into action?'

'Wouldn't be a bit surprised. Not too many openings at the Front for blokes sitting on their arses. They tend to want the fighting fellers. Now don't look so blue! The war won't last for ever.'

'When do you think it'll finish?'

'The officers haven't told me. I'm just a sergeant.'

'From what I hear, it's the sergeants tell the officers what to do,' she said sharply.

He grinned. 'Well, there is a bit of truth to that. When things start to hot up, they want to know what the sergeant thinks. But strategy – that's another matter.'

'Guess, then.'

'A year, maybe two,' he said. He was serious now. 'Nobody can keep this up for ever, not even the mad bloody Jerries. And now the Yanks've come in . . . America's a big country. They could put millions into the field if they wanted. Millions. Germans can't match that. So, I reckon, two years, maybe. Three at the most.'

'Three years.' If he'd said next week, it might have meant something. But the beginning of the war was so far behind it was out of sight, and three years into the future was equally lost in the mist. It meant there was only this one bit of road they plodded along, and it always looked the same, so you never knew if you were actually getting anywhere.

'Could be less,' he said. 'Probably more like two. But either way, it'll be over some day, and then we'll go back to Australia, I reckon.'

Her heart sank. Australia! The whole world away. 'I thought you were sick of it there. Wasn't that why you come back?'

'Yeah, but that was then, this is now. I won't be going back alone, will I?'

So he had a woman after all! Her lips tightened. 'Oh, won't you? First thing I've heard about it,' she said coldly.

He looked at her with broad amazement. 'Whadda you think I've been doing all this week? I've been *courting* you, Ma-a-argaret, or haven't you noticed?'

'I . . .' She was lost for words.

'Did you think it was coincidence I was standing right next to you when the bomb fell? I picked you out, the moment I saw you. "That's the one," I said to meself. So I came over, trying to think of the right way to introduce meself, when the bloody bomb did it for me. Lucky for both of us, the way it turned out.'

'You want *me* to go back to Australia with you?' She was trying to grasp the essentials.

'As my wife. No hanky-panky. This is a serious offer, y'know. I'm not going back to the sheep station, by the way, if that's what you're thinking. No, I thought we'd settle in Adelaide. Nice city, that is. Parts of it look a lot like England. There's even one bit of it called Kensington. You'll feel right at home. I'll use me savings to get meself a little butcher's shop, and I'll make a fortune. You'll never lose money selling meat, I promise you that. Buy us a nice house, with a little garden. And a jacaranda tree – always wanted a jacaranda tree.'

'I don't know what one is,' she said. She felt dazed.

'You'll find out. So whaddaya say?'

'You want to marry me? *Me?*'

'Why not? You're a woman. I'm a man. That's how it works, if I've remembered it right.'

'But – why?'

'Because I like you. You're just what I want. What's the problem?' He sounded a touch impatient.

'You could have someone young.'

'I want a wife, not a daughter. I don't want some scrawny chicken I'd have to be a father to. I want a nice, plump, sensible wife me own age, someone to sit and talk to in the evenings when the shop's shut and the dinner's on the table, someone to grow old with. What's up?' He took her hand across the table, 'Don't you fancy me, then?'

She felt herself blush, and she hadn't done that for a long time. 'No-one's ever asked me before.'

'What – to marry? Bloody good job too, or I'd have to break his neck. Right, so that's settled, then. We'll get this war over and done with, then you and me'll head for the big country.'

'But you're going to France,' she faltered.

'Yeah, bit of a hitch there, right enough. But we'll get over it. You'll give me your address and I'll come and visit you when I get leave. And we'll write to each other, okay? Every week?'

'I'm not much of a hand at writing.'

'So what? I'm not Bill bloody Shakespeare.'

'All right, then.'

'Good girl. And no running after other men while I'm away, understand? All these jokers who tip up at the back door with their eyes on your rock cakes – you send 'em away with a flea in their ear, right?'

'I would have anyway.'

'Too bloody right!'

She sat smiling, wondering at the unaccustomed sensations inside her, of warmth, of belonging, of having someone who wanted to take care of her. In the kitchen, she was in charge, she had to decide everything, she had to be the cross tyrant so as no-one would answer her back. Now – she had a feeling that between her and Fred, he'd be the one taking charge. She could be soft if she liked. That'd be different! There was a soft Joan somewhere in there, believe it or not, if she could just dig her out.

'I like the smile, but you can talk as well,' he said, breaking her reverie. 'What's up?'

'There is just one thing,' she said.

He looked alarmed. 'You're on a promise, remember. No

bloody welshing!' She smiled and shook her head. 'Well?' he said. 'What is it?'

'You got to stop saying that B-word so often.'

He grinned. 'Oh, you're a bloody classy woman all right, and no mistake! I might just do that – for *you*!'

CHAPTER FOURTEEN

Shipping losses and the consequent food shortages had reached such a pitch that something new had to be tried. The idea of having the merchant ships sail in convoy with an armed escort had been proposed by the war cabinet in February, but had been roundly rejected by the Admiralty. The navy hadn't enough ships, they said, and besides, a convoy simply presented a larger target to the U-boats, easier to find and easier to hit.

'I don't know about the first point,' Edward said to Lord Forbesson, when they met in the club one evening, 'but aren't they right about the second?'

'On the first point,' Forbesson replied, between puffs as he got his cigar going, 'they were assuming a ratio of one to one – that is, an escort for each individual merchant ship. Henderson of the Anti-Sub Division put 'em right about that. About eight armed ships to twenty or so merchant vessels, according to him. On the second point – in fact it makes it harder for the U-boats, because instead of picking off defenceless ships at their leisure, they'd have to attack a well-defended position, and they'd only get one chance. As soon as they showed their hand, the escort would strike back. As for being easier to find, that cuts both ways.'

'You mean—'

'If they know where *we* are, we know where *they* are going to be! The Anti-Sub wallahs were looking for needles in haystacks before, but they only have to hang around the convoy, and the bastards are bound to turn up.'

'Yes, I see,' said Edward. 'Then have you persuaded them at last?'

'They're not convinced it will work – no Royal Navy type ever believes a merchant captain can manoeuvre, or keep station properly – but they've agreed to try the system out. So we shall see. I believe it's our best hope. We can't go on as we are.'

'When does it start?'

'The first trial convoy is at sea as we speak. Left Hampton Roads on the twenty-fourth of May, with eight destroyers and an armoured cruiser. Ought to reach port around the ninth or tenth of June. If it works, we'll start up regular runs. The Yanks are very keen on the idea. They'll be shipping men across the Atlantic in large numbers pretty soon. They'll want their troop ships to join the convoys, if they prove their worth.'

'It will be a relief to have one problem solved,' Edward said. 'Of course we'll still have food shortages until the harvests come in, but if we can get normal deliveries resumed across the Atlantic it will make a huge difference.'

Forbesson nodded, reaching for his glass. 'We'd dearly like some good news to announce, to set against those damned Gothas.'

The aeroplanes that had attacked Folkestone had been identified as Gotha bombers, enormous aircraft with a wingspan of over seventy-seven feet, a long range and huge payload. That the Folkestone attack had been the precursor to a regular campaign had been confirmed when they mounted a second raid on the 5th of June, hitting Sheerness and Shoeburyness. There had not been many casualties, but a great deal of expensive damage was caused.

'I can see the future,' Forbesson said gloomily. 'Up the

estuary and hit the docks, just like the Zeppelins – except that they'll be much more accurate.'

'Is there nothing to be done about them?'

'Well, home defence is Lord French's baby,' said Forbesson, 'but even I can see we need two things, and as soon as possible: better air-raid warnings, and a fleet of modern fighters to bring them down.'

'Is that possible?' Edward asked. 'Doesn't the RFC have its hands full in France?'

'Indeed, but we can't leave London undefended. All home defence has got is a handful of obsolete two-seaters. We need six squadrons of first-class single-seaters, set up all round the capital, and an early-warning system efficient enough to get them airborne in time.'

'That will be expensive,' said Edward. 'Won't it involve diverting funds from the Front?'

'That's the devil of it. We've already got Haig tugging one way and Lloyd George the other. The PM and Lord French want to stick to the Pétain solution – sit tight and defend only – until the Americans come in. Haig wants to attack with everything we've got.'

'And which will win?'

Forbesson put down his glass and gave Edward a weary look. 'For me, the French mutinies have decided it. With the Frogs out of action for the foreseeable future, we can't afford to sit still. Haig's right. We had a joint offensive planned for the tenth of June, but it's all down to us now. We must mount some kind of push, or risk the Boche finding out what's going on in the French-held part of the line. Or, rather, what's not going on.'

'So we can expect something big on the Front?' Edward said.

'Within days,' said Forbesson, and added, 'My son Esmond is in Ypres.'

'Is that where the push will be?'

'I'm saying nothing. But you know Haig – he's always believed Ypres is the key.' He drained his glass and stood up. 'Ah, well, fortunes of war and so on. I must be toddling. Meeting with Lord Derby at the War Office. We must find time to have dinner one of these days, Hunter. Jack's becomin' a dull boy.'

You could always tell when a big push was coming by the extra railway traffic. You could hear them in the quiet of night: the endless trains grinding and clanking, one after another, bearing their load of guns, ammunition, heavy equipment and men southwards towards London, the coast and ultimately France.

Cook normally slept like the dead after a day in the kitchen, but on her return from Folkestone she found herself frequently wakeful, listening to the sound, clear across the fields, of the heavy trains struggling up the incline from Rustington. When it was really quiet, you could hear the thump of the signal at Eastwood Lane dropping, to let them pass Northcote Station on the through line. And she would think, as always before, Those poor, brave boys. But now there was an extra dimension to her concern. Now there was Sergeant McAusland.

It hadn't taken her more than a few seconds on her arrival home to decide not to tell anyone about him. They had all been so excited to have her back, so eager to hear her story about the bomb. Had she actually seen the aeroplanes? Had she heard the bomb coming? What did it look like after? Only Ethel had stood aside. She had caught her eye when Lilian excitedly cried, 'What's it like being blown up?' Ethel had curled her lip and walked away. It was the first time Cook had ever felt sympathy with Ethel, in the sense of knowing how she felt. Thanks to Fred, she had talked through her feelings about it all, and wanted now just to put it aside. But Ethel hadn't had anyone like that.

She remembered now, to her shame, how impatient she had been with the girl, wanting her to 'get over it'. And she remembered how she had reduced Ada to tears, telling her not to trust her Corporal Armstrong. It had seemed so unlikely that a man could be interested in Ada for anything but bad reasons. How much less likely was it in her case?

In the stillness of the night, when she was wakeful, she thought about him, tried to remember his face. The voice was easier; the face came to her only in separate features. She remembered how the lines from his eye corners were white in the weather-beaten brown, where he had screwed his eyes up against the sun. She remembered the little crest at the front of his hair-line where a tuft grew the wrong way. She remembered the way his lips curled when he smiled. But she couldn't put them all together to make a recognisable photograph in her head. It worried her that she couldn't. Sometimes she thought she must have imagined him.

Even if she hadn't, was it likely she would ever hear from him again? She was a fat, middle-aged cook, of no wit and no beauty. What could any man find appealing about her? There had been a boy once . . . She took out the memory for the first time in years, and examined it with some amazement. She had been eighteen, in service as a housemaid, fresh-faced, and slimmer then. He delivered the groceries at the door, and took down the order for next time, and Joan, as she had still been then, had been the one to deal with him, day by day. She came to look forward intensely to the little interaction, and had gradually become aware that he enjoyed it, too. Weeks went past, until at last he had asked her if she would walk out with him on her Sunday half-day. She had been so shy and embarrassed she had said no.

But he had asked again. She always remembered that. He had not taken 'no' for an answer. And then it was her mistress who had forbidden it. The cook, who had been a kitchen tyrant and, possibly, slightly mad, had reported it to her, hoping to get Joan into trouble. The mistress had instantly declared there were to be 'no followers'.

When she had told him – Harry, his name was – he had been indignant. They couldn't say that, he had insisted. What she did in her time off was her business. But, in those days, they *could* say that, and they did. Female servants were strictly regimented. If you went against them, you could lose your job, and Joan had been afraid of being without a place. Her backdoor conversations with Harry had become hurried and clandestine – the scowling, brooding cook was always watching for a fault to report. But he had begun to persuade her that the world would not end, and that she was very unlikely to be dismissed, and that if the worst came to the worst, new places were ten-a-penny for a good worker like her. She only had to get up her courage.

She was working on it. She was almost there. And then one day he wasn't. A stranger came to the door with the groceries. The other chap had been taken ill, he said. The newcomer didn't know any more than that, couldn't answer Joan's questions. Two interminable days later, he had some more information. He'd heard that the other chap – Harry? – had been took ill sudden in the night with terrible stomach pains. He'd been rushed to hospital, but he'd died. Appendix, they said it was. It was a shame. Everyone seemed to have liked him.

That had been the end of her one romance. She had shut away that part of herself, turned to cooking as an outlet for everything inside her, worked her way up to be kitchen tyrant, a little like the one she had once hated and feared. And from the age of eighteen to the age of forty-five, no man had looked at her and seen anything but 'Cook'.

Fred. Fred McAusland. As news came in about a new big push starting at the Front, she thought about him being over there, part of it, fighting the Boche. He might be wounded. Killed. And she would probably never know. Who would think to tell her? The greatest likelihood was that she would never hear from him or of him again. He was just another memory to be folded carefully and put in the drawer with Harry. She couldn't remember now what Harry had looked like. Couldn't remember anything about him but the mere fact of his existence.

And then the letter came. It caused a sensation in the kitchen, first because she never got letters, only a card from her sister at Christmas and her birthday, and second because it was in a man's hand and, from the censor's stamp, had come from the Front. Third, it was addressed to Miss J. M. Dunkley. *Miss!* Emily stared at her with such wide eyes Cook was afraid they'd fall out and bounce round the room like ping-pong balls. 'Is it a love-letter, so?' she asked with breathless excitement.

Cook snapped at her to close her mouth, there was a bus coming, and not to talk so daft. 'It'll be from my nephew, my sister's boy,' she said, knowing there had to be an explanation if she was to get any peace. 'Get them potatoes peeled,' she ordered, to distract Emily. 'And then go and ask Mr Munt if there's to be any peas for luncheon. Sooner they gets here, sooner you can pod 'em. You're slow as treacle with peas.'

She heard herself, and wondered who this person was, this barking generalissimo, when inside there was someone pink as a rose and fluttering with silly excitement. She carried the letter in her pocket all day as a talisman, waiting for her bedroom at night to open it.

Well, Margaret, I'm going to call you that, hope you dont mind, it suits you better. Cant think of my special girl being called Joan. Well, here I am at the Front. Cant say where, or they'll cross it out anyway! We are in a cosy billet behind the line, looks like it used to be a school but no desks or anything left, but you cant mistake that smell. Reminds me of a teacher Mr Hook who used to beat me like a dog! Well I expect I deserved it! Getting ourselves ready to go up the line, training and such, Yours Truly being the teacher now, a lot of responsibility, have to bring them up right! Lots of noise going on, which makes the new boys jump at first, but you soon get used to it. Anyway, it never keeps you awake at night after a day running round with packs on. That nice seaside place seems a world away, but its close in my mind, and you with it. Hope your behaving yourself and not getting mixed up with any 'undesirables', you know what soldiers are like! And no sailors or airmen either! You keep yourself for me, girl, because Im coming back for you, so write soon and tell me everything your doing, I want to imagine you in your cosy kitchen when they come up with the mess tins full a burgoo and tea that tastes of petrol. Well thats all now as no more paper. Keep your chin up. Fred.

Her eyes stung with tears at the precious words, the proof positive that he existed and that he cared for her. She was no hand with a pen, having never written anything longer or more creative than a recipe since her schooldays, but she resolved to acquire a piece of paper and an envelope the very next day and write straight back. She couldn't bear to think of his waiting for a letter day after day and wondering if she'd forgotten him. She would maintain the fiction that it was her nephew she was corresponding with, and keep her secret lover to herself for as long as possible, a warm little patch around her heart, not to be trammelled by other people's questions and doubts.

* * *

The British Army had detonated a huge number of mines under the German line at Messines, creating an explosion so massive they could feel it over in England, some said as far away as London. There was talk that it had rattled the chandelier above the prime minister's desk.

The concussion did not reach as far as Hampshire, but David and Antonia discussed it no less eagerly for that.

'Nineteen mines – five hundred tons of explosive,' David read from the newspaper. 'Imagine! Ten thousand Germans killed . . . Most of the fortifications along the Messines Ridge destroyed, as well as the town itself . . . Good Lord! It seems we've been mining the ridge since the middle of 1915!'

'And the Germans didn't know?'

'Oh, they knew, apparently, and took some counter-measures, but they didn't know the full extent of it . . . Now we're consolidating. Fierce fighting . . . Lower slopes . . .' He read on, so absorbed he forgot to read aloud.

'What's the importance of it – Messines Ridge?' Antonia prompted him.

'It's the high ground overlooking Ypres. The Germans have held it since November 'fourteen. It must mean that Haig wants to mount the big push in Ypres, just as your father said.'

'I don't think he's the only one saying it,' Antonia said, with a small smile. 'Everyone know Haig thinks Ypres is the key.'

'Well, who's to say he's wrong? My father thinks he's pretty sharp.' He came to the end of the article and folded the newspaper. 'Shall we go on with Hardy?'

As variety from Latin and Greek, they were reading the poems of Thomas Hardy – 'Can't keep the bow always bent,' Mr Weston had advised. 'And Hardy's poems are easier going than his novels.'

At the end of the garden behind the Westons' house was a stream, and beyond the stream was a meadow, fringed with trees – at present grazed by cows but perfectly nice to sit in, if you were careful where you spread your blanket. They had carried across plenty to read and a modicum to eat in a basket. The stream was spanned by a plank bridge, which had posed a challenge for David with his crutch, but the water was only calf deep and Antonia had taken off her shoes and paddled across beside him, holding his free hand, so they had conquered it.

The cattle had stared, then flounced away when they arrived, but having got used to them, they had slowly grazed nearer. Now, as Antonia read, the words were set to the music of the steady crunch and slurp, the stamp of foot, the whisk of tails and rattle of shaken ears against summer flies, the soft, moist breathing and the occasional wet sneeze.

David relaxed, chewing a blade of grass, watching her as she read. She had pulled off her straw hat so her curly brown head was bare. He noticed how the curls were tipped with gold from the sun, while the darker parts were shot with tints of bronze and indigo. There were one or two freckles on her nose. Her eyelashes were a brown silk fringe lowered over her eyes as she looked down at the book; her pink lips shaped and released the words as though they were creating them from nothing, from the air. He had looked at her a thousand times, but never really *looked* at her before. He was aware of a warm feeling, which, when he analysed it, seemed to be made up of absolute comfort in her company, and a particular affection that was like—

She paused and looked up, as though aware he had stopped listening. The silken fringe had lifted; their eyes met. Hers were blue, not bright blue like Bobby's, for instance, had been, but a rather subtler shade, like water reflecting the sky – rather beautiful. A faint blush came to her cheeks. The warm feeling surged upwards in him, and almost without thinking, as though it were the only thing to do, he leaned forward and kissed her.

Faint shock registered in the back of his mind that he had done it, but the front of his mind was busy with sensation. He had only kissed Sophy before, and this was quite different. Sophy's lips were soft and helpless, like a rosepetal cushion. Antonia's were soft, but also firm, and they responded. He had kissed Sophy; he and Antonia kissed each other. The closeness of her face, the warmth from her skin, the scent of her, the lips giving and receiving under his – something tugged at the deep roots of him, with a pang like hunger. He was innocent for his age, but he was almost twenty-three, and he recognised this as physical desire. He *wanted* her. At the realisation, he broke the contact, leaned back to look at her. Her lips were softly, slightly parted, a bruised expression was in her eyes. He didn't want her to speak and break the spell. He said, 'Is it all right?' She nodded. He searched her sweet, familiar face. 'Again?'

She nodded and closed her eyes.

They kissed again. Her arms crept around his neck, he put his around her and held her to him. She seemed to become boneless in his arms, as though flowing into a different shape to fit him. Longing and loneliness and belonging and sorrow and joy were all rampaging about in him, tugging and tugging at him like the insistent hand of a small, importunate child. *Notice me! Give me what I want!*

Their lips parted again, and this time she lowered her head onto his shoulder in a gesture so like despair that he was afraid for an instant that he had upset her, that it had *not* been all right. 'Antonia,' he said. Her hair smelt of lavender. He kissed her ear, where it peeped through the curls, and the side of her neck, all he could reach. He wanted her mouth again. 'Antonia,' he said more urgently.

212

She lifted her head at that, and looked directly into his eyes, a searching look and, it seemed, with a hint of sadness to it. *What do you want of me?* For a moment he thought she had said it, then realised it was his imagination.

'Will you marry me?' he said. He hadn't known he was going to say it, but now he had, it seemed exactly right. What could be more natural? Why had he not seen it before? As she searched his face, he said it again. 'Will you marry me?'

She said, 'Yes,' and the word came on an outlet breath, like a sigh. Then she said, 'I love you.'

The words gave him a renewed pang, and he pulled her to him again, and kissed her. And now her response was more eager, more hungry, and the desire gripped at him, and tugged, and said *Give me what I want! Give it now!* He stopped kissing her at last, and just held her, his eyes closed.

A cow had grazed its way right up to them, and now stretched out its neck as far as it would go to snuff at the unmoving couple. It startled itself, and jerked away with that stiff-forelegged jump, pivoting on the rear, designed by nature to escape the strike of snakes. At a safe distance it let out a wet, explosive breath, and licked each nostril quickly with a long, muscular tongue. The strangely entwined humans had not moved, and it fell peacefully to grazing again.

'My darling, are you *sure*?' Mr Weston asked. 'Does he love you? It seems—'

'So sudden?' Antonia said. 'We've known each other a long time.'

'And all that time he was in love with someone else.' Mr Weston hated to say it, but she was his only child, and he did not want her to be hurt.

Antonia looked wretched. 'You're against it. You think I should have said no.' He hesitated, not knowing how to answer. 'I love him, Daddy. I never thought he could care for me. Now it's happened. I'm twenty-seven, nearly twenty-eight. No-one's ever asked me to marry them before.'

'Not because you aren't lovely,' Mr Weston said. 'Because you're out of the usual. You're too good for most men.'

She gave a small, sad smile. 'All the more reason then, in your philosophy, for me to seize the day. How many suitable men will I meet before I'm too old?'

'I don't want you to grab at happiness,' he said. 'That never answers. And he's—'

'A cripple?' she said harshly.

'I wasn't going to say that. But he has no means of supporting you.'

'I know what he is, Daddy. And what he can be. You've agreed with me – we've talked, the three of us, about his prospects. And besides,' she added impatiently, 'when have you ever wanted me to marry for money? You didn't bring me up to be worldly.'

'Even the most spiritual couple must have *something* to live on,' he said. He smiled painfully. 'But I love you, and I trust your judgement, and if this is the man you want, we'll find some way to make it work.'

She came and wound her arms round him, and he hugged her. 'You know I love him,' she said. 'You've known it for longer than I have. And now he wants me. Be happy for me, Daddy.'

'I am,' he said. 'You have my blessing.' *And if he hurts you,* he thought, *I will find some way to make him pay.*

A flurry of telephone calls brought Beattie and Edward to Hampshire on the Sunday; Sadie stayed at home with the boys, but sent urgent messages: 'Give David my *special* love. Say I'm so pleased – I like her tremendously.' It would be David's birthday on the Monday, the 11th of June. She had thought he would be home by then, but when his stay had

214

been lengthened, she had wrapped up her present to him to be posted, and now entrusted it to her mother to give to him. 'Wish him happy birthday from me.'

It was a book-mark she had made, an oblong of white card on which she had stuck pressed flowers – heartsease and pimpernels and forget-me-nots – and covered it with cellophane, with a second card glued on the back to conceal the joins. She had punched a hole at the bottom, through which she had plaited a rope of scarlet silk threads ending in a Turk's head knot and a tassel. It had been a labour of love, especially to someone with work-hardened hands who had difficulty keeping the whole thing clean. She remembered with a pang how he had thrown away the white heather she had pressed for him to take to the Front – but he had been in pain then, mental and physical. She hoped now that both were in retreat at Antonia's hands.

Beattie was silent all the way down in the train. She had known this time would come, of course, known it since she first held him as a baby in her arms. She had suspected something when he had extended his stay with the Westons, especially as Ethel had been sent home because 'Miss Weston was attending him personally'. Now she feared the worst. It was well known that young men fell in love with their nurses. If it should be that he saw her in that light . . . Or did he really love her? She was more the right sort of girl for him than Sophy Oliphant. That had been a romantic fantasy. He knew Antonia Weston well, had never, as far as she was aware, had romantic thoughts about her. Perhaps it would serve. Perhaps they would be happy together. And she must be glad for him, if that were the case. She must not be jealous. She wanted him to be happy, didn't she?

Edward also had doubts, also pursued them silently, but they were of the practical sort. How would they live? He

215

did not want to rob his son of the happiness a wife could give him, especially given all he had suffered, but where would they live, and on what? As far as he knew, the Westons were not moneyed. David must work to support her – but what could he do? He was afraid he would have to advocate their waiting, which would place him in the position of denying his loved child the one chance of happiness he might have.

In Mr Weston's study, he, Beattie and Edward looked at each other gravely, while the lovers waited outside, talking in low voices, and the smell of roasting beef wafted from the kitchen, where Mrs Bates wondered whether she was preparing a celebratory feast or funeral baked meats.

'Well, this is rather a pickle,' said Mr Weston at last. 'The young people are very serious about it, and I must declare at once that I would like to find a way to make it work for them.'

'Your daughter is a very sensible, mature girl,' Edward said. 'I'm sure she knows her own mind. And I'm impressed by the difference in David. I had no idea he was so improved. He's walking so much better than when he went away.'

'He has worked very hard,' said Mr Weston. 'And Antonia has helped him. With all due modesty, I can say he would not have progressed so far without her.'

'I'm sure not,' Edward said, remembering how David had been at home, how sunk in inertia and despair. 'But does she realise what she is taking on?'

'Yes, I think she understands very clearly,' said Mr Weston. 'She does know him very well.'

Beattie made a sound, and he looked at her curiously, for she'd said nothing so far. 'Mrs Hunter? What are your thoughts?'

Beattie roused herself. 'That it's impossible,' she said harshly, 'but that if it's what they want, we will find ourselves making it possible.'

'My thoughts exactly,' said Mr Weston.

No, they're not, Beattie thought. *I mean something quite different from you.*

Edward spoke: 'You must, however, be concerned on behalf of your daughter. You will not want her to marry unwisely, and how is David to support himself, and her?'

'There are many things he can do. He has a first-rate mind, and many jobs can be done sitting down.'

'But they require training,' said Edward. 'I could find him a place in my bank, but I doubt he could cope with travelling into Town. Where would they live? As a junior in training, he would not earn enough for an establishment. It would be several years before that was possible. I think we will have to ask them to wait, at least until the war is over, and things go back to normal.'

'If they ever do,' said Mr Weston.

'They won't want to wait,' Beattie said. 'Who knows how long the war will last?'

'David's own thought is that for the moment, until he becomes more mobile, he could work as a private tutor. A crammer. Pupils would come to him – he would not have to travel. And he is certainly capable of teaching. I have seen him teaching Antonia Greek. If they live here, with me, there will be no expense of establishment.'

Edward looked pleased. 'I think that may work. Tutoring will keep him busy, and if his leg goes on improving, there are plenty of professions he can be helped into when the war's over.'

'But they will live with us,' Beattie said decisively. Both men looked at her enquiringly. 'They can have the guest bedroom and make it their own, and he already has a sitting-room upstairs that they can use. If it's cramming work he wants, we have two highly academic schools in the village, and we have large houses and affluent families – plenty of boys who will want to go to Oxford. And

217

Antonia,' she made herself say the name, 'will find plenty of war work in the neighbourhood. We are quite a centre for war activity.'

Weston nodded. 'I see the force of your argument. We are much more remote down here. He will find it harder to acquire pupils. And opportunities will come more readily, as his leg improves, in the environs of London.'

'Quite so,' said Edward. 'Well, if the young people don't mind the arrangement . . .'

'I imagine they'll be happy with anything that enables them to marry. I have, by the way, some money to settle on my daughter. Not a fortune, but enough to make the difference between being comfortable and not, when the time comes for them to set up home. Shall we have them in and tell them the good news?'

'Yes, right away. I'm no advocate of torture,' Edward said, with a smile. 'Regarding the wedding itself . . .'

Weston interposed firmly. 'A girl marries from her own home. It will take place here – I must insist on that.'

Edward nodded. Beattie had nothing to say. It didn't matter to her where they made their vows. She would have him at home a little while longer. She had secured that much; it was enough.

'I dare say they will wish it to be as soon as possible,' Weston went on. 'Three weeks for the banns – that will take us to Saturday, the 7th of July. Does that suit?'

Mr Weston went to open the door and beckon the young people in. Antonia looked grave, David nervous. Beattie saw the crutch and the awkward leg, but saw also that he had put on flesh and looked healthier, brighter, though the fine lines round his eyes – the lines of chronic suffering – would never go now. They made him look older than his age, closer to Antonia's. She was not a pretty girl, but she had a certain something, a firmness in the face and a graceful way of moving. Beattie sighed. She must accept this one, for David's sake. It was, at all events, easier than accepting the vacant, doll-like Sophy.

Mr Weston met their anxiety with a broad smile. 'How does the seventh of July sound to you?'

They looked at each other with wordless pleasure, and David held his hand out to her. Hers slipped naturally into it. 'Thank you. I will make her happy, sir,' he said.

CHAPTER FIFTEEN

The trial convoy had arrived safely, having lost only one vessel, which had straggled far behind the rest. It was an excellent start, and promised better times ahead; but though the beginning of summer had the look of plenty, with the trees in leaf, the grass lush and flowers in the hedgerow, it was the time of the greatest shortage. Animals had long known it: the stored goodness of last winter used up and the current year's harvests not ripe yet. Now humans had to learn it too. Shortages grew more frequent; shops emptier; in towns and the poorer parts of cities there was real hardship, even starvation.

Queuing had become a normal part of life for much of the population; rumour ran like underground water to pop up unexpectedly and cause sudden shifts in population. A hint that there were sausages at Blank's the butcher's, or a consignment of tea just arrived at Thingummy's the grocer's, had crowds pouring from one neighbourhood to another, queues of dozens, sometimes hundreds, forming like magic, so that policemen had to be sent to control them and keep the roads clear.

In mid-June Lord Devonport resigned as food controller and Edward had a new superior, Lord Rhondda. New advertising campaigns were planned, mostly about bread. Posters urged: Save a Loaf a Week and Win the War. Or more simply: Eat Less Bread. Restaurants and cafés had already removed sugar bowls, and sent tea and coffee to the table with the permitted lumps in the saucer. Now they counted out the slices of bread, too. Some had a printed notice on the table: 'If you find you can manage on half a slice, please cut it, rather than tearing it.'

Before the war, the lower classes had lived almost exclusively on white bread. Since March, in an effort to eke out the wheat that was so scarce, bakers had been ordered to use a greater proportion of the whole grain, and to add oats, maize or barley to the mix. The resultant bread was browner, tougher, perhaps more nourishing, but disliked by those who had regarded white bread as the bottom line of civilisation, below which lay degradation. Many was the letter to the newspapers complaining about digestive disorders caused by 'dark bread'.

Now, in summer, worse was to come. Until the harvest came in, grain had to be made to go still further, and the new War Loaf had to be made from dough supplemented with boiled potatoes. The bread had a damp, spongy taste and texture; but for those whose entire diet was bread and margarine, or bread and dripping, it was at least there, and the price was fixed.

Hetherton's Hygienic Bakery no longer delivered. Mr Hetherton was ashamed of the War Loaf, and making it broke his heart. Besides, he had lost his last assistant to conscription, and he needed Con Meyer to serve in the shop. It made it easier for Emily, since she always knew where to find him now. She spent her afternoons off hanging around the shop and getting glimpses of him through the windows.

Cook wouldn't have a War Loaf in her kitchen, and took to making her own bread again. It was more work for her, and it had to be a mixture of whole wheat and oats and a bit of rice flour, but it was better than 'black stuff with lumps of potato in it'. After some experimenting she came up with a recipe she could tolerate. Edward had decreed a ration of one slice per head per day. It was hard on growing boys, and Sadie voluntarily gave up her slice to them at breakfast. She could always fill up at midday at Highclere, where they had army rations.

To everyone's relief at Highclere, the unpleasant Private Higgins had been withdrawn by the army for other duties, though Hugh Stanhill was nervous that it meant he was to be withdrawn too. Sadie thought she would miss him if he went – their special friendship had grown into something comfortable that added a dimension to her days up there – but the original six girls had grown to sixteen now, and it seemed likely that if they needed more hands, there would be no difficulty in obtaining them. Their fame had spread, and the idea of females doing that sort of work was beginning to seem unremarkable in 1917, now that the country had accepted VADs and FANYs, conductorettes and female porters, and even, since March, a Women's Army Auxiliary Corps.

Sadie only learned that Highclere was not alone when a newspaper reported that there were three large War Office remount depots which were completely run by women. And one day in June Mrs Cuthbert told Sadie, with considerable excitement, that a newsreel team was coming to make a film of them at work. 'Horace calls it propaganda,' she confided, 'designed to lift the spirits of the people at home against deaths at the Front, and these damned Gotha raids.'

There had been two more since that first one on Folkestone: the raid on Sheerness and Shoeburyness on the 5th of June, and another on the 13th of June that had hit Margate, the docks, the East End and the City. That had been the worst raid of the war so far, with 160 killed and 430 injured.

'He may be right that it's propaganda,' Mrs Cuthbert

went on, 'but the film will be shown in every cinema up and down the land – think of that! We'll be doing our part to show that women are capable of anything men can do.'

Sadie grinned. 'I didn't know you were a suffragist!'

'When I have the time. Usually I'm too busy. But if we can help win the war *and* do womankind a little good along the way, so much the better!'

So, on the same day that Edward was meeting the new food controller, Sadie was helping the newsreel crew to get the shots they wanted. There was to be 'footage', as she learned it was called, of girls mucking out, strapping, grooming, clipping, and heaving bales of straw about. Hugh was obliged to keep out of the way – they wanted ladies only.

A mobile blacksmith had been co-opted, and there was some footage of girls helping him with the shoeing. The producer asked Sadie which was the most difficult horse to shoe. 'I'd like to show that it isn't all fun, that you ladies face some danger too.'

Sadie could have told him that, thanks to the Stanhill tether – as they called Hugh's idea – they managed even the fidgety horses without having hoofs waving about their ears. They just hauled up a spare leg, and the animal had to learn that it couldn't kick or rear when it had only two odd feet on the ground. But she consented to bring out Pepper and let the smith rap his hoofs for show, as long as she was the one holding him, since she knew his ways better than anyone.

They took some footage of horses being schooled, and then they had to fabricate an exercise ride, with the camera set up beside a track while the girls went past in line, each riding one and leading one. They did it first at the walk, then at the trot, and one or two of the led horses misbehaved in a satisfactory manner, which pleased the producer no end.

Finally they had all the girls gather together for a group shot, in three rows, the ones at the back sitting on the gate, the middle row standing, and the front row squatting. Mrs Cuthbert stood at the side looking proud, and Sadie was in the middle at the front. At the last minute, Nailer wandered over, sniffing, to see what everyone was doing and whether it meant food, and the producer liked the idea so much, Sadie had to clutch him awkwardly to her chest while they all smiled for the camera and waved.

'So you'll be famous too,' she told the indignant dog, when she was able to let him go again.

The film would be in the cinemas in the first week of July, the producer told them as his team packed up their equipment, but they would sell 'stills' – photographs taken from the film – to newspapers and magazines, which might run them sooner. 'You'll have to keep an eye out for your faces,' he said.

When the newsreel team was bumping slowly away down the rough track towards Rustington, Hugh Stanhill came up behind Sadie and said, 'Well, now you're a film star, like Theda Bara or Mary Pickford.'

Sadie laughed explosively. 'I'm not like either of them!'

He looked at her judiciously. 'I think you're quite a bit like Theda Bara. Anyway, you'll be famous, and much too grand for the likes of me.'

'It was a shame you had to stay out of the way,' she said.

'I think they'd have noticed I wasn't a girl,' he said solemnly, making her laugh again. 'Will you allow me to escort you to see your première, Miss Pickford, when it comes out? It might be the last time you'll ever deign to speak to me.'

'Oh, yes, I'm sure to have my head turned and be spoiled by fame,' Sadie agreed. 'You'd better seize the chance while you can.'

The group picture appeared in *The Times* on the Friday,

creating great excitement at home. *The Times* called them 'Gentlewomen who do everything that their grooms did before the war', and mentioned Nailer by name, as 'the one male member of the team, with responsibility for rodent extermination', which made Sadie smile. Everyone agreed it was a very good picture of her, right in the centre, though Nailer had moved and his head was blurred. Peter voluntarily ran down to the village to get a second copy for the servants, as they liked to cut things out for a scrap-book they'd been keeping for some years. What was in there so far was mostly about Diana, so Sadie was flattered to be reaching the servants' hall standard of celebrity at last.

Diana rang at the weekend to say she had seen her sister in the *London Illustrated News*, which had done an article on the subject, and printed two photographs, the group by the gate and one of the exercise ride. There had also been something in *Tatler*, but Diana didn't mention that, as it was mostly about the 'head girl' at the depot being sister to the glamorous young Countess Wroughton, and the photograph of Diana was much bigger than the little one of Sadie cut out from the group picture.

When the film came out, Hugh politely insisted on his right to take her to the cinema and view it, though she would rather have gone with her brothers and enjoyed their pleasure. But she seemed to have promised him, so she couldn't get out of it. He was very nice about it, and brought a packet of Mint Imperials to suck while the second feature was showing. When the newsreel music started up, he reached out and took her hand in the darkness and squeezed it. She squeezed back out of friendship, then disengaged herself to concentrate on the film. It seemed so very professional, so *real*, just like all the other war newsreels she had watched, that she could hardly associate it with herself. When she saw her own face on the screen, it made her gasp, and she felt a twinge in her stomach

225

almost like guilt, like being caught out doing something she shouldn't. But they all appeared very competent, and the horses looked lovely. The voice doing the commentary reported that the inspector of remounts had said he'd never seen horses so well looked after. The only embarrassing part was when reference was made to them riding astride and wearing breeches 'like men', which Sadie thought was unnecessary. How could they have done the work in skirts? It was pandering to people who disapproved of females doing anything but embroidery.

Afterwards, Hugh escorted her home, where he had left his bicycle, and said she had looked every inch a film star: 'as to the manner born'. She told him not to be silly.

'It will be hard to get back to ordinary life after all the excitement,' she said, as he wheeled his machine from the laurels. 'But at least I've got the wedding to look forward to.'

'Oh, yes, your brother's. Saturday, isn't it? You'll be a bridesmaid, I suppose?'

'I shall attend the bride, but I won't be dressed up – it won't be that sort of wedding.'

'I'm sure you'll look lovely anyway. I wish I could be there to see you.'

She wasn't sure what to say to that, except 'Don't be silly,' again, which might have sounded rude. So she said, 'Goodbye, then. I'll see you tomorrow.' He nodded, mounted his bicycle and pedalled off. She watched him go, and he looked back and waved at the turn of the road. She frowned as a sudden unwelcome thought came to her: it wasn't possible, was it, that he was getting 'spoony' on her, as Emily the kitchen maid would have put it? But no, she dismissed the idea – that was silly. He was just Private Stanhill, nice, friendly, good to talk to, yes, but merely a work colleague. He would have been horrified if he knew she had entertained that thought even for an instant. She had embarrassed herself by thinking it, and hurried inside to see if there might be cocoa to be had in the kitchen.

The Westons had a wide acquaintance, Mr Weston was practically the 'squire' and was turned to by everyone for advice, and Antonia was loved for her cheerful temper and many good works. So on the wedding day the church was packed, and there were crowds waiting outside in the July sunshine. It was a gala day for the village. Soldiers from the local camp added a proper dash of khaki to the throng, and there might well have been a few broken hearts behind the smiling faces, for in the tea-rooms she had given homesick boys a place to be and a sympathetic ear.

There was also some press presence, largely because the Earl and Countess Wroughton were going to be among the guests. They arrived in a large motor-car just in time for the service at eleven. Edward, Beattie, Sadie and the boys came down by train, and were to stay the night at the Westons' house. The honeymoon was arranged: all the Wroughtons were in London, leaving Dene Park empty but staffed, and Rupert had suggested the happy couple have a few days there, 'enjoying a bit of privacy, and a bit of luxury, which I don't suppose they'll see much of otherwise'. Diana thought it a very kind notion – even more so when she found he had ordered the staff to feed them like royalty and get out the best wines in the cellar. They were to have the William and Mary Bedchamber, and Rupert and Diana were to drive them to Dene Park on their way back to London after the wedding breakfast.

Antonia slept the night before the wedding at the house of one of the neighbours, rather than oblige David to move. On the morning, she was helped to dress by her other bridesmaid – her cousin Angela – since Sadie's train did not get in until ten thirty. She had a tailored dress and jacket of pale pink shantung: the local dressmaker, who had been

227

thrilled to get the commission, had urged ivory shantung on her, but Antonia had said she couldn't imagine what she would do with a white costume afterwards, whereas she could wear pink any summer. Angela, who was rather a dab at hairdressing, had done her hair into a large, soft chignon behind with lots of curls at the front, and instead of a hat or veil, she had fresh pink rosebuds wound into the arrangement. Angela and Sadie wore their best summer dresses and straw hats.

David had asked his friend Oliphant to be his supporter, and by a stroke of luck Jumbo was on leave at the right time and able to accept. He was deeply touched that his being Sophy's brother had not disqualified him for the job. He wondered at what point to pass on Sophy's best wishes, which he had been charged with, together with the news that she was expecting. Perhaps not today, he mused, as he helped David into position by the altar steps.

Well-wishers had decorated the church with flowers; the organist and choir had volunteered their services and filled the space with joyful sound; and Antonia came down the aisle with her attendants behind her and her face so luminous with joy that David thought first, wonderingly, that he had never realised before how beautiful she was; and second, with a pang of fear, that it was a huge responsibility to be the cause of so much happiness.

Sadie, standing behind the bride, thought David looked touchingly young and unsure of himself. She was glad that he and Antonia had found each other, since she thought they were a perfect match. And she thought of Bobby, who ought to have been there on David's other side, supporting his brother. She imagined him in his khaki tunic with the wings he was so proud of, imagined him catching her eye and winking, with that grin of his she could never resist. *Oh, Bobby!* She wished she could feel he was there with them, watching from some celestial sphere, but she had only once since his death had any sense of him, when she had been packing up his things, sent back from the Front. Since then, she had known only that he was gone. She had come to think that the dead, if they carried on existing at all, went somewhere very far away. She hoped it was a good place. Wherever it was, it could only be enhanced by the presence of her darling brother. He would have enjoyed this wedding so much. *Enjoy it for me, little sister,* she imagined him saying.

'I will,' she whispered back.

And a little while later, Antonia was saying the same thing.

Afterwards, back at the Westons' house, there was the most tremendous party, and since Mr Weston had not only invited everyone from the church but everyone who had shaken his hand outside it and wished him joy, it was fortunate that Mrs Bates had provided twice as much food as her master had ordered. The tea-rooms had been pressed into service, and the party spilled out onto the lawn at the back of the house, plus every room in between.

Rupert said, 'I say, this is what I *call* jolly! What a splendid do!'

Diana was glad he didn't find it too rustic or unsophisticated. She thought he was looking tired. Since his father's death, he seemed often to have the weight of the world on his shoulders. She had not thought he cared so much for the old earl, but the death had plainly been a shock to him; and perhaps the estate was proving more work to transfer than he had anticipated. She smiled, and let him help her to things to eat, and glasses of champagne, and talked pleasantly to the Westons' guests. The bride's costume looked a little home-made, but the style was well-chosen, and she looked handsome and happy. The flowers in the hair were a nice touch – rather Victorian. It was a detail she thought she might copy some time, at a dress ball, perhaps – if there were ever dress balls again.

Edward was thoroughly enjoying talking to Mr Weston. 'You must come and stay with us *often*,' he urged him. 'You'll like to see your daughter – and I rarely enjoy such stimulating conversation.'

'I'd be delighted to,' Weston said. He had been thinking how empty the house was going to be without her.

A little later, Edward managed to make his way through the crowds to his wife's side. 'Well?' he said.

'Well what?'

'You were miles away. I suppose you were thinking of Bobby.' She didn't agree or deny it. 'I know I have been.'

Beattie gave him a painful smile. How did he always manage to heap coals of fire on her head? She had been wishing Louis could have been here to see his son married, thinking how like him David was from some angles.

'Sadie looks very pretty today,' Edward went on. 'I suppose it will be her turn next. Though she never seems to be very interested in that sort of thing.'

'She's young for her age,' Beattie said automatically. Although, when she thought about it, it wasn't really true any more, was it? Responsibility up at Highclere seemed to have made a woman of her.

Edward leaned in and discreetly kissed her cheek. 'I am a very lucky man,' he said softly. 'I have a beautiful wife and six lovely children. Thank you, darling.'

Six! Her heart burned like gall. He didn't say it to be cruel, or even absent-mindedly. He meant it. All six were his, to him; and in his heart, he still had them all, whether they were present or not. He was a good man. Too good for her – and the worst of it was that she must never let him know that, because it would break his heart.

Would this party never end? she thought desperately. Surely Diana and Rupert must want to go soon. 'We'll have a lot to do when we get home,' she said, 'getting the rooms ready for David and Antonia.'

'It'll be nice to have them with us,' Edward said. 'The house seems too quiet sometimes.'

Rupert and Diana dropped the newlywedded at the door of the great house. 'We won't come in,' Rupert said. 'I know you'll want to be alone. I've told them to give you dinner in the Octagon. It's pleasant at this time of year. It opens onto the terrace, and there's a gramophone if you want some amusement after dinner. You might want to use it as your sitting-room. But, please, use any room you like – the whole house is yours.'

The William and Mary Bedchamber was enormous, with a vast four-poster bed sporting a carved crown at the top of each post and hangings of sea-green velvet. There was a carpet in peacock colours of green and blue, and gilded mirrors everywhere. When the servant had left them, Antonia wandered round the room looking at things. 'This room is quite absurd.'

'I expect they wanted us to have the best.'

'Oh, I wasn't criticising – just noting the contrast between *it* and *us*.'

'Think of it as an hotel.'

'Hotel? These figures on the mantelpiece are Meissen, aren't they? Probably priceless. And those portraits on the wall – are they actually King William and Queen Mary? As in William of Orange?'

'Looks like it. Perhaps they stayed here once.'

'I suppose they couldn't have called it the Orange Bedchamber without causing confusion.' She was opening doors now. 'Oh, there's another bedroom in here, with a normal-sized bed.'

'Dressing-room,' David said. 'In case we don't want to sleep together.' He sat down on a little sofa upholstered

231

in green and gold brocade, and watched her with tired eyes. There had been a lot of standing, one way and another.

She tried more doors. 'Closet. Oh – backstairs! Like a secret passage in a school story! And here's a bathroom – how modern! I did wonder.'

'Diana said Rupert's mother had several put in about twelve years ago. Before that, a hip bath and cans of hot water had to be brought upstairs from the kitchen.'

'Via the secret passage,' Antonia said. 'Are we going to change?'

'There's no need. It's only us,' he said. 'Are you uncomfortable in your silk suit?'

'No. Though I might take the roses out of my hair.'

'Pity – I thought they looked pretty.'

'The pins are sticking into my scalp. But I could leave one or two, if you like them.' She walked over to him, looking down with a faintly troubled air. She could see he was tired – but was there anything else? 'You aren't regretting it, are you?'

He took her hands. 'God, no! I can't think why it took me so long to think of it.' She laughed, and he went on, 'You're more likely to regret it than me. I'm no bargain.'

'None of that! I might have to point out my many defects, and that would put a damper on the occasion. Let's just agree that we're equally lucky, and leave it at that.'

'Agreed,' he said. 'Do you suppose we go down when we like, or wait for a bell? I'm strangely hungry.'

'The wedding feast was hours ago. I'm famished too. Perhaps if we go down it will hurry them up.'

'At the least, they'll have to give us something to drink.'

Dinner, served at a small table brought into the Octagon and placed before the open french windows, was excellent, and in enjoying it they forgot any slight shyness in their new situation, and chatted as they always had. After dinner, they played some music on the gramophone, and had a few hands of cribbage, until it was time for bed.

The shyness returned when they reached the bedchamber. This, now, was new territory. At least Antonia was used to helping him with his studs. Freed of them, he went into the dressing-room, leaving her the privacy of the bedroom to prepare herself. When she was ready, she turned off all the lights except his bedside lamp, got into bed and lay down. She felt hollow inside, but with anticipation, not fear. A highly educated young woman, well grounded in the classics, could not be ignorant of the basic anatomy of the business, but she was also a girl in love. Her mind was full of the poetry of passion, and of longing for her Troilus, her Tristan, her Paris.

Eventually he came in, shed his dressing-gown, turned off the last light and climbed in beside her. There was a silence. She listened to his breathing, wondering if he was embarrassed or daunted. She wanted to help him along, but didn't know whether for her to speak would seem immodest to him.

At last he said, 'Um . . .'

'Yes?' He didn't go on at once, and she said quietly, 'I'm your wife now. You can say anything to me.'

'It's this wretched leg,' he said at last.

'Is it hurting?'

'No – I mean it is, a bit, but it's not that.' He was obviously having difficulty with the words. 'You see – well, I've never done this before. I know the theory and – and I'm not sure if I can – if the leg will stand the . . . I mean, you know, there's a usual way of doing things—'

She came to his rescue. 'I understand.' She pushed herself up on one elbow, and leaned over him to kiss him. 'If we can't manage the usual way,' she said softly, 'we'll just have to find some other way, won't we?'

And they did.

On the Sunday night, after a lovely day in Hampshire, the family went home, and Sadie and the boys went to the kitchen to tell the servants all about the wedding. Sadie had brought them back each a piece of the wedding-cake. When they ate it the next day at lunch, Cook pronounced it all right, but not a patch on hers. 'You wait till Miss Sadie gets married – I'll show 'em!'

After having a thoroughly idle weekend with the family away, they now had to put in extra work getting the rooms ready for David and Antonia. 'It'll be lovely to have the blessed boy back,' Cook said sentimentally, already planning his favourite foods for their first meal as a married couple under this roof. Antonia's trunk had arrived, and Ada and Ethel struggled upstairs with it.

'I hope I'm not expected to unpack,' Ethel said.

Ada glanced at her. 'You still sore about him getting married?'

'Don't talk so daft. I'm not a lady's maid, that's all I'm saying.'

'She hasn't got one, so I expect she's used to unpacking for herself. There'll be lots of stuff to press, though, probably. The missus'll ask Nula to come in, I dare say. If she *does* want any maiding, I don't mind doing it. I done it for Miss Diana often enough, when she was coming out.'

'You? They won't ask you, with your hands,' Ethel said. 'I s'pose it'll be me that gets lumbered again – after all, she knows me, and I looked after him for months.'

'You just said you weren't a lady's maid.'

'Said I *wasn't* one. Doesn't mean I can't do it.'

Lilian came in, clutching a framed photograph to her chest. 'This just come,' she said breathlessly. 'Cook says the missus said to put it in their room. Where'd be right, d'you think?'

'Let's see,' Ethel said, wrenching it away from her. A formal portrait, taken in what seemed to be someone's study – Miss Weston's father must have arranged for someone to come along and take it. Mr David, looking handsome and ever so upper class, with his noble features and swept-back hair. One hand resting on a chair-back – so as to do away with crutch or walking-stick, she supposed – and the other arm bent to take his bride's hand. And Miss Weston, not pretty, but looking quite handsome with her face all smiles and flowers in her hair, and the neatly tailored costume – pink, Miss Sadie had said – and the white hand on Mr David's arm displaying the wedding-ring.

Well, he'd done it, she thought, and now he was someone else's responsibility, so she could stop worrying about him. But what was to become of her, a corner of her mind asked. The Hunters had never had more than two house-parlour maids. Would the presence of the married couple mean so much extra work they would need three? Or, if someone was to go, would they chuck out Lilian, last in and first out? Or decide that as Ethel had been sick-room maid she was no longer needed?

Well, she thought angrily, if she got a sniff of a hint they were going to get rid of her, she'd make sure to get her notice in first. She was damned if she'd be sacked! There were plenty of jobs, these days, for a girl – and jobs where you had money in your pocket and could come and go as you pleased! She quite fancied the idea of being conductorette. You met a lot of people that way, and you had a uniform to wear.

Or you could marry Frank Hussey, a little voice whispered. She drove the idea away ferociously. But it had reminded her that her life's plan – to find someone to marry her and set her up in her own home – was in tatters.

When the war's over, she thought, I'll make changes, start a new life. What that might be she had no idea but, thankfully, there was no need to think about it now. The war was not going to be over soon, and as long as it went on they were all saved from deciding what to do next.

'Nice frame,' she said, yielding the photograph to Ada. 'Better put it on the mantelpiece.'

CHAPTER SIXTEEN

So far, Diana had not found life very different since becoming a countess, except for frequently forgetting what her title was, and expecting to be called Lady Dene instead of Lady Wroughton. Lady Wroughton, in her mind, was still her mother-in-law.

There had at first been a lot of extra visitors, distant relatives and old friends of the family 'making their number', as Rupert put it, in case there was anything to be made out of the situation. Since Diana didn't know what they wanted, she was able to receive their congratulations at face value, and won a reputation for being 'charming' and 'unspoiled'.

There was, however, a great deal more in the post every day: not just more social invitations, but many more requests to be on committees and to be patron of various charities and good causes. 'If I accepted all of them, I'd never be at home,' she said to Rupert.

'Refuse them. You're not *obliged* to be charitable, you know.'

But she felt she was. She had been brought up that way, and all this good fortune would make her uneasy if she didn't spread at least some of it around. And 'There's a war on, you know,' she reminded him. They all had to do their bit, and those with a larger bit had to do more.

'Then choose a few and stick to them,' he advised her.

'If you start listening to every request, they'll peck you to death like barnyard chickens.'

There were also the requests for money. Some of them perplexed her – the sad cases described seemed so harrowing, the wavering handwriting so pathetic.

'This is dreadful,' she said to Rupert, one day at breakfast. 'This poor woman: husband and two sons all killed at the Front, a crippled daughter and her aged mother to support. She hates begging, but says if she can just get an operation for her daughter's leg, the girl might be able to go out and earn a living instead of being dependent.'

Rupert held out his hand for it, read it and roared with laughter. 'My dear child! Your poor sad widow-woman is probably a stout fellow with a gold chain across his weskit, a cigar in one hand and a glass of brandy in the other.'

Diana looked hurt. 'What *can* you mean?'

'He'll have an office with four women writing these letters to his dictation, while he picks out suitable victims from the social pages and looks up the addresses.'

'You mean it's a trick?'

'Happens all the time. My mother used to light the fire with them.'

'But suppose it's true? Look, there, you can see the ink's smudged where a tear fell on the page while she was writing.'

'They do that with an eye-dropper. Affecting, isn't it?'

'You're so—'

'Cynical? Look here, darling, I know you want to do good, and I applaud you for it, but the safe way is to give the money to the charities and let *them* dish it out. They have the means and the staff to look into these cases and check that they're genuine. Have you asked yourself why your . . .' He checked the name '. . . your Mrs Paterson – only one "t", nice touch! And a beautifully wobbly signature! Why your Mrs Paterson hasn't gone to the Soldiers' Families Relief or the Churchwomen's Guild or any other of the worthy organisations she must be surrounded by?'

Diana said nothing, looking angrily at the table. She didn't like to be made a fool of, and there was a lingering doubt in her mind as to whether Rupert could be correct. At last she said, in a small voice, 'You think they're all false?'

'I haven't a doubt of it. But I can see it has upset you, and I have a remedy for that.' She looked up. 'You must hire a secretary. Then you need never see any of these things again.'

'I suppose—' she began.

'An experienced secretary will be able to filter out any genuine cries for help,' he said, reading her mind. 'You haven't time for all this stuff.' He waved a hand at the heap of envelopes.

'I think you're right.' She sighed. 'It takes so long, and I keep falling further behind. There are lots I haven't read from the day before yesterday. And I haven't read the papers yet, and your mother gives me such a look if I don't at least keep up with the Court Circular.'

'There we are, then. I'll get Mullet to ask Auden if she can recommend someone. These people all know each other. Matter settled. You're not to worry any more – it will give you creases in your lovely brow.'

'You're very good to me,' she said.

He gave her an oddly stricken look for just an instant, before it was replaced by his usual charming smile. 'Who else should I be good to? You're my wife,' he said.

Yet the other difference the death of the old earl had made was to Rupert. He hardly ever went out alone at night any more, and never stayed out until morning; and sometimes they didn't even have people in. When they were alone together, he often sat thinking for long periods, or played gramophone records and just sat looking at her as she read or worked. She was sure he had something on his mind, but whether it was just the earldom and everything connected with that, or something else, she didn't know. When she asked him if anything was wrong, he dismissed the idea lightly, and immediately started talking about something else.

One evening a message came from Rupert that he had been called away, straight from work, and would not be home to dinner. Diana took the opportunity to go and see her friend, Obby. She was home quite early, and expected Rupert to be very late, but he came in while she was still up, sitting at the table by the window in the drawing-room embroidering a bib for George.

'Hullo,' he said. 'That's a very feminine task.' He strolled across and peered over her shoulder. 'Little Miss Muffet, very nice. I like her bonnet. That, I suppose, is the tuffet. I always wondered what a tuffet was.'

'That's the spider,' Diana corrected. There was brandy on his breath, and he seemed in frivolous mood.

'I thought spiders were black.'

'I didn't want black on the baby's bib.' Purple and blue and green, her spider, with yellow eyes. 'Babies like bright colours.'

'It seems a lot of trouble to go to for something he's going to dribble food onto.'

'You have nice damask napkins at dinner,' she pointed out.

'*Touché!* Though I fancy my eating habits are a little more refined than young Lord Dene's.' He walked over to the fireplace and leaned on the mantelpiece, fiddled with some things, then walked back to the window table and stood looking down at the magazines, his hands in his pockets, whistling softly and tunelessly.

He was obviously restless, and she wondered if he wanted to talk. 'Where did you go?' she asked, setting a purple stitch in the spider's back.

'Hmm?'

'You got called away after work. I hope it wasn't bad news?'

'Oh, all news is bad news,' he said vaguely. 'At Horse Guards, they're all talking about a new offensive, to start at the end of the month.'

Diana nodded. 'We've been expecting a big push.'

'Expecting it too long. Haig's apparently furious. It should have started straight away, as soon as they secured the Messines Ridge in the middle of June, instead of six weeks later, when the enemy's had time to regroup. But the PM didn't want an offensive at all, so they've been arguing round in circles. But the biff-'em boys seem to have won it over the sit-tights at last, so it's settled. I think the public mood's a factor. Sitting tight while the Gotha bombers make hay doesn't look good in the newspapers.'

There had been more air raids on the 4th and the 7th of July, the first hitting Harwich and Felixstowe on the east coast, the second coming up the Thames again and hitting the docks, the East End, and as far west as Tottenham and Islington, with 55 killed and 190 injured. After that raid there had been riots in the streets, shops with German-sounding names attacked and looted, and inflammatory articles in the newspapers, including many popular calls for German cities to be bombed in retaliation. 'We don't do that sort of thing' had not entirely settled public opinion.

Anti-German feeling had risen to such a level of bile that, on the 17th of July, the King had thought it wise to execute an Order in Council changing the name of the royal family. Saxe-Coburg-Gotha sounded altogether too German, and the 'Gotha' part was particularly embarrassing in the circumstances. From now on, it was decreed, all male descendants of the British Royal Family would bear the surname of

Windsor, which was thoroughly English and put people in mind of Good Queen Victoria.

'So what will this new offensive do?' Diana asked.

'Force the Jerries back from Ypres, take over the high ground all round it, then drive on to Lille. If we can take Lille away from them, we'll have their most important industrial base and control the railways.'

It was surprising to hear him talk so seriously about strategy and objectives. Generally he treated the war as either a joke or a bore. She looked up. His frivolous mood seemed to have evaporated, and he was frowning in thought, as if worrying out a problem. Then he met her eyes, and gave an embarrassed sort of half-smile, like the smirk of a schoolboy caught out at something, and said abruptly, 'This evening – I went to see Erskine.'

'Oh,' she said, cooling. 'I didn't know he was back in England.'

'On leave,' said Rupert. 'They're giving as many as possible leave before the next show.'

'I'm surprised you're home so early – you're usually out all night when you see him.'

'It wasn't a friendly meeting,' Rupert said. 'It was in the way of a remonstrance.'

'About what?'

'He's jealous.'

'Jealous? Who on earth of?'

'Tony Lessiter.' He looked at her carefully when he'd said it.

Diana's lip curled. 'Oh, that's so silly. You see it sometimes with schoolgirls, an old friend being jealous of a new one, but one doesn't expect it in grown men.'

He looked at her in wonder. 'You don't know, do you? You really don't know.'

'Know what?' she said, taking another stitch. She often didn't understand what he was talking about, and it didn't bother her any more.

He went on, 'The irony is that I chose you specifically because I thought you *did* know. Because of your aunt. I was a little careless there, making assumptions on too little evidence. But as it happens,' he added, as if to himself, 'it's worked out very well.'

'What *are* you talking about?' she said. He'd brought up her aunt before, and she hadn't understood it then and didn't now.

'Are you happy with me?' he asked.

She looked up again. He seemed to be asking seriously. 'Yes,' she said. 'Aren't you, with me?'

He dropped to his knees in front of her so that their faces were on the same level. 'I am,' he said. 'Against all the odds, I'm very happy. That's rather the point. I don't deserve you, Diana. And little George! To be a father – I never thought it would happen. I never thought I'd care about it. I can't begin to tell you how it makes me feel . . . like the greatest emperor and the lowest rogue in history, both at the same time.' She shook her head slightly. 'You don't understand – I know. But since the gov'nor died, I've been doing a lot of thinking. Turning out the drawers in my deepest soul – and finding they're full of dirty socks. When I think what I was doing when he was dying, instead of being by his side . . .'

'You weren't to know,' she said, as she'd said before. She wasn't sure what the reference to socks meant.

He brushed away her reassurance. 'I've been scattering my luck like a spendthrift. At any time, something could have happened, it could all have been made public, and then what? Exposure, shame, prison even. And it'd be not just the gov'nor and the mater, but you, and George, and the whole bally structure, the name, the title, the family, history – pouff! All gone up in smoke. What was I *thinking*?'

He seemed so genuinely upset about something that she put her work aside and gave him her hands, and he gripped them tight, as if hanging on over a precipice. 'I don't know what you're upset about,' she said, 'but I'm sure you're worrying needlessly. You have me, and George, and everyone likes you. You'll make a fine earl. When the war's over, you can go into government, perhaps, and do all sorts of good things, and go down in history as—'

'No, you *don't* understand,' he interrupted. 'I might be mad to try to make you, but in view of what I've decided, I think you have the right to be – informed.'

'Informed of what? *What* have you decided?'

'I've put in to be transferred to a line regiment,' he said. He searched her face. 'No more cushy staff job. I want to go out there and fight for my country.'

It was a blow. She had got used to having him at home, not having to worry about him. If he went to France . . . Charles had fallen, and Bobby, and so many of the young men she had known. She said the only thing she could think of. 'You're not a fighting officer. You wouldn't know what to do.'

He gave her a wry look. 'Well spotted! But I was in OTC, and I *am* an officer. As for the rest, they'll train me. I won't go straight into the trenches. There'll be trench-training and combat training for several weeks, and I dare say a cushy billet at first, until I've found my feet. If the pressures of war allow. Who knows? Perhaps it'll be head first into the cauldron. I must take my chance with everyone else. But, you see, I've had a lot of things churning about in my mind for weeks now, and this is something I have to do. I have to redeem myself – for your sake and my boy's.'

'Redeem yourself? From what?'

'This is the hard part. Try to understand, will you, dear? There are some men who . . . can only love other men. You must have heard something, some gossip, some rumour.' He searched her face, but it was blank with incomprehension. 'You've heard of pansies, haven't you?'

244

'You mean—'

'*Not* the spring flowers.'

'I know that,' she said with dignity. 'You mean those very artistic men, who wear flowing cravats and velvet jackets and write poetry. Well, I think they're rather silly, but I don't see any real harm in them.'

He gave a painful grin. 'Bless your innocence! I don't think I can go on with this.'

'You can't be saying you're a pansy,' she pursued, puzzled. 'You've never written a poem in your life, or painted a picture, and you dress perfectly normally.'

He lifted her hands one after the other and kissed them. 'Forget about that. The point that matters is that you have redeemed me, you and little George, and I'm going to be a model husband from now on, which means, among other things, doing my duty at the Front as an Earl Wroughton should. And if anything should ever come out – well, it *won't*, that's all. It mustn't.'

He sounded so grim, she was almost alarmed. 'If what comes out? What have you done?'

'You don't want to go into that now, really, do you?' The frivolous look was back. 'However could you deny it convincingly if you knew about it? No, keep your unsmudged innocence, my dear little countess, and I promise you I shall never let you down again.'

'But you *haven't* let me down,' she said, doubtfully. 'Have you?'

He squeezed her hands so tightly it hurt, and seeing her wince, he loosened his grip, leaned forward and kissed her cheek. 'Dear little wife,' he said whimsically. 'How sweet you smell.' He put his hand under her elbow to lift her, and she got up obediently.

'When will you go?' she asked.

'As soon as possible,' he said. And then, 'Not tonight, however. Shall we go to bed?'

He's going to war, she thought. The words seemed ominous and worrying. And she couldn't help thinking that being a staff officer was really Rupert's metier. She couldn't imagine him covered with mud and smoke and standing amid shot and shell giving orders while men died around him.

But he had said they would train him. She hoped it would be all right.

In spite of herself, Beattie got dragged into Mrs Fitzgerald's scheme to have a National Kitchen in Northcote. She was aware that there were poor areas in Northcote, like Church End, the Old High Street, and The Rows – a warren of terraces and alleys off the Walford road – where life was a struggle, even when the main breadwinner was at home. With Father out of work or away at the war, real hardship stepped in.

Bread and scrape for breakfast, bread and scrape for tea, boiled potatoes for dinner – that was what many survived on. Meat or cheese were rare luxuries. If there was a wage coming in, someone might go to the butcher on a Saturday night for a bit of fat bacon or a 'tanner wrap-up' – odds and ends of meat trimmings bundled into newspaper – and they'd be cooked slowly all night in the oven with the potatoes for a Sunday stew. The children suffered most because what food there was had to go first to anyone who was working. It was quite common to see gangs of children hanging about outside the factory gates, waiting for the workers to come off shift, in the hope of begging the left-overs from their lunch packets – a crust here, a bit of stale cake there.

Even those in work were frequently hungry, often having many other mouths to feed on their wages. A place where a hot, nourishing meal could be had cheaply would be one of the best things they could do for the poorest of the locality. But Mrs Fitzgerald's application, even with a little urging from Edward – who did it to please Beattie rather than the rector's wife – was turned down. Resources were limited, and the National Kitchens must go to the areas of the greatest need. Northcote was not one of them.

'So,' said Mrs Fitzgerald grimly, 'we must do it ourselves.'

Beattie had had long experience of resisting her schemes, but this, she felt, was a good one. And Antonia, who was now settled in as part of the household, was eager to help. Mrs Fitzgerald was impressed with Antonia, feeling she was Serious. And she had had some experience of mass catering, in her soldiers' tea-room, on a small scale, but it was more than anyone else on the committee had.

An early breakthrough came when committee member Mrs Hopper secured the help of her best friend, Mrs Braithwaite, who was the wife of the Methodist minister, and persuaded the Church Council to let them have the use of the Methodist church hall in Hastings Road. It involved moving several small groups to other premises for their meetings, but few people objected once they knew the reason, and several offered their help for the project. The hall had a kitchen attached, which was a major consideration, and a supply of trestle tables and benches. Crockery and cutlery could be provided from the parish storerooms. The army camp on Paget's Piece gladly sent a work squad to clean out the hall and give it a coat of fresh whitewash inside. And the usual people gave money – perhaps a bit less wearily this time – to get the thing started.

Once we've got going,' said Mrs Fitzgerald, 'it will run itself. We won't be *giving* the meals away. Ideally, the price should cover the cost of the ingredients, but if there's a shortfall, well, people are very generous in a good cause. And the cooking and serving will be done by volunteers. I shall have no difficulty in drawing up a roster of willing ladies. Everyone enjoys feeding the hungry.'

'Like the animals at the zoo,' Beattie said absently.

'Not *quite*, perhaps,' Mrs Fitzgerald said tautly.

The other main decision was what food to supply, and given that there would be no government support, a good nourishing soup seemed the answer, with bread, and possibly cheese. You could put anything into a soup, someone pointed out, and it didn't have to be the same every day. Antonia, being practical, said that farmers, wholesalers and greengrocers would probably donate damaged vegetables, which could be picked over and the good parts used. And families like the Hunters, who had turned their gardens over to vegetables, might donate what they had spare.

'We may be able to get meat donated, too,' Beattie suggested, 'if we cast the net widely enough.'

'Bread we will probably have to pay for,' said Mrs Fitzgerald. 'But at *cost*,' she added, with determination.

Antonia and Cook put their heads together and came up with a flexible recipe, which could include any kind of meat that came along, including rabbits and pigeons if anyone wanted to trap and donate them. 'And the bones'll go for stock, which all helps the nourishment,' Cook pointed out. 'As long as there's *some* meat in it, and plenty of potatoes, it'll keep the poor souls going. Better'n what they're getting, anyway. That Miss Snoddy at the school says some of the children are so hungry they just fall asleep at the desk, can't work a lick. She gives up her own lunch to the worst cases, divides her bit of bread and cheese out amongst 'em, but she can't do much. She's thin as a winter bird herself, as it is.'

In the interests of getting the thing up and running, Beattie stopped all her other war work temporarily. Once it was established, she told Mrs Fitzgerald, she could give it one day a week – she could not spare more, as she did not mean to give up her station canteen. Mrs Fitzgerald, for once, did not argue or try to wheedle her. She had, she fancied, a better candidate in *young* Mrs Hunter, who might be strong-minded, but was much less experienced in resisting.

Young Mrs Hunter had quickly become an accepted part of the household. Mrs David, as the servants referred to her, was reckoned to be a very nice, agreeable young lady with no 'side' to her, and never forgot to thank a person. But she was no push-over, either. Servants did not like to work for people who were not accustomed to having servants and didn't know how to go on. There was nothing weak about Mrs David. And she was doing Mr David so much good, too. That alone secured her a place in their hearts.

As Beattie had predicted, David had no difficulty in finding pupils, and saw them for several hours a day in his upstairs sitting-room. Another part of the day was dedicated to his exercise, which Antonia supervised, determined to get him properly mobile again. While he was tutoring, she did her war work, or performed little tasks about the house wherever help was most needed: dusting, mending – she was not above shelling peas if she happened to pass through the kitchen and see them waiting. Cook would not normally have liked gentry doing things like that in her kitchen, but Mrs David was very good to talk to. She had a way of drawing a person out, and many a good natter went on at the table while both were busy. Mrs David was interested in cooking, too: they often had absorbing talks about wartime recipes and making do.

And in the evenings, Antonia's presence had brought light and life to the house, and not only because she had got David downstairs and joining in with the family again. She was good fun in her own right, full of ideas, always good-tempered – filling, a little, the space Bobby had left empty. She played the piano, and for the first time since Diana had left home, there was music and singing in the evenings. Edward commented to Beattie that the house seemed like a home again. He did not say it with any intention of hurting Beattie's feelings, but it added to the burden of guilt she carried. She knew she had been neglecting him; betraying him was so bad she could not let herself think about it.

Edward's new superior, Lord Rhondda, was a more energetic master than Lord Devonport, and he was busier than ever, with meetings and campaigns; and he still had his work on the appeals tribunal. The hardship appeals were as difficult to hear as ever, but there did not seem to be any increase in pacifist objectors, as he might have expected as the war ground on. Of the 'conchies', many agreed to be stretcher-bearers or ambulance attendants at the Front; others were sent to the Non-Combatant Corps or labour gangs at home. Only those who refused to do anything at all were sent to prison, and Edward always tried to talk them out of such absolutism, for they were not popular with other prisoners, and were frequently attacked. About twenty a year died in prison. He could be eloquent on the subject; but there were always some who preferred to be martyred for their cause, and the only thing you could do for them, he decided sadly, was to let them get on with it. His fellow judges thought his attitude overly sentimental. It'd be better for everyone, they said, to shoot the conchies and be done with it.

All this activity had to be fitted in with his work at the bank and the servicing of his clients. At least he was not obliged to be away from home so much, persuading landowners to switch from pastoral to arable. There were now local War Agricultural Executive Committees, which could issue a Notice to Cultivate, and if a farmer neglected to comply, he was guilty of a summary offence against the Defence of the Realm Act. DORA, as it was unaffectionately known, gave the government almost unlimited powers to get done what was needed in any sphere, and Lord Rhondda had it vigorously applied to food production. The carrot that went with the stick was that the Corn Production Act had fixed the price of cereals for five years, so that land-owners making the change could be reassured the investment would pay off.

What with one thing and another, he had not seen Élise for many weeks; and when he did manage to call one evening, Solange answered the door, and told him Madame was out.

'Out?' Edward said in surprise. He checked himself – there was no reason she should not have been out: he had not told her he was coming. He tried to smile at Solange, which was not easy when she glowered at him like a particularly grim gargoyle. 'I'm sorry to have missed her. Will you tell her I called?'

He'd have liked to ask where she was, but didn't want to seem to pry. But Solange, unexpectedly, enlightened him. 'Parties!' she said, spitting the word distastefully. 'All ze time, parties! Men! Pah!'

'Men?' Edward couldn't help querying.

'*Musiciens. Danseurs. Acteurs.*'

'Oh,' said Edward. People she was meeting in her new job as dancing-mistress, he supposed. All men? Probably not. Solange was exaggerating. 'I'm sure they're nice people,' he said.

'*Lie de la société,*' Solange spat. Dregs of society. She met his eye challengingly, '*Ils ne sont pas "comme il faut", ces gens.*' The implication seemed to be, I did not approve of you, but you were better than this lot, anyway. And with a final nod, she shut the door on him.

Edward walked away. *Men?* he thought. She had been a ballet girl in Paris, and he knew – he thought he knew – how that game went. He felt a pang of jealousy. It was not, of course, he told himself hastily, *sexual* jealousy. He was sure

251

these new friends were just that – friends. Solange hated anyone coming between her and her mistress.

But Élise had come to him, exiled from Belgium, friendless and alone, and he had helped her. He had befriended her, defended her, taken care of her finances. It was as though he had taken in a bird with a broken wing, and now the wing was healed, it had flown away. But he would not allow himself to feel jealous. He must be pleased for her, if she had found her feet and made new friends. He had always thought it unhealthy for her to rely on him so much.

He did, however, now have to find somewhere to have supper. He turned into Shaftesbury Avenue, and almost ran into Christopher Beresford. 'Hullo!' he said, with pleasure. Since they were no longer going on their jaunts up-country, he had hardly seen the young man. 'Fancy meeting you here!'

'Hullo, sir,' Beresford said with an amiable grin. 'How are things in banking?'

'Oh, pretty well. War is always good for business. Had any interesting trips lately?'

'One or two. I was in Scotland recently – but I'm probably holding you up?'

'No, I was just thinking about a spot of supper. You're not at a loose end, by any chance?'

'Actually, I am. I was eating with someone and they've chucked.'

'Well, what say we strap on the nosebag together? If you haven't any other plans?'

'I'd like that. How about the Garrick? I'm a member, and it's just round the corner.'

They walked off together. 'So how are things at the Board of Agriculture?' Edward asked. 'They must worry about losing you to conscription.'

He gave a rueful smile. 'Unfortunately, I'm not the right material for a Tommy. Trouble with my feet.'

'I would never have known,' Edward said politely.

'I have special shoes made. I wish it were something more glamorous – you can guess I'm always being asked by lovely females why I'm not in uniform.'

'Tell them you're in the Intelligence Corps,' Edward suggested. 'I would.'

Beresford grinned. 'Thanks – I'll remember that. How is your family? Your son got married, didn't he?'

'Yes, and they're living with us for now, which is comfortable.'

'And your other daughter – I saw her picture in the paper a while back. You must be very proud of her.'

'I am. And I'm sure she'd love to tell you all about it. You should come and visit us,' Edward said. He was remembering all over again how much he liked this young man. 'Come and have dinner, and stay the night. We can find a bed for you.'

'I'd really like that – thank you, sir.'

'Excellent. What about next Saturday? That's settled then. And now tell me about Scotland. Was it tractors again?'

'Tractors,' Beresford affirmed with a grin, as they turned up the steps of the club.

School finished for the summer, and William and Peter came home to tear off their uniforms, untidy their hair, and make a joyful noise for a short, celebratory time. Peter had friends ready and waiting for him to go on jaunts on bicycles and into the woods, not forgetting his duty to catch rabbits and fish whenever possible to help out the food budget.

William, having let off steam, was quieter. Edward, coming home on Saturday afternoon, found him unexpectedly – for the day was fine – sitting at the morning-room table with a large book.

253

'Hullo, my son,' he said approvingly. 'That's a good idea – do a little school work every day, so you don't forget it all before September.'

'Oh, well, it's not exactly . . .' William began, with a blush.

'You'll be going into the sixth form next term,' Edward pursued. 'A lot of new challenges. You might do worse than let your brother tutor you for an hour now and then. I'm sure he won't charge, within the family.'

William did not smile at the little joke. He pushed the dark hair away from his brow, met his father's eyes with a worried look, and said, 'The thing is, Father, I don't think I want to go into the sixth form.'

'Not go? What is this? Of course you'll go into the sixth form, and then to Oxford. It was all decided long ago.'

William was the child who looked most like Edward: the long, oval face, dark eyes, the basic gravity. He took things seriously. It was like looking at a younger version of himself. And if William said something like this, it was not because he had not thought about it. 'I don't want to go to Oxford, either,' said William. Absently he turned Bobby's watch round and round on his wrist as he spoke. It was too big for him still.

Edward noted the movement. 'Is this about the war? It's not your fault that you're not old enough to serve.'

'I can't go into the services,' William said, 'but there is something I can do. You see, we had this chap who came and gave us a talk last week. I've been thinking about it ever since. It was so interesting – it was about the new aircraft factory over at Coney Warren. They've started production now, and they need chaps – bright chaps.' He blushed a little at the implied self-praise. 'He said there are opportunities. And you know it's always been something I've been interested in.'

'That's true,' said Edward. Even before the war, William

254

had liked to cycle over to the airfield at Northolt and watch the aeroplanes taking off and landing. 'What are these opportunities?'

'Apprentice aircraft designers,' William said eagerly. 'It's the most important thing for winning the war, he said – designing new aircraft. The Germans do it very well and they keep winning in the sky. We've *got* to catch up. He said they need the best brains, and chaps who are really enthusiastic and can think for themselves. And it isn't just for the war, Dad,' he went on hastily. 'After the war, he said, air travel is really going to take off.' He caught his verbal foot in the unintended pun, stumbled, and went on: 'Everyone will be flying, all over the world, and there'll have to be new types of aeroplane designed all the time. It would be a proper career for life.' He looked anxiously at his father, to see if he'd got his point across.

'I see,' Edward said.

William translated this as disapproval. 'I know I've got the brains to go to Oxford, but this is something I *really* want to do, and isn't it better to do something your heart is in? If it's a good thing anyway, I mean – and this is a good thing, isn't it?'

'It sounds as if it is,' said Edward.

William gave the watch another turn. 'And it's for Bobby,' he concluded. 'I can't bring him back, but I can do this for him. I think he'd want me to.'

Edward laid his hand on his son's bony shoulder. William had put on a spurt of growth this year, but with the tallness there seemed to come thinness, as if his material were being stretched without being added to. He would never be a giant as David was – or had been before he was wounded. William was destined to be tall and thin, like his father. Tall and thin and serious.

'If you want to leave school and apply for one of these apprenticeships – if you've really thought about it—'

'I have, really I have. It's all I want,' William said.

'Then I think that is what you must do. As you say, a man should do what his heart is in, if it's a good thing.'

William beamed with pleasure and relief. 'I won't let you down, Dad. I'll be really good at it, I know I will, and it'll help to win the war. I've already been drawing some aeroplanes, with things I've thought of, features I think will improve them. Would you like to see?' From under the book he drew out a sketch-pad.

'I would like to see them very much,' Edward said gravely.

CHAPTER SEVENTEEN

There had been a letter from John Courcy to Mrs Cuthbert, saying that he was getting leave, but would not be able to come to Highclere as he must go to Scotland to see his father. 'It will mean most of the leave is taken up with travel, but I have hardly seen him since the war began, and I gather he's unwell, so I must do my duty,' he wrote.

He included a note for Sadie, which said,

I just wanted to tell you that we saw the newsreel about Highclere over here, some weeks later than it circulated at home. You looked splendid, and very professional. All the girls looked competent, and I gather from Mrs C that you do a lot of the training, so well done! I'm sorry I shan't get to see you this time. I expect I shan't get back again until Christmas. We are so busy here, and never have enough hands. We could really do with a troop of you young ladies to help out. How is my friend Nailer? Yours, in haste, J. Courcy

Sadie folded it into her pocket and went about her work. How things had changed since before the war, she thought. Then it would have been improper of him to write to a young lady to whom he was not engaged. Now all sorts of people wrote to each other.

But of course, she thought, as she got on with her share

257

of the mucking-out, he did not see her as a young lady: she was just Sadie, the horse-mad little girl who helped out at the stables. There was nothing in this correspondence that any parent could object to. He was not interested in her in *that* way, and he never would be. She had thought at one time that he might, perhaps, one day . . . But she had to face the fact now that her love for him was unrequited, and if she had any sense at all, and any pride, she would dismiss him from her thoughts and get on with her life.

She straightened up, pushing her hair back from her forehead and accidentally dabbing it with a smear of manure, like a chrism. *Horse-mad little girl.* She ought to have thrown away his note but, unaccountably, she forgot to do that. And, even more unaccountably, when she got home and found it in her pocket, she did not take the new opportunity of disposing of it, but put it carefully into the little box in her bedside drawer where she kept her treasures. *There's no harm in it!* she protested inwardly. And *No-one will ever know.*

A few days later, a very pleasant dinner, with lively conversation, followed by some foolish round games, lots of laughter, and songs around the piano to finish, made a nice traditional family evening that Christopher Beresford enjoyed as much as anyone.

In the morning he suffered the usual fate of the house guest staying for the first time, and went down to breakfast too early. But he was soon joined by Sadie, who did not stand on ceremony but went and fetched the coffee, and they had a pleasant quarter-hour talking together before anyone else disturbed them.

'Last night was such fun,' he said. 'I don't have family evenings like that now.'

'Oh dear, why is that?' she asked.

He told her that his father, who had been a book publisher, had died in 1914, and his mother, who was an invalid, had gone to live with his older brother, a canon at Lincoln Cathedral. 'So I don't get to see them very often. It's too far to travel, and the house is so tiny, they don't have a bed for me.' The family home in Highgate had been sold, and he had been sharing a flat in Baker Street with his sister. 'But Catherine's away now, in France, with the FANY, so I don't get to see her, either.'

'I don't know how I'd survive without my family,' Sadie sympathised.

'I suspect you're the sort of person who would always survive,' he said. 'I so admire your work with the remount depot. You must have shown real determination in the beginning to be allowed to do it.'

'Why do you think that?'

'My sister and her friends had to battle like Valkyries to get permission to nurse, or drive ambulances, or do anything else at all interesting.'

'But things are changing now,' Sadie said. 'No-one thinks twice about me wearing breeches and boots. Or hardly anyone. And my parents weren't so bad. I think I benefited from being the second daughter. My sister Diana's such a beauty that all the ladylike ambitions naturally centred on her.'

'I've seen pictures of her in the illustrateds,' Beresford said. 'She *is* a beauty. But, if you'll excuse my saying so, you're very handsome yourself.'

'Me? No, I'm just ordinary,' she said dismissively.

Seeing she was embarrassed by the compliment, he changed the subject quickly, and asked instead what books she enjoyed, and the conversation became lively again, and easy. A thunder on the stairs made Sadie break off to say, 'That's the boys coming down.'

'I've so enjoyed talking to you,' he began, realising his time was short. 'I wonder—'

Peter appeared in the doorway and said, 'Isn't breakfast

in yet?' He cannoned into William as he turned away. 'I'll go and get it.'

'No, don't,' William said, afraid of showing them up before the guest. He made a comical face of regret and resignation and hurried after his brother.

Sadie smiled and shook her head. 'It's always like this in the summer holidays.'

'I wonder,' Beresford went on with determination, picking up his sentence, 'whether you would like to go to the theatre with me one evening. There's a rather interesting play by Barrie I've been meaning to see.'

Sadie could hear Peter's voice raised in protest against William's quiet muttering, and knew they were on their way back, so privacy was about to end. Beresford was looking at her as if it really mattered to him, and she had enjoyed their conversation. Well, why not? she thought. It might be fun. 'I'd like that,' she said. 'If Mother and Father say it's all right.'

She was sure they would. Father wouldn't have invited him to stay if he didn't approve of him. And Mother wouldn't care. She'd given up on Sadie long ago.

'Another letter from your nephew?' Ada said. 'He's getting to be a real good correspondent, isn't he?'

Cook gave her a suspicious look, but it seemed to be said in all innocence. 'Yes,' she said. 'Ronnie's a good boy.' She thrust the letter back into her apron pocket for later and got on with marinating the venison for upstairs dinner. It was good to have a decent-sized bit of meat to work with, and she wasn't going to ask questions as to where it had come from. That new boy from Stein's the butcher's had asked if she wanted any when he brought the sausages and bacon. She suspected if she'd seen the whole carcass there might have been wheel-marks on it, but she just got a shapeless lump of meat wrapped in butcher's paper. When she asked him what cut it was, he stared at her with his mouth open, so she asked no more. The rest wasn't her business.

Fred's letter had to wait until bedtime. She took her cocoa up to enjoy with it.

Well, what you think? I seen some Yanks. I was sitting on a burnt-out car at the sider the road when along comes this company, all in bran new uniforms and shiny new boots, not even dusty. My word! They looked like gods. Your average Tommy is a scratty little runt, five foot five and dressed in rags. This lot was six foot to a man. You never saw such healthy blokes. And white teeth flashing like heliografs, cos they were marching along grinning and looking round like theyd just stepped off a charabang. I see a sergeant and he catches me looking and gives me a nod, so I shout, 'Got a fag, mate?' and he slings me a packet. I was trying to take one out, when he shouts, 'Keep em!' And he gives me a grin and marches on. If they get into the war, my word, the Huns will run like rabbits. I heard they getting all their food and everything sent straight from America, because they dont like 'foreign food', which is what they call everything else. If what we get is 'foreign food', I dont like it either! Now, Pretty Peggy, dont you fret, because Im not where the bad fighting is. Your soldier lad is safe and sound. Theres always something going on, but trust me to duck when a whizz-bang comes over! I got your letter, pretty fair effort, but write more next time. I want to know all about what your doing.

And he finished it with a row of Xs and Os. Cook had to guess they were kisses and hugs, because she couldn't very well ask anyone. She gave a satisfied sigh as she folded the letter and put it under her pillow. It was very nice to have a man write to her from the Front and call her Pretty Peggy.

261

What would happen after the war, she didn't want to think about. That was a long, long way off. Sufficient unto the day, as they said Sundays.

They had never seen rain like it. It had fallen as though the sky were a lake that God had simply flipped upside down. Months' worth had fallen in days. The semi-circular area in front of Ypres was in any case flat and low-lying, and the traditional barrage that had preceded the big push had broken the drains and blocked the ditches, causing even worse flooding. The British assault had foundered in the mud and had had to be halted, for it was impossible to advance, to use tanks, or to bring up guns or supplies.

The violence of the rain had passed, and now it simply rained constantly from a sky like grey dish-rags. Sometimes it intensified and sometimes it lessened, but it never, ever stopped. Laura had ceased to notice any more as it dripped from the end of her nose and plastered her hair to her head. She had abandoned a hat, because the drips from the brim obscured her vision, and any hat eventually soaked through. Once hair was wet, it couldn't get any wetter, she reasoned. She had acquired an officer's gabardine trench-coat, complete with gun-flap across the chest and useful D-rings on the belt, and under that she wore breeches, long boots and an oiled-wool Guernsey, and managed to stay pretty comfortable. But by the end of the day, the water had always seeped through. After a while, you stopped thinking about it.

Despite the cessation of the offensive, they were still busy. There were casualties every day, some due to the Germans, who still sent over shells and bullets, and some to accidents and sickness. But Bessie the ambulance never went further forward than Ypres now. Casualties were brought back from the line by stretcher, because vehicles could not get up there – a hideous journey with the bearers slipping and slithering and trying to pick their way round the mires and the shell holes that reduced the passable land to a kind of lace. Supplies going up to the line had to be taken by trains of pack-horses: you saw them day and night, picking their way along the slatted wooden causeways the engineers had laid. If a horse or mule slipped off into the mud, the chances of getting it out again were not good. Many of them had to be shot where they were, up to their shoulders in the sucking grey clay. There was a special page in the officers' manual on how to shoot a horse: the British Army, though not notoriously sentimental, did not expect the ordinary Tommy to have to destroy the horse he loved.

Even on the right side of Ypres, between there and Poperinghe, where Bessie plied her trade, going was hazardous. With all the lying water, it was impossible to tell which was a shallow puddle you could splash through, and which concealed a shell hole that would break Bessie's back. They kept a six-foot pole in the back, with which to test.

And this afternoon they were in trouble. Everyone wanted to keep to the centre of the road where the going was best, and no-one was willing to yield ground. They had met a gun limber racing the other way, and Louisa, who had been driving, had flinched first. Bessie was now stranded with a wheel stuck in the muddy ditch at the side. Laura had got out to investigate and determined that they needed help, so she was sitting on the running-board waiting for someone to come along. Louisa was staying dry in the cab; Annie and Flora were in the back, comforting the wounded. They had lost Elsie Murray, their qualified doctor, from the team: she had decided her skills were more urgently needed elsewhere, and was volunteering at a hospital in Étaples.

Laura smoked philosophically in the rain, keeping the cigarette dry by holding it under the palm, as the Tommies did. She thought briefly of her brother, how he would sigh at this further proof of her degeneration: not just smoking, but smoking so inelegantly! But she doubted they could have got through the days without cigarettes. Annie and Flora both smoked, and even Louisa, who had held out against it, had one or two in the evening when they were back at their billet in Poperinghe – Pop, as everyone called it. It was a derelict farmhouse on the outskirts, one half of which had been bombed, but it had a sitting-room and kitchen still sound, which they used as their bedroom and living-room respectively, and most importantly, a large barn with a good roof where they kept Bessie, and where Laura, aided by Louisa, carried out the almost daily repairs. Laura doubted poor Bessie was much longer for this world. The terrible state of the roads was taking its toll. And what, then, would they do?

A cart was coming from the direction of Ypres. It was pulled by a very weary horse, plastered with grey mud right up to the traces; mud hung like stalactites from its belly hair and the ends of its tail. A squat Belgian in shapeless work clothes was driving it, and in the back were four Tommies, one lying on a heap of sacks and the other three sitting with their legs hanging over the back. Laura got up and held up her hand. The horse didn't wait to be told, but stopped, hanging its head as soon as the reins were slackened. It was too tired even to cock one hind foot, but stood in the rain, steaming faintly, knees sagging.

'Can you give us a hand?' she called to the soldiers. 'Or are you hurt?'

'Sid here is,' said one of them, in a Cockney accent. 'But he ain't too bad – busted ankle, we reckon. You nurses?'

'FANY, ain't you?' one of the others improved the offer.

'No, we're volunteers, but we've all done first-aid courses, and one of us is a trained nurse. Would you like her to have a look at your friend?'

'That's right nice of you, miss.'

'And, in return, can you help us get out of the ditch?' She looked speculatively at the horse.

264

The first Tommy saw the direction of her gaze and grinned. 'He can't help you. He's about done for, poor bugger. Couldn't pull the skin off a rice pudden. Me and me mates'll get you out, won't we, lads?'

They jumped down, and Laura went round the back to open the doors and call Annie and Flora to get down and lighten the vehicle.

'We've got some wounded in here,' she told the Tommies. 'Heading for the hospital in Pop. Can't ask them to get out.'

'Don't you worry, miss, we can manage.'

Laura mentioned the injured lad on the cart to Flora, the trained nurse, who climbed up to examine him, while the other three soldiers, along with Laura and Annie, found hand-holds on Bessie's carcass, ready to push, and Louisa turned on the engine. In a few minutes, they were back on the road.

'Thank you, gentlemen,' Laura said. She fumbled under her coat and drew out a rather squashed packet of Woodbines from her breeches pocket. 'There's only three in there, I'm afraid, but perhaps you can share them.'

'Ta very much,' they said. And 'Maybe you better foller us to Pop, 'case you come another cropper.'

'Is that where you're heading?'

'Yeah. We got separated from our platoon when Sid got hurt, and this officer we met told us to go and report to the HQ in Pop to sort us out. And this geezer,' he jerked a thumb at the patient Belgian, who sat on the front of the cart like something carved out of it, 'stopped for us when we give him the thumb.'

'Well, we must get our wounded back as quickly as possible. Thank you very much for your help.'

''Sall right, miss. What's gone of Sid's leg, then?' he added, as Flora got down from the cart.

'Not broken – just a bad sprain,' she said. 'I've bound it up as best I can. Don't let him walk on it. He'll need to rest it several days at least.'

They all got back into the ambulance, waved to their protectors, and drove off.

'I'm sorry,' Louisa said, after a bit. 'I shouldn't have pulled over so much, but he was coming at such a rate—'

'It's all right,' said Laura. 'No harm done.'

'Keeping the wounded waiting like that,' she mourned. 'But I really thought he was going to hit me. And I'm so tired,' she added pathetically.

Laura looked at her properly for the first time that day. They had been too busy for any personal interaction. 'I think you've got a cold coming,' she said. 'You look a bit feverish.' Louisa was flushed, and her eyes were glassy. 'How are you feeling?'

'Not terribly well,' she admitted. She shivered. 'It's being wet all the time. I get cold, and then I can't seem to get warm again.'

'You'd better let me drive,' said Laura.

'No, I'm all right.'

'Pull over – look, there's a wider place just there – and we'll swap.' The change-over was quickly accomplished. 'And there's a dry sack behind the seat. Put that round your shoulders. I really should have been keeping an eye on you,' she chastised herself, as she put the ambulance into gear and eased forward again.

'You're not responsible for me,' Louisa said.

'Well, I rather think I am,' Laura countered cheerfully. 'I persuaded you to come out here.'

'It's just a bit of a cold. I'll be all right once we get home,' Louisa said, listlessly.

The long summer days started to shorten noticeably in August, and the low grey sky brought on dusk yet earlier. It was not terribly late when they delivered their four wounded to the hospital, but Laura called Annie and Flora to conference, and when they learned Louisa was unwell, they agreed – with some relief – to call a halt and go back to billet. It

266

was always hard to know when to stop, because there were always more wounded out there, and their suffering was so much greater than any inconvenience Bessie's team might endure. But they were not new to the job now, and had learned that a balance had to be found because they were no use to anyone if they did not take care of themselves.

At the farm they drove Bessie into the barn. Annie and Flora got on with cleaning her out while Laura hustled Louisa into the farmhouse. There was a closed stove in the kitchen, which they had left banked for the day, and happily it was still warm. Laura opened the dampers, poked it up and put in more fuel, while ordering Louisa to take off every scrap of wet clothing and wrap herself in a blanket. When the stove was roaring she said, 'I'm making you a hot drink, and then it's a hot bath for you.'

Louisa had no argument. She sat shivering, lethargic with fever. When the water was on to boil for cocoa, Laura found a towel and rubbed Louisa's hair vigorously. She made the cocoa, filled the bath, and got Louisa into it, with the mug in her hand, blankets draped over a towel horse to screen out draughts. Meanwhile she warmed some clothes against the hot stove, and by the time Annie and Flora came back in, she had got her friend out, dry, and dressed in a motley assortment of underthings, trousers, jumpers and socks.

'How is she?' said Annie, dripping into the kitchen. Looking at her, Laura only then realised how wet they had all been.

Flora went across to feel Louisa'a forehead, look in her eyes and peep into her throat. 'A bit feverish,' she said. 'I expect it's a cold. We all got pretty soaked through yesterday. Even I was shivering.'

'How are you feeling now, Lou?' Laura asked.

'Warmer. Sleepy,' Louisa answered.

'Well, bundle yourself into that armchair and put the blanket round you, while we see about supper.'

'I'm not hungry,' Louisa said.

'Never mind. You have to eat. Doesn't she, Flora?'

'Feed a cold and starve a fever,' said Annie. 'That's what my nanny used to say.'

They all had some cocoa to warm them up while they were waiting, and Annie, who was proving quite a dab at making meals out of not very much, created a kedgeree out of a tin of salmon and a bag of rice she found in the cupboard, a handful of raisins, and a spoonful of curry powder which was one of the stores she had brought with her from home. This proved unexpectedly tasty, and they followed it up with several slices of bread and jam. The bread was a bit stale, so Laura toasted it slightly on the stove. The jam was only plum and apple, in a tin, army standard issue – they had finished their home-brought jam weeks ago – but they all craved sweet things and it was a great deal better than nothing. Afterwards they had more cocoa.

'What would we do without it, blessed stuff?' Annie said. 'I can't remember what coffee tastes like.'

Flora fetched a dry packet of cigarettes from the kitchen cupboard where they kept their stock. The cigarette made Louisa cough, and coughing made her sleepy, so Laura took the rest away to finish herself, and they put Louisa to bed with all the extra blankets they could find.

'Nice,' she said drowsily. 'I'm warm now. Thanks.'

Flora laid a hand on her forehead and said, 'See if you can sweat it out. You'll probably feel better in the morning.'

Back in the other room, they drew up close to the stove to finish their cigarettes. Outside the rain fell busily, gurgling in the downpipes, and setting up a counterpoint of drips and patters from broken gutters and holes in the roof.

'If she's not better,' Flora said, after a bit, 'she mustn't go out in this. I suspect it's only a cold, but colds can turn into pneumonia.'

Laura said, 'I think this life is too much for her. She's not tough like us.'

Flora looked surprised. 'I always thought she was tough as nails. I'm the weakling of the group. I can only just hold up my corner of a stretcher. And I'm no help with changing wheels.'

'Yes, but you've robust health, and a mind to go with it,' Laura said. 'Louisa's more delicate inside. I'm beginning to believe she's had enough of this job.'

Annie looked at her cannily. 'Does that mean *you* have?'

Laura looked uncomfortable. 'You make me feel guilty. I know it's important work, but—'

'You're restless. You want a change.' She sighed. 'The weather is tiresome, but it can't go on raining for ever.'

'Can't it?' Laura laughed. Then she said, 'Don't worry. I won't abandon you without warning. But—'

'You're giving your notice,' Annie finished for her.

'Perhaps. We'll see. Just now, I'm for turning in, while I'm still warm.'

In the morning, Louisa was feverish, and had a racking cough. She obviously was not well enough to go out on the road.

'And I'm not happy about leaving her here,' Laura frowned. 'This place is cold and damp, and what if she gets worse? We'll have to find somewhere better for her – a hotel or something.'

Louisa didn't feel well enough to argue, a telling point.

'We'd better drive into Pop, then,' Annie said, 'and see what we can find.'

They had breakfast – bread and jam and cocoa – then Laura went out to the barn to coax Bessie into life and backed her out. They all squeezed into the cab and drove up the road into Pop. It was looking a bit battered now, partly from stray shells and air raids, but mostly from the

269

passage of thousand upon thousand of soldiers. They said everyone in the army passed through Pop at some point: it was the jumping off and landing place for many going to and coming from the Front. Short leaves were spent there, transit troops were billeted there, and convalescents from wounds not bad enough to require repatriation enjoyed its pleasures. As Bessie crept through the traffic in the cobbled central square, it looked as though most of the Allied troops were milling about.

In Garenstraat they saw a bed-and-breakfast sign, and pulled over, Laura kept the engine running while Annie went inside to make enquiries.

'It looks clean,' she reported, 'and they have a single room vacant on the second floor. I spoke to the landlady, and she seems a nice, motherly sort. She speaks English, and she said she'd keep an eye on Louisa. I'm not sure we can do better.'

They looked at Louisa, who nodded, heavy-eyed. 'I don't mind, as long as I can get into bed and sleep.' She coughed again, hollowly.

When they had seen her settled, and all had agreed that the landlady, Madame Vermeulen, was a decent sort and safe to leave her with, they headed out again to Bessie and cranked her into life, ready to start their day's work rather late and short-handed. As Laura eased her through the crowds, she noticed for the first time how many women were about. There were VADs and WAACs as well as FANYs, and quite a few civilian volunteers like themselves.

'I wonder where they all go,' she commented.

'At night, you mean?' Annie said. 'Back to their billets, I suppose.'

'They could hardly join in with the night life of the town,' Flora said. Pop had a reputation for rather rough bars and louche clubs – the soldier's delight.

'They ought to have a club of their own,' Laura said. 'Somewhere decent they could go and be safe, chat to each other and – I don't know – play cards or something. Somewhere with a piano so they could have some music.'

'A parlour away from home,' Annie said drily.

'Why not?'

'The men have a place in Pop, don't they?' Flora said. 'That Toc H place – Talbot House. Serving men can go there regardless of rank.'

'Isn't it run by chaplains?' Laura asked.

'Yes, but I've heard it said they're decent chaps, quite jolly and so on, not pulpit-thumpers, only they discourage swearing and drunkenness, which is all to the good.'

'If the men have a place, the women should have one, too,' Laura said.

'Nice idea, but impracticable, I'm afraid,' said Annie.

'Why?'

'Well, who would run it, to begin with?' Annie said. She glanced sideways at Laura, who was frowning over the steering-wheel, and gave a little sigh. She thought she saw the end of this particular adventure. If Laura left the team, she'd take Louisa with her, and they couldn't function with just two of them. Apart from anything else, neither she nor Flora could drive.

They cleared the narrow streets of Pop and headed out on the road to Vlamertinge and Ypres, and Laura let Bessie out a little, jolting over the ruts and keeping an eye open for water. 'There must be plenty of empty houses,' she mused. 'Most of the well-to-do natives made a run for it long since. I'm sure there'd be no difficulty in renting a suitable place.'

Annie and Flora exchanged a glance. It looked as though Laura had found her next adventure.

It was obviously not going to be possible to resume the offensive until the rain had stopped and the ground had dried out somewhat. With the suspension of the attack, the opportunity was taken to send some personnel on leave, those who had not had any in June or July.

Louis warned Beattie in a letter that he was coming back, hoping she could arrange her time so as to be with him. He wanted them to go away somewhere together, but it was not possible for her. What excuse could she use? Now that Edward was not making his trips up country, she could not even stay away for the night. She told them at home that sickness and holidays meant she must take over extra shifts at the station canteen, and go every day instead of twice in the week, and felt horribly guilty, the lies tasting sour in her mouth. What was even worse was that when Edward looked at her enquiringly, she was able to meet his gaze steadily. She was becoming a hardened criminal.

But she had to be with Louis while she could. He told her a little about the fighting at Ypres, and the terrible conditions that had brought them to a standstill. He could not convey in words the horror of the mud, but she felt it through his skin and his bones as they lay wrapped together. She had seen it in his face, thinner, older than six months ago.

'It was awful to see the horses suffer,' he said. 'Horses are designed for galloping across dry grassland. Labouring through the mud kills them. It simply breaks their hearts.' He told her how he and his runners had come across a gun limber that had gone over, with the horses stuck up to their mid-line. They had stopped to help. When the last one was got out, it was found to have a broken leg. It stood, trembling, holding a forefoot clear of the ground, exhausted from the struggle. Its trooper had held its head, pressing his cheek to the hairy forehead, stroking and stroking it and weeping, until his officer had come with his pistol to put the poor beast out of its misery. 'They love their horses,' Louis finished. 'More than their wives perhaps – at least out there, where their wives are far away and out of reach.'

She understood that he spoke of the death of horses because he could not speak of the death of men. She held him tightly, like the poor trooper, and stroked him.

They had four days together. She left the house early in the morning and returned as late as she dared at night, and at first was in a sweat of fear of being discovered. Supposing someone saw her? Supposing someone went by the canteen and saw she was not there? Supposing – she remembered the occasion when Rupert had seen them together. Supposing he took it into his head to expose her, and rang Edward? At home she made herself ill with worry, and couldn't eat, and slept only fitfully. But she could not stay away from him. And by the second evening she was so exhausted with anxiety, she felt as though she was in a dream.

Edward said, 'That canteen work is too much for you. I wish you would be kinder to yourself. But I dare say you wouldn't give it up, however tired you were.'

She said, 'I can't,' and it was the truth, but not the truth he thought he was hearing.

'What will happen?' she asked Louis.

'In Ypres?' She nodded. That was enough for now. 'I suppose we'll have to wait for the rain to stop. We'll keep on, at all events. We've *got* to keep the Channel ports. And wipe out the submarine bases. And if we can take the high ground around the Ypres Salient, we can cut their railway line.'

'People say,' she tried tentatively, 'that we ought to wait until the Americans can join in.'

The lines of weariness in his face tightened into grimness. 'That won't be for many months, not until next year, and we can't wait. The Russians are in trouble. There's been another revolution. The moderates held on, but only just, and if the Reds manage to take over, they'll make peace. We've got to hit the Huns while their attention is divided. If the Eastern Front troops are turned against us as well—'

He stopped, took a breath, controlled himself. 'We can't wait,' he said in a gentler tone. '"There is a tide in the affairs of men . . ."'

'". . . Which, taken at the flood, leads on to fortune,"' she finished the quotation. 'Is this the flood? It's just that there seem to have been so many of them. Every time we hear, "This time we'll beat them," and the war goes on.'

'It's a different kind of war,' he said. 'Nobody really knew how to fight it.'

'And do they know now?' she asked.

'We're finding out,' he said. 'As we go along. God, I'm tired of it! Let's talk about something else. Tell me about your son's wedding.'

Inwardly, Beattie winced at his choice of topic. David! There was so much she would have liked to tell him about David, but she could not. She was a bad woman, a sinner, but that was a betrayal of Edward too far.

CHAPTER EIGHTEEN

Sadie thoroughly enjoyed the visit to the theatre with Christopher Beresford. After so long toiling in the mud and manure, it was nice to get clean and put on smart clothes, to go up to London, to mingle with elegant people, to watch an entertainment that stretched her intellect just a bit – more than a Charlie Chaplin film, anyway. And Beresford was a pleasant companion, attentive to her, and with plenty to say for himself. At first, she tended to let him do all the talking, but when they came out from the theatre, she found she had opinions about what they had just seen, and that led on to other topics of discussion. She was using mental muscles that had lain dormant for months.

They had time, it turned out, for a little supper before the train, and Beresford took her to the Café Royal for omelettes. It was fun to have him point out some of the famous people there: the actor-manager Charles Hawtrey entertaining his star, Lydia Bilbrook, and an engaging bat-eared fellow Beresford thought might be a young actor called Coward; a stout man with a large moustache whom Beresford said was Conan Doyle, the author, talking very earnestly to a thin man with large eyes, long hair and a flowing necktie. Beresford thought he might be a medium – Conan Doyle had become very interested in spiritualism. The large, gentle-faced man eating cutlets and listening to a garrulous baldpate in pince-nez, he said, was Fabian Ware with Rudyard Kipling, discussing war memorials. It made Sadie feel, at least briefly, like a woman of the world.

It was astonishing, too, to see a very rich-looking dowager taking sugar cubes from the bowl on the table and slipping them into her handbag.

'Lots of people do it,' he said, when Sadie whispered to him. 'Sugar's hard to find in the shops.'

'But stealing sugar! Look at her diamonds,' Sadie protested.

'Not really stealing. And they're probably paste,' he said. And then, 'How do you think rich people get rich in the first place? Not by wasting sugar.'

And she laughed.

When they parted, he asked if he might see her again, and she agreed. Perhaps, he said, he could take her out for a drive one Sunday. He had a friend in the department who had a motor-car he could borrow. She said he might, and they shook hands goodbye.

I've had a real proper walk-out with a real proper man, she thought, as she got undressed later. *My first!* Beresford was nice. It would be no hardship to go out with him now and then. But when she lay down in bed and turned off the light, it was John Courcy's face that swam into her head. She sighed – then grew firm with herself, dismissed it, and thought about horses instead.

It was one thing to think about giving up on the ambulance, quite another to do it, when every day the work was there. Though the main action had halted, there were still little local struggles going on, attacks and counter-attacks, each side trying to keep a foothold on some ruined farmhouse or battered copse or ridge; and there were still shells.

In the middle of August there was a short but fierce action at Langemarck, which resulted, after four days, in the high ground being taken, but a lot of casualties. An aid

276

station was set up a little way along the Menin Road, and Bessie had to bring casualties back from there to the hospital. The Menin Road being a main thoroughfare from Ypres into the war zone, they were in danger on these runs from German fighters, which could come over at any time and liked to bomb and strafe anything on the ground that caught their eye. The red cross on Bessie's roof did not confer immunity, and Laura had to have Annie beside her in the cab, to keep a look-out for enemy aeroplanes while she concentrated on the road. If they were attacked, there wasn't much they could do except either drive on hell for leather if there were any shelter ahead, or if there were not, to stop, throw themselves out and hide under Bessie's body, while Flora and the wounded in the back simply lay flat and hoped for the best.

Louisa was very ill at first, with a tight, scalding fever and a dry, racking cough. Madame Vermeulen admitted herself worried, hinting at pneumonia, but after five days the fever broke and the illness resolved itself into the streaming eyes and nose and wet coughing of a normal cold. But Louisa was much debilitated, and obviously not fit to get back to work. It was all she could do to lie against the pillows and apologise feebly when any of them came to visit her. The coughing fits left her exhausted, and she had little appetite.

Laura visited her every evening, though it was an effort after a long day to get cleaned up and drive over to the house when all she wanted to do was to collapse in a chair by the stove. She now had to do all the driving, and only three of them to lift stretchers meant more strain on each of them. The fear of German air attacks also took its toll. And Bessie had developed a worrying noise, an intermittent loose, metallic sort of clang that she couldn't identify.

But she felt responsible for Louisa, and except on the evening when there was an air raid and they couldn't get back from Ypres, she went every day. Sometimes the others would go with her, but Laura didn't miss. During the second week of her illness, Louisa went through a weepy stage, beginning with floods of tears over her brother, who had died at sea when his ship was torpedoed, and going on to the war in general.

'I don't think I can keep doing this,' she sobbed, against Laura's shoulder one evening.

'Doing what, lovey?' Laura asked, soothing her head with a work-roughened palm.

'This – this ambulance thing,' Louisa said. 'I know it's important, and we're needed, but, oh, Laura! The wounds are so awful, and the suffering – those poor men! The blood and the pus . . . the smashed limbs . . . I can't bear it! If I have to see one more poor soul in agony, I shall die! And the smell! How do you bear it?'

Laura didn't answer what she knew was a rhetorical question. She didn't bear it, of course – none of them did. They just shut it down somewhere deep inside with a heavy lid and didn't listen to it. There was fire in the hold, but they kept sailing on. What else could you do? At some time, somewhere down the line, they would have to deal with the fire, and see what was left of the ship. But not here, not now.

Louisa found her handkerchief and blew her nose. She looked up at Laura with wet eyes, and said, in a dead voice, 'You've got blood in your hair. By your temple.'

'Oh!' Laura put up her hand automatically. Her hasty wash must have missed it. She said, 'It isn't mine.'

'I know,' said Louisa, and caught the hand on the way down. 'Look, there's blood under your fingernails as well.' Their eyes met. 'Don't you see?'

Laura knew what she was saying. 'It's a job,' she replied. 'Someone has to do it.'

Louisa didn't answer. She held the hand a moment longer, then lifted it to her cheek in silent tribute.

'You're hot,' Laura said. 'You've cried yourself into a fever again.'

'I'm all right,' Louisa said. 'I'll be better in a while. But I don't think I can go on doing this. I'm not brave enough.'

'Of course you're brave. You were a militant suffragist,' Laura reminded her. 'You faced all kinds of dangers.'

'Dangers to *me*,' Louisa said. 'That's different. It's other people's pain I can't bear. I'm sorry, Laura darling, but I've reached the end of my tether.'

Laura patted her hand. 'All right. Just concentrate on getting well again, and then we'll see. We'll work something out.'

On the 22nd of August, it finally stopped raining in the Salient. After the constant pattering, drumming, rushing and gurgling, the silence that followed, punctuated only by the sound of drips, was extraordinary. The occasional gleam of sunshine raised a little steam here and there from the abused earth. People came out from their houses and looked around like sleepers awakened. People stopped on street corners to talk, instead of scurrying for shelter. They talked about what would happen next. Obviously, there must be time for the ground to dry out, but the action would be resumed. Haig was not one to give up. The Salient was vital, and the high ground from Langemarck via Passchendaele to Zandvoorde must be secured. The rumour was soon abroad that Haig was changing his commanders: a new battle plan was being drawn up. And when the blood-soaked mud was firm again, the frightful pounding would be resumed. And the soldiers would march up from Pop to the Salient, and the wounded would be carried back down, and the narrow streets would echo to the clamour of wheels and hoofs on cobblestones.

Laura decided she dared not risk the strange knocking sound any more, and took Bessie to see a mechanic she had discovered in a yard behind Patersstraat. He didn't speak any English and Laura didn't speak Walloon, but the language of suffering motor-vehicles was universal. He performed his miracle, slapped his patient encouragingly on the rump, but shook his head over her long-term future. She was, Laura understood from his Basset-hound eyes and downturned mouth, on her last legs.

On the way back to the billet, she stopped at the hospital to tell them Bessie was operational again, and found one of the medical officers she regularly dealt with standing on the steps in a gleam of sunshine, smoking a thin cheroot with an air of one emerged, blinking, from a deep mine. She had never seen him outside his office before. Major Ransley was about her age, tall and thin and slightly stooping, with a thin face, thinning hair, a magnificent thin beak of a nose, and the warmest brown eyes, now she came to look at them, that she had ever encountered.

He smiled, gestured with his face to the sunshine, pulled out his cigarette case and offered her a cheroot. 'I don't know if you can stand these things,' he said. 'I find I like 'em better than the standard-issue gasper, but it's all a matter of taste.'

'Always willing to try something new,' she said, accepting one.

'Glorious, isn't it?' he said, as he lit it for her. She gathered he was not referring to the smoke, but the watery sunshine struggling through the remaining clouds.

'It will be,' she said. 'Once it gets going. I can't believe it's August. It's seemed more like March these past few weeks.'

'How's your friend? I heard on the grapevine one of you fell ill.'

Laura shook her head in wonder at the gossip-circuit of Pop, which seemed to know everything, almost before it happened. 'Yes, Miss Cotton. It was just a cold, but a nasty one. She's recovering.'

'Good,' he said. 'I'm surprised we haven't had more

280

sickness, with that atrocious weather, but I suppose people keep going when they have to.'

A pair of nurses came out and clattered down the steps, arms folded under their capes, and he moved over slightly to let them go by.

'Where do they go?' Laura said aloud, watching them walk off down the street.

'I beg your pardon?' said Ransley.

'I've noticed lately that there are a lot of women in Pop – serving women, I mean: WAACs and VADs and so on. Far more than there used to be, even last year. And yet there doesn't seem to be any arrangement made for them, anywhere for them after their duties.'

'You're right. I hadn't thought about it,' he said.

'No-one has. There's the Toc H club in Gasthuisstraat for the men, and I hear it does sterling work, but why haven't they done anything for women?'

'If you mean the army, they would never have expected there to be so many women around. No-one did. It will take time to catch up. On the other hand, if you mean the Talbot House chaps,' he went on, 'well, you've never been there, of course, but it's like – like the Remove at Greyfriars. Jolly japes and pranks and clean-minded fun. Good thing, too – I don't criticise it – but they're the sort of chaps who simply never think about females at all.'

'Whereas, you?' she said, teasing.

'Whereas I,' he said, with dignity, 'have sisters, so women are in my blood, so to speak. And you're quite right, there should be somewhere for them to go – a safe place to rest, perhaps to get advice and talk over their problems.'

'I'd like to start up a club for them, like Toc H. What do you think?'

He barely paused. 'I think it's an excellent idea.'

'Really?' She was pleased. 'It sounded good inside my head, but when I said it out loud, it was less convincing.'

'Women are rather adrift in a man's world – they need a haven. I do see. And if anyone can do it, you can,' he said. 'I've heard a lot about you. And your colleagues,' he added, but Laura had already accepted the compliment and the warmth that went with it.

'The first thing, I suppose, is to find premises,' she said, energised by his belief in her. 'I know there are lots of empty houses around.'

'You should talk to Lady Beningbrough at the Red Cross depot,' he said. 'She knows everyone in Pop. She'd be jolly helpful with raising funds, too, because I expect you'll need them. Look here, I know her quite well. Why don't I have a word with her? I could set up a meeting between you.'

'As long as you're there too,' Laura said.

'Me? Well, I'd be delighted, if you think I can help. Though I wouldn't have thought you were the type to need your hand to be held.'

'Every woman likes to have her hand held sometimes,' Laura said, then blushed because it sounded like the most blatant flirting. Fortunately, she was of an age where blushing only happened inside, not visibly; and fortunately, he seemed to find the remark amusing rather than shocking.

August had brought more Gotha raids, on the 12th, the 18th and the 22nd, but the numbers hurt had been small and, even more encouragingly, the early-warning system and the extra defences, both AA guns and aeroplanes, had proved effective. Gothas were meeting heavy fire from the ground, and aircraft, from the Royal Naval Air Service and from the Royal Flying Corps bases now encircling London, had been able to get up in time to hit the invaders heavily. Intelligence suggested that something like thirty-two of the Gothas had been destroyed or seriously damaged, which represented a great cost to the German command. Bombers were being turned back or brought down before getting as far as the coast, and fighters were learning quickly how to hit the monsters in the air. In just three months, the situation had been turned around. What had happened at Folkestone would never happen again.

On the 24th of August, the War Cabinet decided unanimously to act on a recommendation from Lieutenant General Smuts, that the RNAS and the RFC should amalgamate. It had first been suggested at the beginning of the war, but neither service would give up its air wing. The rivalry between them had bedevilled the provision of adequate air cover for three years. Now, the Gotha menace had shown that things had to change. In his report, Smuts predicted that, one day in the future, destruction of populous and industrial centres from the air on a vast scale might become the principal operation of war. Britain had to be prepared.

So in eight months' time, on the 1st of April 1918, the Royal Air Force was to be born, a third service operating independently of the other two. All RFC and RNAS personnel would be transferred to the new service, but only with their consent.

'Forbesson says they'll have their own uniform as well,' Edward told Beattie, knowing the detail would mean more to her than the wider fields of policy. 'Something quite distinct. He thinks possibly green or blue – a lighter blue than the navy.'

'Bobby would have looked good in blue,' she said, as he had known she would. 'I hope it's blue.'

William had had his interview at Coney Warren – it was the name of the farm on which the aircraft factory had been built, but had now come to signify the factory itself – and had been accepted for a place. He was to start on Monday, the 3rd of September, so he had a few more days to be a boy and roam the woods with his friends. Being William, however, he spent most of his remaining freedom reading every book about aircraft design he could get hold of, and drawing ever more elaborate flying-machines on his sketch pad.

His conversation at mealtimes was mostly about Sopwith Camels and Pups, which had proved so effective in combating the Gothas, describing their flying qualities and weaponry. He had collected a series of cigarette cards on British military aircraft, from which he gleaned much of his technical information. Only Sadie listened to him with any attention, and that was because she loved him, not because she understood. Peter, who might have been expected to be a more sympathetic audience, was more likely to leap instantly into his imitation of a fighter pilot in action and spray the table with machine-gun bullets, accompanied by what he fondly believed were realistic noises, until one or other parent told him to stop.

William was proud of getting his place, but Peter thought him a mug. 'As soon as I'm old enough, I'm going to join the cadets, and then I'm going to be a flyer. It's flyers who'll win the war. I'm going to be a famous Air Ace.'

'The war will be over before you're old enough to fly,' William said dampeningly. 'And, anyway, there wouldn't be anything for flyers to fly without the designers and engineers. They're the *real* heroes.'

Peter only said, 'Huh!' in a profoundly disbelieving voice, and went on to strafe the sideboard and window-seat into submission.

Up at Highclere, later that day, Sadie decided to tackle Inkpot, one of their problem horses. Stanhill had named the gelding: a nice-looking dark bay, with four black stockings and a curious black splotch on its rump. Inkpot was good to handle, but had an objection to being ridden: he would go along quietly for a few minutes, then explode into bucks, which did not stop until he'd rid himself of his rider. Sadie was determined to best him. The alternative fate for an unbreakable horse was the slaughterhouse.

'He's too handsome for that,' she said to Stanhill. She was caressing the bay's ears, and he was nibbling affectionately at her jumper, his eyes dreamily half closed.

'The trouble with him,' Stanhill said, 'is that he thinks. You can see him working things out and plotting. That's not natural in a horse.'

'It could be awfully useful, though,' said Sadie. 'In a well-behaved horse,' she added honestly.

'That's rather the point. What do you want to do?'

'Lunge him for half an hour to settle him down, then I'll slip quietly up and you can go on lunging him. Perhaps he won't notice the difference.'

'We can give it a try,' Stanhill said doubtfully, comforting himself that if it didn't work, at least there'd be two of them to hold on to him.

Inkpot didn't mind being lunged. He trotted and cantered easily on either rein, looking about him brightly as if enjoying the exercise. He shouldn't, of course, have been doing *that*. The steady repetition should have had him dropping his nose and going into a trance-like state, but there was something in Sadie that couldn't help being glad that he was happy in his work. She was all for freedom and enjoyment, even though in this case it boded more difficulty for her.

At last she told Stanhill to call him in, and they both made much of him. 'He's not really concentrating, you know,' Stanhill objected. 'I can practically *hear* him thinking.'

Sadie grinned at the conceit. 'He's probably thinking how nice it is that the sun's out at last.'

'He's probably thinking up new recipes for serving humans,' said Stanhill. 'Rider cutlets. *Homo rissolus.*'

'Nonsense! He loves me – look at his eyes,' Sadie said, rubbing the soft muzzle.

'Eyes tell lies,' said Stanhill. '"By their deeds shall ye know them."'

But Sadie led the horse out to the track, gave Stanhill, at the other end of the lunge rope, a nod, and quietly and smoothly mounted. She felt Inkpot's back go up as she eased her weight into the saddle, but then it went down again, and he shook his head vigorously, mouthed his bit, and seemed quite relaxed. She nodded again to Stanhill – she wanted all the commands to come from the lunge. She was just an extra burden, like the saddle. She hoped that way to get him used to the presence of a rider before the rider began to give commands.

And it worked. Inkpot walked on, and she could feel him adjusting to the weight, finding his balance. She had agreed with Stanhill beforehand to walk or canter only, since trotting would be uncomfortable for the horse if she didn't post, and distracting for him if she did, so at her next nod, he sent the gelding straight into a canter. Sadie sat close, rocking with the movement, being as much as possible a part of him, and he seemed to accept her. He was cantering smoothly, his ears pricked, not seeming to notice her at all. Triumph filled her, and she had to stop herself petting him.

It was when they changed rein that the trouble came. As soon as the office came to canter, his ears flattened, and Sadie caught a glimpse of white eye as he rolled it back at her. He gave a great leap forward, throwing his head up to try to shake off the rope, then put his head down and began to buck. He bucked like a professional rodeo horse, with slamming energy and dedication, without pause, arching his back and throwing an extra twist in from time to time at the height of the curve. He was determined to get that thing off his back, and Sadie knew she couldn't hold out for ever. At the next high snap she went flying.

It was a long way to the ground, and she slammed into it so hard the breath was driven out of her and everything went black. When sight came back to her, she struggled to breathe – somehow her rhythms had been interrupted and she couldn't remember exactly how to do it.

And there was Hugh Stanhill, kneeling beside her, clutching both her hands and babbling something. She wanted to say, *The horse! Don't lose the horse!* But her lungs were empty. Things were going black again, when nature took over and she gave a great crowing gasp and sucked in the life-giving air. 'I'm all right,' she croaked. 'Just winded.'

'Oh, thank God!' Stanhill cried. The next moment his arms were round her, he had pulled her up against him, was clutching her tightly and frantically kissing her hair.

Horrified, she struggled, and managed at last to push him back, but he used the space only to kiss her cheek and was evidently heading for her mouth. 'Stop! Don't!' she cried, twisting her face away, pushing with determination and getting free at last. 'Don't do that!' she cried.

He transferred his grip to her hands, and said, 'I thought you'd broken your neck! I thought you were dead! Oh, my darling!'

'Don't *say* that!' she cried. 'You mustn't—'

He was kissing her hands, one after the other. 'I must! I thought I'd lost you.'

She snatched them back. 'Please, Mr Stanhill,' she said, trying for calmness. 'You really mustn't kiss me. It isn't right.'

'You mean, someone might see,' he said, with a smile of complicity that made her want to hit him.

'No! I mean I don't *want* you to!'

That gave him pause. He sat back on his heels, looking puzzled, hurt.

Sadie began brushing herself off, so as not to look at him. 'You'd better catch Inkpot, before he breaks the rope or trips himself.'

But he was not so easily put off. He stood as she did, and

287

placed himself before her. 'I don't understand,' he said. 'You don't want me to kiss you? You mean, not *here*?'

'Not anywhere,' she said firmly, not meeting his eye.

'But – I thought we were walking out.' She didn't know how to answer. 'We've been to the pictures. To cafés together. We— I thought – I thought you liked me.'

Now she had to face up to it. 'I'm sorry,' she said, aware that her cheeks were red, ashamed that she had not been more careful. 'I *do* like you, but only as a friend. It was – a misunderstanding. I thought we were going out just as friends. I could never—'

'Never?' he anticipated her. 'If you like me, surely I can hope? If we go on spending time together . . . You enjoyed it, didn't you?'

'I did – I do. I like your company. But, I'm sorry, it can't be more than that.'

He looked down. 'I'm too old for you,' he said.

'It's not that.' Oh, this was awful! 'I'm so sorry. I didn't mean to – to mislead you,' she said. 'You see – there's someone else.'

He looked up. 'You're walking out with someone else?'

She couldn't speak of loving John Courcy, and not only because it was a hopeless love. But Christopher Beresford – that was a proper walk-out, wasn't it? That counted. 'With a colleague of my father's. In London.'

He seemed offended now, but perhaps that was better than the dumb misery. 'I see. Well, I have been a fool. Obviously a young lady as attractive as you would have suitors. I should have realised. I'm sorry if my behaviour alarmed you. It will never happen again, I assure you.'

She wanted to put a hand on his arm, to cry, 'Don't say that! We can still be friends! We can still go to the pictures and have tea!' But she had just enough wit to stop herself. Underneath, she felt peeved with him, that he had deprived her of a perfectly good friendship; and underneath that there was a faint, a very faint, sense of triumph, that she had *two* men interested in her at the same time – she, the plain one, so unlike her lovely sister. But stronger than those reprehensible feelings was the topmost layer, a genuine sympathy for him. It must be horrid to be rejected, she thought, and she wished with all her heart she could fall in love with him, because he was such a very *nice* person; or, at least, that she could take away his present embarrassment.

Well, probably they could never be easy with each other again, and that was her fault for not being more careful. For now, all she could do was to distract him.

'I think Inkpot was going quite well there, for a while. Catch him up, and we'll give it another try – perhaps stick to a walk for now. I'm sure we can cure him, if we're patient. He's too good a horse to waste.'

'And he loves you,' said Stanhill. 'Look at his eyes.'

But he said it so quietly, as he was turning away, that she decided afterwards she had misheard him.

'I won't suddenly abandon you,' Laura said. Annie and Flora regarded her from the other side of the stove, their hands wrapped around cocoa mugs for comfort. 'It will take a long time to arrange. Nothing will happen for ages, if it ever does – I may not be able to get the money together. It may be just a mad dream.'

'If it's something you want enough, it will happen,' said Annie. She had wanted to bring an ambulance to France, wanted it enough to bring it into being against probability and much opposition.

'You don't think it's a worthwhile thing?' Laura said, a little hurt at the lack of enthusiasm.

There was a telling pause before Annie said, 'Yes – yes, I suppose so. Anything that helps the war effort . . .'

Flora was less tactful. 'It's Louisa, isn't it? She's squeamish, and where she goes, you go.'

289

'Flora, don't,' said Annie. 'Everyone has to find their own path through life. We wish you well, Laura, really we do.'

'I'll keep driving until you find someone else,' Laura promised. 'And, as I said, it may never happen.'

Annie sighed. 'I'm not sure how long poor Bessie can carry on – and when she goes, we may all have to pack up and go home. It's taken all my spare money to keep her going this far. I'll never be able to buy a new one.'

Laura couldn't deny that Bessie was in poor shape. 'If she does die, you'll find something else to do. Your skills and experience won't be wasted.'

'I wish I could drive,' Annie said. 'It's dawning on me now that the most useful thing any of us women could have done at the beginning of the war was to learn.'

That had been exactly what Laura had thought, but she had thought it in 1914 and acted on it. But she wouldn't be smug. 'You can still learn,' she said. 'It's never too late.'

Edward finished the appeals tribunal session, and stepped out into the limp August air of London with a slight head-ache and a sense of oppression. Élise had said he was too sensitive for the work, and though he rejected the idea vigorously – *sensitive*! It made him sound like the pudgy boy at prep school! – it was true that the cases were usually divided between the genuine and pathetic, which made him sad, and the sly and opportunistic, which made him angry.

London didn't empty in August as it used to, but there was certainly a lessening of traffic and crowds, as some families still adhered to the tradition of the summer exodus. To counteract that, there were more soldiers about, leave being taken ahead of the resumption of the offensive in France, he supposed. It had been raining again while he was inside, and though it had stopped now, the pavements were wet, and there was a smeary, stale smell, like unwashed bodies, in the air.

And he was hungry. Thinking back, he realised he had not eaten since breakfast. That might account for the headache. Hungry, a little oppressed – and a little lonely. He missed his gay trips with young Beresford, who had always cheered him up. It was interesting that he seemed to have taken a shine to Sadie. He was glad she had found an interest outside horses, for once, and at nineteen, it was natural for her to begin to notice the opposite sex. He was glad it was Beresford, who he knew he could trust to behave properly: he had not even felt it necessary to warn the young man that Sadie was extremely innocent for her age. He wondered if anything would come of it. Wartime romances, popular wisdom said, did not last. But at least it gave Sadie a chance to practise without endangering herself.

And the culmination of many strands of thought led him to wonder whether Élise de Rouveroy was at home and if she would give him supper. It had been their routine; this had been his usual evening for calling round. All that had been disrupted, first by his extra work for the food controller, and then by her sudden acquisition of a social circle. Still, it was only a step to Soho Square. He had nothing to lose by calling round, and if she was out, he could go to his club and absorb a chop with a glass of claret in solitary state.

He was aware of music all the way up the stairs, but did not associate it with his destination until he reached the door and heard it loud within. His ring was answered by Élise herself, her face flushed and bright. Behind her he could see a crowd of people, hear voices and laughter as well as what seemed to be Tchaikovsky playing on a gramophone disc.

'Édouard!' she cried, with pleasure, as she registered who it was. '*Vous voici!* How charming it is!'

'I'm sorry, you have company,' he said stiffly. 'I'll call another time.'

'*Mais non! Entrez!* You must!' she cried, catching his arm to stop him turning away. 'Some friends, it is all. *Voyez*, a party. Come and join us! There is food, there is beer, there is wine. I wish you to meet my new friends. They are all *très gentils, très amusants.* You will like them.'

She had dragged him inside and closed the door behind him, and he saw now that it was a very Bohemian crowd he was being towed towards. He felt a fool in his stiff collar and Town suit. There were bright prints, peasant blouses, dangling earrings, flowing hair, Corsair shirts. One young man's shirt was open almost to the waist, and he had bare feet. Another, he could have sworn, was wearing maquillage. There was a smell of Russian cigarettes. In the babble of conversation he detected quite a bit of French and another language he took, on the evidence of the cigarettes, to be Russian. Most of them were younger than him, though he saw one elderly woman in a fantastic turban of red and gold and a scarlet plush gown, below whose hem her feet in flat gold slippers were turned out to either side as though she was on a stand. And there was a thin ugly old man, in black Turkish trousers and a black shirt, whose white hair flowed over his shoulders; he seemed to be keeping three young women fascinated.

Élise, holding tightly to his arm, was introducing him to people, but he could not catch their names, and there were too many to distinguish them one from another. They did not seem very interested in him, anyway, and as soon as they had nodded vaguely towards him they plunged back into their conversations, held at screaming pitch to counteract the noise of the music. The old man in black, Edward saw over the heads, suddenly put down his cigarette, laid hold of one of the girls in front of him and lifted her with astonishing ease straight in the air, talking all the time as though nothing odd was happening.

He pulled Élise back as she tried to thread him through the crowd, and said, 'Who are these people?'

She raised a smiling face to him. 'My new friends,' she

replied. 'Some from the school of dance. Some I met through them. People of the theatre. From the ballet company. *Les artistes.*' She made an expressive gesture with her hands that said, Here they are, you see them, what more can I say?

Before he could summon the breath to try another sentence, a young man came up behind her, and reached past her to thrust a glass of beer into his hand. Edward had to take it or drop it. He mouthed, *Thank you*, and the young man rested his chin a moment on Élise's shoulder as he said something into her ear, then slithered away. She met Edward's eyes and shrugged. The record came to an end, and the conversation at once rose a notch, as though, against all evidence, it had been held back. Edward felt his headache tighten.

He bent his head to Élise's ear so that he needn't howl. 'I should go,' he said.

'But you have only just come,' she replied, into his ear. Her breath on his skin, the smell of her perfume so close to him, made his hair rise. 'Do not you like my friends?'

He tried to think of a polite excuse. 'I wasn't expecting – I'm not dressed for it – I'm afraid the noise is rather – I have a little of a headache.'

She pulled back to look at him and said, '*Tiens!* I see it. Poor Édouard. You came for a quiet talk and you find this!'

'I'm sorry,' he said.

She nodded kindly. 'Come tomorrow,' she said. Then she put her mouth to his ear again to be sure he heard. 'Come tomorrow. I shall be alone. We shall have a quiet supper and talk, *comme autrefois. Ça va, chéri?*'

Had she called him *chéri?* He must have imagined it. He pulled back to look at her, and she smiled at him, made a little 'bye-bye' wave of the hand, and mouthed, *Tomorrow.* He nodded, and she had turned away and slipped through the crowd before he could say anything else.

He worked his way back to the door, only then discovering

that he was still holding the glass of beer. The last two people he had to squeeze past were a young woman leaning against the wall and a young man standing over her, resting one hand beside her head as if to stop her escaping. Edward tapped his other hand, and when he looked round, put the glass into it. Then he slipped out, before anything else could happen.

All the way home, he thought about the Bohemian party, the very louche-looking young people, the crowd, the noise, the foreign languages. How could she have thought he would fit in with all that? Her new circle, he thought. Perhaps, remembering where she had come from, it was rather her *old* circle. She was reverting to her younger self, and he should be pleased for her that she was happy, among people she understood and who were like her.

He thought about her invitation for the following evening. He thought about her warm breath and her perfume. He thought about her calling him *chéri*. Had she really called him *chéri*? He could go tomorrow evening, and he could tell himself that he did nothing wrong, and he could *mean* to do nothing wrong, but he knew in his heart that that was no longer true, if it ever had been. She was Temptation, and he suspected she was deliberately placing herself in his way. If he – he shivered at the thought – if he kissed her, touched her, she would not pull away, protest. She would draw him in. They would kiss, caress, and then—

He had never been unfaithful to Beattie. He had never wanted to. He did not want to now – it was just that the old Adam, buried deeply in him, had been neglected for a long time, and was stirring restively. *Lonely*, said the deepest voice in his stomach. And above that, a lighter, fainter voice whispered sadly, *What are you for? Why do you toil? Who cares for you?*

There were always voices, if you listened for them. Best

that you did not. Shut the cellar door on them, let them whisper in their darkness, out of earshot. Life was what it was, and they all had their furrows to plough. He would send a note round to Élise tomorrow to say he could not come. And leave it at that. He had her business to keep an eye on, but anything he needed to tell her, he could do by letter. He need never see her. She would understand. She knew he was a married man; she would know he must avoid temptation.

Lonely, said the deep voice, and *Who cares for you?* came the counterpoint. Over and over, nagging at the edge of his thoughts, crying for attention. But it was only the sound of the wheels on the lines, the music of the railway. It was not real.

CHAPTER NINETEEN

September came in fine, to the relief of all. Warm days of gentle sunshine and light, drying winds were welcome not only in the Salient, but at home, where harvests were being brought in, and were good. The food shortages were much eased, thanks to the extra vegetables and potatoes that had been grown, and thanks to the success of the convoy system, which was bringing American wheat safe to shore in large quantities. The government brought in a bread subsidy, reducing the price of a loaf from a shilling to ninepence, to be paid for by an increase in income tax. And the campaign urging the well-to-do to eat less bread and leave it for the poor became more emphatic. The food controller did not want to bring in rationing, and it was hoped that this easing of the crisis would make it unnecessary.

During the summer a transformation had come over Munt, shifting him from surly rebellion to enthusiasm. He was becoming quite a bore about 'me veg'.

'Look at them onions!' he said, coming in with a basket of pale golden globes. 'You never seen onions like them in the shops!'

They were beautiful, but Cook never thought it a good idea to encourage the old man. He was uppity enough without help. 'Very nice, I'm sure, and I'll have half a dozen in my box in the larder, but you can take the rest away and plait 'em like you always do, so's I can hang 'em up.'

He was unabashed. 'Beauties, ain't they? And me runners – gor, you never seen such a crop! All that rain done 'em good. You'll have to start salting 'em, girl – there'll be too many to eat fresh. Enough to last through the winter, I wouldn't wonder.'

'How am I going to salt beans when I've got no jars to put them in?' she said, distracted. It had been bad enough with the cherries and early plums in August, when she'd no sugar to make them into jam. She'd had to bottle them instead and used up all the jars. And she had the big Victoria plum harvest, always the heaviest, hanging over her in September, looming like – like some pagan god, and she was the sacrifice. And then there'd be the apples and pears. She couldn't be dealing with all these extra vegetables as well. And she certainly didn't want to talk to Munt about them.

'You'll have to get some,' he said calmly. That was another thing – those blessed veg seemed to have turned his character. He was calm as a blessed vicar, these days, and it made her want to hit him.

'Oh, I'll *have* to, will I?' she said menacingly.

''Sright. Tell the missus to get you in a 'ole load of 'em. I got tomatoes coming on lovely, what you'll want to bottle the surplus, *and* make relish out of. Cucumbers too. Nice bit o' cucumber relish for your cold meat, come winter suppers, can't beat it.'

'Oh, go away and leave me alone!' Cook cried. 'I've got luncheon to get.'

'Ar. I'll fetch you up a nice cauli – they'll like that upstairs. Lovely and white they are. I heard you can get 'em green and purple as well. Dunno if they tastes the same,' he mused, 'but I like a nice white head, me. Talk about white, you should see my parsnips—'

'I don't want to see your parsnips, you horrible old man. *Go away!*'

His eyes gleamed maliciously. 'Seen blackberries in the hedge when I was walking up this morning. Ought to get young Master Peter to pick you a lot. Blackberry an' apple pie – lovely! And jam. Like a bit o' blackberry jelly on one o' your rock cakes, I do. You may be an awkward old besom, but you can make a rock cake, I'll give you that.'

'I'll give you the sider my hand if you don't go away!'

He reversed out of the kitchen, chuckling, and she fanned her hot face and tried to compose herself. The mention of rock cakes had made her think of Fred, her secret fancy-man. Blackberries! As if she had time to cope with the fruits of the hedgerow when she was drowning in the stuff Munt kept bringing in! Blackberry jelly, my eye! And then there were elderberries – she'd always liked to put up a bit of elderberry wine, just for emergencies. A nip of it was good in case of funny turns. And sloe gin: make that in October, and it was ready come Christmas, better than all your fancy French brandies to sip after dinner, in her opinion. Not that she'd had much experience of French brandies, but never mind. Would Fred get leave at Christmas? Would he come and see her, like he'd promised? She imagined having him at the table for the servants' Christmas dinner, and it made her go pink and warm again. But jam, jelly, wine, gin, they all needed sugar, and where was she to get that? And if she didn't get it, how was she to carry on? The Victorias, for instance: there was a limit to how much bottling was reasonable. You needed jam. The army had jam – they issued it to the soldiers, part of their rations. So the army must have sugar. A thought came to her, took hold, and she examined it from all angles, before taking off her apron, smoothing her hair, and going along to the morning-room, where the missus was working – writing letters, it looked like, as she paused at the open door.

298

Beattie looked up, and in a gesture so smooth as to be almost undetectable, she slid the sheet on which she was writing underneath a blank one. Cook noticed, without appearing to, and was first a little hurt – *as if I'd read her blessed letter!* – and then intrigued: *Who's she writing to that she doesn't want me to know about?*

'Yes, what is it?' Beattie asked.

'I beg your pardon, madam, but I been thinking about jam.'

'Jam?'

'I've hardly made any this year, with there not being any sugar about, and the plums are coming in any time, and what'll the master put on his toast? I know plum's not his favourite, but it's better than nothing, and you know what Victorias are like, madam. It'll be a flood, and what'll I do with 'em if I can't jam?'

Beattie saw the problem. 'I'm not sure I can do anything,' she said, 'except keep looking in the shops.'

'Well, madam, it did occur to me,' Cook said diffidently.

'Yes?'

'The army must have sugar. And the master's brother-in-law makes jam for the army.'

Beattie gave her a level look. 'You want me to ask the master to ask Mr Palfrey to let him have some sugar?' She considered. 'I'm sure he wouldn't do it. He'd think it was wrong.'

'There's still some late raspberries coming on,' Cook said cunningly. 'And elderberries. It's not too late to make a pot or two, just for him.'

Poor Edward, Beattie thought. He really would suffer if there was nothing to put on his breakfast toast. He worked so hard, he deserved a good breakfast. And raspberry was his absolute favourite, and elderberry was not too different from blackcurrant. 'It would be – hoarding, wouldn't it? Or profiteering?' No, it wasn't either of those. She couldn't think why it would be wrong, but she was sure Edward would think it shady.

'I don't see it would be any harm, madam. Such a tiny amount out of all the tons they must have. And they're bringing more in all the time – must be – so it's not as if the soldiers'd go short. There's no law says you can't buy sugar if you can find it. P'raps Mr Palfrey could put a few extra pounds on his next order, and the master could pay him for them, same as if he was a shop.' She paused a beat, then said, 'It'd be a crying shame to let all those plums go to waste. Wasting food's a sin, specially in wartime.'

Beattie couldn't see what harm it would be, either. It wasn't stealing. These days, when you had people to tea, if you put out a sugar bowl it would be empty the next time you turned around. People put it in their pockets to take away when you weren't looking. *That* was stealing. And it would be wrong to waste the plums. 'All right,' she said. 'I'll ask him.'

She'd find some argument to talk him round. The raspberry jam ought to do it.

Christopher Beresford borrowed his colleague's car, and took advantage of the sweet golden weather to take Sadie out for a Sunday drive. Beattie invited him to come back to tea afterwards. They had a pleasant toodle about the lanes, and talked like old friends. Sadie was a little on her guard, remembering the unhappy Hugh Stanhill episode, and determined to keep an eye on him for any signs of sentimentality so she could nip them in the bud. But the afternoon passed pleasantly without any spooniness on his part. She couldn't say that it was exactly like an outing with William, because she was intensely aware of him being a man and *not* a relative, but he said and did nothing to alarm her.

They stopped on Boxwood Heath to stretch their legs and give Nailer a run (he had insisted on coming with them – Beresford didn't seem to mind, though Sadie got it into her head that Nailer had set himself up as a chaperon), and found lots of bushes laden with blackberries. 'If only we had a basket,' Sadie said.

'We'll fix something up,' Beresford said. There was a tool box in the boot of the car, which he emptied, and lined it with dock leaves for the sake of cleanliness.

Sadie was proud of both of them when they presented Cook with several pounds of 'absolute beauties', and so enjoyed telling her how clever Beresford had been in devising a container that she didn't notice Cook's absence of enthusiasm over the gift.

'Madame de Rouveroy, sir,' said Murchison, and Edward had only time to look up, startled, before Élise was there, standing before his desk, her face taut with some emotion. He stood up hastily, waving Murchison away, hoping she would not speak until he was gone, because her unannounced presence here did not bode well.

'I – I wasn't expecting you,' he said, as Murchison closed the door behind himself.

'Do not blame that old man,' she said. 'I did not let him stay me. I was afraid if he asked, you would say no.'

'That would not happen,' Edward said, coming around the desk and gesturing for her to sit down. 'You are always welcome.'

She did not sit. 'Am I?' she said. 'You did not come to supper. I asked you to supper and you did not come.'

'I sent a note—' he began awkwardly.

'Oh, I received a *note*,' she said, pronouncing it with scorn. 'A *note*, from you, that you could not come. And then, nothing. In two weeks, nothing. So now it is me that has to come and ask – what have I done? You are angry with me.'

'Of course I'm not angry with you,' he said unhappily. 'How could I be?'

'How? I do not know. But you are – *ça se voit.*'

'I'm not, I assure you. It would be – inappropriate.'

'What is this "inappropriate"?'

'You are a client.' Even to him it sounded bald – almost insulting.

She made a face. 'Oh, is that what I am? A client. How foolish of me to think that I was perhaps a little more. Perhaps a friend.'

He reached out a hand, and drew it back. 'Please don't,' he said. 'I didn't come to supper because I was afraid. I found myself caring too much about you. I was afraid that if we were alone together, my feelings would – might – overcome me.'

She regarded him seriously, as though examining him. 'I thought perhaps you were jealous of my new friends.'

'I am delighted that you have new friends. You should have everything that makes your life pleasant.'

'Except you.'

He felt something inside him jolt at the words, as though they were a blow. 'You mustn't say that,' he said in a low voice. 'You know that I am a married man.'

'Yes, I know. You tell me so – oh, often! But, Édouard, does she love you? Do *you* love *her?*'

He did not answer for a moment, looking at her, a beautiful, desirable woman, offering herself to him. She was making herself vulnerable, holding nothing back from him. Whereas Beattie was closed and mysterious and, for him, cold. It would be easy, so easy—

The words came, it seemed, without his volition. 'In the end,' he said, 'it isn't a matter of that.'

'*Not* a matter of *love*?' she said. She considered. 'What is it, then?'

'It's a matter of honour,' he said unhappily. 'I gave my faith to her. I find I can't take it back.'

She stared. Her eyes shone, as though tears were close. 'Honour,' she said.

He felt wretched. 'It was very wrong of me to allow matters to develop as they have. Our friendship has been very precious to me. But it must not go on in this way.' He cleared his throat, unnerved by that bright gaze. 'If you like, I can refer you to someone else, who can take care of your business. Perhaps you would feel more comfortable—'

'No,' she interrupted him. 'You shall take care of business, as you have. I trust your judgement. As to *friendship*, I shall not trouble you for any more of that. You are safe from me, *Mr Hunter*.'

She was turning away. Again his hand went out, but he stopped himself. To show any warmth or tenderness at this point would be to abuse her further. Yet 'I'm sorry,' he heard himself say – not commandingly, but like a guilty child.

She turned back, and there were certainly tears in her eyes now. 'Oh, Édouard,' she said, with profound sadness. She pulled out a handkerchief from her sleeve and touched the moisture away from her eyes. Then she straightened. 'Have the kindness to open the door for me,' she said.

He hurried to comply, and as she passed him, without a look, she said quietly, 'You know where I am. If your mind changes. *Au revoir*.'

Not *adieu*, he thought. He felt as bad as she could possibly have wanted. The trouble was, he didn't believe she did want. She was a better person than him.

On the following Sunday, the 16th, Diana came to tea, bringing little Lord Dene with her, for his grandparents' sake. She was looking well, beautiful and rather glamorous in a lovely pale yellow silk suit that made her hair shine like gold coins, with pearls round her neck and at her ears, and the enormous diamond engagement ring on her finger, but she hugged everybody in a natural way, and seemed unaffectedly happy to be 'home'. She did not forget to greet the servants, and when she held George on her lap, allowed him to suck the finger with the diamond on it and use the stone as a teething-ring. She seemed, Sadie thought, less grand now she was a countess than she had as a mere Lady Dene.

Nula had come over, especially to see the baby, and took him away to the kitchen to be entertained while the family talked.

Edward asked after Rupert.

'I don't know where he is,' Diana said, 'but he's not in the Salient, I do know that. He's seen some action, and writes proudly about it. His letters are very droll. Almost like a boy writing home from boarding-school.'

'Bad food, hard beds and lack of hot water,' David said. 'There are similarities.' He was trying to be jolly about it, for Diana's sake, but he couldn't help adding, 'He won't be droll about it if he gets wounded.'

Diana wasn't upset. 'Oh, he *has* been wounded,' she said. 'Not seriously, but a piece of shrapnel cut his hand quite badly, and he had to have stitches. He's terribly proud of that, too. He says the worst thing is not being able to keep the bandage clean. He's very fastidious, you know – can't bear anything dirty near him.' She smiled round at them, and said, 'Tell me all your news. Sadie, how are things at the stables?'

'Much the same,' Sadie said. 'Except on a grander scale. We're getting two new girls next week. And . . .' She was about to add that Mrs Cuthbert had heard a rumour that Hugh Stanhill was going to be moved away, but she found herself reluctant to mention his name. It would perhaps be as well if he *did* go, though she would miss him. 'It's almost like a factory line now – horses in, horses out. We don't even give them all names.'

'I hear you've got a gentleman friend,' Diana said.

Sadie made a face. 'Don't say that. It sounds horrid.'

'What else can I call it?'

'Anyway, how did you know?'

'Issy and Lavvy Manners saw you in the Café Royal with him. He's from a literary family, isn't he? Very nice.' She nodded approval. 'Publishing's quite respectable. Obby Marlowe's cousin Dick used to work for Greene and Beresford, where your friend's father was editor.'

'Well, as you know all about him,' Sadie said, 'I don't need to say anything.'

Diana smiled. 'You're growing up,' she said. She examined her sister. 'This war's been good for you. And, William, how are you liking your job? Is it better than being at school?'

'Gosh, heaps,' William said. 'Of course, I've not been there long, still finding m' feet, but they're a topping set of chaps, and it's all *terribly* interesting.' He had been about to go on, but her attention had passed from him; and, of course, he knew no-one else was *really* interested, not in the detail. One day, he thought, when something I've helped design goes into production, *then* I'll tell them, and they'll be proud of me.

'And, David,' Diana was saying, turning her golden eyes on him, perhaps with the faintest reluctance, as if afraid of what she might see or he might say. 'you're looking so much better. Are you better?'

He nodded, with a faint, amused smile as if he knew exactly what she was thinking. 'Gosh, heaps,' he said, imitating William.

Diana flushed slightly. 'You're downstairs,' she pointed out. 'It's good to see you joining in again.'

'It's good to have some work to do, to feel I'm not just a helpless cripple,' he said, then stopped teasing her and said seriously, 'I owe it all to my lovely wife. She's the one behind the transformation.' She was standing beside his chair, and he lifted the hand that rested on his shoulder and kissed it. 'What would I do without you?'

'As it happens,' Antonia said, 'we have some news, and it seems a good time to tell it, with all the family here – don't you think, David?'

'As you please,' he said.

She waited for him to go on, and when he didn't, she said, 'You've probably guessed what it is. I'm going to have a baby.'

There were delighted exclamations. Beattie said, 'Are you sure, dear?' They had only been married two months.

She nodded. 'I saw Dr Postgate on Thursday, and he says it's definite.'

'I didn't see him arrive,' Beattie said. 'And why him? We've always had Dr Harding.'

'He didn't come here – I went to him,' Antonia said. 'I didn't want anyone to know until it was sure. And I knew if I saw Dr Harding, everyone would hear about it.' The Hardings lived in the same road, and their servants knew the Hunters'.

Edward came over to kiss her and shake David's hand. 'I'm more pleased than I can say! It's wonderful news. When is it due?'

'Not until April, I'm afraid,' Antonia said.

'If we could get it here any quicker, we would,' David said. He obviously meant it as a joke, but Sadie looked at him sharply, thinking she heard something else underneath. But he was smiling up at Antonia. He looked tired, but he always did, these days, tired underneath the day-to-day animation Antonia had given him. But he must be so happy about the baby, she reasoned. Everybody always was, but in his case, it was new life coming out of the wreck of his past, and that must make it extra special for him.

'I hope it's a boy,' she said.

'A playmate for little George,' Diana agreed. 'They'll be cousins. Won't that be nice?'

'I hope it's a girl,' David said unexpectedly. 'A girl who looks just like Antonia. And will never have to go away and fight a war.'

There was a little spiked silence. And then Edward said, 'There won't be any more wars. Once we've settled the Germans, we must make sure nothing like this ever happens again.'

David looked at him. 'Unfortunately, it isn't the men of goodwill, like you, Father, who make wars. It's the idiots and madmen. And there'll always be plenty of them.'

'However did we get so serious,' Beattie intervened diplomatically. 'Antonia, you're nearest – ring the bell, dear, and we'll have tea. I wonder how the kitchen is doing with George. They may want to hand him back by now.'

Antonia said, 'I'll go along and see if all's well. I want to tell the servants our news, anyway. I'll ask for tea at the same time.'

David's eyes followed her out of the room, and Sadie's were fixed on him. He looked so *sad*, she thought. Perhaps new life, though a great blessing, also reminded you of what you had lost.

'Will the baby live here when it comes?' William asked, breaking into her thought. 'It'd be awfully jolly – we could play with it, and teach it things. If it's a boy, it ought to learn about machinery and suchlike as young as possible. I've got an aeroplane construction kit I've never done yet. I suppose,' he added doubtfully, 'if it's a girl it will have to play with dolls and things.'

'Sadie didn't much, as I remember,' Diana said, amused.

'I'd sooner have a white rat,' Peter said. 'They're awfully intelligent. A boy at school has a white rat, and he teaches it tricks. They're not like the ordinary brown ones, Mother,' he added hopefully. 'They're very clean.'

'No rats,' she decreed.

And Sadie said, 'Poor thing, it wouldn't last long, with Nailer.'

Major Ransley had been very helpful. He set up the meeting with Lady Beningbrough, who turned out to be Belgian. She had married an Englishman and lived in England for forty years. On being widowed, she had come back to her native Pop and, having just got herself settled in 1914, refused to leave again when the war broke out. She was quite peeved about the war, seeming to regard it as a personal affront to her, and anything she could do to help defeat the Germans, in however indirect a manner, she would do.

She was a tiny creature in an old-fashioned black dress to the ankles and a tower of white hair, with a front of false curls, like a true Edwardian, and a quantity of tinkling jet ornaments and decorations. She obviously adored Major Ransley, who bowed over her hand in a courtly manner and twinkled when she flirted with him.

She listened to his introduction of Laura, then Laura's exposition of what she wanted to do, with silent attention, examining her minutely from head to toe. Finally she said, 'Good. An excellent idea. I do worry about those young women, alone in a foreign country.' She spoke good English, but with an accent. 'They are dedicated, but it is natural that they should want to have fun, as well. Let us make a safe place for them to enjoy themselves.' She nodded to herself, as though that were decided. 'I will find you a suitable house. I have one or two in mind that may serve. Have you money?'

The abrupt question took Laura by surprise, but she answered, 'I have a competence. A private income enough to live on.'

'That may not be enough. There will be rent to pay, the running expenses, staff. How will you staff it?'

308

'With volunteers,' she said.

'Ladies like you? Yes, very well, but you will need some paid staff. You will not want to be cleaning and cooking and making beds yourself.'

Laura laughed. 'We are not dainty, Madame.'

'No, I see that. But your talents will be needed for other things.'

'I agree,' said Ransley. 'The Talbot House fellows have an NCO and four privates to do the menial work. But, of course, they have official army status.'

'You,' Lady Beningbrough concluded for him, 'will have to manage some other way. You will need money. I shall give you letters of introduction to some benevolent ladies in England. Everyone applies to them, but the amounts you will need are not large, and I think you will be able to persuade them.'

But the offensive in the Salient resumed on the 20th of September, with an attack on the Menin Road Ridge, followed on the 25th with a ferocious battle for Polygon Wood. The objectives were taken, but at the cost of heavy casualties, and the fighting went on through the rest of September as the Germans counter-attacked and had to be repulsed.

So Bessie was in demand again, and Laura had little time for writing letters or looking at houses. Louisa was back with them, but even with her sharing the driving and the carrying, it was an exhausting business. Ransley was a great help, and undertook to look at houses on Laura's behalf. He came out to meet her whenever Bessie arrived at the hospital, and they had hurried but effective conversations about her preferences and needs. He had taken her scheme deeply to heart, and was determined to see it up and running before the end of the year.

'Sooner than that, I hope,' Laura said in surprise, rubbing a grimy hand over her forehead and not improving the situation. 'Three more months, with these girls having nowhere to go?'

'Then we had better find a furnished place,' he said calmly. 'Have you enough money at least to get things started?'

'Oh, I have a cheque book, and I haven't been spending a great deal over here,' she said with a smile.

'Well, I'll see what I can do. Madeleine Beningbrough has made a list of possibles, but I dare say many of them will be in a poor state, and you won't want to waste time and money on heavy repairs. Look here, can we meet in a few days' time? Properly, I mean, not like this,' he added, as Annie waved from the ambulance to say they were ready to go.

'In the evening, when we've stopped for the night,' Laura agreed.

He named a day. 'I shan't be on evening call then. And will you let me treat you to dinner? Camille's in the square does decent grub.'

'I have nothing to wear,' Laura said.

'My dear girl, this is Pop! Come just as you are.'

'Perhaps I may wash my hands and face,' She grinned, and ran back to Bessie, pleased with the idea of a proper meal at a table, and pleased that he felt enough at ease to have called her 'my dear girl'.

Despite the counter-attacks, no ground gained was lost, but the casualties were heavy, and on the 27th of September the 33rd Division had suffered so many losses it had to be withdrawn, to be replaced by the 23rd, which had been only two days out of the line. The good weather held, and the ground was firm, allowing heavy guns to be brought up; the dust and smoke were sometimes so thick, though, that advances had to be made by compass bearing. The army was moving forward and gripping what it grasped, but it was, as the Duke of Wellington had said, 'hard pounding'.

By the end of the month, Major Ransley had found what he thought was the perfect house from Lady Beningbrough's list, and took Laura to see it one evening. He collected her from the billet in a motor-car, and drove into Pop with the headlamps off because, he said, they were expecting air raids. There were almost no lights in the town, either – blackout conditions prevailed – and those people out and about had to feel their way along the walls, or use torches shaded with their fingers.

'Another reason to get our refuge open soon,' Laura said. 'It isn't safe for young women to go out in the dark, in a town full of soldiers. I know most of them are decent chaps, but there's always a rogue. And there's always temptation.'

'I'm glad to know you don't see life through rose-tinted glasses,' Ransley said, easing the motor down a narrow street. 'It makes it easier to talk to you.'

'I'm not sure I ever had any rose tint about me, but if so, it would all have been washed away by my experiences as a lady-policeman,' she said.

'That must have been fascinating,' he said.

'I'm not sure "fascinating" is the word. It opened my eyes to a number of facets of the human character, however.'

'And I admire you for doing it. And for remaining so positive and cheerful.'

'The worse the world is, the more we have to do to counter-balance it,' she said. 'But most people are good and decent, I find. We could hardly survive as a species, other-wise.'

'That's true. Here we are. This is it. What do you think?'

The buildings along the narrow roads of Pop were all joined together in terraces, so it was one section of a contin-uous façade she was looking at. It was faced in stone, three stories high and, as well as she could tell in the gloom, had

311

the usual sort of shaped gable at the top. There was a large window, shuttered, to either side of the front door, which was set back up a shallow flight of steps – a wide, handsome door of highly varnished wood, with a fanlight over it, on which, in curly gold letters, was a monogram, an A and an H intertwined.

Laura stepped out and stared up at it, and said, 'It's an hotel, isn't it?'

'Yes, it was the Hôtel Amiel Hubert – hence the letters over the door. It's been empty since the beginning of 1915, but it's been well shuttered, and it hasn't been shelled, so it's in fair condition, only very dirty. And,' he went on, as though producing the winning card, 'it's furnished.'

They looked around by the light of torches – the electricity had been turned off. There was a foyer, with a staircase straight ahead, and a room on either side. One was empty, except for stacks of dining chairs around the walls; in the other, drawing-room shrouded furniture loomed mysteriously in the twilight. Ransley pulled off one or two of the sheets to reveal heavy armchairs and settles with plush upholstery, some of it rather mouse-bitten. The floor was bare wood, but there was a rolled-up carpet against the wall. A large fireplace, with fancy tiles and an elaborate over-mantel, was topped with a huge mirror, also shrouded. In the centre of the ceiling was a dangling wire where the chandelier had been removed.

'Good thing too,' Laura said. 'A chandelier? We don't want to frighten our girls to death.'

Behind the foyer were the kitchen, associated offices and storerooms, and upstairs there were four large bedrooms on the first floor, eight small ones on the second, and a bathroom on each. Best of all, Laura thought, was the conservatory across the back of the house. Quite a few panes in the roof were broken, and the tiled floor was covered with dead leaves and one or two puddles, but it would make a wonderful place, as she said to Ransley, for tired, homesick girls to sit quietly, drink a cup of tea, and gaze at the soothing shapes of nature in the form of the garden.

'There *is* a garden?' she asked, suddenly anxious. It was too dark out there to see anything.

'Yes, a small one, with some fruit trees, winding paths, and some sort of shed at the bottom. All very overgrown, of course.'

'Oh, good,' said Laura. 'One does so crave a garden after all the mud and desolation. Just a bit of green grass and a tree with branches and leaves.' She turned to him. 'It's a bit bigger than I imagined, but the bedrooms will be a great bonus. Somewhere safe for the girls in transit to stay the night, or if they have a short leave and can't get home. I wonder what state the mattresses are in.'

'There won't be bed bugs, if that's what you mean. They've been empty too long.'

'We'll have to buy linen,' she mused. 'Two sitting-rooms is good – one can be the quiet room and the other for noisier fun. I suppose the electricity works?'

'I think I can arrange for a sapper to come and look at it. And the plumbing. I have a friend, a major in the RE, who owes me a favour.'

'Crockery, cutlery . . .'

'You can buy that sort of thing quite cheaply at Gerard's, in Gasthuisstraat.'

'And we'll need at least one table, for meals. It needn't be more than a trestle, really.' She stopped in the middle of her musing. 'At all events Lady Beningbrough was right about the cleaning. I'll need to hire someone to come in and scrub it from top to bottom. How did Talbot House manage?'

'They've got the army behind them. When they want

something done, they just request a work detail from whichever regiment is billeted here.'

'Yes, of course. Well, I'm sure there are plenty of civilians in Pop who wouldn't mind working for a few extra francs. I'll need money,' she said bluntly.

'I thought you would,' he said. 'Have you still got those letters of introduction?'

'Yes, and corkers they are! Lady Smith-Dorrien, Lady Haig, Lady Portland, and Lady Overton. I know of the first two, of course. Lady Portland?'

'The Duchess of Portland. Better known for her devotion to animal welfare, but she's a humanitarian as well. And they're extremely rich.'

'And Lady Overton?'

'She might be your best bet. She's one of the richest women in England, and she's very active in benevolent schemes. Runs a hospital in London, and operates the X-ray ambulance scheme almost single-handed. You know, where they give an ambulance a woman's name, and invite every woman in the country with that name to donate something towards kitting it out and running it? Works like a charm. She comes over from time to time, too. This might be just up her street. She's been involved in the women's franchise struggle for years. Something over here for women might appeal to her.'

Laura was thoughtful. 'I'm not sure I can put the case eloquently enough in a letter. And ladies of that sort must get hundreds of "begging letters" every day – probably don't even read them. It would be better if I went and saw her in person.'

'Good idea,' he said. 'You come across as very personable to me. I'm sure you could persuade me to anything.'

'Ah, but you haven't any money, have you?' Laura said, missing his expression in the comparative gloom. 'All the same, I think I'll *have* to go. The question is, when? I can't leave the girls in the lurch.'

'Miss Cotton can drive, can't she?'

'Yes, but she's still not strong, and air raids frighten her. I wouldn't want to leave her to do everything. And she can't fix Bessie, unless it's something very simple.' She sighed. 'I think I'll have to wait for a break in the action. I hate all this delay. Now I've seen – what was it called, the hotel?'

'Just call it AH,' he suggested.

'What's that in soldier language? I know A is Ack.'

'Ack Harry,' he supplied.

'Perfect. Now I've seen Ack Harry, I want to be getting on with it. I want it to be ready *tomorrow*.'

'I bet you drove your nanny to distraction when you were at the tantrum age.'

She grinned. 'You have no idea! I've never been good at taking "no" for an answer.'

'Well, you can't do anything more tonight, so why don't we go and get a bite of supper before I drive you home?'

'I oughtn't to, really. The girls will expect me back at the billet.'

'More for them, if you don't turn up,' said Ransley. 'And, by the way, I'm not known for taking "no" either.'

'Oh dear. What quarrels we shall have!' she said.

Afterwards, back in the motor-car and driving to the restaurant, she thought that had been rather a presumptuous thing to say, open to misinterpretation. It sounded as though she assumed they would be in a position to quarrel with each other for a long time into the future. But he hadn't seemed to mind. And it would be easy enough for him to disentangle himself from her scheme, if he wanted to.

But he didn't seem to want to. Over supper – a dish of cassoulet that was mostly beans but no less tasty for that – they talked non-stop about Ack Harry, what might be done with the building, and what happy times there would be

315

when it was open for business. Anyone listening would have thought it was something they had devised together from the beginning.

Bessie finally gave up the ghost on the 4th of October. There was a muted explosion under the bonnet, and she coughed, then slid to a halt half a mile short of Ypres. Laura got out and opened her up, but she couldn't get her going again. It was lucky that they were on their way up empty, rather than back full of wounded. A new assault had gone in that morning at Broodseinde, and the Germans were counter-attacking at Zonnebeke. It would have been a busy day, as Louisa remarked, with what sounded to Laura like deep relief.

They had to wait until a motor-lorry came past, heading towards Pop, to give them a tow. There were half a dozen Australians in it, the first they had met, and they were immensely cheerful and friendly, but called them all 'miss' and did not flirt with them, seeming respectful of woman-kind, which Laura liked. She dropped the others off at the billet, and had them tow Bessie to her mechanic's yard. They accepted her thanks with broad grins and a certain shuffling shyness, but would not accept the packet of cigarettes she offered in payment.

'What'd me ma say?' said one, putting his hands behind his back as if she might force it on him.

'Couldn't leave a sheila in distress,' said another, and when he was fiercely nudged by his mate, 'Beg pardon, I mean *lady*.'

'Well, thanks again, and good luck, lads.'

'Hope your wagon gets better.' And they drove off.

But the mechanic-wizard shook his head and sucked his teeth, and conveyed that Bessie would have to be admitted overnight, and that Laura must come back in the morning. And in the morning, he read the last rites over the faithful old girl, and offered to strip out any equipment and useful parts and bring them over to the billet for her in his lorry.

'Well, that's torn it!' Annie said, when Laura reported back.

They looked at each other helplessly.

'What do we do now?' Flora said.

'I know what I'm going to do,' Laura said. 'Go back to England, visit these great ladies, and see if I can get my scheme off the ground. You all ought to come, for a holiday.'

'We couldn't,' Annie said, sounding shocked. 'With all this going on?' She gestured towards Ypres. In the distance, you could hear shell fire, a sound like heavy doors being slammed at the far end of a big house.

'No sense being here if you can't do anything,' Laura said briskly. 'And you all need a rest. Even *soldiers* get to go on leave, and we've all been here for fifteen months.'

'I'd like a holiday,' Louisa said abruptly. 'I'm so sick of dirt and rubble and broken things and – and *everything*!'

'Well, *I* can do something,' Flora said. 'I'm a trained nurse, and they can use me at the hospital.'

'I think I'll stay,' Anne said. 'I can help at the hospital too.' She looked unhappily at Laura. 'I hate to think we're breaking up. But if I stay, perhaps I'll hear of another vehicle we could use.'

'I'll be back,' Laura said. 'I promise you. And if my scheme doesn't come off, I'll jolly well find an ambulance for you, and we'll be back on the old run.'

Louisa didn't say anything. She looked at Laura as though she could burn her thoughts into her head without speaking them aloud. But, just for the moment, Laura wasn't attending.

'And if it does come off,' she was saying, 'I still might be able to find an ambulance for you. I shall ask the great ladies while I'm at it. My view is, if you're going to ask for something, better to ask for more than you need and fall short than ask for less and get it.'

Annie smiled. 'I can't imagine anyone saying "no" to you.'

CHAPTER TWENTY

The new strategy in the Salient was called 'bite and hold'. Instead of a major set-piece, advancing the whole Front at the same time, the idea was to mount small local offensives, seizing an important position, then consolidating it. The plan seemed to be working. Little by little the Germans were being driven back, and were suffering unsustainable losses.

British casualties were heavy, and once again the hospital trains were rolling into London's termini. Though Laura had been aware from her own viewpoint how busy they had been, it was salutary, now she was in London, to see the thing more on a national scale. Bessie had been a small drop in a large ocean, and while it was axiomatic that every little helped, it somehow assuaged any guilt she had been feeling to see that the entire nation was mobilised to succour the wounded.

'Thousands are doing what we did,' she told Louisa, 'but Ack Harry is something only we can do. Or, at least, that only we *are* doing.'

Louisa was perfectly willing to be diverted. Some of the things she had seen as a lady policeman had been shocking, but they had not torn her heart as the ambulance work had. This new scheme would be hard going, she suspected, but at least it would not be harrowing.

Laura had an appointment with Lady Overton.

'Do you want me to come with you?' Louisa asked.

Laura thought her friend was looking pale and worn. 'I think you should rest a bit – you've been hard at it for weeks now without a break. Why don't you potter about, do a little shopping? You could take the opportunity to catch up with your old friends.'

Louisa looked relieved. 'I really would like to see some of the girls,' she said, 'if you don't mind seeing Lady Overton on your own.'

'Not at all. We can meet later for dinner and exchange news.'

Before her meeting with Lady Overton, Laura called in on Edward at his office to tell him about her latest plan. He listened with some reserve, which she realised in the end was not disapproval but suspicion.

'What is it?' she asked, with an urchin grin. 'You suspect me of double dealing of some kind, and I can't fathom what it is.'

'Of course I don't. It's just that you seem to have been leaping like a mountain goat from one peak of danger to the next, but *this* – I can't see the mortal peril in it. It sounds positively safe.'

'Poperinghe is pretty close to the Front, within shelling distance if the war takes a turn for the worse. And there are always air raids. I might still be killed,' she reassured him. 'I gather you're not in fear for my respectability.'

'I've passed beyond that. I remember how once I worried simply about your taking paid employment . . . How long ago that seems.'

'Dear Teddy, the war *has* changed you. You're much less stiff, you know. Much more patient.' Sadder, too, she thought, but she didn't say that. 'What can you tell me about Lady Overton?'

'She's not a client of ours, but I know of her,' he said. 'She's very wealthy. She must be a woman of strong character, because she trained as a doctor in the days when it was an outrage for a woman to do so. And she's been a leading light of the franchise movement almost since the beginning.'

'She sounds terrifying,' said Laura.

'You sound notably *un*terrified.'

'I have nothing to lose. And if she doesn't help me, I have three other letters of introduction, so *nil desperandum*.'

'Come back and tell me all about it afterwards,' he said. 'Dine with us at home tonight.'

'I'd love to, but I'm promised to Louisa. Tomorrow?'

'Tomorrow. They'll all be so pleased to see you. David's much improved, Antonia's going to have a baby – and Sadie's walking out with a very nice young man.'

'Goodness, how you all change when my back's turned for a moment! What about you, dearest? You look tired.'

'I'm fine, just too much work. I don't change.'

'Hmm. I need to have a private lunch with you to probe the truth of that statement. Before I go back, perhaps?'

'I'd be delighted to have lunch with you, but there's nothing to be probed,' he said. 'I'm just your same dull old brother.'

'Not that. Never that,' she said.

Lady Overton turned out to be tall and thin, with a hard-worked boniness that put Laura in mind of an honest horse, yet her sharp eyes and brisk intelligence were far from equine. She listened attentively, asked a few to-the-point questions, then delved straight into the finances, making notes on a piece of paper in front of her and assembling a column of figures that Laura was afraid would add up to the answer 'no'.

Finally she sat back, and subjected Laura to a long, thorough examination. 'You remind me of myself when I was your age,' she said. 'And since that self of mine could never bear a put-off, I won't keep you waiting for an answer. I have been in Poperinghe several times, and other places close to the Front, and I know about conditions there for women. A club house, such as you describe, will be invaluable. It will help the morale of *all* the women out there, to know that they are taken seriously. In time, perhaps, the government and the army might consider their welfare, but that time is not now. I will fund your hostel. I have an idea now of the costs involved.' She tapped her pencil on the page. 'I shall undertake the whole cost, as it stands, but if anything important changes you will let me know at once. I expect you to be frugal—'

'Of course,' Laura said.

'—but not Spartan. It is a hostel, not a workhouse. Simple home comforts, is what you should aim for.'

'Yes, ma'am. That accords with my own ideas.'

Lady Overton nodded, and held out her hand. 'Then it is done. What date is it? The sixth. I'd like to hear that the hostel is in operation before the end of the month. That gives you three weeks.'

'I hope we can do it in less. The sooner the better, in my view.'

'Good. Now, is there anything else?'

'I don't think so, ma'am.'

'Now is the time to ask me, when I have my cheque-book at my elbow.' Laura hesitated, and Lady Overton gave her a bright, amused look. 'I know a good deal about you, Miss Hunter. I did not invite you here without doing some research into your character and actions. I know that you have been driving an ambulance in France for over a year. What has made you decide to exchange the ambulance for a hostel?'

'The ambulance died,' Laura said, and seeing Lady Overton was interested, she told the whole story. 'It seemed the right time for me to move on. But I do feel guilty about Lady Agnes and Miss Hazlitt. Or not guilty, perhaps, but sorry, and anxious for their future.'

322

'I know Agnes well,' Lady Overton said. 'She's a very energetic young woman, and she will dislike enforced idleness. Miss Hazlitt I know slightly from the Women's Hospital. As a trained nurse, she will readily find a place for herself, but a niche for Agnes is more difficult.' She mused. 'She does not wish to help you?'

'She really wants to go on doing what she was doing, working with an ambulance.'

'Hmm. But she does not drive? Pity. However,' she said, at the end of a train of thought, 'I think I can find a place for her. You perhaps know about my X-ray ambulances?'

'Yes, ma'am.'

'I want to get two more to the Salient very soon, and I am always looking for suitable staff for them. Do you think she would be willing to go to the Curie Institute in Paris for two weeks, to train to operate an X-ray machine?'

'I'm sure she would,' Laura said and, for an instant, felt a small pang of envy. That would be an adventure! But she had her own adventure ahead of her. And for some reason the face of Major Ransley popped into her mind. Well, he would be helping her, wouldn't he?

As she was leaving, Lady Overton asked, 'By the way, what will you call your hostel?'

Laura explained about the AH on the fanlight. 'We've been referring to it as Ack Harry, but as you are funding it, I wonder if you would agree to our naming it Overton House?'

Lady Overton thought for a moment. 'I'm not so vain,' she said. 'And you will be doing most of the work. Given the initials, why not call it Artemis House? Artemis being, of course, the huntress of the heavens.'

Laura laughed. 'I'm not sure I'm so vain either, ma'am, but I suppose few people will ever associate Artemis with Hunter. Artemis House it shall be, if that's your decision.'

'It will be our joke,' said Lady Overton. 'And one day, when I have time, I shall come out and inspect you. It won't be for many months, however – not until next year, certainly. By then, I expect, I shall find that everyone is calling it Ack Harry. Nicknames always have more sticking power than formal names.'

'You want to do *what*?' Cook said in outrage.

Lilian and Emily, standing close together for comfort, flinched a little, but Lilian repeated it bravely. 'We want to go and be munitionettes.'

'We want to go and make bombs to kill Germans,' Emily added defiantly.

'You hold your tongue!' Cook snapped, scowling. 'Munitionettes – the very idea! You'll do no such thing!'

They exchanged a glance, and Lilian said, 'But – we've done it. Yesterday, on our afternoon off. We signed up.'

'You went behind my back, without so much as a by-your-leave?'

Lilian was anxious to explain. 'You see, last week, when we was coming out of the pictures, there was this boy with leaflets—'

'I'll give you leaflets!'

'Saying "Women Wanted for Munitions Work". And it said a recruiter would be at the Station Hotel next week—'

'—which was yesterday. So we went,' Emily concluded. 'We signed.'

'Well, you can just go and *un*sign!' said Cook.

Another exchanged glance. They moved even closer together. 'You can't,' said Lilian nervously. 'It's like signing on with the gov'ment. They can send you to prison.'

'We don't want to unsign,' Emily said, bolder now the explosion was over. 'We *want* to go.'

'My brother helped build the factories, and I want to work in one,' said Lilian.

'It's dirty, dangerous work, not fit for girls. And where will you live?'

'There's boarding houses,' Lilian said. 'They give you a place when you start. You stay with other girls from the factory.'

'Dregs of the gutter, everybody knows that,' Cook said. 'You want to mix with girls like that? You'll be in trouble before you know it.'

Lilian was tearful now, but Emily was hardening. 'We can look after ourselves!'

'First I've heard about it!'

'You get a uniform an' all, and loads o' money in your pocket, and you can go out whenever you like, every evening, if you're not working. You can go to the pictures *every day*, if you want.'

'Pictures! Is that what this is about?' Cook said scornfully. Though in the back of her mind she knew it was, in a way. Domestic service was safe – you were looked after – but your freedom was curtailed, and the young were the ones who rebelled against it. To go out whenever you wanted, without asking . . .

'Anyway,' Emily said quickly, 'you can't stop us.'

'We'll see about that. We'll see what the missus has got to say.' Cook started for the door.

Emily pinched Lilian hard to put spirit into her, and she jumped. 'It's patriotic!' she gasped.

Cook paused, turned, stared at her through narrowed eyes. She knew they had her there. 'What did you say?' she asked as menacingly as possible.

'It's our duty to – to help the war effort,' Lilian managed. 'And – help kill Germans.'

Cook would only dignify that with a snort.

Beattie and Antonia were together in the morning-room, going over some accounts for the Hastings Road canteen. Antonia had agreed to take over the book-keeping for the project, since she had been doing it for her father's tea-room

325

and was the only one on the committee who understood double-entry. They were using vegetables, like Munt's, from private gardens, and the question was how this should be entered, and what the money saved should be spent on.

They were getting on nicely when Cook brought the news about Lilian and Emily.

'I don't see that there's anything I can do,' Beattie said, when she'd finished. 'It's a nuisance, but they are free to give their notice if they want to. Can't we manage without them?'

'Well, madam, we can probably manage without another housemaid, now Ethel's not looking after Mr David special, but I must have a kitchen maid.'

'We can all pitch in and help,' Antonia said. 'I've peeled potatoes and chopped carrots many a time for Mrs Bates back home.'

Cook reeled at the idea of gentry doing menial tasks in her kitchen. 'I'm sure it won't come to that, madam,' she said stiffly.

Beattie, who had known Cook a long time, stepped in. 'I'll make enquiries for a new kitchen maid, but in the meantime, you'll just have to manage as best you can. Ethel and Ada will have to do Emily's jobs, and we'll help with some of the upstairs work to take the strain off them – dusting and tidying and so on.'

'Yes, madam,' Cook said gloomily. She didn't mind them dusting, but in her mind anything like that threatened to be the thin end of the wedge.

'We all have to pull together,' Beattie said, to get rid of her. 'There is a war on, you know.'

'Yes, madam,' Cook said again, and went away.

Ethel was furious. 'I'm not doing kitchen maid's work. What a cheek! I'm house-parlour maid.'

'You'll do as you're told!'

'Catch me for that! I've never been a skivvy. Let Ada do it.'

'Ada's head and you're under,' Cook pointed out. 'As for talking about skivvies, you've got no call to be putting on airs, my girl, you as had a baby and not married! Think yourself lucky the missus took you in, else where'd you be now? In the workhouse, that's where.' And before Ethel could make the furious retort that leaped to her lips, she added, 'Lucky for you that baby died, that's all, or—'

Ethel's face seemed to sag for an instant in an expression of intense misery, which stopped Cook in mid-sentence. It was only a momentary lapse. Almost before Cook had registered the look, it was gone, and Ethel's jaw was jutting again in her usual expression.

'I'm not scrubbing floors,' she said, shifting position. 'You can say what you like.'

'You won't have to. Mrs Chaplin'll come in extra, till we get a new girl. It's only temp'ry.'

It was a climb-down, Ethel recognised it; but since she had no choice, all there was to do was save face. 'On your head be it, if I have to wait on the master at dinner with me hands smelling of onions. Or me nails dirty.'

And Cook knew a flag of truce when she saw one. 'You won't,' she said, and added her own face-saver. 'There's a war on, might I remind you. Everybody's got to pull together.'

On the 5th of October, in the Salient, the rain came back, and fell again in torrents. On the 9th of October, there was a joint French and British action at Poelcapelle, with the intention of moving a long section of the Front, over thirteen hundred yards, half the distance from Broodseinde Ridge to Passchendaele Ridge. The northern part of this section took its position and held it, but in the centre, in front of Passchendaele, the ground taken was lost to German counter-attacks. General Birdwood reported that the heavy rain and

327

mud sloughs were the main cause of the failure to hold the captured ground. But the Germans had suffered heavy losses which they would struggle to replace.

On the 12th of October, there was another Allied attempt on Passchendaele, but the torrential rain made movement desperately difficult: the mud prevented artillery from being brought up, and the soldiers, already exhausted from the previous attacks, foundered in the dispiriting morass. The advance was less than had been hoped for, and much of it was immediately lost to counter-attacks. It was a horrible day.

Even the perennially cheerful Lord Forbesson looked grey when he called in at Edward's office on his way to the War Office on Monday, the 15th.

'Thank goodness you're here,' he said, 'and not off gallivantin' on one of your committees. I need a large sherry before I go and face the war again.'

Edward settled him by the fire with a glass of the best, and said, 'The newspapers never tell the whole story. I gather it's not good news from the Salient.'

'Conditions are impossible out there,' said Forbesson. 'Lakes of water. Bottomless mud. Men sinkin' to their waists, horses dyin'. It takes the heart out of 'em, man and beast, coated head to toe in grey slime, every step a labour of Hercules. Most miserable business you could imagine. Haig and the other commanders had a conference on Saturday, agreed to call off the attack until the weather improves. Meanwhile, they've got to build miles more roads, causeways above the mud, to get artillery and ammunition forward – and wounded back, of course.'

'Were the casualties heavy?' Edward asked.

'About thirteen hundred, all told,' Forbesson said. 'Bad enough for a day's work, but hundreds of them are still out there, stuck in the mud in no man's land, dead and wounded. Rotten for morale.'

'What will happen now?' Edward asked.

'Well, we need the Frenchies to take the Huns' attention off us for a bit. Pétain's been promising for weeks to renew the attack at Chemin des Dames, and now's the time if ever it was to get on with it. Haig's naggin' at him as we speak. Persistent man, Haig. I wouldn't like to say "no" to him. So we'll see what we shall see.' He sighed and rose to his feet. 'Thanks for lettin' me bend your ear. You're a good fellow. By the way, what's this I hear about your daughter going to Ypres to open a Toc H sort of place for women?'

'My sister, not my daughter.'

'Ah! I didn't see how it could be. Is that the sister who went for a policeman?'

'The same.'

'Gritty people, you Hunters,' Forbesson said, with a grin. 'Give us a battalion of Hunters, we could knock Jerry over in a week.'

It was later that same day, the 15th of October, that Edward received news that Warren, his former secretary, had been killed in the Salient in the attack before Passchendaele. A letter came by the afternoon post from Warren's father. His section had been hit by a shell during the German counter-attack. His body had not been recovered yet, but several men who had made it back had reported that they had seen him fall.

From what they say, there is no room for doubt, I'm afraid, that our dear boy is indeed gone from us. I do not wish to harrow you, knowing how fond of him you were, but I would not have you harbour painful false hopes. He always spoke of you with both respect and affection, and had the war not intervened, I feel sure he would have wanted to remain with you for his whole career.

Warren, dead. Edward put down the letter, feeling sick and shaken. Hit by a shell. Reading between the lines, he guessed there would not be much to recover, when and if the ground was retaken and the dead could be brought in. Officers writing letters of condolence from the Front traditionally told families that their loved-one had been shot through the head or through the heart and had died instantly. It was easier to live with the thought of such a swift and tidy death. But Edward was in a position to know a little of the reality out there. It was horrible to think of Warren, that cheerful young man, being smashed by a shell. He hoped – God, how he hoped – that it had been instantaneous. Better blown to rags than to lie hideously wounded, in terrible pain, to bleed to death slowly in the mud, beyond all aid.

Warren, dead! He put his hands over his face, trying to keep himself in one piece, to stop himself trembling. In one way, it was worse than losing Bobby, because he had worked with Warren all day, every day, while Bobby had been away at school, then at university, and then with the RFC. He had an intimate knowledge of Warren's character and thoughts, could remember his expressions and his voice. Bobby was his son, his child, his own flesh, and that was something that could never be got over. He had known him from his birth, had raised and nurtured him. But he had known Warren as an adult.

His thoughts turned to Beattie, searching for comfort. But though she might say the right things, she would not feel it. She was shut away in her own sorrows, and would not understand how a man who had lost a real son could be devastated by the loss of an employee. And she would not hold him when, like a child himself, he ached to be held. But a man must be strong, always, must never faint or fail, must offer comfort but never ask it. So she would not know that he wanted, just for once, to be weak.

His mind turned to Élise, but sternly he forbade it, turned

330

it away again. He must not think of her. Emphatically, he must not go to her. She would have comforted him – but he had no right to that comfort. He lowered his hands, took a long breath, and reached for the paper on the top of the pile awaiting his attention. He read it, and it was written in English, but it took him a long time to understand what it said.

It took a week to conclude the legal entanglements over leasing the Hôtel Amiel Hubert, but Laura did not wait until the contract was concluded before starting work on it. Lady Beningbrough assured her the owners would lease, and that was good enough for her. Through Lady Beningbrough she found two charwomen and a handyman happy to work for good English money, while Major Ransley fulfilled his promise to get a team of sappers in to go over the electricity and plumbing.

Laura pitched in and helped with the cleaning – there was so much of it to do. It was amazing how dirty an unused place could get in three years. She put on the overalls she had used when servicing Betty and acquired a mob-cap, and as she scrubbed, rubbed and beat, she sang, to the tune of 'Rock of Ages', a version everyone gradually picked up:

> Dust of ages, shed on me,
> Let me hide myself from thee.
> From the plaster and the soot
> And the cobwebs and the grit,
> We shall scour Ack Harry's face,
> With the power of elbow grease.

When the floorboards had been scrubbed, the carpets unrolled and beaten, the furniture rubbed up to a gleam, the windows and mirror made to sparkle, the old place did not look half bad, she thought. A bit shabby, but none the

331

worse for that – it was home-from-home they were aiming at, not a daunting luxury. Where the upholstery was too ragged, they fashioned loose covers from clean, plain holland. The shutters were all put in order and painted, and given that Pop was under black-out every night, it was decided there was no need for curtains as well.

When the cleaning was almost done, Louisa, with Annie's help, went to shop for crockery, cutlery, mattresses and linens. Word was spreading about the project – probably through Lady Beningbrough, Laura thought – and donations of objects from the useful to the frankly odd came in. A restaurant sent over a cartload of rather battered but service-able pots and pans for the kitchen; an officers' mess donated a tea-urn, scavenged from the ruins of Ypres, saying they already had one; a lady living down the road in Helhoek sent plants from her garden, and her own gardener to put them in; another lady sent a fern stand and two enormous vases, while a 'well-wisher', who preferred to remain anon-ymous, sent six oil-paintings 'for your drawing-room', which would have been kind had they not been very bad paintings and set in exceptionally ugly poker-work frames.

Major Ransley threw himself into the business with enthu-siasm, whenever he had time free from his duties. He seemed to become a clearing-house for offers, and Laura was always receiving little notes from him, such as 'Would you like a piano? Lt Jones of the Sherwoods has three, and I can scrounge one from him if you wish.'

And: 'Major Bedford of the 47th has a large mantel clock he wants a home for. Have not seen it but promised that it "goes"! Liberated from Ypres, I imagine. Should you care for it?'

And: 'Office desk and six wastepaper baskets on the way to you. M. Lemmens offered them in a hurry so I had to decide for you.'

He even managed to 'scrounge' – one of his favourite

words – a whole lot of cane furniture for the conservatory. An hotel in Ypres had been bombed to oblivion back in 1915, but not before the owner had managed to get a good deal of his stuff away. In the enterprising manner of refugees, he had set up again in the outskirts of Pop, but his new premises had no conservatory, and having hung on to the cane furniture in the hope it would come in useful, he had finally decided he needed the space. He had been in the hospital to be treated for a septic wound, and Laura guessed that his 'finally deciding' had been helped along by a certain major of her acquaintance.

Things were going so well that Annie was almost sorry when the moment came for her to depart for Paris. 'I wish you were coming with me,' she said, as she hugged Laura goodbye.

'I half wish it myself. But I've got my teeth into this now.'

'I'll be coming back to the Salient with the ambulance,' Annie said, 'so I'm sure to see you again. I shall come and visit when I'm off duty, and see how you're going on.'

'Visiting when you're off duty is what Ack Harry's for,' Laura pointed out.

Annie smiled. 'Lady Overton was right. That nickname's going to stick.'

Rupert came home on leave, thoroughly elated. 'I don't know why I held out so long,' he told Diana, the first evening. He had gone straight upstairs for a long bath on his arrival, telling her to put dinner back. She had taken advantage of his telegram to cancel her evening engagement and order something special. He came down, fragrant with bath essence, damp of hair and wearing his velvet dressing-gown with the hussar frogging instead of a jacket. 'I'm so glad you haven't got people in, by the way,' he mentioned. 'I really relish the idea of a quiet dinner, just the two of us. What are we having?'

'There's a little pot of caviar I was saving for a special occasion. Game soup. Then a duck, and a savoury. And some apples and pears, if you want a dessert.'

'Sounds just the ticket. Pour me a glass of sherry while I go and choose the wine, and then we'll talk.'

When they were settled, he reverted to his previous sentence. 'I don't know why I held out so long against going to the Front. It's the greatest adventure – beats playing polo into a cocked hat! Of course, the Aged Ps never wanted me to go – and I dare say the mater thought I'd be a complete rabbit and bring the family name into disgrace. But I have to tell you, wife of my heart, that it turns out I am a natural-born soldier!'

'Really?' Diana said in surprise.

'There it is, you see – the astonishment! Rather insulting. But it turns out that I'm really frightfully good at officering. Got an eye for terrain, so the colonel told me – I'm his blue-eyed boy. *That* comes from hunting. I can read a map and make it pop up in my mind in three dimensions, and spot cover and possible enemy strongholds. After that, it's just a matter of giving orders in a clear, firm voice as if you know what you're doing – whether you do or not. Gives the chaps confidence. *That* comes from amateur dramatics – playing the part, d'you see? If you play it well enough for long enough, you become it. I base my voice and delivery on Grandpa Hexham, the mater's father. You wouldn't think of not obeying him. When the shells begin to whistle down, I absolutely *am* Grandpa H. Of course, he had a gimlet eye, which I can't quite manage, but I'm working on it.'

'I suppose the men are all afraid of you,' Diana said, enjoying his performance.

'Afraid of me? Bless you, they love me! They're like dogs – you give them a thrashing and they respect you, then you pet 'em up, and they adore you. I have them all eating out of my hand.'

'That doesn't surprise me,' Diana said. The one thing he had always had, when he cared to use it, was charm.

'So, what with one thing and another, I'm on my way to making a great success of this war business. Of course, there are disadvantages.'

'The shells and bullets?' Diana hazarded. 'Aren't you awfully afraid?'

'The odd thing is that, once you get used to the noise, you don't really think about them. Or *I* don't. It's like going out in the rain. Once you've made up your mind to it, you forget about getting wet. No, I was talking about the food, and the dirt, and the discomfort. But I suppose you have to put up with that sort of thing when you're on an adventure. It's a bit like going camping. Of course, I never cared for that much – Charles was the one for canvas and camp fires – but sometimes you reach some remote place with a wonderful view and it suddenly becomes worth it. Or almost,' he added honestly.

'I'm so glad you're enjoying it, and doing well,' Diana said. 'You weren't in the Salient, were you?'

'I wasn't, but I shall be when I go back. Oh, Lord, I shouldn't have told you that! Well, can't be helped now – just don't tell anyone, will you? Not that I can see the point of trying to keep it secret, since the jolly old Boche must know what we're up to by now.'

'But – isn't it awfully dangerous in the Salient?' Diana asked anxiously.

'Oh, war's dangerous everywhere,' he said lightly. 'And you've got to go where the action is if you want to distinguish yourself. I'm aiming to get a DSO at least, to impress little George when he's a bit older. When he asks, "What did you do in the war, Daddy?" I want him to know his pater was a hero.' He yawned suddenly. 'Lord, this fire's making me sleepy. It's wonderful to be clean and comfortable again. And I'm hungry enough to eat a horse. When I go back, I must make sure to take a good big hamper with me – that was my mistake last time. Just didn't think about it. But it can make all the difference. Simple things like mustard and pickles for cheering up ration food. And coffee – you can't take too much coffee. The French stuff is awful. Full of chicory.'

Dinner was ready. He ate with relish, and talked between mouthfuls, telling her about patrols and sorties and raids, the other officers and the chaps under his command. He drank most of the two bottles of wine that came to the table, and grew more elated and more garrulous under their influence. After dinner he wanted to go and see George, and she went with him, to stand silently at the foot of the cot for a while, watching him sleep.

'I'd forgotten how absolutely perfect he is,' Rupert whispered. 'Like something carved out of ivory.' He took her hand and pressed it, and her heart tripped.

They went back to the fireside for coffee and Rupert had several cups, which perhaps counteracted the several large brandies he had too. Finally he seemed to wind down. 'Play something on the piano,' he commanded her. 'I haven't had any music in weeks.'

She got up obediently. 'Ragtime?' she asked, picking up the bundle of popular songs that lay on the top of the piano and leafing through them.

'No, no. Proper music. Something grand – Bach, or Chopin, something like that. What's that piece I always like?'

'The Berceuse?' she hazarded.

'That's the one. Play that.'

She had to take it quite slowly, because once the intricate right-hand stuff started, she had to concentrate not to muff it. When she finished, and turned round, she thought she had sent him to sleep, because his eyes were closed and he seemed so relaxed. But he opened them and smiled at her, a slow, drowsy smile, unlike his usual sharp and satirical look.

'Lovely,' he said. 'Thank you. Let's go to bed.'

336

She remembered the press of his hand in the nursery. 'Together?' she dared to ask.

She had missed him – and he would be going away again soon, and she would miss him more. She wanted to feel close to him. She had liked it, when they were first married, when he had got into bed with her and held her against him, her back to his front, 'like spoons in a drawer', as he had put it. Even after she was pregnant, he had used to come and hold her like that and talk to her for a while, before going back to his own bed. It had been so comfortable – and what she had thought of as really being married. But he hadn't visited her bed since George was born.

'Would you like to?' he asked, with unexpected diffidence. She nodded. He offered his arm, she put her hand through it, and they walked to the door. 'I was thinking,' he said, almost dreamily, as they passed out into the hall and towards the stairs, 'that little George ought to have a brother. What do you think about that?'

With a sensation of hot and cold chasing each other through her body, she discovered that he intended more than just holding. 'I'd like to have another child,' she managed to say.

Beattie noticed, on the Saturday evening when Rupert and Diana came to dinner, the extra glow in Diana's cheeks. She looked invigorated, as if she'd just had a brisk walk in the fresh air, and she gazed fondly on her husband, so Beattie concluded, thankfully, that it was a case of love. Diana was pleased with her husband and her marriage, and that was good.

Rupert was in great form, charmed everyone and kept the party going. The Olivers were there, Christopher Beresford had been invited for Sadie's sake, and William had been allowed to ask a friend from work, a solemn young fellow of seventeen called Dangerfield, who watched Rupert in a dazzled sort of way, like someone encountering their first bird of paradise.

Beattie watched him with reserve. She couldn't forget the night he had met her and Louis at Baker Street Station, the sense of menace she had got from him; she couldn't forget that he held it in his power to ruin her. Louis had said, 'Why would he do that?' But why do people do most of the things they do? There was something odd about Rupert, she had always thought. At the very least, he was not *reliable*.

He seemed to catch her looking at him from time to time, and threw her dazzling smiles, and once a slightly quizzical glance with a raised eyebrow. None of it seemed hostile. But he was an actor, she felt. You would never really know what was going on in his mind.

They talked about the war, of course, and William's new job, Sadie's work, David and Antonia's good news, Laura's adventure. The discussion kept circling back to Ypres, the terrible conditions there, the struggle, which could be the most important of the war.

'We've *got* to hold the Germans there, while the French are still in disarray,' Mr Oliver said. 'Keep them so busy they won't notice what's happening elsewhere.'

'Like a flurry of punches in a boxing match?' Beresford said. 'Won't knock him out, but stops him landing a haymaker on you?'

'My dear chap, *boxing*?' Rupert said. 'You do lead a colourful life!'

'Oh, it was thought to develop character at my school,' he said easily.

'Mine too,' Rupert said with a shudder. 'Savagery was positively encouraged.'

Mr Oliver looked at him curiously, but went on, without comment, 'And more importantly, this "bite and hold" strategy seems to be working – wouldn't you say, Hunter? You're closer to the centre.'

'It's a workable system of offensive tactics, against which the Germans have proved to have no long-term answer,' Edward replied cautiously. 'It doesn't play so well in the newspapers as a grand, all-out battle, but tactics must be adapted to the terrain. Anything else is madness.'

'*War* is madness,' Mrs Oliver said. 'The casualties in the Salient are shocking. Every day I dread opening the newspaper.'

'Father lost his old secretary, Warren,' Sadie said. 'He was terribly fond of him, weren't you, Father?'

Edward said neutrally, 'Everybody's lost someone.'

'But the Germans are losing more,' Mr Oliver said, 'and they can't replace them, whereas we have the Americans coming.'

'Eventually,' David murmured. He took no part in war discussions. It was not his war any more. Antonia, beside him, laid a hand a moment on his knee under the tablecloth.

'When we have the Salient secured, we can capture the German submarine bases,' Edward said. 'You'll allow *that*'s an important objective.'

The telephone had rung, and now Ada came in to whisper to Beattie, who sighed and stood up, saying, 'I'm so sorry, I shall have to take the call. It's Mrs Fitzgerald, something about the canteen. She's on duty there.'

'Shall I go?' Antonia offered.

'No, dear, thank you. She just wants to make sure I'm on the end of her string.'

It was an unusually sharp comment from Beattie, who usually kept such thoughts to herself.

When she had finished the call, she turned to go back to the dining-room, and found Rupert lurking on the stairs, evidently waiting for her. Her heart jumped into her mouth. Was this it? Did the blackmail begin here?

'I made an excuse,' he said. 'I wanted to talk to you privately.'

339

She reached behind her and took hold of a chair-back to steady herself. 'Very well,' she said impassively. 'What is it?'

He said, 'When I go back, I shall be going to the Salient.'

'Oh?' said Beattie. She had no idea how he wanted her to react.

'We're not supposed to tell people, but Diana knows. I don't think it's fair to hide the dangers from one's women, do you?'

'I – have no opinion on military matters,' she managed to say. *It was dangerous in the Salient. He might be killed.* The thought went through her mind without her volition. She gripped the chair-back till the carving on it hurt her hand. *I don't mean it,* she placated the Fates. *I'm not that person.*

'This is more a domestic matter,' Rupert answered her, and he seemed serious. There was no gleam of malice or black humour in his face. 'I thought you ought to know that – I happen to know Colonel Plunkett is there.' She managed not to react to the name. 'In the Salient, I mean. He – he won't have been able to tell you. As I said, we're not supposed to.'

She said, 'Thank you, but I hardly know Colonel Plunkett. He was—'

She was going to say, 'a friend of my father's', but Rupert interrupted her impatiently.

'Oh, look here, we're quite alone, and there's no need to pretend with me. God knows, I've got enough dark secrets. I behaved badly when I met you that evening, teasing you. It was ungentlemanly. I've wanted to apologise for a long time. I want you to know you've nothing to fear. Your secret is safe with me. Wild horses wouldn't drag it out of me. It'll go with me to the grave.'

A goose walked over hers at the words. 'I don't know what you're talking about,' she said faintly.

He shrugged. 'All right, play it that way, if you like. Just so long as you know. The game's changed. I have a wife

340

and child now, and I won't do anything to endanger them. So all secrets are now sacred – do you agree?' He looked at her searchingly.

'I would not do anything to hurt Diana and the child either,' she said. 'And I am very good at keeping secrets.'

He smiled just a little. 'I imagine you must be,' he said and, quite abruptly, turned and left her, to re-enter the dining-room.

Beattie had to wait a moment until her heart slowed down. She unclasped her hand from the chair-back and massaged away the red marks on her palm. What was he talking about? What were his secrets? But if he kept hers, that was the important thing. If he could be trusted. What could she do but trust him? She had no choice.

CHAPTER TWENTY-ONE

The dowager Lady Wroughton was still at Dene Park, though she was preparing to depart for a house-party in Scotland. Rupert and Diana stayed the night after the dinner party at The Elms, and on the Sunday morning, when they got back from church, Rupert sought out his mother in her private sitting-room.

'You're not going to like this,' he said, 'but before you even think of arguing, let me tell you my mind's made up.'

'As it always seems to be, since your father died,' she said. 'What is it now?'

'Death duties,' he said, and saw her flinch at the words. 'Boardman's been doing some ferretin' – useful cove, Boardman – and it seems we can get a reduction in death duties if we let the government use Dene Park for war purposes.'

Her response was instant. 'No,' she said.

'No use sayin' no, Mater dear. You know the alternative is sellin' something, and I want to keep the estate intact for George.'

'*You* – care about the estate?' she said scornfully.

He grinned. 'Amazin' isn't it, what fatherhood can do for a fellow? I'm a reformed character. Understand now all those old shibboleths about family and duty and what-not. Yes, I want to leave things to little George in as good heart as possible. Now, if we let the government put in a hospital or a military camp—'

'Unthinkable!'

'Would you sooner I sold Wroughton House? Or Dersington?'

'You could sell Park Place,' she said viciously. 'It's disgraceful that you keep a separate establishment in London.'

'Oh, Park Place don't cost much, and we're comfortable there. When the war's over, we'll use Wroughton House all right. I thought you'd sooner have it to yourself just at present. Listen, old dear,' which was kind, but not respectful enough for Lady Wroughton, who bristled, 'Boardman's gone over everything very carefully, and the least bad option is to take the reduction in return for a requisition, and fund the rest by selling Scalford Hall.' This was the hunting estate near Melton Mowbray.

'Sell Scalford?' Lady Wroughton was surprised – Rupert had always loved hunting.

He shrugged. 'It's easy enough to rent a place for hunting parties. It stands empty most of the year, and you'd sooner we kept Dersington – you use that much more.'

'What about the Irish estate?'

'Irish land prices are too depressed at the moment, Boardman says. Bad time to sell. No, it's settled. Scalford goes, and we welcome the war to Dene. Either a hospital or a training camp. I favour the hospital – less likely to do damage. Soldiers are destructive beggars. I've had a chance to see what they can do now.' His mother was silent, contemplating the unpalatable choice. 'Look here,' he said, more kindly, 'they won't take over the whole house. We keep the east wing to ourselves and give them the west wing, and let them put up huts in the grounds. Oh, and perhaps let them use the dower house for staff accommodation – I know you don't care to use it.'

'I suppose,' she said, 'if it must be, it must be.'

'You don't have to be here much – or at all,' he said. 'You can stay in Town, and use Dersington in the summer.'

Lady Wroughton rallied. '*Somebody* has to be on hand to make sure they don't destroy the place,' she said.

'Diana can do that,' he replied.

To which suggestion, Lady Wroughton merely snorted derisively.

There was further action in the Salient from the 20th to the 22nd of October, to distract the Germans from the French preparations at Chemin des Dames, where their attack began on the 23rd.

On that Tuesday, Beattie was on duty at the canteen in Waterloo, and watched the hospital trains roll in with fresh casualties. She hadn't heard from Louis for a while. Was he still in the Salient? Had he been in the recent action? It was part of canteen duty to take tea to the injured coming off the trains, but she would not go near that platform for fear of seeing him. 'You go. I'll take care of things here,' she said as each new engine huffed and sighed to a halt beside the waiting ambulances.

He might be wounded, he might die. He might already be dead. She knew he would have arranged some system by which she would be informed if anything happened to him, but there was always a delay. And he didn't know about David. It troubled her all that long, hard day.

On the train going home, tired to death, her head aching as much as her legs, she rested against the carriage window, stared out blindly, and thought of Louis. Her whole life had been governed by the one wrong thing she had done when she was very young – giving her body to Louis outside the sacred bonds of marriage. After that, there had been nothing else she could do but survive in the only way open to her. Edward had offered her salvation, and she had taken it. Her life since then had been laid down, as though running along rails, with no decisions to make, no choices: the consequence of her wrongdoing.

She had not dared allow herself to think of 'after the war' – but the fact was, she had a choice now. If Louis survived. He did not know about David. It seemed to her a wrong thing, as wrong as her original sin, that he faced death every day in ignorance that he had a son to follow him.

After the war, whatever happened, she knew she would have to tell him. She would have to give him that much, at least.

The assault on Passchendaele Ridge was resumed on the 26th of October, once more in the rain. To the background sound of distant shelling, Major Ransley and Laura walked around Artemis House, with the shutters closed and the lights on, examining the work.

'You'll have to think about laying down some rules,' he said.

The place was clean, and smelt of soap and furniture wax. The leaks in the roof had been mended, broken panes in the conservatory replaced. The boiler had been overhauled, and a new pump installed, so there was hot water to the first-floor bathroom as well as the kitchen. The second-floor bathroom would have to wait, but the bedrooms were all furnished with mattresses at least, even if most were on the floor instead of on a bedstead. The chimneys had been swept and a wilderness of old nests and bones removed from the grates and flues. The kitchen range had been cleaned out and blackleaded, and every mousehole properly stopped up with zinc mesh and plaster, against the day when there would be food enough to attract the little beasties back.

Laura and Louisa had moved in, and had one of the big bedrooms, with their pick of the furniture – and their beds *did* have bedsteads. There were some final touches to undertake, but essentially they were ready for action, and would be officially open the next day, well on time. Lady Overton would be pleased.

Laura knew she couldn't have done it without Major Ransley. His encouragement alone, and his faith in her, had been worth thousands.

'Rules?' she said. 'What do we have to have rules for? I just want to women to feel comfortable and at home.'

He smiled at her naivety. 'Well, for instance, Toc H is a dry house. How do you feel about alcohol?'

'Well, I certainly don't mean to become teetotal myself.'

'You have to think about reputation,' he said. 'These young women will have families back home who will want to know they are not getting into undesirable situations. The slightest suggestion that you are running an irregular house, and they'll be ordered to stay away.'

Laura put her hands to her cheeks. 'Irregular house? My goodness! With Lady Overton behind it, do they think I would open a brothel?'

He laughed. 'Trust you to call a spade a spade! But you know how spiteful people can be, especially against a woman doing something different. And they won't necessarily know Lady Overton's behind it. It's a pity you couldn't name it after her.'

'We can make sure there's something on the door – a plaque naming her as patron, or something. And how about a large portrait of her in the lobby – the first thing you see as you come in? I wonder if she would send me a photograph.'

'Preferably looking stern. Good idea. So – no alcohol?'

'Nothing but tea, coffee and cocoa,' Laura said. 'I see the necessity. What else?'

'Separated ranks?'

'Definitely not,' Laura said. 'Everyone is equal when they come through those doors. No saluting, or anything of that sort.'

'What about gentlemen visitors?'

'I can see you're laying a trap for me,' Laura said. 'We're back to reputation, aren't we? On the other hand, the idea that I could never entertain you, for instance, to tea, to thank you for all you've done . . .'

'There are other places we can meet,' he said mildly.

She thought about it. 'I think it would be pleasant for our young women to be able to meet someone of the opposite sex in a safe environment, rather than some insalubrious *estaminet*. The streets are not safe after dark. And there'll be brothers, and fathers, and cousins. They shouldn't have to stand out in the rain to talk to these women. What do you think of allowing *well-behaved* gentlemen guests in the drawing-room from, say, five p.m. to nine p.m., on Saturdays?'

'I think that might contribute to a pleasant atmosphere. As long as you or Miss Cotton or some other responsible lady was present the whole time.'

Laura laughed. 'So I'm to be a chaperone now, am I? I doubt whether most mothers would think me respectable enough.'

'I'll write you a letter of recommendation, if you like,' he said. They had reached the end of the conservatory, and stopped. She turned to face him. 'You've done so much for me – for Artemis House. I can't thank you enough.'

'I've never enjoyed myself so much,' he said. 'It's a wonderful change to be involved in something so cheerful and positive, after dealing with broken bodies all day. It's for *me* to thank *you*.' He took her hands, looking down at her. For a wild moment she thought he was going to kiss her, and felt light-headed.

But at that moment they heard the front door open and slam shut, and Louisa's voice called, 'Where are you? I've got the flyers from the printers.'

Laura found her hands released, and they walked back through into the entrance hall, and saw Louisa there, rain glistening on her coat and hat, and a canvas satchel over one shoulder, bulging with the leaflets that would let the serving women of the area know they now had somewhere to go. 'It's raining again,' she said, taking off her hat and shaking it. Then she looked up and saw them, and something about them must have struck her because she said, 'Oh,' in a disconcerted way.

Laura said, 'I've come to the conclusion that what Artemis House needs most is a cat. Some nice, friendly tabby who'll sit on people's laps and purr when they come in worn out by the war. There's nothing so soothing as a cat in the lap, I always think.'

'I'm sure it won't be hard to acquire one,' said Major Ransley. 'You may only need to light the fire. Cats always find the warmest places.'

Louisa didn't comment, only continued to look from him to Laura and back.

Hugh Stanhill had been moved on from Highclere by the army, to some place he was needed more. Sadie was sorry to see him go, but also relieved. After the first uncomfortable days, he had got over his chagrin and they had been able to work together on something like their old terms. But it couldn't be as easy as it had been before. She felt guilty about having hurt him, and even when he seemed to speak to her perfectly normally, as if nothing had happened, she was always wondering what he was thinking. There was a restraint between them.

Now the Cuthberts' long-established head man, Podrick, was the only man about the place apart from Mr Cuthbert, except for the occasional visit from the vet, or an inspection by someone from the Remount Service.

It made her all the more glad of her friendship with Christopher Beresford, with whom, by contrast to Hugh Stanhill, she was becoming more at ease. He seemed happy to squire her once or twice a week, as their free time dictated, without making any romantic demands on her. Occasionally she wondered if he intended there to be anything more at some point in the future, but he made it so easy for her, she was able to forget for much of the time that they were not just old childhood friends.

He had planned to take her out for a drive in the borrowed motor-car again on Saturday the 27th, but it was raining steadily from a leaden sky, and rather chilly, too, so they changed their plans and went to the pictures instead where, as well as the feature films, there was a newsreel about the war.

'They always sound so cheerful on the commentary,' she remarked, when they came out afterwards. The rain seemed to have stopped, but there was such a misty, foggy dampness in the air it was hard to tell.

'They have to keep up morale,' he said.

'But we *know* about the casualties,' she said. 'At the beginning of the war, everyone thought it was all glorious charges and so on, but there can't be anyone now who hasn't lost someone, or seen the wounded, or convalescents in the street.'

'That's the cost of war,' he said. 'And as a nation we've agreed to bear it. There's a difference, of course, between the national cost, and the private cost, but it would be counter-productive for official sources to talk about it. We have to grit our teeth and carry on, if we're to win.'

'I know,' she said. 'And *not* winning doesn't bear thinking about. It would mean it had all been for nothing.'

He nodded, and after a silence said, 'Are you hungry? Would you like to go for some supper?'

She grinned. 'You know me, I'm always hungry. Where could we go?'

'There's the Regal Café over there. Anything less regal would be hard to imagine, but if your tastes are not too dainty we could get sausages and fried potatoes.'

'Sounds like heaven,' said Sadie. 'Look at the steam on the windows! And a cup of tea?'

'And one of those buns, afterwards, with the white icing and the coconut shreds on top.'

'It sounds to me, Mr Beresford, as if you have very depraved tastes,' she said sternly.

'It's the war,' he said meekly. 'I was brought up on caviar in silver spoons. My mother wouldn't know me now.'

Coal rationing was brought in – the first enforced rationing of the war, and unpleasant in its sense of coercion. Every household had to register with a coal-merchant, from whom alone they could get supplies. An allocation of coal was then guaranteed, but as it was the same amount regardless of the size of the household, it affected the middle classes the most. The poor, in small houses with only one or two rooms to heat, were now able to enjoy a regular fire. At The Elms, they had been practising frugality with fires for some time, but now things became really difficult. The cold, damp weather required regular fires to keep the house tolerable. The kitchen and David's room had first call on the fuel. Now there was no morning-room fire through the day, and the drawing-room fire in the evening was lit only from six to nine. It was perhaps the biggest blow to morale of the war so far. It was hard to go on being cheerful when there was no comfortable place to gather. Now the sense that the war had been dragging on for ever began to take a grip. 'War-weariness', they called it. Three years since those heady days in the autumn of 1914, and it seemed now as if it would never end.

October passed into November, and there were only three rainless days, between the 3rd and the 5th of November. These, however, were a great help to the Canadian Corps, which had been transferred to the Salient from Lens, in their preparations for a fresh assault on the Passchendaele Ridge. By the 10th of November, all the high ground had been taken, and the objectives of the campaign were secured.

Throughout the naked, war-ruined, sodden territory of Ypres, the troops sank into weary stillness. They might hope that the weather would now, perhaps, be their friend, dissuading the enemy from further action as much as it dissuaded them.

At Artemis House, there were cosy fires and a warm welcome, and at first shyly, then eagerly as the word spread, the women serving in their various capacities came. Some were stationed in and around Ypres, some were passing through on their way to other theatres, some were on leave or simply off duty. But here was a place they could go and be safe, meet like-minded sisters, have a little fun. There was music – there was almost always someone who could play the piano. There were parlour games – it was a good way to release the tension of war, by indulging in the sort of innocent silliness remembered from nursery days. There were cards – most evenings would find a couple of tables of bridge, and cribbage or picquet pairs. A Belgian lady from Poperinghe donated a chess set that had belonged to her husband, and was often found there hoping for a game. It had not taken long before the Ack Harry invitation was extended to all women, not just those in uniform. Laura argued that they were all in their way helping the war effort, and that they all needed the home comforts.

And, of course, there was always, always conversation. Sometimes Laura would pause on the stairs on her way down to the public rooms, and listen to the hum. It reminded her of the sound from a beehive, and it made her feel that what she had done there was worthwhile.

She was enjoying herself, though the hours were long and the work was tiring – not so much physically as emotionally. She had to be housekeeper, older sister, headmistress and occasionally mother superior to a wide selection of mostly young women, from a variety of backgrounds, who had questions and problems and doubts and heartaches, and no-one else to tell them to. She had to adjudicate when there were quarrels, or infractions of the few rules. When trains came in late she had to wait up to admit travellers with nowhere else to go. The mattresses in the bedrooms were occupied more often than not, and on one evening there had been four VADs sleeping in the armchairs in the drawing-room.

Her only real doubt was whether Louisa was enjoying it as much as she was. Most of the time she seemed committed to the project, but there were days when she was low, indifferent, perhaps a little depressed. Laura wondered whether it was simply homesickness. When Louisa was down, she sometimes snapped at Laura, and once even muttered that she wished she had never come to Belgium.

She also seemed to not like Major Ransley, though when Laura talked to her she acknowledged that they couldn't have managed without him. Even now they were open, he was still helping, finding equipment and sponsors for them, spreading the word of their existence. Laura had thanked him early by inviting him to the first Saturday gentleman visitors' time, and since then he had shown up whenever he could get off. He had been quietly helpful in keeping the said gentlemen in order, and giving the right tone to the evenings so that there should be no malicious gossip. But though he was unfailingly polite and pleasant towards Louisa, she spoke to him coldly, and seemed to try to avoid him. But when Laura taxed her with it, asking why she disliked him, she had said that she didn't, and that Laura was imagining things.

It was thanks to the major that, when they had been open for three weeks, a journalist came to interview them for a piece in *The Times*. Laura made a point of emphasising Lady Overton's patronage, and described their activities in the most respectable of terms. The article, when it came out, was approving, and they received many letters from people back home saying how good it was that the daughters of England should have a safe haven in the midst of war. Their fame spread, their position seemed secured, and Lady Overton promised to come and inspect them before Christmas, if she could possibly get away.

'We must do something special for Christmas,' Laura said to Louisa. 'It'll be sad for the girls who can't go home. We must make it as much like a Christmas at home as we can. Turkey and pudding, decorations – a tree. That shouldn't be hard to find. Silly games. Carols round the piano. And perhaps a little present for each of them – just some small thing, hand cream, a lipstick, a pair of stockings – to remind them of happier days.'

Louisa listened to this without enthusiasm. 'You mean, we're not going home for Christmas?'

Laura looked surprised. 'No – how could we? We can't close at the time of year we're most needed. Did you think we would?'

'I supposed we would have some sort of break. If everyone else gets leave, why shouldn't we?'

'Because this is not just our job, it's our life. This is our home now. Don't you feel that way?'

'Oh, I suppose so,' Louisa said.

'Dearest, aren't you happy here? Don't you want to carry on?' Laura said, with concern.

'There's nothing else I can do, is there? I sold Auntie's house, so I haven't a home to go to.'

'There's our house in Westminster.'

'*Your* house. And if you won't go, I'd be there alone, which wouldn't be much fun.'

'It'll be fun here,' Laura said. 'I promise you.' Louisa continued to look moodily into the fire. 'And, look, I promise we'll have a little time away from Ack Harry. I'll get someone in to take charge one evening – Lady Beningbrough, perhaps – and we'll go out to dinner on our own. And next year I'm going to look for some more volunteers to share the work with us, so we won't have to be here all the time.'

'And what would we do with our time off?' Louisa asked suspiciously.

'Well, we can have a few days in London,' Laura said. 'Or Paris – would you like to go to Paris?'

'I don't suppose Paris is much fun, these days,' Louisa said.

'Major Ransley says you can still have a good time if you know where to look,' Laura said.

'Oh, Major Ransley says so, does he?' Louisa said. 'I think I'd sooner go to London. At least I have friends there.'

CHAPTER TWENTY-TWO

Though activity in the Salient had largely died down after the 10th of November, there was a major action further south at Cambrai, beginning on the 20th of November, where, thanks to a number of new techniques that had been developed, including the use of tanks, the Hindenburg Line was breached for the first time. German counter-attacks recovered some of the ground taken, and the fierce fighting went on into December, with heavy casualties, but there was hope now that what had been achieved once could be achieved again.

The fighting in the Salient and at Cambrai meant that more hospital capacity was sorely needed. In the second week of November, the first wounded men arrived at Dene Park, to the wing which had been converted with admirable speed into a hospital. Edward reflected on how long such a transformation would have taken before the war. In the three years of the conflict, efficient systems of organisation had grown up, and the sleepy country of separate individuals that had been Edwardian England was no more. Even when the war was over, things would never be the same again.

Beattie had not managed to find a new kitchen maid.

Ethel grumbled, 'Most like she didn't bother to look.'

'How can you say such a thing?' Ada protested. 'You couldn't have a better mistress.'

'When it suits her,' Ethel said sourly. 'And it don't suit

355

her to go looking for help. She'd much sooner mess about playing patty-cakes down her canteen. And her committees, drinking tea and chatting and pretending it's work.'

'Ooh, I won't listen to such talk,' Ada said crossly. 'Anyway, I do as much as you of Emily's work – more, even – so I don't know what you're complaining about. You're lucky to have a position at all. Lots of girls would give their hair for it.'

'I don't see 'em lining up outside the door,' Ethel said. 'And you know why? They're all getting work in the new factories at twice the pay and ten times the freedom. I don't know why anybody sticks it out in service.'

'You don't want to be a munitionette,' Ada said. 'It's nasty, dangerous work.'

'They've taken on girls at the aircraft factory,' Ethel said. 'That's not dangerous.'

Ada sighed. 'Well, if you want to go, I can't stop you. But I think you should know when you're well off, that's all. You wouldn't have good food and a nice home if you had to live in a boarding-house. And what'd you do with all this free time? Just get into trouble, if I know you.'

'Better get into trouble than be bored to death,' Ethel muttered.

Ada's side of the argument was given more force when there was a knock on the back door one evening in late November.

'Now, who on earth can that be?' Cook said, looking up from her knitting. A balaclava helmet for Fred, for the winter out in France, that was what she was working on, but she had never been much of a knitter, and the pattern was proving more complicated than she had expected. Her piece now had a big hole in the middle, which she supposed was for the face, but she couldn't see how it worked. Ada said she'd see it better when it was sewn together, and she had to hope that was true.

'It's raining cats and dogs out there,' she went on. 'Who'd be out in weather like this?'

'Maybe it's a telegram,' Ada said nervously.

'They'd come to the front door,' Cook objected.

The knocking came again. Ethel threw down her sewing in exasperation and got up. 'Well, why doesn't someone answer it? Then we'll all know!'

'It might be some tramp,' Cook called after her nervously.

'Might be the Germans, come for you,' Ethel retorted unkindly, over her shoulder.

It wasn't the Germans or a tramp. It was a drowned rat that she recognised only after an amazed stare as Emily. She was hatless, clutching a soaking coat around her with one hand and holding her battered carpet bag in the other.

'Look what the cat dragged in,' Ethel said. 'What do you want, then?'

Emily tried to speak, but her teeth were chattering too much. She looked up at Ethel in pitiful appeal. Taking in the bag, which had contained all Emily's worldly goods when she left, Ethel smiled cruelly and said, 'Got yourself into trouble? The missus won't go for it twice.'

'N-n-no, I've n-not—' Emily began.

But Ada appeared behind Ethel and gave a little shriek. '*Emily!* Oh, my Lord, what's happened to you? Let her in, Ethel, don't keep her standing out in the rain.'

Ethel shrugged and stepped back. Let Ada take the blame for someone dripping on Cook's kitchen floor. Ada took Emily's arm and helped her over the threshold. In the light of the kitchen, she looked even more pathetic. Her face and hands were stained yellow, she looked thin and feverish, and she shook uncontrollably.

'I c-came back,' she said, addressing herself to Ada, who had always been the kindest of the staff. 'I d-didn't know what to do.'

'Are you in trouble?' Ada asked. She didn't want to think

357

ill of anyone, but it was what jumped to mind all the same, after Cook's warnings.

Emily shook her head, too exhausted to take offence. 'I can't work there no more,' she said feebly. 'I want to come home.' And she concluded the statement by collapsing quite gracefully onto the stone flags.

When stripped of her wet clothes, she turned out to have a nasty wound on her left arm, clumsily bandaged but inflamed. She was also obviously feverish. Cook's sympathies were engaged so immediately she didn't even have time to think of pregnancy. 'What have they been doing to you? Who did this to you?'

''Twas an accident at work,' she said. 'A chain come loose and lashed across me arm. I was lucky.' Her eyes looked enormous as she stared up at Cook. 'There was another girl killed.'

'Oh, my precious lamb,' said Cook.

Emily blinked, never having been Cook's lamb before. 'I don't want to go back. I don't have to go back, do I? The work's something awful, and the other girls are so mean.'

'Doesn't Lilian look after you?' Ada said.

'She's not on the same shift as me. I never see her.'

'You look ever so thin,' Ada commented. 'Aren't you eating?'

'You have to buy your own food,' Emily said pathetically. 'And I've no money.'

'What d'you mean, you've no money?' Cook demanded. 'They've got to pay you.'

Tears squeezed out of Emily's eyes. 'The other girls take it off me.'

'Take your money? You mean *steal* it?'

Emily shook her head, unable to explain.

Ethel thought she knew. 'Trick her out of it, more like,' she said. 'You always were a fool. Come down off the last Christmas tree. Sharp girls like that'll know one when they see one.'

'There's these two in the same boarding-house. They're always on at me. And you have to pay your rent, or you're chucked out, so I've never enough for food as well,' Emily said. 'I never should ha' gone. The factory – 'tis awful there, the noise, and the smell o' the powder, and the foreman always shouting at you. And I'm all yellow, and girls get killed. There was one fell under a truck and had her leg cut off. I want to come home. Can I come home?'

She gazed urgently from Ada to Cook, while Ethel in the background gave a snort of amusement.

Cook heard it, and was incensed. 'Of course you can, you poor child. As if we'd let you go back after this! Ada, make her some cocoa, and Ethel, go and get her something dry to put on. I'll have a word with the missus.'

'Sooner you than me,' Ethel said, heading for the door.

Beattie wasn't pleased, especially when Cook told her about the injured arm, which, if it required medical attention, would cost money *and* stop Emily working. However, she had set up a precedent with Ethel, and could hardly now refuse to help Emily, who had not been delinquent, and who, more than Ethel, had nowhere else to go. It was an annoyance – but at least it was Christian work without any moral shading that Mrs Fitzgerald could fasten on to. And when she followed Cook to the kitchen and saw the state of the child, she sincerely pitied her.

'You can have your old job back,' she told Emily, since that seemed to be the question most exercising her, 'but if you leave again, that will be the end of it.'

'Oh, no, ma'am, never, I'd never go again. I just want to stay home,' Emily babbled, through her tears.

Home, Beattie thought. Well, if that was what it was to her, she couldn't begrudge her. It was lucky, she reflected, that she hadn't found a new kitchen maid, or an awkward situation would have arisen. She told Cook to clean the

359

wound thoroughly with salt, bind it up, and put Emily to bed with an aspirin. 'And we'll see how she is tomorrow.'

German counter-attacks at Cambrai were ferocious. The action went on until the 7th of December, and casualties were rumoured to be around forty thousand over the whole period.

At The Elms, the blows came in quick succession, first a telephone call from Aeneas Palfrey, on the 13th, to say that Donald had been wounded near Armentières and was being shipped home to the 2nd London General in Chelsea. 'Shell explosion,' he said shortly, obviously not able to risk his voice in a longer sentence. 'Shrapnel wounds. A leg is involved, and the abdomen. Don't know yet how bad it is.'

But it must be bad, they all knew, if he was being sent home. The 'Blighty wound' feared by many, hoped for by others who found soldiering intolerable. What made it harder to bear, Audrey later confided to Sadie, when the families met, was that he had not been in action at the time but leading his men back from the line to go out on rest. It seemed doubly cruel to be grievously hurt 'for nothing'.

And the following day, David received a letter from Sophy Oliphant, now Sophy Hobart, to inform him that her brother, David's friend Jumbo, had been killed at Cambrai.

We had a letter from his commanding officer, saying that he had been shot through the heart while attacking the ridge, and died instantly. It is a comfort to know that he did not suffer, and would have felt no pain. There never was a better brother, and I do not know how to bear his loss. I must be everything to Mother and Father now, for they feel it keenly. I know that you will grieve with us, because you loved him, and whatever disappointment you may have suffered, you will not allow it to prevent you from writing a word of comfort to my poor parents. They would appreciate it very much.

The reference to his 'disappointment', meaning Sophy's rejection of him, passed David by. He read the letter at breakfast and sat heavily, staring at the words, his mind revolving over thoughts, none of which held any comfort. Shot through the heart? Sophy believed it, just as anyone who had ever cared for her would wish her to. But he had seen men torn open like envelopes, seen men disembowelled, men decapitated, stumps of men with all four limbs blown off, men with no faces. *Not Jumbo!* Please, God, let it be true that he had not suffered. They had volunteered together, that August a lifetime ago, in fresh-faced eagerness. Jumbo had remained, fighting on, carrying the flag for both of them, as well as for his country. Now he was gone, was never coming home, was rotting somewhere in the mud of France.

Once, David could have believed that his soul had soared free and was looking down on them, would comfort him somehow from Beyond. But such beliefs had withered away in the trenches, watching his own men die in ways unimaginable before the war. Life was nasty, brutish and short, and death was an outrage, not to be sanitised or explained away. Jumbo was dead. His friend was dead. It was not noble, it was horrible.

He felt sick. He pushed his chair back, grabbed his crutch clumsily, and heaved himself up. Antonia's face was turned up to him, her hand coming out to him, but he could only say, low and desperate, 'Leave me alone,' and stump away, misjudging the doorway, hitting the frame and almost falling, before limping on.

'It must be bad news,' Antonia said. 'The letter—'

But he had taken it with him. It was not until much later that she was able to coax the truth out of David, and by then he was sunk in a gloom that she could not penetrate.

'Leave him be,' Beattie advised. 'He'll come out of it in his own time.'

It was something she hoped, but did not entirely believe.

She knew how much Jumbo had meant to him, and was afraid that this new blow would be too much for his fragile mind. He had seemed to be getting stronger, with Antonia to care for him and the baby on the way. But ever since he had first gone to France, she had had a sense of balancing on a narrow ledge over an abyss. She had been afraid he would be killed, and now he was home, she was afraid of something much more nebulous and therefore more daunting: that he would lose his mind.

When Donald could be visited, his wounds proved to be serious but not life-threatening. His side had been torn open, and a severe gash had laid his thigh open to the bone, but provided gangrene did not set in, both wounds should heal in time. Aeneas and Audrey visited him. Sonia said she could not until he was better: her nerves would not bear it. To see her son grievously injured . . . No, it could not be borne. Audrey gave regular bulletins to Sadie, who passed them on. Donald was very weak from shock and loss of blood, but remained cheerful and talked of getting well so that he could go back. 'He says there'll be the dickens of a fight next year,' she said. 'All the talk over there, apparently, is about the Russians making peace.'

There had been another revolution in St Petersburg on the 8th of November, and the 'moderate' government had been ousted by the Bolsheviks, whose leader had sworn to end the war if he came to power.

'If they do,' Audrey said, 'all the German troops on the Eastern Front will pour back into France.'

'But we'll have the Americans,' Sadie said.

'Yes,' said Audrey. 'I suppose it depends who gets there first.'

Christmas was something to look forward to in the dark days of December, with war-weariness in every bone, and sadness in so many hearts. Cook had secured, through an elaborate series of go-betweens, the promise of a very large turkey from a farm in the neighbouring village of Goston. It soothed her mind a little from the contemplation of her puddings, which were suffering from wartime shortages. The usual dried fruit and peel had been impossible to get, and she had used the last of her stores on the Christmas cake. And sugar was still in short supply. She managed to get hold of some dates, and she had dried some of the cherry crop in the summer; and there was still a barrel of treacle in the cellar, which helped with colour and sweetness; but the poor old puddings suffered from a superfluity of apples, carrots and beetroot, which, before the war, she would have died rather than allow near them. At least stout and brandy were in full supply, and she could only hope that a large measure of alcohol would disguise their shortcomings.

Coal was still being rationed. Peter went out with his cartie, helped by William when he was not at work, and they collected as much wood as they could. Diana, visiting one day, became aware of their efforts, and dispatched an order to Dene Park to send over a load of logs. Peter asked her if they had any fir trees in the park, and she told him to go and look, and if he found a suitable tree, she would have it cut down for him. Once they knew they would have a tree, Sadie and William made gilded apples to hang on it, along with the icicles and coloured baubles from the box in the attic, which had been brought down every year since they were children.

Lady Wroughton would be going to Sandringham as usual, so Diana promised to spend Christmas at The Elms, unless Rupert was home. Edward's cousin, Jack had written to his wife Beth to confirm he would be home at Christmas, and they promised a visit.

Antonia had hoped her father would come and stay with them, rather than be on his own for the first Christmas since her marriage, but he had written to say that he had to keep the tea-room open, for those soldiers who could not go home. 'It would be too bad to let the poor fellows down,' he wrote, 'but Mrs Turnberry has promised to come over every day and be mother to the poor boys. In return I shall give her Christmas dinner, so you needn't worry that I shall be all alone.'

'Who's Mrs Turnberry?' Sadie asked.

'She's a lady who lives in the village. A widow, very rich, and does a lot for charity,' Antonia said, poring over the letter.

'An old lady, is she?' Sadie asked.

'He's written about her quite a bit,' she went on, and reaching the end of the letter, looked up and said, 'What did you say?'

'I said, is she an old lady?'

'Why do you ask? No, she's not particularly old. Younger than Papa – about forty or forty-five, I think. Awfully ener-getic. She kept horses before the war, and hunted, and she was always up with the leaders. I suppose helping with the soldiers is a way to use up her energy.'

'Yes, I expect that's it,' Sadie said, hoping Antonia wouldn't be upset if it wasn't. After all, her father had been a widower for a long time.

Her own hopes rested on the chance of John Courcy getting leave for Christmas. Nothing had been said yet, but if he did, he'd probably spend it at Highclere, and she would get to see him.

Emily's return did not lead to a lessening of work for the other servants. Quite the opposite – for she developed a severe chill and became feverish, and was confined to bed. More seriously, the wound in her arm was obviously infected, and Beattie was obliged to call in the doctor. He cleaned out the wound as best he could, shook his head over her, and told Beattie that there was nothing more he could do.

364

'The body has to fight the infection with its own resources – and, sadly, this young woman's seem to be depleted. She needs feeding up. Good nursing and good nourishment are all that can help her. Give her the very best of both, and her youth may do the rest.'

At least he didn't recommend prayer, Beattie thought distractedly.

Good nourishment presented no difficulty. Cook liked nothing better than preparing invalid food – beef broth, chicken soup, puréed fish, little dishes with extra eggs and cream in them. It was a novelty for her to be preparing them for a kitchen maid, but the missus had endorsed the doctor's orders (her mind had been on other things, but Cook was not to know that) so she fell to with relish.

The good nursing was a different matter. 'I'm not waiting on her,' Ethel said indignantly.

'You were sick-room maid. You know more about it,' Ada pointed out.

'I looked after Mr David. That's different. I'm not running up and down for some Irish kitchen maid.'

'She's ill, poor thing. Where's your Christian charity?'

'Where's *yours*? If you're so sorry for her, you nurse her.'

'All right, then, I will,' said Ada. 'You'll have to do my work, though.'

'Catch me!'

The impasse was solved, in the event, quite simply, because without having heard any of the argument, Antonia quietly stepped in and appointed herself nurse. 'But I'll need you to keep an eye on Mr David for me,' she said to Ethel. 'You looked after him so well before, I'm not afraid of asking you. If he needs anything and I'm upstairs, he'll ring. I just want to be sure *you* will answer, because you know his ways, and you can be tactful.'

'Well, *you*'ve fallen on your feet again,' Ada said to Ethel, with unusual sourness for her. 'I don't know how you do it.'

'Luck favours the fair,' Ethel retorted.

'That doesn't even make sense,' said Ada, fretfully.

'All very well,' Cook said later, when the arrangement was explained to her, 'but I've still not got a kitchen maid, and now I've only got half a housemaid to help me. And Christmas coming up. I wish—' She'd been going to say, she wished Emily had never come back, but at the last minute cancelled the thought as unlucky.

The third blow came out of nowhere, in the form of a letter to Beattie, in a hand she didn't recognise. She hadn't heard from Louis since a brief note when he had come out of the line after Passchendaele was taken, had been expecting a letter, and now wondered if, for some reason, he had got someone else to address the envelope and post it. But it had a London postmark. Caution had become instinctive to her now, and she concealed it from all eyes and later took it to the bathroom, where she locked herself in for privacy.

The letter inside, on a single sheet of lined paper, was written in pencil, in the careful, round hand of the elementary-educated.

Mrs Hunter,
Dear Madam,
I write with great regret to tell you that the major has been wounded. I hope you will forgive the liberty but I know he would have wanted you to know. It happened during a night attack north of Poelkapelle. He was wounded first in the arm, but carried on, and then was struck in the head. At Rouen they thought he was done for, but he rallied, and they sent him back to Blighty. He lies at the

second London General. He is seriously
wounded but doctor says he may live.
With great respect, madam,
Albert Waites

Sitting on the edge of the bath, she read the words with a
slow, dull pain in her stomach. It was strange how physical
a mental hurt often was. *Seriously wounded.* What did it
mean? Waites, his soldier-servant, had written, which meant
he could not. *He would have wanted you to know* meant he
was unable even to ask Waites to write. *He may live* – but
he couldn't, he *couldn't* die! He had come out of the hell of
the battle for Passchendaele, where tens of thousands fell.
It had been all over. This must have been a skirmish, as
they called the unplanned bursts of fighting that flared up
and died down all the time. An unimportant, random skirmish, that would never even be written about in the history
books. Something so insignificant *could* not take him.

She jerked her head up. She must go to him. The 2nd
London – that was where Donald was. It was in Chelsea.
She must go straight away.

At the beginning of the war, she had prayed, 'Please,
God,' for her sons. 'Please, God,' over and over. That part
of her mind was silent now. She had no right to ask this;
and she no longer believed God heard, or perhaps even
existed. Such prayer was a telephone that rang endlessly in
an empty house, unanswered.

As the war continued, the war hospitals had begun to
specialise. David had been sent to one that dealt particularly
with wounds of the femur. The 2nd London specialised in
head wounds and, as well as its general wards, had a dedicated optical ward. When she arrived there and asked after
him, that was where she was directed.

The sister of the ward met her at the door and looked

her over with a frosty eye. 'Are you a relative?' she asked abruptly.

Beattie was about to say, 'No,' when her wits caught up with her and she said, almost without hesitation, 'I'm his – sister.'

The eye did not warm. 'We had no information about his next of kin, you see.'

Beattie could not quite meet the gaze. 'There is no-one else,' she said. 'May I see him?'

'I'll ask the doctor to have a word with you,' said the sister. 'He's on the ward. Wait here, please.'

The doctor was young, tired, his eyes sunk in their sockets, but he looked at her with sympathy. 'I'm glad he has someone,' he said, not questioning her relationship. She suspected he knew what it was, really. 'We find they respond much better when there's someone nearby.'

'Can you tell me what happened?' Her voice sounded very calm, and seemed to be functioning on its own.

'A bullet passed through his head, behind the eyes, and lodged in the skull on the other side,' he said. There was no drama in his voice, for which she was grateful. The only way to speak of such things was dispassionately. 'They were able to remove the bullet in Rouen, and also removed the right eye, which was badly damaged. They sent him here in the hope that we could save the sight of the left eye, but I'm afraid the optic nerve is severed, so there is little hope.'

'But there is some?' she asked.

'Nerves have been known to grow back,' he said, 'but I would not like you to depend on it.' His gaze grew kinder. 'He is conscious, and rational, which is a great deal. Would you like to see him?'

She could only nod.

As the hospital had expanded to accommodate the wounded, it had been forced to build huts in the gardens behind the buildings, and it was in one of these that she found Louis, propped up on pillows, in his neatly tucked bed. His upper body was in striped pyjamas. His head was heavily bandaged, and the bandages covered the place where the right eye had been. The left eye stared blankly at nothing. It was the same dark blue of David's eyes, but the intense, brilliant stare was gone. His face was pale, and looked not so much thin, but lessened, as if his substance had melted away. Almost, he seemed smaller. His long, strong, beautiful hands rested on the sheet, and were restlessly turning something over and over – his silver cigarette case. In an instant of sympathy she realised that, seeing nothing, he needed the stimulus of touch.

She came up beside him, and could not immediately speak, but he sensed that someone was there, and turned his head, trying vainly to *see* who it was. Then his nostrils flared, and he strained his face towards her. 'Who's there?'

He had caught the scent of her, she thought. Her throat closed, and she couldn't answer for a moment. Then she managed to say, 'Louis.'

'You came,' he said, with such gladness she would have wept then, if she ever wept. His hand reached out. She caught it, and let him take hers back, and he held it as if it were anchoring him to the world.

There was a chair at the bedside. She sat, her legs trembling. 'Waites sent me a letter,' she said.

'Good old Waites,' he said.

It seemed important to keep the conversation banal. Neither of them could have borne anything profound or emotional just then.

'Is he here?' she asked.

'He's hanging around somewhere. He looks after me as much as they allow. He shaves me in the morning. Better him than the nurses. He knows my face.'

'He brought your kit back, I suppose?'

'He has my razors, so I suppose he must have.'

369

'Are they treating you well?' It was an absurd question, but her tongue was having to operate without her brain, which was engaged with trying to comprehend the shock of his changed appearance.

'Oh, yes,' he said. 'They have the best eye doctors here, best in the country. They—'

He stopped abruptly. *He knows*, she thought. *He knows they can do nothing for him.* In one instant, like a landscape viewed in all detail in a flash of lightning, she saw that his life was utterly changed. He would never see another sunrise, flower, tree, the rain. Blind, dependent, for the rest of his life. He would never see her face again.

He would never see David.

And in that silence, which needed so desperately to be filled, she found herself unable to speak. There was nothing she could say of comfort. He must have imagined already all the possible responses a civilised person could make.

In the end, he filled the gap himself, began talking about the nurses, the other patients, the daily routine of the ward. His voice was feeble, and he spoke slowly, holding her hand in both his, and she made sounds of agreement and response, and grew used, bit by bit, to the sight of him.

At last he ran out of things to say. She thought he was tiring, and tried gently to withdraw her hand, but he clutched it tighter and said, 'Don't go. You don't need to go yet, do you?'

'No, I don't need to.'

'What date is it?'

'The 16th.'

'Of December?'

'Yes.'

'It will be Christmas soon.'

'You'll be in here for Christmas,' she said.

He heard the tone of her voice. 'I know you won't be able to come. I expect they'll do something special for those

370

of us who can't go home. They do try, bless them.' He pressed her hand anxiously. 'You'll come when you can?'

'Every day,' she said.

'Except Christmas Day.' The blind eye closed.

'You're tired,' she said. 'I should leave you.'

'Wait until I'm asleep?' he asked.

'How will I know?'

'You'll know,' he said.

Leaving the ward, she met Waites, who stopped and looked at her with such an expression of relief, it was as if he thought she could cure his master. 'I knew you'd come,' he said.

It all flowed upwards in her at the sight of him – the shock, the pain, the fear. He put his hand out as though he would touch her, and drew it back. 'He's alive, ma'am,' he said earnestly. 'You got to think of that.'

'Yes,' she said; and unable to say any more, she nodded to him, and walked on.

CHAPTER TWENTY-THREE

Emily was out of bed, but her arm was still bandaged and in a sling. It had not healed, and Beattie had said she should not use it. 'But it will be better for her to be up and about,' she decreed. 'I dare say there are some little tasks she can perform one-handed.'

Cook had no argument with that. At least it meant no-one had to wait on her in bed. As for one-handed tasks – 'I never knew anyone so fumble-fingered in my life,' she complained. 'Just sit there out of the way and try not to be a nuisance.'

'I'm sorry,' Emily whispered, tears in her eyes.

'I dare say you are,' Cook snapped. 'Pity you didn't listen before when I told you not to go. Here, stir this batter. At least you can't make a mess of that.'

She'd have been kinder had she not been in something of 'a state', thinking about her poor old puddings, which she really didn't want to have to send upstairs, and the fact that she had only two jars of mincemeat left from last year, and no chance to make any more, so mince pies were going to be on ration – a nice thing at Christmas!

And she hadn't heard from Fred recently. Had something happened to him? Or had he decided to let her go? She admitted she had not been a good correspondent: she was no hand at letter-writing. She had received a lot more from him than he'd had from her. Perhaps she should have made

372

more of an effort. She never seemed to have a minute to spare, what with managing without Emily and then managing *with* her, and when she sat down by the fire at the end of the day she was as likely to fall asleep as have the will to take up a pencil. She had finished the balaclava helmet, but she hesitated to send it, partly because if he had finished with her she would end up looking silly, and partly because it was such a strange shape she'd look silly anyway.

In the end, she decided she couldn't go wrong at least sending him a Christmas card, and writing in it that she had not had a letter for a while, and that she hoped all was well with him, which was the truth and Christian, whether she was still his sweetie or not. And in the end, she put in a nice cotton handkerchief wrapped in tissue paper for a present, because a nice handkerchief never went amiss. And then she just hoped for the best.

Laura had acquired a new assistant. Veronica Mildmay arrived one day asking for her, and when Laura came out from the office to ask how she could help her, Miss Mildmay said, with a cheerful smile, 'I'm hoping, on the contrary, that *I* can help *you*.'

She seemed in her late thirties, with a plain but pleasant face, was dressed in a serge skirt and jacket and sensible boots, and her hair, which was an astonishing dark red in colour, was neatly out of the way in a plait wound round her head, like a crown, and pinned with a firm hand. She looked ready to undertake any job of work thrown at her, and Laura liked her immediately. She held out her hand, and the lady pulled off a fleece-lined leather glove and gave her a warm shake.

'You don't know me,' she went on, 'but I know a lot about you. Let me give you my credentials first. My aunt-by-marriage, Mrs Mildmay, is with the FANY in Calais, and she heard of what you were doing here, thoroughly approved, and wrote to her brother, who is Colonel Lansdown, with the 43rd in Ypres. He is a friend of Major Ransley of the RAMC, who said you were in need of volunteer help. So Uncle Claude, as I call him, wrote to me, and said I should write and offer myself. But I couldn't wait. I suppose I ought to have done everything by form, but I thought if you needed help you must need it quickly with Christmas coming, so I just packed a bag and dashed to the station, and here I am.'

She concluded her statement with a look so eager and hopeful, Laura could only laugh and say, 'I'd have done exactly the same, so there's no need to apologise. Welcome aboard! Though when you've seen the place, and know what we do, I shall understand if you want to disembark again. It's not like being in the FANY. But I think it's useful work.'

'Oh, I know what you do here, and I agree – it's very much needed. If I'd wanted to be a FANY, I could have joined a long time ago. Aunt Beryl has asked me often enough. Everyone understands what FANYs do and there's no chance of their going unregarded. But there are so many other women now, doing men's jobs, without much in the way of acknowledgement. They *ought* to have somewhere to go where they can be with their own sort, and be comfortable, and understood.'

'My feelings exactly. I'm sure we shall get along, Miss Mildmay.'

'Oh, Ronnie, please. Everyone calls me Ronnie.'

'I'm Laura. Come and have a cup of tea and tell me more about yourself. My friend, Louisa Cotton, is somewhere about. We founded the place together.'

'Yes, I know the story. And I know about you and Miss Cotton. I met her years ago when I was in the WSPU, though I don't suppose she'll remember me. We have a common friend in Sylvia Partridge, who often talks about you both.'

'How is Sylvia?'

'Still busy with her daubs. Not so involved in the Bedfordite salons any more, though. She helps out at a women's centre in the East End now – one of the Pankhurst ideas. Advice on contraception and childbirth.' She gave a frankly boyish grin. 'If anyone could make the wretched women use contraception, it's Sylvia. She'd frighten them into it.'

Laura laughed. 'She's a strong-minded person, all right.'

'She says the same about you. She speaks with admiration about your police work. Pushing the frontiers, she calls it. When the war's over, they won't be able to put women back in the box again.'

'I hope not. But most of the time I feel as if the war will never end.'

'Never mind, by next year we should have the vote – think of that!'

'Has it gone through? I didn't hear anything about it.'

'No, the women's clause comes on in the Lords in January, but they're saying it will definitely go through this time. They've added up the numbers, and there'll be a big majority.'

'I shall believe it when it happens,' Laura said cautiously. 'But it is an extraordinary idea – going to the polling station, casting my vote like . . .'

'Like a human being,' Ronnie concluded for her, and they both laughed.

They chatted with animation over a cup of tea, and were interrupted finally by the arrival of Louisa, who stopped at the door of the bureau, as they called the little office behind the entrance hall, and said, 'Oh,' in a discovery sort of voice that did not, however, include much pleasure.

Laura looked up at her and smiled. 'Lou, there you are! Come and meet Veronica Mildmay. She says she knows you.'

'I don't suppose you'd remember me,' Ronnie began.

'Of course I do,' Louisa said. 'How could I forget?'

'Ronnie's come to volunteer herself as a helper,' Laura said. 'We've been talking about more help,' she explained to Ronnie, 'but we can't afford to pay for it.'

'Don't worry about that. I'm independently wealthy,' said Ronnie.

'Isn't that splendid?' Laura urged, for Louisa's expression was blank where it should have been welcoming.

'Yes,' Louisa said woodenly. 'I suppose it is. You'll find it a bit rough here,' she said to Ronnie. 'We don't have a furnished bedroom for you. You'll have to sleep on a mattress on the floor.'

'Better than the tents the FANY sleep in,' Ronnie said. 'And I'm not made of glass. Now, if I'm acceptable, why don't I drop my bag somewhere and get straight to work?'

'That's the sort of attitude I like,' Laura said. 'It reminds me of Major Ransley.'

'Does he have a hand in this?' Louisa asked.

'In a roundabout way,' said Laura. 'Ronnie's aunt's brother knows him, apparently.'

'Ah,' said Louisa. 'What a lot we have to thank him for.'

Laura led Ronnie away to show her her room and then take her round the house; and it was only afterwards that she thought Louisa's last comment had sounded strangely ironic, rather than sincere.

John Courcy would not be having leave at Christmas, but Mrs Cuthbert said he hoped to get his time after the New Year. 'He hasn't said if he'll be coming here, to Highclere, but we can hope, since he went to Scotland last time. Unless his father's worse, of course. He doesn't say anything about that in his letter.'

Sadie accepted it philosophically. Christmas at home would be nice anyway. Rupert would not be in England, which would mean Diana would come. David was still gloomy and withdrawn, but surely even he must find his spirits lifted by reliving the old traditions that had made their childhood Christmases so lovely.

Realising belatedly that The Elms was suffering from shortages, Diana paid a visit to the Dene Park kitchens, and had a number of things sent over, including lemons, oranges, dried figs, nuts – and half a dozen jars of mincemeat, which reduced Cook to tears. 'I was that worried, my lady,' she told Diana, who came to see that everything had arrived safely. 'Apart from the family, we always get the carol singers on Christmas Eve, and I was at my wits' end what to give them. It's *always* mince pies and punch, my lady. And then there's the tradesmen, that call for their boxes – they always get a mince pie as well, and a tot of something.'

It was a pity, she thought afterwards, that she had already made the puddings, because she could have put some mince-meat in them to make them more like the real thing. She was worried about them puddings. She even wondered whether the master would be able to flame them with brandy in the usual way. She wouldn't put it past the blessed things to catch fire or melt or something.

Beattie went every afternoon to see Louis, giving the excuse, when anyone asked, of the canteen at Waterloo. Antonia was the only person at home who ever wondered where she was going, and that was only because she was neglecting the Hastings Road canteen, whose duties fell more and more to her daughter-in-law. 'Wouldn't you like me to do the station for you?' Antonia asked one day. 'You could do Hastings Road instead, and be saved the journey. You're looking awfully tired.'

'I'm not tired at all,' Beattie said quickly. The last thing she wanted was Antonia involving herself in her life. 'And don't forget, you're expecting a child. *You* are the one who must rest. I can't think of letting you go up and down to Town on the train – they're so slow and crowded, these days. In fact, after Christmas, you ought to think of giving up the canteen entirely.'

'Oh, I like helping,' Antonia said. 'I don't want to stop. And I do take care of myself, I promise.'

Beattie hurried off. Louis was so desperately glad that she came. When she entered the hut, she would see him sitting upright, his face turned towards the door with a strained look, as though trying to make his other senses take the place of sight. It gave her the feeling that he had been sitting like that for hours. When she spoke, his face was transformed. She sat beside him, and he held her hand, turning it over, tracing its shape with his fingers, as they talked.

She tried at first to tell him things about the outside world, what the weather was doing, what was in the news, but he had no interest. What animated him was to talk about their past, about Dublin, about the time they had spent together since they had met again. He went over and over that first meeting, when he had come up, quite by chance, to buy a cup of tea, and found her there. 'It was meant to be,' he said often. 'I was meant to find you again.'

He had moments of depression, but on the whole he was remarkably resilient – or, at least, he was when she was there. Waites told her that at other times he could sink into a silence from which it was hard to rouse him. ''Sonly nacheral,' Waites said, 'when you think of what he's lost.'

Beattie did, on the way there on the train, on the way back, in every quiet moment. For such a powerful, energetic, independent man, it must have been a devastating shock. She would expect him to be bitter, to rail against the unfairness of Fate. But when she was there, he seemed resigned, never spoke of his loss. Indeed, he spoke only once directly of his blindness, and that was on the Friday before Christmas, the 22nd.

'Had a visit from a padre this morning,' he told her. 'He was a captain in the Blues, blinded last year. He belongs to some church group, and they're experimenting with ways to make sightless officers independent. Teaching them Braille, for one thing. How to do everyday things. Finding them jobs for when they're discharged. He offered to take me on when I'm out of here, said I could go into the church. Parish priest.' He was silent a moment, and Beattie almost held her breath. She could not see him in a cassock, feeling his way into a pulpit; if he could think of himself in that way, she must not discourage him, but it distressed her to think of him so defeated. He *ought* to rail a little – he was Louis! He ought not to go meekly into the darkness.

And then he laughed. 'I told him that sort of thing wasn't me. I told him I had a job, thank you very much. I told him about my plantation, and he was very interested. I think he envied me.'

And he went on to talk about his life there before the war, and she listened, glad for his enthusiasm, but with a worm of dread in her stomach that she couldn't quite identify.

Donald's wounds were healing, and he was expected to make a full recovery. He would still be in hospital at Christmas, but in the relief at his better prospects, the Palfreys were planning the biggest celebration they could contrive. Beth and Jack would be with them on Christmas Day; they would come over to Northcote on Boxing Day.

Beattie was restless and unhappy on the Sunday, for she could not visit the hospital, and though she had prepared Louis for it, she had a low sense of dread that something would happen in her absence. Monday was Christmas Eve, and she would see him, but then there were two days when she couldn't get out – it would raise too many questions.

Edward was surprised on the Monday to learn that she would be going in to the canteen, and even protested mildly. 'The trains will be so crowded. Surely you can miss one day.'

'I can't,' she said; and when he seemed likely to argue, she added, 'There's a war on. I can't just please myself.'

'I suppose not,' he said. He touched her hand. 'You are an example to all of us.'

She snatched her hand away. '*You* are going in today,' she said.

'It's my job,' he said, slightly puzzled.

'Then try to think of this as my job,' she said.

'Just don't get too tired,' Edward said. 'You are looking rather worn, you know.'

'We're all tired,' she said shortly.

Cook was making the pastry for a batch of the mince pies that would be needed later for the carol singers, when Ginger put his head round the door.

''Ere,' he said, 'there's a bloke out 'ere asking for you.'

'Bloke? What are you talking about? And don't bring them muddy boots into my kitchen. If it's the butcher's boy, tell him to come and speak to me himself.'

'Ain't no butcher's boy,' said Ginger. 'You'd better come and see, Ma.'

'Don't you "Ma" me, you cheeky 'ound!' she said, wiped her hands on her apron and hurried over to give him a box on the ear, at the very least. But he had withdrawn like a rabbit down a hole, and when she stepped out onto the back-door mat, she almost ran into a great big tall man, who so surprised her that she let out a shriek.

'Steady the Buffs! No need to holler, I'm not the bogey-man,' said a familiar voice.

'Fred!' she breathed, looking up, and the next instant he had swept her off her feet, given her a swift hug and put her down, to follow it up with a kiss on the lips that made her tingle all over, and gave her a jolt of alarm at the same time.

'Don't do that! Anyone might see,' she said breathlessly.

'You can't come here grabbing a person and – and kissing 'em without so much as a by-your-leave.'

'Oh, I thought we'd done all the by-your-leaving,' he said, with a cheerful grin. 'You're my girl, remember. You're spoken for. I can kiss you whenever I like.'

'Not *here*,' she hissed, aware that Ginger would be hiding somewhere, watching and sniggering, the little toad!

'All right, invite me in, then, and I'll kiss you inside,' Fred said irrepressibly.

'I *can't*,' she moaned.

'Can't invite me in? Whyever not? Don't you fancy me any more?'

'They don't know about you,' she said.

'Time they did, then,' he said, and he was inside before she could do anything about it, looking round, and saying, 'So this is where you work? Very nice.'

Emily came in from the scullery, and almost dropped the vase she was holding. She gave a little shriek, too.

'Is that the way you greet people round here?' Fred said, feigning interest. 'Funny customs in these parts.'

'What do you want?' Cook snapped at Emily.

'Miss Sadie wanted this for some holly,' Emily said faintly. Her eyes were huge.

'Well, take it to her, then. Don't stand gawping.' Emily didn't immediately move, her eyes stuck to Fred, like fish-glue. 'This is – my nephew, come to visit,' Cook said. 'Now *go!*' Emily scuttled out, and Fred looked down at Cook reprovingly. 'Your nephew? Oh, Ma-ar-garet, you disappoint me. How's *that* going to work out?'

Cook blushed. 'You took me by surprise. I got flustered. I didn't know what to say.' They could hear Emily's voice in the passage talking to someone excitedly. 'Someone else coming,' she said, distracted.

'All right, but no more lies,' said Fred. 'If you don't tell 'em, I will.'

Ada came in, saying, 'What's Emily in a state about? She says—' And stopped as she saw Fred. 'Oh!'

Cook's brain was stuck, but Fred administered an unseen pinch from behind her back, which made her jump, and she said, 'Ada, this is Sergeant McAusland. My – my friend.' And she felt herself going scarlet.

Ada looked from one to the other in amazement, then closed her mouth and got hold of herself. 'Please to meet you, I'm sure. I'm Ada Cole, head house-parlour maid.'

'You're the one with the lovely singing voice,' Fred said, shaking her hand. To her surprised look, he added, 'Joan's told me about you.'

'Joan? Oh, Cook. Has she? Have you?'

Some explanation was necessary 'We've been writing to each other,' Cook said, with an attempt at dignity. 'We met down in Folkestone, that time I was staying with my sister.'

'Now I got a bit of leave, so I've come to visit you all,' Fred said genially.

'How nice!' said Ada. 'How long have you got?'

'Four days,' said Fred. 'I'm staying at the Coach and Horses, nice and handy.'

'I s'pose you've got family to visit,' Ada said politely.

'Nope. No-one but Joan here. All my time's my own, which means it's yours.'

Ada's face lit in a smile. 'So you'll be able to have Christmas with us?' she said. 'We have a lovely Christmas dinner down here, and we're allowed to have friends. I'm asking my friend Corporal Armstrong. We're going steady.'

'Going steady?' Fred said. 'Now there's a nice expression.' He put an arm round Cook's waist, making her jump. 'I reckon Joan and me are going steady – what do you say?' He looked down at her with as much mischief as tenderness.

'You can come, and welcome,' she said awkwardly, 'but there won't be no Christmas pudding. I'm doing a plain suet duff for down here, with treacle. You can't get the dried fruit.'

This tickled Fred so much he went off into a very infectious chuckle, which, oddly, laid down Cook's feathers and made her feel more at ease. Normally she was wary of being laughed at. But perhaps to talk of suet duff had been odd, in the context.

'I'll come,' he said, wiping his eye with the back of a finger, 'and it won't be for your pudding, though I don't doubt it'll be very good. She's a grand cook, isn't she, Miss Ada?'

'The best,' said Ada, proudly. 'And after dinner, we'll have a sing-song. My Len sings lovely. Do you sing at all, Sergeant McAusland?'

'That's Fred to you,' he said. 'And I do sing. If I say it myself, I can warble with the best of 'em. I'll sing you a few ditties from Australia, if you like.' He winked at Cook. 'Don't worry, only the decent ones.'

And she didn't even blush. 'Oh – *you!*' she said.

Beattie arrived home on Christmas Eve late and footsore from standing all the way on the packed train, then walking from the station. She went straight upstairs to her bedroom, ignoring the sounds of the children's voices from the drawing-room, not wanting to speak to anyone.

It had been hard to tell Louis she would not see him for two days, but he had not reacted much and she wondered if he had even taken it in. His world had contracted, and time did not mean much to him any more. He had no days or nights. For the whole of her visit, he had been talking about South Africa, about his plantation, describing it to her, remembering times past. He told her what he had done to improve the house, and what more he would do. He told her about yields, about picking, about packing and transporting, about his workers and his servants. He told her about his horses, and dogs he had owned. He told her about his neighbours. And when he had done, he started again.

She wondered if he was delirious. The hands that held hers did feel hot, but his face was as pale as ever, and the blank, sea-blue eye that looked only on darkness did not shine with fever.

And then he talked about their future together. As soon as he was discharged, he said, they must book their passage. 'Even if the war's not over, there are ships going to the Cape, and the convoy system makes it safe enough,' he said. 'Once we're there, we can forget all about the war. The house is a bachelor's home. You'll want to put your own touches to it. You must change whatever you like. I have plenty of money, so don't worry about that.'

He talked on, and there seemed no need for her to reply. He never mentioned his blindness, or any difficulties it might throw up. He was seeing the plantation and the house in his mind's eye; she wondered if he even remembered, at that moment, that he would never see them in reality again.

And all the way home, there had been nothing to distract her from the contemplation that, as his life had changed utterly and permanently, so must hers. She had thought that after the war she would have to make a choice; Louis had accepted that it must wait until then. But now suddenly the choice was upon her. She did not know how much longer he would be in hospital, when he would be released and discharged from the army, but it could only be weeks, surely. Then he would expect her to sever herself from her old life, and go with him.

And given how much more he needed her now, how could she refuse? She remembered thinking that she had choice again, where her whole life had been laid down before. Now she saw that there was no choice after all. She would have to leave Edward, her home, her children, her country, and go with Louis, and it would not be her own, free decision. The railway lines along which she had been borne without volition had branched, and she would go *that* way whether she wanted to or not, while Edward and her other life would go *that* way.

Edward! It would be, she knew, a terrible betrayal. He had been good to her, he had loved her faithfully, and if he knew where David had come from, he had never so much as hinted at the knowledge. Now it would all have to be dragged out into the blinding light, and she would have to hurt him, humiliate him, break his heart – and have him hate her for the rest of his life.

She loved Louis, with a deep, blind passion that was like the hunger of some insatiable beast deep in her guts. But she had loved Edward, too, and he had never done anything to forfeit that love. She wished to God he had. She wished him faithless, shiftless, a drunkard, a wife-beater, so that he might deserve the cruelty she would have to inflict on him.

When? Not now. Not at Christmas. Not until Louis was ready to leave hospital. She must continue with the lie. She must be the deceiver a little longer. And she must do it with a smile, so that no-one suspected. She sighed, from the depths of her body, and stood up, to change her clothes for the evening.

And Edward came in. 'I got off a little early,' he said, answering her surprised look. 'I have some news. Oh, my dear, you do look tired,' he interrupted himself. He crossed the room to her and went to stroke her hair, and without meaning to she flinched away from his touch. For an instant there was a lost look in his eyes. Then he said, 'Was it hard work at the canteen? Seeing all those boys going home for Christmas . . .'

'It was all right,' she said. Another moment, and he would mention Bobby. She couldn't bear it if he talked of Bobby. 'What is your news?'

'I'm going to tell everyone tomorrow, when we're all assembled, but I wanted to tell you alone first. It's something you'll like.' He was searching her face, hopefully. 'Something that will please you.'

She tried to find some warmth somewhere to put into her face, her voice. 'Well?' He waited, savouring the moment. She made an effort. 'You're like a little boy with a secret in your pocket. I hope it's not a white mouse.'

He laughed. 'It's *my* white mouse. I had the formal letter today. Lord Forbesson hinted at it before, but I didn't want to tell you until I was sure. I'm being honoured in the New Year list. I'm being knighted.'

It was so far from anything she might have expected, she could not at first take it in. And then the reality tumbled through her head with all the other thoughts that had just been tormenting her, another complication, another layer to the hurt she would do him. All she could think was that it was ghastly.

He was scanning her for reaction. 'Don't you understand, my love? I'm going to be Sir Edward Hunter. And you'll be Lady Hunter. I thought you'd like that. No-one deserves it more – you've been a wonderful wife and mother, and an inspiration to everyone who knows you.' Still no reaction. He took her hand and pressed it. 'Just think how furious it will make Mrs Fitzgerald,' he urged.

And then, to his horror, he saw she was crying. He had never seen her cry, never, in all their years together, not when her father died, not when David was wounded, not even when Bobby died. Beattie didn't cry. She never cried.

'Darling,' he said, in anguish. And this time, when he put his arms round her, she didn't resist. He drew her against him, and she wept onto his shoulder, so that he could feel the hot, wet tears on his neck.

It was good to have all the family together again on Christmas Day. Diana was back in what had been her usual place, looking more lovely and elegant than before, but otherwise their same Diana. She had brought bags full of beautifully wrapped presents, and Rupert's good wishes, and little

George, stout and healthy and full of smiles for everyone. David came down, and seemed to be trying to be cheerful for everyone's sake. Bobby's place was not empty, because Antonia sat there now, and no-one minded that. She was a part of the family; and Bobby would always be with them.

Edward told his news at the beginning, and there was excitement and marvelling and questions.

'Does that mean David will get a title?' Peter asked. 'Like George is Lord Dene?'

'It doesn't work like that, idiot,' Diana said, from the depths of her newly acquired knowledge. 'A knighthood can't even be inherited. But Mother will be Lady Hunter. It sounds rather nice,' she added, a touch wistfully.

'If anyone should be lady something, it's Mother,' William said loyally.

Beattie smiled, and was glad there was no need for her to say anything.

The turkey was a triumph, and nobody said much about the pudding. William and Sadie ate it, out of loyalty to Cook. Diana refused any, saying she had lost her sweet tooth; the others picked, and set their plates aside as soon as was decently possible.

The cheese was put on, and the port came round, and they drank to the King, and then Edward proposed, 'Absent friends,' and after a hesitation, added, 'and those who have gone before.'

There were so many now, not just their own Bobby, but friends like Jumbo and Hank Bowers, Charles Wroughton, Peter Warren, and so many from the village, young men Diana had danced with, boys who had served in the shops and delivered to the house and swept their chimneys and cleaned their windows. A shadow army, Sadie imagined, marching away down the road, their boots making no sound, each turning his head for one last look before they disappeared into that perspective point where all lines meet.

And the saddest thing of all, she thought, was that this had become their world now, and they no longer found it strange. The war was where they lived; it seemed sometimes that it was where they had always lived.

The little silence that followed was broken by Diana, who cleared her throat and said, 'I have some news. I was going to tell you earlier, but I didn't want to spoil Father's.' She looked round them all. 'I'm going to have another baby.'

Congratulations erupted with a delight that was warmer for the sharp sadness that had come before.

Diana smiled and received their love like a tribute. 'Rupert would like another boy,' she said, 'but I don't mind which it is. A girl would be nice too.'

Sadie looked at her mother, and saw the sorrow behind her smile, and thought that she was thinking about Bobby. And she thought of him too. It wasn't as easy as a life for a life. But there was a little of that in it, somewhere. Nothing could replace Bobby; but new life was the only antidote to death. It was a cause for happiness.